D0444514

Praise for Tabitha Suzuma:

'One of the most powerful and tense books I've
read in ages – outstanding'
Independent on Sunday on *Hurt*

'Suzuma's writing is compelling and the quality
without question' *Irish Times* on *Forbidden*

'An exhilarating, emotive and at times exhilarating
read, which I couldn't put down'
TES on *A Note of Madness*

'A writer of great sensitivity who tackles big
issues while sustaining a thrilling plot'
The Bookseller on *From Where I Stand*

www.totallyrandombooks.co.uk

Also available by Tabitha Suzuma:

Hurt

Tabitha Suzuma

Definitions

HURT
A DEFINITIONS BOOK 978 1 849 41520 0

First published in Great Britain by The Bodley Head,
an imprint of Random House Children's Publishers UK
A Random House Group Company

Penguin
Random House
UK

Bodley Head edition published 2013
Definitions edition published 2015

1 3 5 7 9 10 8 6 4 2

Copyright © Tabitha Suzuma, 2013

The Random House Group Limited supports the Forest Stewardship Council® (FSC®), the
leading international forest-certification organisation. Our books carrying the FSC label
are printed on FSC®-certified paper. FSC is the only forest-certification scheme supported
by the leading environmental organisations, including Greenpeace. Our paper procurement
policy can be found at www.randomhouse.co.uk/environment.

Definitions are published by Random House Children's Publishers UK,
61–63 Uxbridge Road, London W5 5SA

www.**randomhousechildrens**.co.uk
www.**totallyrandombooks**.co.uk
www.**randomhouse**.co.uk

Addresses for companies within The Random House Group Limited can be found at:
www.randomhouse.co.uk/offices.htm

THE RANDOM HOUSE GROUP Limited Reg. No. 954009

A CIP catalogue record for this book is available from the British Library.

Printed and bound in Great Britain by CPI Group (UK) Ltd,
Croydon, CR0 4YY

In loving memory of my kind, funny and loyal friend

Camille Lloyd-Davis
28th November 1974 – 29th October 2012

Forever missed . . . Never forgotten

Sins cannot be undone, only forgiven.

Igor Stravinsky

PROLOGUE

He opens his eyes and knows instantly that something is terribly wrong. He senses it through his skin, his nerves, his synapses, even though, spread-eagled on his back, all he can see is the frosted light-fitting on his bedroom ceiling. The room is white, violently bright, and he knows that it is a sunny day and he forgot to close the curtains, just as he knows, from the belt cutting into his side, the denim against his legs, the clammy cotton sticking to his chest, that he slept in his clothes. Arching his foot and finding it weighted down, he lifts his head just high enough to see that he even failed to take off his shoes. And then, slowly, his eyes focus beyond his mud-caked trainers and begin to take in the rest of the room. For a moment he holds his breath, convinced he must still be dreaming. Then, with a gasp of horror, he snaps upright as if from a nightmare.

The walls around him immediately begin to sway, colours bleeding together, fraying at the edges. He screws his eyes tight shut and then opens them again, hoping not just to clear his head but to rid himself of the vision – the chaos of his wrecked bedroom around him. But sunlight is pouring in through the windows, illuminating the anarchy of this usually immaculate space. Fractured furniture, crippled objects, torn clothes and smashed glass are all that remain. The room looks like a scene from a crime show. The breath is wrung from his lungs. Things are beginning to take on a particularly tactile, vivid, saturated look. He puts his hand to his mouth and tears at a hangnail, and then just sits there, stuck like an old vinyl record with no more play.

Beyond the windows, the day is still. The branches of the trees don't move; the sky is a deep, impossible blue. The sun appears to blaze brighter for a few seconds. He seems to be in some kind of trance, staring around with a kind of guardedness, a horrified fascination. From the wall hangs a brutally twisted picture frame, like something salvaged from a furnace. On his desk, pieces of a smashed mug catch and reflect the late-morning light like scraps of glass adrift in a pool of coffee, the surface shimmering with oily iridescence. Spread out beneath his bookshelves is a tapestry of splayed books, pages ripped from their spines and scattered like leaves. Broken diving trophies, splintered and ragged, lie nearby like the contents of a suitcase lost at sea. There isn't a single surface or stretch of carpet that isn't covered with the flotsam and jetsam of the night.

Slowly he slides himself down to the end of the bed and levers himself onto his feet, a time-consuming manoeuvre which requires great orchestration and willpower. His muscles are stiff and sore and unyielding. A sharp scorch of pain rips through his leg – he looks down to find that his jeans have a tear just above the left knee, threads darkened with blood sticking to his skin. Prickles down his arms reveal a multitude of scrapes and scratches. Pain corrodes his body – his head, his neck, all the way down his spine and into the backs of his legs. He focuses on the humming in his skull, the maelstrom in his head. Below him, his body hovers, unattached. Then, all of a sudden, the breath is kicked out of him and he is shoved onto the cold hard concrete floor of his life.

He takes a step forward in the ransacked room. Abject horror slides under his skin, burrowing into his body without asking: his hands are its hands, and its hands are filled with an otherworldly strength. Fear, like a pinball, bounces against his heart, his head, his throat, until finally settling in his gut, hard and cold. His chest churns with unspecified, wretched thoughts. He wants to hurt someone for all the hurt he is feeling right now. He wants something that will knock him flat and keep him there until the world goes away.

His first thought goes to his brother. He wrenches open the bedroom door, skids across the marble landing, and halts in the doorway of the adjacent bedroom, staring at the perfectly made bed, vacuum paths still fresh on the carpet. He continues through to the other rooms, the empty, hollow house seeming suddenly sinister and ghostly, like a mausoleum. But nothing is out of place, everything is in its usual immaculate state. The front door, the back door, the windows – all locked. No sign of anything missing – stolen. No sign of forced entry.

Back in his room it is as if he is looking through a shattered windscreen. His mind is running on several planes at once. Everything he sees seems freighted with significance but he cannot put the pieces together to create a comprehensible whole. His mind races back to the previous night and chases it, failing, scenes stuttering, disappearing. Memories pull and bend, mixing and blending like watercolours on an abstract canvas. He is on a carnival ride, being sucked to the wall, glimpsing faces, colours, lights. His life is disintegrating, bits and pieces of it flying off into the dark. His mind hits the self-preservation button and turns blank, like a ream of unmarked paper. He can remember the diving competition in Brighton, the day before. He can remember leaving the Aquatic

Centre after the press conference. But after that, nothing.

He lays out the facts the room has provided him with, side by side, in his head. Nothing of value seems to have been taken; in fact at first glance he can detect nothing missing at all. His desktop, his PlayStation, his laptop – all smashed beyond repair but present all the same, mashed gruesomely into the carpet. Muddy footprints crisscross the floor but, on inspection, perfectly match the soles of his trainers. The windows are locked from the inside.

Slowly, painfully, he begins to pick through the remnants of his belongings. He tries to avoid his reflection in the mirror but finds himself glancing at it periodically even so, like a motorist peeking at the gruesome remains of a roadside accident. Suddenly he can take it no more, and straightens up to face the stranger before him. He barely recognizes himself. Running his fingers through his tangled hair, he watches in stupefaction as twigs and dead leaves fall at his feet. His face is pinched and bleached – violet staining the skin beneath his eyes. There is a cut on his cheek and dark shadow beneath it. The corner of his mouth is encrusted with blood, and what appears to be the beginnings of a bruise blooms purple across his forehead. He looks shocked and thin and in-substantial, his collarbone visible through his cotton sweater, his cuff torn and his jeans streaked with mud.

What the hell happened?

His mind refuses to answer. Silence fills the room, as fragile and intricate as frost; so much silence, refusing to be stirred. His world suddenly appears before him as an unmarked road, with visibility down to almost zero. His headache persists, a heavy pounding that refuses to let go of his temples. Then, abruptly, fear is replaced by rage, fanning through his veins, his own fury seeming to spike the very air around him. What if he suddenly just goes crazy and starts to scream? It scares him because he feels that is exactly what he is about to do – any second now.

He is filled with a deep, black desire to fall to his knees and weep. It's as if he knows that he will never recover. He senses himself desperately trying to cling to the person he once was, hanging on with both hands while spinning away from the real world.

His life is over . . . His life has just begun.

1

Just one week earlier he was lying in the long grass with his friends. Such a short time ago, but it might as well be a whole lifetime. Another life. He was a different person. One who knew how to laugh, how to crack jokes, how to have fun. He was just an ordinary teenager back then, although he didn't know it. He thought he was amazing; everyone thought he was amazing. School had just finished for the day and the long weekend beckoned – three whole days of turbulent freedom, off with his coach to the south coast to compete in the National Diving Championships. A-levels were finally behind him, the final weeks of school were just a formality now, and all those painstakingly stacked stale hours of closeted revision had led to this: lying back against the soft, pulpy earth, the grass tickling his ears, staring up at a violently blue expanse of sky, while movement and general conversation buzzed around him – a pleasantly dim hum, like the noise of a badly tuned radio.

Here in the park is where most of the sixth formers hang out during free periods. In the shallow dip between the two hills, far enough from the lake not to be bothered by squawking geese but close enough to see the sequined light dancing off the water. The sun is a pure, transparent gold, stroking the local hangout with light and filling it with delirium. It's a particularly warm day in June, and today feels like the first proper day of summer – the kind of weather where you can kick off your shoes and enjoy the feel of the soft, cool ground beneath your soles. Where ties are scattered in the grass and blazers are bunched together to prop up heads. Where shirt-sleeves are rolled up, exposing anaemic white arms, and collars flap loose, buttons undone down to the curve of breasts or the tops of bras. Where guys like him with six packs wear their shirts hanging open, or shed them completely to engage in a raucous game of football.

All around, Greystone pupils sit in pairs or in groups: guys with their arms slung proprietarily round their girlfriends' shoulders, amoeba-like clusters picnicking from pizza boxes or swigging bottles of Coke. A gaggle of girls is drawing on each other's bare arms with thick black felt-tips – hearts, messages, cartoons with speech bubbles. Someone has organized a piggy-back race: girls clambering onto guys' backs, shrieks echoing through the park as they wobble precariously or go tumbling into the grass. The sun, approving their languor, is making its way lazily down the sky, in no hurry to end the day. He can almost taste the freedom and release in the air – summer, like an infection, spreading across the park.

'Are you playing, Matt?'

Mathéo considers for a moment, then decides to let them wait, his eyes squinting in the needling brightness of the sun.

'Matt?' Hugo sounds irritated and prods him with his foot. 'We need you on our team.'

'I think he's asleep,' he hears Isabel say, and realizes his eyes are half closed against the blinding white light, amorphous silhouettes blurring and fading around him. 'As I was saying, my parents are away that weekend,' she continues eagerly, 'so we can all come home after the Leavers' Ball and have our own party—'

'He's faking!' Hugo's voice cuts through. 'Lola, will you tell your lazy sod of a boyfriend to get up?'

Whispers. A muffled giggle. Mathéo presses his lids tightly closed as he becomes aware of Lola shuffling over towards him on her knees.

Trying desperately to relax, he inhales deeply, fighting to keep his lips from twitching upwards. Her

9

breath is on his cheek — what the hell is she up to this time? He tenses his muscles, ordering them not to move. Her theatrical snort cues the sound of laughter exploding from all around him. Something tickles his nostrils. A blade of grass? He bites down on his tongue, his chest tightening, lungs contracting, threatening to explode. The feathery wisp brushes back and forth.

'Maybe he really *is* asleep,' Isabel says again, clearly keen to turn the conversation back to her end-of-year party. 'So I was thinking we should have the barbecue by the pool—'

'He moved!' Hugo declares triumphantly.

Silence. Hugo is imagining things. Then Isabel's voice: 'Lola, what are you doing?'

Mathéo braces himself and is suddenly aware of an intense itch — a blade of grass, up one of his nostrils. His eyes fly open and he rolls over to sneeze violently into the grass. 'You! That's not even funny!' He kicks out at her but she dodges his bare feet with ease.

'I respectfully disagree! Missed. Missed again. Your flies are undone, Walsh.'

Mathéo jack-knifes up. 'Liar!' His attempt to grab Lola fails spectacularly as she bounds lithely to her feet and runs over to the muddy edge of the water. Grabbing a long, sturdy stick, he follows her, the grass prickly against his soles, determined to get his revenge. Lola backs away, giggling, as he advances menacingly, stick held out like a sabre. Hugo joins them at the lip of the pool as, ducking his fencing moves, Lola splashes into the turbid water, luring them in.

'Push her over! Push her over!' Hugo urges him, his voice rising with glee as he scrambles in the grass for a weapon of his own.

'Isabel, get over here, I'm outnumbered!' Lola implores as they both start prodding her with sticks.

Isabel jogs over reluctantly, collar flapping open, sunglasses crowning her head. 'Guys, I thought we were going to finish planning the—'

But she doesn't get a chance to continue as Hugo runs up behind her and gives her a good shove, which almost sends her tumbling in.

'Bastard!' Isabel spins round, splashing water all over his school uniform.

Soon, the four of them are wrestling at the water's edge. Mathéo grabs Lola round the waist and lifts her up, swinging her towards the murky depths. Her screams turn heads and draw amused looks and envious stares from pupils close by, but as one of the most revered cliques at school they are used to it, even play up to it slightly: the higher their pitch, the more they feel they are enjoying themselves. The four of them have been friends for nearly two years now. It started out with just Mathéo and Hugo, best friends since starting secondary school. Then, two years ago,

Hugo started dating Isabel; six weeks after that Mathéo hooked up with Lola.

Hugo has always been the embodiment of the archetypal private school alpha male, a young Prince Harry: closely cropped ginger hair, rosy skin, a compact, muscular build. Captain of the rugby team, vice-captain of the cricket team, keen rower – obsequiously British to a fault. At times he can be a bit of a narcissist, delighted by the sound of his own voice and the humour of his own jokes, but still manages to exude the smooth charm and make the kind of flirtatious overtures that girls find hard to resist. Isabel has an elongated feline grace about her, abundant dark hair, playful eyes and a classical refinement to her porcelain features.

Mathéo, like Hugo, has always taken for granted that he should be part of the elite clique. Taken for granted the other guys' looks of envy whenever he slung his arm casually over Lola's shoulders as they walked the school corridors or high-fived Hugo after some spectacular sporting win. At times he even feels smug for constantly having beautiful Lola by his side, thrives on Hugo's pranks and dirty jokes, basks in the cacophonous, cosy comfort of all four of them giggling and laughing at others, satisfied in their insular, privileged existence.

'Lola, come here, I want to show you something!' Mathéo reaches out to Lola from where he stands, ankle deep in green weed, trousers sopping from the knee down.

She flashes him a look. 'You really think I'm that gullible?'

He stares intently at something down in the brown water. 'Oh, cute, a baby frog . . .'

She inches towards him to get a closer look – and suddenly he has her by the arm and is yanking her through wet leaves and muck. She squeals and clings to him, about to topple over, their feet slowly sinking into the soft mud. Hugo splashes over and tries to grab Lola's legs while Isabel watches in hysterics from the safety of the shore. Suddenly finding herself horizontally suspended in mid-air, Hugo gripping her ankles and Mathéo hooking his hands beneath her arms, Lola begins to panic, and on the third swing screams in anticipation of the inevitable launch into the water. But Isabel has come to her rescue, dragging Hugo backwards, and suddenly everyone is flailing about in the mud and the wet, yells and shrieks piercing the somnolence of the afternoon.

Brushing the tousled hair back from his face and rolling up the clammy sleeves of his drenched shirt, Mathéo climbs the bank. He sits down in the shade of a large tree, its long branches heavy with thick green leaves, creating shadows across his body, dancing to the trilling of birds' joyous disharmonies. Leaning back on his hands and stretching out his

13

mud-streaked legs, he looks back at the others tussling at the pond's rim, splashing and screaming and laughing, their voices echoing in the trees. But mostly he watches Lola, her long brown hair glinting in the sun.

It's hard to believe that it was nearly two years ago that he met her. Here, in this park, after the first day of the new school year. Hugo and Isabel were locked in a friendly argument about the merits of *Dexter* versus *Homeland* – a conversation that as usual he had no part in, his intensive training rarely giving him a chance to watch TV. As he leaned comfortably back on his hands, blinking rapidly while his eyes slowly grew accustomed to the sun hanging low in the sky and casting a golden glow across the grass, he allowed his gaze to travel casually across the few remaining clusters of pupils, past the game of Frisbee and beyond, to the grassy slope. And there she was, sitting slightly apart from the other pupils, close to the foot of the hill. Her head was turned away, legs pulled up, arms resting on her knees, torso limp as she gazed at an indefinable point on the horizon.

Mathéo was used to a lot more than his fair share of female attention. He had been out with a couple of girls before – even one from the year above – but quickly lost interest when they began to make demands on his time, preferring instead to spend his rare free moments with Hugo. But for some inexplicable reason, this girl-in-the-distance captivated him. There was something different about her. She appeared lost in thought, elsewhere, only switching on the automatic smile and slapping on a superficial gloss when forced to engage with the other girls sitting nearby. The difference was so slight as to be barely noticeable, but once he had detected these hairline cracks between her and the rest of the group, he could not turn his eyes away. He found himself studying her as if she were a figure in a painting. She was tall and slender, pretty – no, beautiful – in a long-legged, coltish kind of way. A loose-fitting white shirt hung over the regulation grey school skirt, cuffs undone, flapping around her wrists. Unlike the others in her group her face was devoid of make-up and tanned from the long summer. Her hair was the colour of conkers and hung loose to her waist, long and dishevelled, cloaking her legs as she sat. At rest, her face wore a wistful, slightly dreamy expression, and her wide green eyes gazed far off into the distance, as if indulging in the fantasy of another possible life. There was a look on her face that captivated Mathéo in a way he couldn't quite define.

Knowing she could not see him, he watched for as long as he dared and found himself unable to take his eyes off her. Why exactly, he could not tell. In some indefinable way he felt drawn to her, as if he already knew her, as if they had been close friends, soulmates even, somewhere in a previous existence. Her mere presence seemed to calm his thoughts, saving him from the vicissitudes of his mind. She appeared before him as familiar, a kindred spirit. Perhaps it was something in her face, her eyes. She seemed to know . . . what, exactly, he was not sure. She seemed to understand. Or rather, he had detected in her the capacity to understand.

With a little smile, he raised his hand.

She returned the gesture, her face igniting for a moment, and then she was gone, striding back to join her friends. The feeling hit. Mathéo stared after her, drawing his lower lip in between his teeth and biting down in confusion. Disappointment yawned open like a cavern in his chest. Was it a gesture of farewell or a friendly acknowledgement of his existence, an invitation even to go over and say hello? But she was back chatting with her friends, denying him the possibility of any further communication.

Her group was packing up, about to set off home. The sun had started to dip in the sky, the early evening colours, soft and roseate, falling like dust over the water. He had missed his chance — if indeed there had even been one in that brief, ephemeral moment. Frustration welled up, pressing at the back of his throat. He watched her wipe her feet clean on the grass before putting on her shoes, stuff the remainder of a sandwich in her mouth and gesticulate wildly while talking to her friends. Chatting animatedly, she followed the others across the expanse of greenery, through the trees and out of the gates without so much as a backward glance.

He felt cheated somehow. As if the wave had been a tease, or a signal to alert him to the fact that she had caught him staring; a warning that he wouldn't get away with it again. He pressed his fists against his eyes and inhaled deeply, a disappointed, sinking feeling in his chest. It was time to train, time to leave the emptying park, time to go . . . Slinging the strap of his bag across his chest, he said his goodbyes to Hugo and Isabel and slowly got to his feet, his muscles protesting. Passing the pond, he stopped for an instant to soak in the last of the golden rays, the grass drenched in low evening sun, watching the shimmering interplay of light and dark and the gentle arrival of dusk – the conclusion of another day. Spread out before him, the water's surface was wrinkled and whispering, reflecting thin clouds that stretched across the indigo sky. The geese had reclaimed their territory and glided seamlessly across, serene and proud, melting into the glaucous evening. They brought him peace, and for a few moments he stood there, transfixed by the beauty of the scene . . . Then he shook the fog from his head. *Get a grip*, he thought. There was only so long he could stand here.

But as he turned, his gaze sweeping over the patch only moments ago alive with the sound of girlish chatter, a sparkle of silver amongst the long blades of grass caught the fading sunlight, reflecting it so brightly it burned his eyes. He blinked, the flash of white light repeating itself on the back of his eyelids. Crossing over, he picked up a watch, its black face no larger than the pad of his little finger. The strap was more of a bracelet – fine, interwoven loops of white gold. He felt its cool weight in his hand: solid, real, the needle ticking soundlessly round and round, making it feel somehow alive.

'Thief!' The word was called out casually, teasingly, but caused him to inhale sharply in surprise. The girl was striding down the slope towards him, her long hair tossed by the rising wind. The world quivered around him, and for a moment he was too startled to respond, but then he came to his senses and stepped back, nonchalantly slipping the watch into his pocket.

'Finders keepers!' He raised his eyebrows at her with a teasing grin.

She stopped just a few metres away. She was taller than he'd realized, almost the same height as him, and a smattering of freckles covered her cheekbones. Grass stains streaked the hem of her school shirt, one of the buttons was missing and the shape of her slim arms was visible through the sleeves. Dried mud marked her long, pale legs, blood crusting a small scrape just above her knee. A curled leaf was caught in her windswept hair, small pearls adorned her ears, and hanging from a delicate chain, a silver teardrop lay against the smooth skin of her collarbone. For a moment her green eyes widened with incredulity at his response. Then she latched on to his smile and gave a wry shake of the head.

'Very funny – give it back.'

He took in a quick lungful of air. If he messed this up, the moment would burst. Hands in pockets, he hunched his shoulders, scuffing his heels against the ground and narrowing his eyes in mock-suspicion.

'First I'm afraid I'm going to need some proof that this – uh – seemingly valuable item does in fact belong to you.' He cocked a grin and stepped back tauntingly. But he was aware of a warmth rising in his cheeks: it was clear that he was flirting now, and so this was the point at which she might just demand the watch back and stride off. How fine that line was between connection and interruption – one false move, one misspoken word, and you found yourself on the wrong side of things.

But she only let out a little sigh of mock irritation. 'My name is Lola Baumann,' she informed him, dragging out the words with exaggerated tolerance. 'It's engraved on the back.'

'Oh, really . . .?' He removed the watch carefully from his pocket and pretended to inspect it. 'I'm

Mathéo, by the way.' He kept his eyes narrowed on the watch.

'Where are you from?'

'Here – London. But it's French – my mum's French.' He felt himself flush and tried to mask it by cocking his head and pretending to narrow his eyes at her. 'So I'm guessing you're a Greystonian like the rest of us?'

'Unfortunately. We moved here from Sussex last month for my dad's job.'

'So are you in the Lower Sixth too?'

'Yeah. Not doing any science-y subjects like you, though.'

He felt himself start. 'How do you know which subjects I'm doing?'

She smiled. 'You're the Olympic diving guy. Everyone knows everything about you.'

He flushed at that. 'Well, what subjects are you doing, then?'

'Art, English and Music.'

'Ah, that explains why I haven't seen you around school.' He turned away, tossing and catching the watch with exaggerated nonchalance.

'Hey, careful!' She lunged forward, but he was too quick.

'Hold on, hold on.' He moved backwards, holding out his hand to keep her at bay. 'An engraving, you say? Pity I'm not wearing my contacts—'

'Oi!' She lunged again, and this time caught hold of his wrist. 'Open your hand!'

The look of fierce determination on her face made him chuckle. 'No!'

'Fine, then I will!' She attempted to prise open his fingers. 'Oh God, why are guys always so freakishly strong?' As she dug her index finger into his fist, he allowed her to gradually unclench his hand until she found it empty.

Sucking in her breath, she appeared shocked for a moment, her eyes meeting his, her fingers still round his wrist. For a second she was so close he could almost smell her hair . . . He stepped back with a jolt, blood thrumming in his cheeks.

'What?' she asked sharply, noticing the change in his expression.

He managed a quick laugh, galloped back a few steps and pulled the watch out of his pocket. 'Catch!'

She squawked and had to jump for it, only just making contact as it arced over her head.

'Oh, my poor watch!' Lowering her hands, she inspected it carefully, polishing its face with the hem of her shirt, then holding it up to the light to scrutinize it for scratches. 'This is brand new, you know – a leaving present from a friend back home. God, if I'd lost it—'

'You're welcome,' he interrupted with a sarcastic grin.

She slipped it back on her wrist and pinned him with a stare. 'Oh, I'm sorry! Thank you for trying to steal it and then nearly throwing it in the water!' Brushing the hair back from her face, she shook her head with a long-suffering air, but he detected a glint of humour in her cut-glass eyes.

Leaving the park and its orchestra of summer scents, they exchanged crunchy gravel for the unyielding asphalt of the main road, striped with long, spiked shadows, the tall buildings robbing the pedestrians below of the final minutes of sunlight. Almost immediately they found themselves swallowed up by the rush of commuters hurrying towards the gaping mouth of the Tube, while the open doors of bars spewed out laughing, chattering people, before sucking others back in again. From a café somewhere the pounding bass of a drum seemed to shake the ground, and the whole cacophony of the street rose to greet them as if someone had just turned up the volume, raised voices reverberating inside his skull. Crowds eddied around him, their faces looming large as in a telescope, filling the lens. Ahead of him, swept away by the current, Lola had almost reached the street corner. Half turning, she called back: 'So I guess I'll see you around school . . . ?'

But already she was disappearing from view, fading into the crowd.

He took a deep breath. 'How about you give me

your number? My friend's having a party this weekend . . .' A lie, but he knew he could count on Hugo.

A brief moment of hesitation, and then she was elbowing her way back towards him. People swarmed past them like ants round an obstacle. He produced a leaky biro from his pocket and felt the nib tickle and scratch against the palm of his hand. Then she flashed him a smile before once again being engulfed by the human tide. As she was washed away by the mass of seething bodies, he moved back, away from the flow, sagging against the glass of a department store, utterly spent but unable to stop smiling.

'Aargh!' Lola grabs him by the shoulders and topples him backwards so that he finds himself with his head in her lap, staring up at the sky. 'What are you daydreaming about? Winning Olympic gold?'

He lets out a snort. 'Yeah, right.'

'Hey, I'm counting on you winning that gold medal next year!' Lola teases. 'I mean, why else would I be going out with you?'

He gives her an evil smile.

'We'd better make a move. It's Orange Wednesday,' she reminds him.

Wednesday evening is movie night for Lola. Every week, without fail, her father takes her to the cinema. Both movie buffs, it's one of many fun routines they started way back when Lola was still at nursery school and lost her mother to cancer. When she and Mathéo first started going out, she would try and persuade him to come along too, but despite being flattered to be included, he always firmly refused, not wanting to encroach on her time with her father.

Lola gathers her things, and he levers himself to his feet and slings the strap of his school bag across his chest, shoving his damp feet back into his shoes.

'Hey, guys!' Hugo calls out from his spot in the sun with Isabel. 'You off already?'

'Yeah, unlike you lazy sods, we have better things to do,' Lola shouts back teasingly. 'See you tomorrow.'

The kitchen door of the Baumanns' house is open onto the courtyard, the smell of cooked apples billowing out with the steam, and Lola's dog, Rocky, scampering around in circles on the grass patch, chasing a leaf into the early evening breeze.

'Come in and say hi to Dad – he's been asking after you.'

As they approach the gate, Mathéo can already make out Jerry Baumann at the cooker, his favourite Guns N' Roses apron tied beneath a slightly sagging stomach, rattling a saucepan with gusto to the blast of Queen on the radio.

'Dad, you're gonna get in trouble with the neighbours again!' Lola shouts by way of greeting.

Jerry sets the pan down on the hob with a clatter, turns round with a broad grin and, in his usual manner, envelops his daughter in a bear hug as soon as she steps through the door.

'Ow, I can't breathe. Why are you cooking already?'

Ignoring her protests, Jerry turns to Mathéo and claps him heartily on the back. 'How's my favourite diver?'

'The only diver you know,' Mathéo responds automatically, playfully swatting Jerry away and circling the table to tussle with Rocky. Mathéo has always loved this house. So warm and snug. So small and cluttered and messy. So very different from his own.

'Sit down, sit down,' Jerry urges him as Lola disappears upstairs to change. 'I got off work early so I thought I'd be a good dad and do some baking.'

'Thanks, it smells great but I'm not really hungry.' Mathéo holds out a hand in an attempt to restrain Jerry from passing him a piece of apple pie.

'You're looking undernourished as usual,' Jerry counters, taking no notice and pushing the plate towards him. 'You need fuel for all that training!'

'Hardly.' But he sits, breaks off a small piece of burned crust and surreptitiously feeds it to Rocky, salivating expectantly under the table.

'Dad, it starts in ten minutes!' Lola rushes in with her handbag, narrowly missing Mathéo's plate as she dumps it unceremoniously on the table. 'I'm sure your pie is divine but I really want to get good seats for once, so can we please go?' She rushes over to the oven and turns off the heat. 'Daaad! One of these days you're going to burn the house down.'

Jerry intercepts her at the fridge, holding out a spoon. 'Just a taste. I made it from scratch from the new recipe book you got me.'

Glancing at Mathéo, Lola shoots him a long-suffering look and reluctantly accepts the mouthful. 'You're force-feeding Mattie too?' she exclaims in-distinctly, her mouth full. 'Aargh, Dad, that burned my tongue!' She strides over to the sink and bends over to drink straight from the tap.

'Do you think it's a bit overcooked?' Jerry carries on blithely, ignoring his daughter's antics. 'I'm worried I left it in the oven too long.' He takes a bite himself.

'I think it's delicious,' Mathéo assures him.

'Mattie, stop being polite! Would you please just tell my father to get his butt out of here?' Lola implores.

But Mathéo is quick to raise his hands with a small laugh. 'Whoa, you know I never take sides between you two.'

She scowls at him. 'Coward.'

With the help of Rocky, Mathéo manages to finish his slice, watching the interaction between father and daughter with customary amusement. Lola and Jerry have a relationship like no other he has seen before. They are mates, partners in crime. Mathéo's own parents always comment that Jerry allows his daughter to do as she pleases – run wild and have whatever she wants – because he is trying to make up for the loss of her mother, but Mathéo doesn't agree. For the majority of Lola's life, it's just been the two of them, and so they seem to have formed a bond so strong it sets them apart from the rest of the world.

Mathéo's parents tend to dismiss Jerry as a hippie – and no doubt he once was – but now he is more of a middle-aged rocker. Former lead singer in quite a well-known band, Jerry seems to have passed his talent down to his daughter. The two of them are passionate about music – seventies rock in particular: David Bowie, Bruce Springsteen, Lou Reed, Queen, Led Zeppelin, the Rolling Stones . . . Jerry and Lola even have a little band of their own: Jerry composes and plays the drums, Lola plays the guitar and sings.

But over and above their shared passion for music, what Mathéo has always found remarkable about the two of them is the way they interact. It helps that Jerry is laid back and that Lola is not known for her wild streak, but they share a camaraderie usually only found between best friends. Sometimes it seems as if Lola is the adult – reprimanding her father for leaving his camera gear lying around or for shopping for ready meals. Materially they aren't wealthy – Lola is at Greystone on a music scholarship, and he knows Jerry struggles to pay the mortgage out of his salary as a freelance photographer – but on the other hand, when Jerry receives assignments he gets to travel the world, usually taking Lola out of school for days at a time, and almost every wall in their small but cosy little house is covered with prints of Lola at every age in all sorts of exotic locations. When he is working locally, Jerry always seems to be home to greet her after school – chatting about her day, plying her with snacks and drinking in every little detail. He is always on hand to help with homework, and in the evening they take Rocky to the park together. After dinner they might watch some TV, or download a film or, if Lola isn't too tired, head for the studio-shed at the bottom of the garden and work on Jerry's compositions . . .

The first time Lola brought him back to introduce him to her father, a couple of weeks after they started dating, Mathéo was nervous. He expected Jerry to be very protective of his only daughter. And he was, in a way. But he approved of his daughter's first serious boyfriend, Mathéo could tell. Jerry was friendly and took an interest in Mathéo's diving, right from the start. Even now, even though his training usually gets in the way, they always make an effort to include him. Mathéo shouldn't feel envious. And yet sometimes, watching them together creates an ache inside him.

2

After parting company with Lola and Jerry at the end of their street, it takes Mathéo less than ten minutes to walk the nine blocks home. Hawthorne Avenue, otherwise known as Millionaires' Drive, always seems especially austere after the cosy little street of small terraced houses where Lola lives. Everything about the avenue seems twice the size: the wide, residential road is lined with people-carriers and four-by-fours, interspersed with the odd sports car or motorbike. The trees here are thin and tall, their topmost branches level with the roofs of the identical four-storey houses with their painted white exteriors and shiny black doors. Passing the neighbouring houses, where crystal chandeliers catch the afternoon rays behind the windows, he turns between the pillars out-side number twenty-nine and climbs the five steep steps, reaching into the back pocket of his jeans for his key. Pushing open the heavy front door, he steps into the silent hallway. Virtually everything inside the house is white or cream, from the heavy marble tiles downstairs to the thick carpets that muffle every footstep on the upper three floors. Each room is painted white – it makes your eyes ache after a while. The ground floor is open plan: the hall leads to the living room, which in turn opens out into the dining room and then the kitchen. The size of all the rooms is further magnified by the sparse furniture, mostly black or silver – even the light fittings are made of brushed aluminium. The kitchen holds only the essentials: white-topped surfaces, a silver heavy-duty fridge-freezer, eye-level cupboards and a long breakfast bar separating it from the living area. This then contains a black leather sofa with matching armchairs, a glass coffee table, floor lighting, a sound system built into one wall and a flat-screen TV built into another. To the right of the hallway a spiral staircase, still in white marble, leads to the first floor: a second living room, rarely used, a guest room and a bathroom. The second floor belongs to his parents: their bedroom, ensuite of course, his father's study, and the spare room that no one seems to know what to do with – empty save for a broken exercise bike and some weights. The top floor is the one his parents still refer to as 'the children's floor'. First, a spacious bathroom, and next to that a large room that until recently was

Loïc's playroom. Now it's more of a games room, with a television, a computer, a variety of games consoles, a football table and mini pool table. Across the landing, the two bedrooms are more or less identical: king-sized beds, built-in closets and French windows that open onto balconies overlooking the garden. This is quite large by London standards, about the size of a swimming pool, and consists of a patio strip, followed by a long stretch of closely cropped grass, mowed weekly by the gardener. There are few plants or flowers – the brick walls are free of weeds and vines. Mathéo can't remember the last occasion he spent any time out there. Even in the summer the garden remains largely unused except for parties. The conservatory doors open straight out onto it, and at the far end of the lawn a small black iron door leads out onto a narrow footpath that runs along the backs of all the gardens and opens onto the street – a useful short cut or escape route when his parents are entertaining.

Back on the top floor, posters of any description are strictly prohibited. The cleaner makes the beds and picks up after them daily, so every evening Mathéo comes home to find his scattered books neatly stacked against the wall, his laptop closed and his desk bearing the telltale smears of a polishing cloth. The discarded clothes have vanished from the floor and the crumpled bedsheet has been replaced by a fresh one. However messy and lived-in Mathéo tries to make his room, by the time he gets back it has always reverted to its customary clinical neatness. It never used to bother him before; in fact, he'd always thought it perfectly normal. It was the only home he'd ever known and his friends' houses were much the same – although perhaps not quite as large. Until he met Lola. Until he met Jerry and started hanging out at theirs more and more. At first he'd been astounded by the clutter, the lack of a dishwasher, the breakfast things still sitting casually in the sink when they got back from school. The mosaic of photos and sketches and postcards on the fridge door. Dog hair every-where, crumbs littering the kitchen table. But he soon found out that it was the clutter, the lived-in feel that made it one of the few places he could be completely at ease. One of the few places he could relax, prop his feet up on the furniture, fall asleep on the couch.

Glancing into his own kitchen, Mathéo notices that the dirty plates and bowls and half-drunk mugs of coffee have vanished off the counter, as if breakfast were no more than a figment of his imagination. Loïc is doing his homework with the new nanny, Consuela, at the dining-room table. She is younger than the previous ones: petite and sinewy, with pointy features and a kind of nervous energy.

Loïc looks bored and fed up, blond head resting against his outstretched arm, picking at the end of his pencil, while Consuela tries, in broken English, to explain a comprehension question to him. He looks round hopefully as the front door slams, and Mathéo sees the disappointment in his eyes. 'What time is Maman coming home?'

'Hello to you too. I don't know. Hey, Consuela.'

'Mathéo, I try to call you. Your mother, she ask me for making chicken but this morning when I come there is only steak, so I defrost steak, but I thinking now maybe I should buy chicken?' She is very shrill and her words pelt out rapid-fire in a strong Portuguese accent that makes them hard to understand.

'No, really, I'm sure steak will do fine—'

'But what about chicken? Should I buy chicken?'

Oh Lord. Only her second day here and she is already a nervous wreck.

'No, I'm sure Mum will be fine with steak,' he tries to reassure her. 'Do you want me to put it on? Have you started dinner?'

'No, no, I start dinner.'

He hesitates, confused by her use of tenses. 'Do you want me to help Loïc while you sort out dinner?'

She appears appalled by the suggestion. 'No, no! Mathéo, you do homework now?'

'My last exam was yesterday. I don't have any homework.'

'You have training then? You do training now?'

'Yes.' Her way of telling him what to do by phrasing everything as a question is already getting on his nerves, so he turns towards the basement stairs. 'I'm just saying – if you need help with anything just give me a shout.'

'You change for training now, yes?'

'Yes,' he responds wearily without turning, beginning his trudge downstairs.

'Mattie?' Loïc's voice is quiet but plaintive.

Mathéo stops a few steps down and looks back up at him. He can tell Loïc wants him to stay, but . . . Soon his parents will be back, arguing about whose day has been the more stressful; Consuela will be in a flap, with his mother quizzing her about Loïc's homework; and his father will be demanding to discuss Mathéo's training for this weekend's competition.

'Can you help me?' Loïc gives him a mournful look. 'Consuela doesn't understand English.'

Mathéo feels himself cringe. 'Loïc, don't be so rude, of course Consuela—'

'I understand, I understand!' she shrills at him. 'Loïc, your brother must do his training now. I explain to you again. Listen—'

'But what time's Mummy coming back?' Loïc tries to ignore her, still looking at him with that frustratingly plaintive look of his. Mathéo never knows what his eight-year-old brother wants from him – only that whatever it is, he never seems able to provide it.

34

'Really soon. That's why you've got to get a move on. We're all having dinner together this evening.' He gives Loïc what he hopes is a reassuring smile.

'Is she going to put me to bed tonight?' Loïc looks hopeful for a moment.

'Yes!' He nods enthusiastically.

'And read me a story?'

'Yes! But only if you do your homework now, OK?'

Loïc eyes him doubtfully for a moment, as if trying to gauge whether Mathéo is telling the truth or just telling him what he wants to hear in order to get away.

'Are you going to the pool?'

'No. Just the workout room.'

'Will you come back to the kitchen when you've finished?'

'Yes,' he replies, safe in the knowledge that his parents will be home before it comes to that.

In the basement is the home gym that his father put in when Mathéo started winning medals at national level. He is the only one to use it – his parents prefer to work out at their country club – and so it is purpose-designed for his diving needs: the size of the whole basement, with wall-to-wall mirrors, sprung foam flooring, a tumbling harness, large trampoline for practising flips and somersaults, a running machine, rowing machine, and various bits of apparatus designed to stretch or strengthen different muscles. He is supposed to use it for an hour a day

35

when he has diving or gym training, and for two hours if he is recovering from injury, recuperating after a bug, and on Sundays, his only day off. He is usually pretty good at sticking to the schedule, but as his parents never come down here and it has its own exit into the garden, it has become a useful place to retire to in order to sneak out to see Lola.

As he enters, the lights come on automatically and the air conditioning starts to hum. Mathéo crosses over to the music player and, fiddling with the remote, kicks off his shoes and sheds his uniform, pulling on a pair of grey jogging bottoms and a blue T-shirt from the closet of workout clothes he keeps down here. After the mandatory hour of stretches, weights and floor tumbling to the blast of Eminem, Mathéo removes his socks and trainers and climbs up onto the trampoline. It is Olympic-sized and set beside the main gym in a purpose-built space that runs up the side of the house so that the ceiling is almost four storeys high. As he begins to bounce, gazing out of the glass panelling at the gathering dusk in the garden, the lights coming on around the lawn, he allows gravity to do most of the work, shaking out his tired muscles and tilting his head from side to side. He slowly allows himself to gather height until he reaches the marker on the opposite wall, and then he begins to flip. Front somersault in the tucked position, bounce twice and repeat. He goes through a set of ten before switching to a front somersault in the straight position, his body held as taut as a board, twirling through the air. A set of these, then somersaults in the piked position: legs straight and toes pointed, ankles gripped, his head almost touching his knees. Whenever he even slightly loses his form in the air, or lands more than a few centimetres away from the cross in the centre of the trampoline, he does the set again. Only a perfect set will do – there is no point in cheating: he will only pay the price when he has to perform these same twists and somersaults diving from the ten-metre board, and a bad landing headfirst into water from such a height is far more painful than landing wide of the cross in the centre of the trampoline. He repeats the sets in the same order, with the same positions, but this time somersaulting backwards, before finishing with a series of combinations: double somersaults and twists. As he pushes himself further and further, he begins to make mistakes – landing on the side of his foot, missing his landing altogether, crashing down on his shoulder – and he stops, goes back to warm-up bounces, refocuses his mind, tempers his breathing . . . before going for it again. He has passed the two-hour mark and knows he should stop now, so he sets himself a final target: five 'full outs' and he's done. Five, but in a row. He can do it. He just needs to believe he can do it . . .

* * *

Stepping out of the scalding shower at the top of the house, Mathéo enters the hush of his white-walled room, pulls on jeans and a T-shirt and, his hair still dripping, flops down on the bed, staring up at the opaque glass light-fitting hanging from the ceiling. The room is violently bright, and there is a sinking feeling inside his chest at the prospect of the evening ahead. Dinner with his parents is always an ordeal and he feels sleepy suddenly. Like most days, he has been up since five and diving at the Aqua Centre from six till eight, before catching the bus straight to school. The last couple of weeks have been rough, with A-level exams almost every day and last-minute cramming at weekends, and he is exhausted. But although there are still two weeks before term officially ends, school is now a mere formality. Several big names in some of the most popular fields of work – law, medicine, politics, science – have been drafted in to give talks; a lot of career counselling is still going on, as well as all the other end-of-year stuff. A big cricket tournament led by Hugo, which he foolishly agreed to help organize and referee, despite not being able to take part for fear of injury. A musical in the lower school that Lola is masochistically directing. Sports Day, which the sixth-formers must help organize, and things like yearbooks to sign, an auction for Save the Children, and of course the Leavers' Ball on Saturday night, which he will no doubt have to help set up as Lola is on the committee, but will miss completely as it coincides with the National Championships in Brighton. All very tedious.

Rolling onto one side, he removes his mobile from the pocket of his trousers in an effort to get more comfortable, and the familiar sight of an origami crane, made out of notebook paper, flutters down onto the duvet beside him. Settling himself back against the pillows, he picks it up and opens out its wings with a smile. Lola and her cranes . . . Somehow, she constantly manages to sneak them into his pocket, his school bag, once even into his shoe. She started doing it shortly after they first got together, when he had to take a whole week off school to compete in the Worlds in Hong Kong. She had stashed seven in his bag, with strict instructions to only open one each day. It had been a little like an advent calendar and, jet-lagged and nervy and so far from home, he had felt strangely comforted.

This one reads:

Good luck at dinner tonight. Hope your dad sees sense about the holiday. But don't worry if he doesn't — we'll find a way of kidnapping you!

P.S. I'm missing you right now. xxx

With a smile, Mathéo folds the bird's wings closed again and slides it under his pillow. Lola rarely comes to the house because his parents have made no secret of the fact that they don't approve of her. Partly because they are snobs, partly because they think she gets in the way of his training. So coming back to his sterile house to find one of Lola's cranes always makes him feel as if he has brought a little piece of her, a little part of her essence, back home with him.

He must have dozed off: when he hears the dinner gong, time seems to have escaped him. Dazed, still riding fluorescent dreams, he opens his eyes to find the light in the room has changed. The colours of evening fall like dust across his bed and a bluish haze fills the still room like water. Outside the window the garden trees are melting into dusk. The air has turned cold and smells of pine; a breeze enters the room through the gap left between the French windows, sending the curtains into an unchoreographed dance. He runs his tongue over his chapped lips and sits up slowly, his head filled with a heavy fog. Outside, lights are coming on in the living rooms where other families like theirs are gathering, fitting their day inside a single dinner hour before retreating for the evening, so much left unsaid.

Mathéo reaches for the switch by his bed, and at once the room plunges into a harsh brightness, obliterating the world behind the window. He gets up

40

and crosses the landing to the bathroom, skating in his socks over the polished floor, the tiles cool against his soles. After going to the loo, he splashes cold water against his face. A moth blunders in through the window and ricochets back from the mirror. Following its trajectory, he briefly inspects his reflection: his face looks flushed with sleep, the imprint of his pillow still fresh on his cheek. His shaggy fair hair is badly in need of a cut. He has inherited his father's blue-eyed stare, although Mathéo's eyes are larger, giving him a slightly startled look. His skin is almost translucent – pale threads of blue visible on his temples. He reaches up to touch the hot ridges in his skin. According to Lola, his greatest assets are his lopsided smile and his dimples. Although on the skinny side, years of intense training have given him a well-defined body.

He is rubbing ineffectively at an ink stain on the hem of his T-shirt when the gong sounds again, alerting him to the fact that he is only postponing the inevitable. It is rare for them all to have dinner as a family. Over the Easter holidays he ate at the Baumanns' almost every evening, and on days when his parents were likely to show up early, he managed to keep the peace by having dinner with Loïc and his nanny. But the last nanny was older, more relaxed and, having worked for his parents for the last three years, relatively unafraid and willing to cover for him. He has a feeling that Consuela is not going to be so accommodating; he will have to try to win her over.

As he hurries downstairs, he senses his parents' presence before actually setting eyes on them. He smells his mother's perfume, his father's aftershave. Their suit jackets both hang in the hallway, waiting to be put away. His can hear his mother in the kitchen, already castigating poor Consuela. Tall, slim and blonde, his mother has never, in all the years she has been in England, managed to shed her strong Parisian accent. Impeccably dressed at all times, never leaving the house without full make-up, she is regularly told she looks far too young to be the mother of a teenage son. Tonight she is still in her office clothes: silk blouse and tight pencil skirt slit at the side, high-heels increasing her stature by a good three inches so that she positively towers over the diminutive Consuela. Loïc circles round them like a cat, meowing for attention, trying to show his mother some wooden object he made at school. His father is already seated in his usual chair at the head of the table, his tie slung over the armrest, nursing a Scotch and leafing through *Sports Illustrated*. He too is tall – broad-shouldered and athletic, a keen golfer with a year-round tan and closely cropped salt-and-pepper hair.

'*Loïc, arrête!*' his mother snaps in French. 'Go and show Papa. I need to finish preparing dinner.

Consuela, please just go and lay the table and let me finish this.' She catches sight of Mathéo as he goes to take the plates from the cupboard. 'Mathéo, get your brother out of the kitchen, will you? We're never going to have dinner at this rate.'

Mathéo quickly passes the plates to a frazzled Consuela and takes Loïc by the hand, propelling him gently towards his father. 'Hey, Dad, look what Loïc made at school.'

His father glances briefly at the spinning top Loïc is now holding dejectedly in his hand. 'That's nice, Loïc. What is it, a ball?' But before Loïc can respond, his eyes alight on his older son.

'Did Mr Harrington-Stowe tell you he's going to be giving you private lessons twice a week starting in September?'

'Yeah,' Mathéo replies. 'I was kinda surprised. I thought we'd agreed I'd ask Miss Bell. I mean, she *has* been my teacher for the last two years—'

'I called the school before work this morning. Didn't want you wasting another day with that dim-witted Canadian.'

He feels himself flinch. 'She's actually pretty nice, Dad. She got me through my GCSE and this year's A-level – or at least I hope—'

'Pretty nice?' His father chuckles as if Mathéo has just cracked a good joke. 'The woman only has half a brain – I don't think I've ever met such an inarticulate teacher at parents' evening before. Mr Harrington-Stowe – now, he's a solid guy, Oxford-educated, and rumour has it he really stretches his students—'

And is also one of the most hated teachers at school, Mathéo thinks to himself. 'But twice a week for two hours?'

'Next year's not a gap year!' his father exclaims for the hundredth time. 'Just because you're deferring your university place for a year to compete in the Olympics doesn't mean you can slack off on study. If you're serious about reading Economics at Cambridge, then you need the best tuition you can get between now and then. It's bad enough that you're wasting your time on that English A level. I don't know why you insisted . . .'

You're the one who is set on me doing Economics at Cambridge so that I can end up going to work in the City like you. Mathéo tunes out his father's continuing eulogy and surreptitiously aligns the glasses with the plates as Consuela lays the table. His mother is chopping carrots with an energy bordering on mania, and marches over to the dining table to throw a stash of parsley, diced tomatoes, peppers and carrots into the salad bowl, like confetti.

'Oh, Mrs Walsh, I do that—' Consuela protests desperately.

'It's all under control, Consuela. Just get the boys to sit down, will you, please?' With a click of exasperation his mother goes to wash her hands and then returns to the table, taking her usual seat at the far end, nearest the kitchen, opposite her husband. 'Mitchell, please put the paper away now. We're about to start dinner.'

'Then why is no one else at table?'

Loïc slides quickly onto his chair, sucking his middle finger. Mathéo brings the heavy steak dish over from the kitchen and joins them. Consuela finally takes her place beside Loïc. There is a moment's silence while everyone holds back, waiting for his father. Taking another swig of his Scotch, he surveys them all for a moment, as if to check everything is in its place, then folds his hands in his lap and looks down.

'For what we are about to receive, may the Lord make us truly thankful.'

Mathéo lowers his head like everyone else, but refuses to close his eyes or chorus 'Amen'. When he looks up, his mother is eyeing him with one of her pinched, angry looks. Pretending not to notice, he unfolds his napkin.

'Consuela, would you cut up Loïc's meat?' His mother speaks sharply, the tone of her voice a clear reprimand to the nanny for daring to begin her own meal before attending to her charge's needs.

Consuela starts, almost dropping her knife. Mathéo can't help feeling sorry for her, already so

45

jumpy and yet still to witness one of his mother's meltdowns. Or one of her three a.m. rows with his father after he'd embarrassed her by getting into some drunken political argument at a cocktail party. One thing Mathéo is about to introduce her to, however, is the parent—son dinner-table argument, and he feels almost guilty for subjecting her to it so soon after her arrival. But he has little choice. He is unlikely to catch his parents together again for the rest of the week, and he needs to let Hugo know about the holiday.

Mathéo takes a bite of overcooked steak and chews it for longer than necessary, struggling to swallow, his mouth suddenly dry. It's not exactly that he is afraid of his parents – they have never hit him or anything. He just doesn't particularly relish confrontation of any sort – especially not with his father, who has a quick temper, has been known to smash the odd plate or glass after a drink too many, and excels at shouting Mathéo or anyone else who disagrees with him into submission. And of course there is Loïc, who always turns into a quivering wreck when tempers flare . . . Mathéo had always thought these kinds of tensions were present in all families, until he met Lola. But seeing her with Jerry, hanging out in a house that actually felt like a home, witnessing a family dynamic where disagreements rarely evolved into arguments, and when they did, were quickly settled by an apology – an apology from both sides, and often a hug too –

had made him see his own parents in a whole new light. And it saddened him, made him resentful of an upbringing which consisted of far too much money – for which he was supposed to show eternal gratitude – and an almost cruel absence of attention and time.

'So, I had a chat with Coach Perez on the car phone this morning and he warned me—' his father begins.

'Maman, I made a spinning top at school today!' Loïc interrupts.

'That's nice. How did you do in your spelling test?'

His father puts down his knife and fork with a clatter. 'In case you hadn't noticed, I was in the middle of speaking,' he snaps.

'I'm aware of that, Mitchell, but could you wait one minute please? Loïc, take your elbows off the table and sit up properly. Consuela, you need to cut his meat into much smaller pieces—'

'OK, that's fine, just go ahead and ignore me as usual.' His father's voice begins to rise.

'No one's ignoring you, Mitchell. I'm just trying to teach our son some table manners, that's all.'

'Well, you could start by teaching him not to interrupt.'

'Dad, what were you saying about Coach Perez?' Mathéo interjects quickly. If they start on each other now, he will miss his only chance.

'I was saying' – his father takes a deep breath and looks pointedly at his wife – 'that when I spoke to him this morning he made it very clear you would have to be on top form at Nationals. Apparently there's a new lad threatening to make the team – an Aussie, but with dual citizenship. Sam Natt, only sixteen. Just moved here but competing in Brighton against you this weekend and already creating quite a stir. Perez reckons he'll not only make the Olympic team but give you a run for your money this season.'

Mathéo chews the inside of his cheek and fiddles with the stem of his glass, trying to appear nonchalant. 'Yeah, I heard. Perez already told me.'

But as usual his father keeps on at him.

'It's like I keep telling you: there's always someone younger and hungrier snapping at your heels. A few months ago they were hailing you as Britain's greatest and youngest hope for the Olympics. But if you don't up your game, that could all change over the course of a single weekend.'

Matéo winds his napkin round his fingers. He is going to have to go for it now, he realizes, before his father gets completely carried away.

'Dad, you know school's ending soon—' He takes a nervous stab.

'Yes?' His father's eyes narrow immediately.

'Well, my friend Hugo – you know, the one whose father is a partner at Glaxo . . . he has – well, his parents have a villa in the South of France. I used to

48

go and stay there for a few days every summer, remember?'

His father puts down his fork. 'I remember.'

'Well, Hugo and a couple of his friends are going out there for two weeks when school ends, just – just for a holiday, and—'

His father stares at him, a chillingly still, open-mouthed gaze. 'You want to go too?'

'Well, yeah,' Mathéo says quickly. 'It's just that Lola really wants to go because she's never been before and – and the others are going off to university soon so it'll be my last chance to, you know, spend time with them . . .'

His father continues to stare at Mathéo, his eyes cartoon-huge. 'You want to take two whole weeks off training to go partying in the South of France?'

'We wouldn't be partying. It would be to relax, just me, Hugo, Izzy and Lola,' Mathéo tries to explain. 'Like an end-of-school thing. I wouldn't have to go for the whole time. Like maybe just a week—?'

But his father is already beginning to lose it, his face reddening, the veins standing out in his neck.

'Is this is why I spend ninety-hour weeks in the City to pay for all that exorbitant training?' he begins to shout, his eyes darkening with rage. 'So that you can piss off with your mates on holiday and go boozing every night with the Games only thirteen months away?'

'No!' Mathéo shouts back, his heart pounding with

a mixture of fear and frustration. 'I just want to be able to go on holiday with my friends for once!'

'Mathéo, don't take that tone with your father!' his mother chips in from the other side of the table, her voice low, fire in her eyes. Loïc gives a whimper and leans in towards the equally terrified-looking nanny.

Heat scorches Mathéo's cheeks. 'But he won't even listen to me!' he appeals to his mother. 'He just starts shouting whenever I say anything he doesn't want to hear!'

'Damn right I do! It's thanks to your mother and me that you have food on the table, a roof over your head, a top-class education and the best diving coach in the country!'

'I know that, Dad, and I appreciate it.' With an effort, Mathéo forces himself to speak in more measured tones. 'But I'm just asking for one week off. Or – or five days—' A note of desperation begins to creep into his voice that he immediately tries to quash.

'This is about Lola, isn't it?' his father says suddenly.

'What? Well, yes, but not just that—'

'You spend far too much time with that girl and her hippie father, Mathéo, and I want it to stop. She's getting in the way of your training, she's breaking your focus. You won't have time for a serious relationship once your training is stepped up—'

'If you think for one second I'd ever break up with

Lola!' he shouts, the blood rushing to his cheeks. 'She's the best thing – she's the only thing that – that—' He feels his throat constrict and forces himself to stop, to bring himself under control.

'Look,' his father says, more steadily now. 'A thorough training schedule, the moment term ends, is vital to put you firmly on the map for the Olympics. You want to compete in next year's Olympics, don't you?'

'Of course!'

'Then don't let this opportunity slip away! Most seventeen-year-olds can only dream of competing in the Games. For you, it's a reality. You've no idea what I'd have given, at your age—'

'I know, Dad, I know,' Mathéo replies. His body slackens as he realizes he isn't going to win this one.

'In just over a year's time you could be in with a shot at gold, while other guys your age are getting drunk down at the local pub, watching you on TV.' Sensing Mathéo has given up, his father's voice softens slightly. 'Now, take a look at this!' With a flourish, he pulls a newspaper out of his briefcase and unfolds it carefully, handing it over to his son. Mathéo spots his name in the headline, and a grainy picture of himself falling through the air.

Recognizing this as an attempt at reconciliation, he forces a smile, even though reading about himself always makes him uncomfortable. 'Cool.'

17-year-old Mathéo Walsh became Britain's first individual diving European champion last month, producing a remarkable last-round performance to land gold. He is rapidly becoming Britain's new diving superstar, determined to turn his talent to Olympic gold next summer. Walsh was only 14 when he became both British champion and Commonwealth champion in the space of just six months. A year later, he won a bronze medal at the World Championships in Shanghai – further raising already high hopes of something quite spectacular at next year's Olympics – and now he is European champion.

Walsh admitted he was 'shocked' after winning gold.

The London teenager recorded 10s in five of his six dives to score 540.85 – a new personal best. 'It was a very high-standard competition so I'm pretty chuffed,' said Walsh. 'I was thinking I would be lucky to get a medal, let alone win gold. After all the hard work and speculation it feels unreal. I'm totally overwhelmed.'

After a shaky start, Walsh produced flawless dives in rounds four and five, each earning four marks of 10 from the judges. 'I missed one of my dives. Normally I can do that third dive a lot better, and because I didn't, I got quite worried, and knew I had to turn it around. To be able to get the 10s after that and win gold was utterly unexpected. To finish up standing on the top of the podium with the national anthem playing is not something that happens every day. Now I just want to do it again at the Olympics next year.'

As he walked on to the platform for his first dive, Walsh looked tense and nervous. His opening dive – a back 2½ somersault with 1½ twists – earned him 88.40, putting him top of the leader-board. But his main rivals also produced their best opening scores, and it was clear it would come down to who would hold their nerve. Walsh had slipped to third place after round three, but his fifth dive, a reverse 4½ somersault with tuck, gained 97.15 and lifted him back up to second. Walsh kept the expectant crowd waiting until the very last round to see whether he would overtake the Russians. Then the teenager completed a powerful reverse 4½ to claim gold.

It was a dream come true for Walsh. 'I was so nervous, but there were loads of Union Jacks flying in the crowd, so the support really helped.'

Walsh has been breaking records since the age of 10. Quickly exchanging the 5m for the 10m board, he was British under-18 champion by the age of 14. The hard work put in to achieve his gold medal was carried out at the Ashway Aqua Centre in West London, under the guidance of his coach, Juan Perez, who is keen to stress that the Olympics is still the main goal. 'By next year he will be 18 and physically mature enough to give the top divers in the world a run for their money.'

But Walsh is trying to play down expectations. 'I am really looking forward to the Games,' he said. 'Getting any medal is going to be tough though: the Chinese are going to be really hard to beat.'

Walsh shows absolute devotion to his sport, even training on Christmas Day! Within 24 hours of winning gold in Berlin he was back at school, studying for A-levels and training three hours, five days a week.

At competitions, Mathéo makes it all look so graceful and easy, but every time his toes leave that board he is literally taking his life in his hands. In the nanoseconds before he hits the water, at more than 34 miles an hour, there is the potential for so much to go wrong. 'I'm always scared, but that's part of the rush,' says Walsh. 'I've gone through stages in my training when it's gone wrong, and it's terrified me. It takes time to build up that courage and go again. But you can't let it affect you.'

by Jim Rickets

Lying in bed, his arm bent beneath his head, Mathéo finishes reading the article and then flings the paper across the floor, in the vague direction of the filing cabinet that houses all the articles about him since he first started competitive diving. Switching off his bedside lamp, rolling onto his back and staring up at the darkness, he knows he will not sleep. Still riled by his father's attitude, he is tempted to pick up the phone and call Lola. But Jerry goes to bed early, he doesn't want to risk waking him, and anyway, he feels the need to move, to stretch his legs, to run. With one swift motion he swings his legs off the side of the bed and reaches for his clothes. He has to get out – of this room, of this house – before it stifles him. Crossing the floor, he opens the French windows and steps out onto the narrow balcony. Night has fallen; he feels the thick blue dark gently pressing its fingers into his eyes. The air is mild, the sky made of velvet, so soft and heavy it seems you could gather it up in your hands. A few streaks of colour remain tucked into the folds of the night; the lights have come on in the garden below. But the conservatory is dark, Consuela has left and his parents must have turned in.

Opening his door quietly, he strains for sounds from below and, hearing none, begins his careful descent down the three flights. Letting himself out of the conservatory, he walks quickly down to the end of the garden and exits through the door and out onto the footpath.

Streetlights smear behind him like neon streamers as he jogs the nine blocks to Lola's house. Beneath the orange glow of a lamppost he skids to a dizzy halt, staring up at the darkened windows. The heavy silver watch on his wrist indicates that it is gone midnight. Shit. Even though he knows Jerry would be cool about it, he can't possibly go waking him up at this time. But he aches to see Lola. She is the only one he can talk to about the stuff at home.

Pulling out his mobile phone, he runs his thumb over the screen and begins to text:

Awake?

A long wait. He leans against the trunk of a tree, suddenly spent, his eyes flicking hopefully from his phone to her bedroom window, praying for a light or a reply . . . Nothing. Her window remains dark.

Damn. He is about to return his phone to his pocket when it starts to vibrate, startling him so much he almost drops it.

No.

He smiles in relief and empties his lungs with a sigh, feeling better already.

Flashing thing in sky!

What???

UFO? Look quik!

Suddenly her curtains part and he feels his face light up as her ghostly silhouette appears behind the window. He can just about make out the contours of her face, tilted back to look up at the sky. His thumb skims the screen of his mobile again:

Beaming up from ground!

Grinning, Mathéo watches in amusement as Lola glances back at the phone in her hand and then down into the street below. He begins to quietly chuckle as she heaves open the heavy sash and leans out, blinking down at him sleepily, her long dishevelled hair catching the moonlight.

'Oh, fuck off!' She is laughing.

'Shush – you'll wake your dad!'

'You know he sleeps like the dead.' She brushes her hair back from her eyes and yawns. 'Jeez, I was just dozing off, you know. You do realize you have to be up in less than six hours? Where are you going at this time, anyway?'

Her tone is jocular, but Mathéo suddenly realizes he has no idea. Has he woken his girlfriend just to have a moan about his spoiled little rich boy's life?

His sudden silence seems to catch her attention, because all at once the tone of her voice changes. 'Are you OK?'

'Course.' He peels himself off the tree trunk. 'Just passing by. Checking to see if you still felt threatened by UFOs.' He forces a laugh. 'I see that alien abduction is still posing a real danger. I'll come round tomorrow after training.'

'Mathéo, wait.' She isn't buying it, he can tell. 'I'll be down in a sec.'

'No, don't, it's late—'

But she has already slammed the window shut, retreating from view.

The sound of the key in the door makes him start, and Lola slips out, pulling it gently closed behind her. Her white cotton nightdress hangs over a pair of skinny jeans and she is wearing what appear to be hiking boots, forcing a smile to return to his face.

'Don't you dare laugh!' she hisses. 'Couldn't find my shoes in the dark!'

'I didn't know we were going mountain climbing.'

'Shuttup – you've just dragged me out of bed. You're lucky I didn't come down in my underwear.'

'Wouldn't have complained.'

She thumps him on the arm and he finds himself envying her lightness, her apparent lack of gravity.

He empties his lungs with an audible sigh. 'D'you want to – I dunno – walk around for a bit?'

'Sure . . .' She pins him with a quizzical look, concern registering in her eyes. 'Has something happened?'

'Nothing different from the usual.' He starts walking fast, too fast. Lola has to break into a clumpy trot to catch up, and grabs his arm to slow him down.

'Hey, you said a walk, not a marathon sprint! Look, you don't have to tell me if you don't want to.'

He forces himself to walk at a more reasonable pace, and for several minutes they just trail along the tree-lined terraced avenues, the silence between them broken only by the clump of Lola's boots.

'You sound like an elephant in those things.' Mathéo manages a weak laugh, but the words catch in his throat.

'Hey! You should know better than to compare

your girlfriend to an elephant! Are we headed anywhere in particular?'

He rubs his forehead. 'I dunno. I'm being stupid, I shouldn't have woken you. I just – I just had to get out of the house . . .'

'I know,' Lola declares suddenly, pointing to the twenty-four-hour supermarket across the road. 'Let's get some booze!'

'Here's to a crappy life, a stupid school, brain-dead teachers, endless diving competitions and fascist, dictatorial parents!' Mathéo shouts out across the river, and takes another heavy swig of vodka, holding the bottle aloft by its neck and wiping his mouth with the back of his hand. The alcohol seems to be going straight to his head, filling his body with a warm buzz, blurring his thoughts and blunting his emotions. He takes an unsteady step forward and feels Lola grab the hem of his T-shirt.

'Sit down, will you? If you fall into the water, don't think I'm gonna dive in and rescue you!'

Despite her jocularity, Mathéo detects a note of alarm in her voice. They are sitting on the flat stone rooftop of a boathouse overhanging the Thames – one of their regular hangouts. The two of them have been coming here ever since they started dating, seizing whatever scraps of time could be salvaged from Mathéo's busy training schedule. To sunbathe or watch the rowers or just chat, expanses of unscheduled time receding towards the horizon. However, it's the first time they have been here at night with the sole purpose of getting wasted.

Lola is still tugging persistently on his T-shirt, nagging at him to sit down on the roof beside her. 'Come on, you're making me dizzy.' Cross-legged at his feet, she looks wild and windswept in the moonlight, her green eyes flecked with gold, the vodka making her cheeks glow, the shape of her long, slim arms visible through the sleeves of her nightie. 'Mattie, come on, you're too close to the edge.'

Ignoring her, he continues to hold his arms aloft, as if presenting himself on stage. Taking another deep swig, he feels the satisfying burn of vodka in his throat. He laughs down at Lola, teasing her by balancing on the edge of the roof on the balls of his feet. The river snakes away below him, reflecting the lights from a nearby bridge, the water's surface black and wrinkled.

'Stop it, I'm not looking.' Lola covers her eyes with one hand and holds out the other for the bottle. 'And it would be chivalrous to share that, you know.'

'Whoa—' For a split second Mathéo loses his balance as he attempts to take another swig. Lola extends her arm just in time and he grabs her hand, allowing her to drag him down beside her, suddenly shaken by his near-fall. She takes the bottle from him and thumps him hard with her fist.

'Ow!' Mathéo exclaims, rubbing his arm for effect and scrunching up his eyes. 'What the hell was that for?'

'Showing off and trying to scare me,' she replies matter-of-factly, placing the bottle out of his reach.

Side by side, they sit quietly now, legs dangling off the edge of the roof. Mathéo stares down at the inky water scissored with flashes of neon light, transfixed by the shimmering interplay of light and dark. For a few moments it brings him peace and he feels the inside of his mind fill up with the absence of thought, until there is nothing but static inside his brain. He is overcome by a sense of being nowhere – for a few minutes at least he can forget who he is, forget the endless treadmill of his life.

'Ah, that's better.' Lola leans back on her hands, staring up at the moonless sky. 'It's true what they say: vodka *does* warm you up, and having a boyfriend *is* overrated. Thanks for offering to lend me your jacket, by the way. Such a gentleman you've turned out to be. I should have let you fall in. In fact I should have pushed you in myself . . .' But when Mathéo fails to respond to her ribbing, her voice melts away into the darkness.

He continues to stare down, transfixed by the dancing lights on the water. Moonlight trickles on

61

the river's surface and a small boat bobs in the distance. The weight in his chest has returned suddenly, and he feels drained and heavy and slow, unable to even keep up the banter.

He heaves a sigh.

Lola moves closer, resting her head on his shoulder. 'What was that for?'

'Wish I didn't have to go away this weekend.'

'But it's the Nationals.' Lola sounds surprised. 'At least you know you're going to come back with a medal. Everyone in the press has you tipped for gold.' She raises her head to scrutinize his face. 'Hey, what's happened to all that self-belief you've had drummed into you over the years?'

'I dunno. I just don't have a good feeling about this one.'

Silence. He can tell that Lola's searching for the right words to say.

'It's probably just 'cos you're not coming,' he says lightly with a laugh. 'You're my lucky mascot!'

'You've no idea how much I wish I could come,' Lola says quietly. 'If I hadn't agreed to be on that damn committee—'

'I know, it's fine,' Mathéo says quickly. 'It's not that. Dinner tonight was just another embarrassing attempt at playing happy families . . .'

Lola exhales slowly. 'So, your dad said no to Hugo's holiday?'

'Of course.'

She looks deeply despondent for a moment. 'Don't they realize you need some kind of a break?'

Mathéo snorts. 'Clearly not. And my father rang the head and arranged for me to have private maths lessons next year with that fucker, Harrington-Stowe.' Staring down at the inky water to avoid her gaze, he is nonetheless aware of her eyes on his face, her look of astonishment.

'Oh, you're kidding. I thought the whole point of deferring your university place was to train full-time for next summer's Olympics.'

'So did I. And speaking of training – he's already on my case about the new schedule. Perez is still drawing it up for September, but my father thinks I should be starting it now. Oh, and he's also suddenly decided that spending time with you is affecting my focus.' The kaleidoscope of lights on the water's surface is hypnotic. Suddenly he feels horribly tired.

'Do *you* think we spend too much time together?' Lola asks. The question is posed lightly, almost teasingly, but it pulls him sharply out of his growing stupor.

'What?' He meets her gaze, feeling mildly stunned, and narrows his eyes as if to read her thoughts better. 'No . . . No way! Why – do you?'

Her face looks very white in the moonlight, contrasting sharply with her dark hair, and her eyes are bright, almost luminous. She appears ephemeral, as if she might suddenly disappear, and for a brief moment he is paralysed by a fear so strong, he can hardly breathe. He wants to reach out and touch her; feel the warmth of her skin against his, her breath against his cheek; hear the beat of her heart, the sound of the blood thrumming through her veins.

'You brought it up,' she counters, her tone reflective, pensive. 'Sometimes I just wonder . . .'

'What the hell's that supposed to mean?' The words come out sounding angry, defensive.

'I know how much you want to make the Olympic team, Mattie. I know how hard you've worked for it!'

'I'd give up diving tomorrow if you asked me to.'

She stops and looks at him as if trying to gauge if he is serious. 'Really?' Her voice resonates with disbelief. 'But it's your passion – it's the most important thing in your life. You've been competing since you were a kid. Hugo told me you would even skip school trips just so you wouldn't miss out on training.'

Mathéo raises his eyes to meet hers, so bright and intense in the moonlight, framed by her wild, tangled hair. And is aware of a pain, somewhere deep inside him, a stab of longing, a fear that she could one day be taken away from him.

'I do love diving,' he tells her, quietly now, struggling to keep his voice steady. 'More than anything. Except for – except for you.'

Her eyes widen and she sucks in her lower lip. She seems to be holding her breath.

'I love you, Lola.'

His heart stutters and threatens to stop. For a moment he thinks she might not respond. He has said it too soon – this wasn't the right time, the right setting. And yet he feels it with all his heart, has done for a while now, and perhaps the alcohol and the veil of night have finally given him the courage to actually articulate his thoughts.

Tears glint in her eyes, making him flinch. 'You don't have to say anything back, Lola.'

'I want to.' She crinkles her nose and presses her fingertips to her eyes. 'I love you too, Mattie. So much. I've been wanting to say it for ages. I just – I was just scared you would take it the wrong way—'

Her words begin to sink in and he feels as if all the air is exiting his body. 'Really?'

Lola wipes her eyes on her sleeve, sniffs and gives him a disarming smile. 'Why do you think I only applied to drama colleges in London?'

He stares at her, momentarily stunned. 'I thought – I thought that was so you could save money by living at home—'

'Of course not, silly. It's so that I can still spend time with you while you're training.'

'Wow.' He is speechless for a moment. 'Does Jerry

know?'

'Of course! He totally understands. He was the one who found me that job in the bookshop so I could save enough money to travel to watch you compete.'

'But I thought that was to help pay for uni fees—'

Lola shakes her head slowly with a small smile. 'No, the trust fund he set up for me out of my mother's life insurance will pay for that.'

'Cool!' Mathéo tries to smile but feels his throat constrict. 'So . . . Does that mean you want us to stay together for—' He breaks off suddenly, unsure how to continue. 'For – for a long time?'

'Yes. Or maybe even a very long time?'

He nods, unable to speak for a moment. 'A very long time,' he finally manages to whisper. 'Maybe even for ever.'

She smiles suddenly, fresh tears pooling in her eyes.

'Don't!' he says with a quick laugh. 'Or you're going to start me off too. Just—' He inhales raggedly. 'For God's sake, just come here, will you?'

She scoots over onto his lap and he wraps his arms around her and pulls her into a tight hug, high up on their perch above the moonlit water.

As Lola unlocks the front door to her house, Mathéo leans his head back against the strings of ivy that have grown down from the bricks over the years like a carpet unravelling.

He closes his eyes with a sigh. 'Don't go . . .'

She steps in, hesitates, and then reaches back for him. 'Stay over.'

'But you didn't ask Jerry—'

She laughs at him. 'Oh, you know he never minds.'

His eyes meet hers and he gives her a shy smile. 'OK. Just remind me to set the alarm.'

He tiptoes up the stairs behind her, past the softly snoring Jerry, and into her room. Sinking down onto the side of her four-poster bed, he shrugs off his jacket and kicks off his shoes. Lola disappears into the bathroom, and with an effort he unbuckles his belt and lets his jeans slide to the floor. Clad in his boxers and T-shirt, he switches off the light and lets himself fall back against the sheets, leaving space for Lola beside the window.

The door creaks and Lola pads in barefoot in her nightie, long hair cloaking her bare arms. As she comes round to her side of the bed, Mathéo turns his head against the pillow, smiling up at her sleepily. Even though his lids feel hot and heavy, he forces them open to stare at her silhouette. The light of the streetlamps falls across her face, highlighting her tousled hair. She climbs onto the bed, but instead of getting under the covers, kneels up beside him, her eyes opalescent in the half-light.

'Are you tired?' she whispers.

He feels the breath catch in his throat. 'No.'

He turns towards her abruptly, a sharp edge to his gaze. As she moves in closer, he feels his breathing quicken and a strange hum fill the air. Sitting up, he reaches out for her, pulling her towards him. Silence descends, as thick and tangible as the velvety darkness that surrounds them. All he can hear is the faint sound of her breath, soft and whispery against his face. He moves his hand so that his fingertips touch the warmth of her cheek, sliding his hands into her hair. Tilting his head, he closes his eyes and leans in until their lips meet.

He breathes her in, smelling her in the heat that rises from her skin. She tastes of strawberry lip salve and toothpaste. Her lips, her tongue – always so soft. He takes a startled breath and places his hands on either side of her face, pulling her closer, kissing her harder. He wants to press up to her, fall into her, feel her hands over him like the sea. His heart is pounding, the blood pumping through his veins. Every nerve and synapse and neuron is on fire, as though channelling electric currents: crackling and spitting sparks. He reaches for the hem of her nightie, pulling it over her head in one swift motion, then dragging off his own T-shirt, kneeling up on the bed so that their bodies are pressed together, so that he can feel the warmth of her breasts against his chest, her hair tickling his shoulders, her hands on his bare skin, muscles shuddering beneath the brush of her fingertips.

As he grips her by the shoulders, her hands ball into fists in his hair. They are kissing wildly, violently now, without a shred of control. His lips and tongue ache with the force of it. He presses his teeth against Lola's bottom lip, sucks at her neck as her hands stroke and pull at his shoulders, travel down his back. He is acutely aware of their mingled breath tearing and shredding the air around them. Falling back against the pillows, he tries to pull her down on top of him, but she resists and he feels a stab of panic rush through him.

'Lola, why? That's not fair—'

'We've run out of condoms,' she whispers with a wince.

He snatches his jacket from the floor. Shoves his hands into its pockets. Pulls out his wallet and fumbles through it. 'Ta-da!'

They collapse back on the bed, naked now, their bodies pressed into one. They are kissing hard, frantically – there is no one to stop them, no fear of interruption, no limit on their time. But instead of making them languorous, it adds a new element of excitement and urgency to the situation. Between kisses, he pants gently against her neck, the pain of longing pulsing through his whole body. He kisses every part of her face, her ears, her neck. He needs to touch every part of her, feel every inch of her. He wants to inhale her. He longs for her so much, it physically hurts. As he enters her, he curves forward, sucking in his breath, tensing and staring down at her face as if seeing it for the first time. A small sound escapes him and he closes his eyes.

He is having to hold himself so tight, he can feel himself shaking. It's been almost a week since they last had sex – he knows he isn't going to last long.

'Slow down – slow down!' he implores in a hoarse whisper, forcing out each word.

'Shh, OK!' Flushed and exquisite beneath him, she stares up into his eyes, breathing hard.

He buries his face in her neck. Taut as a wire, he inhales sharply, and again holds his breath and closes his eyes, hands scraping and scratching at the rough cotton sheets. His heart thuds hard in his chest, his breath shudders in his lungs and he tries to remember to keep breathing. The tingling feeling grows inside him like an electrifying warmth, almost a pain, all his muscles twitching. Then the rush fills his body and he feels he will burst from the strength of it. His whole being is taken over by an electric current, and he trembles with repercussions that send him reeling and gasping for air.

'I'm going to come,' he tells her in an urgent whisper.

Arching her back, Lola stares up at him, letting out a small cry. He feels himself tense so violently he seems sure to implode. He shudders again and again, scarlet madness rushing through him at full tilt. Unable to breathe without heaving, the gasps catch in his throat. He scrunches up his eyes, clenches his fists, and Lola holds him tight until the convulsions die away and slowly, gradually, the madness begins to fade.

Panting hard, he rolls onto his side and allows his head to fall against the pillow. Lola strokes his head, making him jump; he can feel the sweat on the back of his neck, down the length of his spine. He feels enveloped in warmth, heat even, his heart still pounding against his ribcage, the sparkling, tingling feeling still rushing though his veins. Inhaling deeply, he raises his head and kisses Lola, then rests his head against her chest, his body still caught up in sporadic shivers as she encircles him with her arms. The sweat between them is warm and slippery, and he clings to her as if to a yacht's mast on a stormy sea, their two bodies panting in silent unison.

3

He wouldn't have made it home in time if Lola hadn't had the presence of mind to set her alarm for four a.m. He dresses hurriedly and kisses her while she buries herself beneath the duvet, barely awake, warm and flushed with sleep. By the time Mathéo has jogged home through the first light of dawn, crept in through the back of the still sleeping house, changed into his swim trunks and tracksuit, he hears his father begin to stir. Mathéo finds him seated at his usual place at the kitchen table in his suit, drinking a large cup of coffee, as thick and black as tar. He holds out the usual banana and energy bar as Mathéo walks in, slinging his sports bag over his shoulder.

Whenever his father can go into work late, he drives Mathéo to training. If he doesn't have any early morning meetings, he may even stay for the whole two hours. Usually, though, he has to set off for work before the training session is out, leaving Mathéo to catch the bus straight to school. Unfortunately today his dad doesn't have to be in the office until mid-morning and intends to sit out the whole session – as he informs his son as soon as they meet.

They leave the slumbering house in their usual silence and slam into the front of Dad's BMW. Gravel crunches beneath the tyres as they make their way up the drive, Mathéo turning his head to look out of the window in the hope that his father won't notice the violet hollows beneath his eyes. Despite his painfully short night, he feels elated that he got to spend it with Lola.

People always seem to think that because he has been diving for so long – nearly half his life now – he must be used to it, must find it easy, must have conquered all his fears. But the truth is, a diver never entirely conquers his fears. You learn to manage them, as he began doing aged thirteen, when his father dragged him off to see a sports psychologist because he refused to attempt a back dive. Throwing himself backwards and plummeting down ten metres without being able to see where he was going was just too horrific to contemplate, and when harangued by Perez, then his father, Mathéo ended up sobbing at the very back of the board, refusing to budge. Since then he has learned to control his fear rather than conquer it, but it is always there, and with every step up the chain of seemingly endless iron ladders, his heart rate increases. People also seem to think that a competitive diver – especially one who excels at the ten-metre board – cannot be afraid of heights. But in fact diving makes you hyper aware of heights: the difference between a dropped dive from five metres and one from ten is extreme. A bad entry from the ten-metre board is like a car crash – at best it will wind you, at worst knock you unconscious. Mathéo knows of divers who have split their faces open by hitting the water at the wrong angle, divers who have been killed. When you are jumping and spinning and twisting through the air at thirty-four miles an hour, you had better get it right or the result can be fatal.

But nailing a dive, particularly a high-tariff one in competition, is an almost indescribable experience. The rush of pure adrenalin as you achieve that perfect rip entry, the rising feeling of euphoria as the muffled applause from the stadium reaches you underwater, the sudden burst of unbridled energy as you kick for the surface, searching for the display board, for your score, and the roar of the crowd when the giant digital numbers flicker you into the lead – ahead of your teammates, ahead of the consistently perfect Chinese, ahead of the world. Mathéo lives for those moments, he thrives on them – they are what keep him going: through the treadmill of training, the hours in the pool, the hours in the gym, the hours in the workout room. There is always another competition on the horizon, another competition to be won . . .

Losing hurts, of course; losing hurts like hell. Getting distracted by the lights, the flashing cameras, the fluttering banners and flags, the screaming supporters – it can all cause you a momentary lapse of concentration, a nanosecond of losing yourself in the air, mistiming a takeoff, mistiming a somersault, mistiming an entry. And you know it – feel it in your bones and muscles the moment you hit the water. And whether it's a bread-and-butter dive or the most difficult one in your set – the one you have been practising every day for months – it hurts. Far worse than a painful landing. It drives a stake through your heart. And you pull yourself up onto the side, shaking the water from your ears, trying to ignore the sympathetic applause, trying to keep your composure as you glance at the score board and see your name slip down through the rankings. But then the anger sets in – the anger with yourself, the anger with the universe; and it's how you use that anger, his coach and psychologist always say, that makes the difference between a champion and an also-ran. If you can channel that anger, that sense of injustice, into your remaining dives, you can claw back the points, some-times even make a complete comeback and go on to win the competition. You think: *I'll show them – I'll show them what I'm capable of, I'll show them I won't be beaten, can't be beaten, that one dropped dive is nothing.* And then you go back up to the ten-metre platform and execute the perfect dive, and you know the other competitors are thinking, *Damn, this guy just can't be beaten.*

From the top board at the Ashway Aqua Centre, Mathéo arches his neck to stretch his muscles and stares up at the blinding white concrete roof just above him. From up here, the diving pool below is nothing but a small, rectangular slash of fluorescent blue. Beyond it, miniature people swim up and down the lanes of the regular pool, getting in their early morning workout. Sounds bounce and echo all around him, but up here he always feels oddly removed from it all, in a world of his own. The air is hot and humid – he dries himself with his cloth so that his hands will not slip when he holds his legs while somersaulting down. Slipping out of a dive is just one of the many dangers.

The challenge when preparing for a difficult dive from the ten-metre board, whether in competition or in practice, is always to keep himself from imagining the many things that could go wrong. Today he is practising one of the toughest dives, The Big Front: four and a half somersaults with tuck, and it scares him. But down below, way down below, both his coach and father are waiting, squinting up at him, already assessing his attitude, his confidence, the amount of time it is taking him to psych himself up, and there is only so much stretching and bouncing on his toes Mathéo can get away with before he knows he will have to go for it.

After walking up and down the board a few times, he finally takes up his position at the back, breathes deeply, closing his eyes to visualize each movement in his mind – every tuck and turn and spin his body will make in the air as he falls; all the moves etched into his mind through endless practice dry-diving into the foam pit, on the trampoline with a harness, as well as in the pool. He focuses on his spot, raises himself onto the balls of his feet, counts aloud to three and runs four steps, launching himself off the board and into space.

He pulls his taut legs against his chest, spins down into four somersaults. His eyes constantly search for the water: the slash of blue. One, two, three, four, five. Then he stretches out as hard and fast as he can, left hand grabbing the back of his right, before punching the water like an arrow.

It hurts, and he knows it was an imperfect dive as the vacuum sucks him under, slowing until it allows him to turn and kick straight for the surface. Bubbles rise above him; he can feel the riptide created by his mistimed entry and he shoots towards the light, emerging with a painful gasp, his hair stuck down around his face, chlorinated rivulets pouring down into his eyes. He feels bruised all over. Although it wasn't a terrible dive, he already knows he over-rotated his entry and landed slightly flat, knocking the air from his body. He pulls himself onto the side and sits, fighting for breath, as Perez comes over, gesticulating at the giant screen on the wall as it replays Mathéo's dive in slow-motion, highlighting his error.

'Too much momentum in the run-up; you jumped too wide – that's why you over-rotated your entry.'

'I know,' he gasps, shaking his head to clear the water from his ears and the dizziness before him.

'You're still aiming for more clearance than you need. Stop worrying about hitting the board!' his father shouts from his plastic poolside chair.

It's not so much a board as a fifteen-centimetre-thick concrete platform. You try somersaulting through the air with that jutting out in front of your face, Mathéo thinks acidly.

The second slow-mo on the big screen comes to an end, and both coach and father are waiting for him to do it again. In a two-hour training session, it is usual for him to clock up over thirty dives from the high board. One dropped dive already – he is already analysing his mistake. He won't make it again. The next twenty-nine will be perfect. Mathéo jumps to his feet, picks up his cloth, strides over to the ladders and begins his ascent once again.

* * *

Shovelling down his huge high-protein breakfast in the Aqua Centre's canteen, he tries to explain the extension at the end of The Big Front to Eli, who has been trying to nail the dive for months now.

'The trick is to extend as soon as the top of your head is level with the three-metre board,' he says between mouthfuls of scrambled egg on toast. 'If you wait until you think you're level, it's actually your eyes that are level, so you've left it too late.'

'But how do you know when the top of your head is level?' Eli jabs his fork against his plate in frustration. 'Do you use another visual marker, or what?'

'You can tell because you're looking down,' Mathéo replies. 'That's the thing: you've got to keep your head straight but really keep your eyes on the water.'

'Hey.' Aaron and Zach come over, carrying similarly laden trays which they set down noisily at the table.

'Perez says if we all finish in the top five this week-end, he's taking us out for a night on the town!' Aaron declares with a grin.

'What, like, to a bar?' Eli's mouth falls open.

'Yeah, maybe!'

'He told you that?' Mathéo shoots Aaron a sceptical look. 'Perez letting us drink? I don't think so.'

'I was there. He said "a night on the town",' Zach chips in. 'What does that expression mean to you?'

'Cool!' Eli's face is quick to light up. 'Top five – we can do that, right, guys?'

'Means at least two of us have got to win a medal,' Aaron points out.

'Duh! Matt's gonna win gold!' Eli retorts.

Zach's face instantly darkens. 'Why the hell do you always assume that Matt—'

'Yeah, any one of us could win gold,' Mathéo says quickly, feeling the heat rise to his cheeks. 'I was really over-rotating my dives today.'

'You're still the only one who's got The Big Front—' Eli begins to argue.

'It's not all about that one dive, dickhead!' Zach flicks one of his peas into Eli's face.

'I reckon we can all get into the top five, easy,' Mathéo interjects.

'Yeah. Gold, silver, bronze.' Aaron points at Mathéo, himself, then Zach.

'Oh, in your dreams, mate!' Laughing, Zach kicks Aaron under the table.

'What about me?' Eli protests.

'Fifth!' the other two shout triumphantly.

Mathéo catches Eli's eye and gives a quick shake of the head. Despite being nearly a year older than Mathéo, Eli has been home-schooled all his life: an only child, mollycoddled and cocooned by fiercely protective parents who live for his diving. As a result, he often acts young for his age, susceptible to a fair bit of ribbing.

Fortunately, Zach is too busy examining his food to continue winding him up. 'I can't believe I've got to eat this shit for another thirteen months.' He holds up a spoonful of oatmeal and lets it glob back down into his bowl. Both his parents are overweight; he has begun to broaden out in recent months and so is on a strict low-fat diet. 'After the Olympics, I'm gonna eat at McDonald's every day for a month, I swear.'

'I'd kill for a Big Mac and fries,' Matéo agrees with a grin. 'Chocolate milkshake, apple pie, blueberry muffins—'

'Beer!' Aaron adds. 'And not just to celebrate winning a fucking medal! I tell you, I'm gonna get so wasted. Like that time after Worlds, when Zach snuck all that gin into the hotel room and we—' He breaks off, perplexed, as Matéo frantically mimes slitting his own throat.

'So!' Perez startles Aaron by approaching from behind him to join them at the canteen table. Short, lean and wiry, he is an overly familiar figure in his usual black tracksuit, an assortment of whistles, keys and ID badges hanging from his neck. 'I hope you boys are discussing your dives. Just three days till Nationals. We want a clean sweep.' He leans back against the plastic chair, folding his arms and pinning them each with a look, narrow eyes almost black in his perennially tanned, weather-beaten face.

Matéo nods along with the others, relieved that

81

Perez appears to have just missed the tail end of their conversation. He wouldn't have found it funny. Perez is a tough coach, doesn't suffer fools gladly; he can be painfully blunt, and in the world of diving has a reputation for being extremely quick-tempered, which is true. Nonetheless, Mathéo respects him, likes him even. Perez has been his coach for almost six years now, has pushed, bullied, yelled and dragged him to where he is now – number one in the country, right up amongst the top ten in the whole world. Perez always reminds his divers that he only expects one thing of them – and that is to put in as much work and dedication as him. No mean feat, as Perez himself is a former three times Olympic gold medallist. Twice divorced and now married to his job as the UK's top diving coach, he specializes in producing future Olympic medallists, and over the last twenty years has coached some of the biggest names in diving history.

'I'm counting on you guys,' he continues with furrowed brows, watching them eat. 'I expect perfect sets from all of you on Sunday. Especially you.' He is looking straight at Mathéo, who feels himself flush. 'We'll sort out that over-rotation once and for all on the dryland springboard after school.'

'We've got dryland training this evening?' Eli squawks in surprise.

Perez barely looks at him. 'No, just Matt.' His phone bleeps and he gets up from the table. Pats

Mathéo on the back as he passes. 'See you in the gym at four sharp.'

Lola is busy with the school musical all morning so it isn't until lunch that he manages to catch up with her. She meets him at their usual table, setting her tray down across the table from him with a clatter.

'So, last night was fun!' She laughs and drops her jacket, bag and keys on the chair beside her, unwinding a multicoloured shawl from around her neck and gathering her windswept hair into a bunch behind her head, twisting it into a hastily made bun, her cheeks pink with exertion. 'How's the hangover?'

Mathéo puts down his fork down with a clatter and gives her a sarky smile. 'Not good. And not helped by the fact that someone shook me awake at the crack of dawn and then ruthlessly kicked me out of bed—'

'Hey, I saved your arse,' she reminds him. 'Your dad would have gone nuts if you'd missed training! You're not going to the pool this evening, are you?'

'No, but I've got a one-to-one session in the gym with Perez straight after school. And then I've got to have dinner with Loïc and the new nanny.'

'What? Why can't you have dinner with us?'

'Don't worry. I'll sort something out with Consuela after this weekend.'

She frowns. 'You'd better. Oh, Dad and I are

83

rehearsing some new songs tonight. Will you come over and listen after dinner?'

'Sure . . .' He chews at his thumbnail, his mind suddenly pulled elsewhere.

Lola raises a questioning eyebrow. 'Nervous about the weekend?'

Damn it, she can sense everything. At home, he has always been adept at wearing masks, but with Lola that's impossible; she sees through them all. 'Bit. Training wasn't too brilliant this morning. Still having problems with The Big Front.' He looks down at his plate, arranging his rice into patterns with his fork.

He starts at the touch of her hand against his wrist. 'It's hardly surprising. You only had about three hours' sleep.'

'I know, but I just – I don't have the best feeling about this weekend.'

'You always get nervous before the big competitions,' she reminds him. 'And then on the day you turn those nerves into adrenalin and just go for it.'

He works his teeth against his lower lip, unable to look up. 'Yeah . . .'

'Mattie, you always rise to the pressure, you know you do. That's why you're European champion! And why the TV commentators nickname you the Iceman!' She gives his hand a little shake and chuckles. 'Although after last night, I should probably suggest they come up with something else—'

He laughs, despite himself. 'Shuttup!'

'Speed Demon?' she suggests, taking a mouthful of juice and half choking on her own wit. 'I'm joking, I'm joking!' she splutters as Mathéo reaches across to thump her.

He leans back in his chair and looks at her from beneath lowered eyelids. 'You're evil. I want a divorce.'

She grins. 'No you don't. You'd never manage without me, Mathéo Walsh!'

By half seven that evening, he is finally free. The afternoon felt endless: Perez kept him at the gym until he produced a consecutive string of ten perfect landings in the foam pit, Consuela was in another of her flaps when he arrived home, Loïc was whiny and refusing to eat dinner, and by the time Mathéo was finally able to go downstairs under the pretext of using the workout room, he felt ready to jump out of the window. Ten minutes after arriving at Lola's, he takes up his favourite place in the Baumann residence: the damp-smelling, faded green couch in Jerry's music studio at the bottom of their garden. It is not so much a studio as a shed – the windows are smudged and some of the wood has begun to rot, but thanks to Jerry's regular repairs it is still just standing. Mathéo rolls onto the couch, head propped up on one armrest, legs stretched out and crossed at the ankles.

Lola plonks herself on top of him, squashing his legs.

'Ow! Make yourself comfortable, why don't you?'

'Kiss.'

He obliges, pulling her back against his chest.

'Missed me?' she asks teasingly.

'Of course.'

'Good. Where's my coffee?'

'Over here on the floor where you left it.'

'Well, pass it to me, will you?'

'Do you need me to pour it down your throat as well?'

She narrows her eyes and wrinkles her nose. 'So much for chivalry—'

'Hey, my days as your slave are over, Baumann,' he counters. 'Now training is about to be cranked up, I don't plan to exert any more energy than strictly necessary. So from now on you will have to start reaching for your own mug once in a while, carry your own bag, open doors yourself—'

She turns her head against his chest in order to give him a nasty smile. 'Would you like your coffee poured over your head?'

'I think we both know that's an empty threat, Lola Baumann.'

By the time Jerry finishes setting up his new drum kit, Mathéo is dozing comfortably on the couch, head half buried amongst the musty cushions. Lola is messing around with new kit and Jerry comes in backwards through the door, carrying a large tray of snacks and drinks. Lola executes an flourishing drum roll followed by a mighty clash on the cymbals which makes him laugh.

Helping himself to a mouthful of crisps and lying back on the couch, Mathéo is aware of a sudden weight beside him. Something presses against his foot, and Mathéo props his head up on his arm and sees that Jerry has sat himself down beside his outstretched legs.

'Tired?'

'A bit.' He smiles apologetically.

'Lola tells me you didn't get much sleep last night.'

Mathéo feels the heat rise to his face, but Jerry is holding back a smile and his eyes are twinkling.

'Uh – well—'

Jerry gives a warm laugh and slaps Mathéo's leg. 'Hey, you know I'm just messing with you!'

Mathéo pulls a face and rolls his eyes in an attempt to cover his embarrassment.

'Hey,' Jerry says quickly, as if sensing his discomfort. 'Exciting weekend ahead! I'm just so sorry I won't be able to make it, but the shoot was booked nearly a year ago.'

'I know, I know. Don't worry about it.'

'We will, of course, be recording the TV coverage to watch in the evening, though.'

'Wait to hear from me first. It might be a total embarrassment!' Mathéo half jokes with a smile.

Jerry smiles back, but there is a slight furrow between his brows. 'Nervous about it?'

'Nah,' Mathéo begins, but the warmth in Jerry's face and the fold of concern between his brows reminds him that he doesn't have to pretend here. And much like his daughter, Jerry seems instinctively attuned to the sensitivities of everyone around him. 'Well, actually, yeah. It's just that I'm expected to win at Nationals, and that's worse, somehow. I prefer being the underdog.'

'Oh yeah, I can understand that. But the way you cope with the pressure in all your competitions is really remarkable. I know it's easy for me to say, but try not to worry, OK?'

'Yeah, OK . . .'

'When are you off?'

'Tomorrow morning,' Mathéo replies. 'Got an hour's train journey to Brighton with the squad. Then training in the new pool. Then we go back to the hotel for the night and prelims start in the morning.'

'It's gonna be really exciting to see you on TV again.'

'Hm.'

'Are your parents going down to watch?'

'Mum's got some meeting. But Dad – yeah, un-fortunately.' He meets Jerry's eye and pulls a long-suffering face.

Jerry makes a disapproving clicking sound with his

tongue and shakes his head with a wry smile. 'Your mum works too hard. Both your parents do.' A pause. 'They work you too hard as well . . . Have you been getting enough rest?'

'I'm OK.' Mathéo feels himself flush slightly. They always throw him slightly, Jerry's looks of concern. It's as if he knows how few of them he gets at home.

Leaning over to ruffle his hair, Jerry says, 'Just be careful, OK? Diving's not the safest sport in the world and Lola would be devastated if anything happened to you.' He pauses for a moment. 'And I would too.'

'Oh, don't fuss.' Mathéo swats him away with a laugh. 'I'll be fine.'

'Oh, I know. You're about to hit the big time. But between you and me, Lola needed a bit of reassuring the other night,' Jerry says in a low whisper, leaning forward with a conspiratorial wink.

'About what?'

'About the two of you – about how you becoming a big Olympic star next year might affect your relationship.'

'I'm not going to become—' Jerry suddenly has his full attention. 'Lola thinks it would affect our relationship?'

'I think she sometimes worries about some of the girls on the women's squad. As well as those squealing teens who follow you and the rest of the team around the country.'

Mathéo laughs but feels the heat in his cheeks. 'I rarely hang out with them. It's not— She's being silly!'

Jerry is smiling. 'I told her I didn't think she had anything to worry about,' he says. 'I've been around long enough to see that what the two of you have got is something really special.'

He pats Mathéo's knee, gets up and leaves the shed to make some tea. And Mathéo stares after him, struck by the realization that for the first time, Jerry has broken his daughter's confidence by telling him of her worries. He wonders why on earth he felt the need to do so. It almost felt like some kind of veiled warning – a warning to not ever hurt his daughter . . .

Lola is still messing around on the new drum kit; it's past nine and he's going to have to go home soon. He turns to give her a look that she is quick to recognize.

'OK, OK.' She puts down the drumsticks and comes over, leaning nonchalantly against his arm and flicking through Jerry's new score. 'I wanna be a drummer,' she informs him plaintively. 'I think I'd be good.'

'You're not doing my headache any good,' Mathéo retorts. 'Stick with what you know.'

She starts to hum the first bars, then breaks off. 'I'm gonna miss you this weekend.'

'No you're not,' he jokes. 'You'll be too busy at

the ball, dancing with all the guys who fancy you.'

She doesn't respond to the tease in his voice. 'It scares me to watch you dive on TV when I can't be there. I would have never agreed to be on the Leavers' Ball committee if I'd known it would coincide—'

'If I win a medal at the Olympics, I'll embarrass you by climbing up the bleachers and kissing you in front of the whole world.'

'You'd better!' She laughs. 'And then I'll embarrass you more by jumping into the pool!'

She levers herself off him, crosses to her spot in the centre of the room to set up the mic, and he swipes at her with his leg as she goes.

With the mic and amp finally adjusted to her liking, she hops onto the guitar stool and opens the score, looking at him with a mischievous smile. 'Ready to be blown away?'

'Not particularly, thanks to my three-hour night . . .'

She conceals her smile with a long-suffering look.

'Fine, fine.' Mathéo sits up and rests his chin on the back of the sofa as Lola strums the opening chords, leans towards the mic and starts to sing.

He watches her profile as she sings to the window looking out onto the garden, now fading in the gathering dusk. In the house opposite, he can just make out Jerry in the kitchen, clearing away dinner. Lola swings her shoulders to the song, almost dancing to the upbeat tempo, and her long fine hair bounces against her back as she does so, catching the weak light of the naked bulb. Just like every time she sings, her cheeks are flushed, her eyes glowing. The daughter of two musicians, both reasonably successful in their time, Lola was always destined to show talent – the reason she got a music scholarship to Greystone in the first place and has now been accepted by the prestigious Central School of Speech and Drama to start pursuing her lifelong ambition of becoming an actress. But it is more than just the mixture of purity and soul in her voice that pulls people in. She has that indefinable ingredient, that magic spark that, whenever she performs, lights up the air around her.

Ten o'clock comes around too soon – he has to be in bed early before a competition: anything less than eight hours' sleep could affect his performance. Jerry wishes him good luck again and envelops him in a bear hug at the front gate, the familiar smell of weed and tobacco on his favourite checked shirt. Lola insists on walking Mathéo home, and as it's not yet dark, he lets her. The sun still hasn't quite set, the last of its orange rays touching the roofs and glinting through the treetops.

Hand in hand, they take their time, walking slowly down the leafy, residential streets, still warm, but quieter now after the hot, busy day. Pollen falls like gold dust from the lime trees and the air is heavy with the thick, sweet smell of summer flowers blooming in the hedges and front gardens. Dusk is taking its time to fall, stretching out each remaining minute for as long as possible, in no hurry for the day to end. And Mathéo finds himself wishing it never had to, wishing this walk could last for ever. He usually looks forward to competitions, even if they take him abroad and away from Lola, but this time something is different; this time he wishes he didn't have to go.

'If we walk any slower, we'll start moving backwards.' Lola glances across at him after several moments of silence, pressing her tongue into her cheek to hold back a smile.

'Hey! You didn't *have* to walk back with me—'

'I'm joking.' Sliding her arm round his waist, she pulls him close, kisses his ear. 'I know it's only three days, but I'm going to miss you.'

'I wish you could come.'

'So do I. It'll be the first time I've missed one of your home competitions. The first time Dad has too.'

'I'll miss his giant banner.' Mathéo smiles. 'Gah – I can't believe you told him I snuck over last night!'

'What? You know he likes it when you stay over!'

'Likes it? Jeez, Lola, you must have the most liberal dad in the history of all parenting.'

'He's only like that with you. He adores you. You're like the son he never had!'

'He's like the dad I *wish* I had!'

Lola laughs. 'Your parents aren't . . . the easiest,' she says diplomatically. 'But deep down, you know they love you and just want what's best for you.'

'I dunno about that. I'm just waiting to see how long it takes Loïc to start accidentally calling the new nanny *Maman*, like he did with all the previous ones—' He breaks off suddenly, feeling uncomfortable, almost ashamed. How can he complain about his life – his privileged existence, his opportunities, his parents – when Lola and Jerry live on a shoestring and . . . 'Do you – do you sometimes wonder about your mum?' He watches her expression carefully in the fading light, afraid of upsetting her. But they have had this kind of conversation before, and Lola has always been quite laid back about it. But still, he wonders: what must it be like, growing up, even in the happiest of environments, wondering what might have been?

'Sometimes,' Lola replies lightly, swinging his arm. 'On my mum's birthday, or the anniversary of her death, when Dad goes all silent and withdrawn. But when I look at photos – it's weird, I feel kind of detached, like I can't really believe she was once my mother. I guess it's because I never knew her, or at least not for long enough to remember anything. Sometimes I try to think back to my earliest memory, but I can never quite reach her.'

'Do you ever wish you had two parents though? Or is Jerry enough?'

'He's more than enough!' Lola exclaims with a laugh. 'I can't really imagine having two parents. That's why I'm so glad Dad never remarried or had a serious girlfriend.'

'How come he never did?'

'I think my mother was the love of his life,' Lola replies, her smile fading a little. 'The few times he does talk about her, he just says she was his saviour.'

'Wow.'

'Yeah. He was kind of a mess when he met her. He was touring with his band, got into drugs big time, was even homeless for a while.'

'And your mother turned his life around?'

'Well, not immediately. Apparently it took some time. And there's still part of him that's kind of . . . I dunno. Like he does drink and smoke the odd joint . . . But after my mother – well, he tried. He used to go out on, like, one date a month when I was in primary school, but I think he felt guilty leaving me at home with some random babysitter, so it sort of petered out. I mean, obviously I want him to be happy, but because he stayed single all these years I think it brought us even closer together, so we're like friends – best friends – the two of us against the world!' She laughs again. And Mathéo thinks: *She looks so happy.* Yes, one really good parent *is* better than two mediocre ones.

'I thought I was your best friend!' he protests.

'You're both my best friends,' she says with a grin. 'I can have two best friends, can't I? You're my two favourite people in the world.'

He kisses her goodbye at the front gate under the soft glow of the streetlamps, in no hurry to go inside.

'I miss you already,' Lola says plaintively, hanging her arms round his neck.

'It's only three days. I'll be back from Brighton on Monday.'

'So, I'll still miss you.' She pouts, teasingly. 'Are you saying you won't miss me?'

He pulls her into his arms and bites her nose. 'Course I will.'

She snuggles her head against his shoulder and looks up at him with a mischievous glint in her eye. 'Don't forget to say you couldn't have done it without me when you're sitting in the press conference with the gold medal round your neck!'

He looks down at her with a long-suffering shake of the head.

She giggles. 'What?'

'You're silly,' he informs her.

'But you love me,' she whispers with a soft smile.

He leans down to kiss her again. 'I do.'

4

His clock bleeps, startling him out of his trance. Almost three in the afternoon. Sitting on the edge of his bed, elbows resting on his knees, surrounded by the wreckage of his room, Mathéo is aware of the need to move. He has lain immobile here for far too long. Consuela will be home with Loïc any minute now: Lola, Hugo and Isabel will shortly be leaving school. Mathéo realizes he is going to have to do something about this mess. God forbid Consuela should see this: she would call the police, and for some reason, as yet indefinable, he knows that matters. The only person who can put things right is Mathéo himself. He needs to return his bedroom to its usual orderly appearance.

Although there is nothing but a black hole where yesterday should have been, other memories still remain, anchoring him somewhat to the present, even if, in this pool of utter chaos, he still feels lost, like a cork at sea. With a concentrated effort, he excavates the most recent memories from his brain. Yesterday he was in Brighton, competing in the GB nationals. Not only did he make the cut but he won, he came first – he remembers calling Lola, and then his parents; he remembers the press conference with Aaron, who won silver, and Sam Natt, who beat Zach by a tiny margin to claim bronze. He remembers leaving the Aquatic Centre to go out and celebrate with the squad. He doesn't remember coming home – no doubt pretty wasted after celebrating with a night on the town. Now he is home, and so today must be Monday, which explains the empty house: his parents are at work, Loïc is at school, Consuela food shopping. But what happened to his room? The only explanation is that he trashed it himself, but why? *Why?*

Hurrying downstairs, wincing at the pains darting through his whole body, he returns with a handful of bin bags. Most of his possessions will have to be chucked. The twisted, broken trophies could possibly be salvaged, so he pushes them against the very back of his cabinet, out of direct view. The books he returns to the shelves, roughly shoving the torn, crumpled pages back between the covers. His laptop he hides beneath his bed – there's a guy at school who might be able to fix it. His desktop computer, however, is smashed beyond repair and the keyboard is in several pieces. He wraps them up in one of the bags and starts piling torn clothes, snapped DVDs, crushed cases, smashed photo frames, and even a mangled comb into the other. Blood and mud stain his sheets and pillow case – he drags them off his bed and bins these too.

In the shower he discovers more cuts and bruises. The knuckles on his hands are cracked and bloodied; his elbows and knees are scraped raw. His right foot hurts like crazy, his toes are a violent shade of purple. There are crimson scratches on his arms, his back, his legs – as if he'd been attacked by a particularly vicious cat. His knees feel weak and he aches all over, as if he'd been punched repeatedly in the head, the chest, the stomach. The shower burns his lacerated skin and the pain dizzies him. He appears to be still bleeding – the water pink as it spirals into the drain. He must have got into some kind of brawl at the pub after the competition. There is simply no other logical explanation. But as for the mayhem in his room . . . Did he get into an argument in his own bedroom? No, that's ridiculous. Yet his mind seems vaguely aware of some sort of fight – raised voices, clenched fists, the crunch of his knuckles meeting bone. And blood . . . No. He screws up his eyes until the flickering images fade. No. He cannot remember, *will not* remember.

Dressed in clean jeans and a long-sleeved T-shirt, he walks out into the bustling afternoon – and finds himself trying to memorize his surroundings, as if attempting to rediscover his place in the world. The identical rows of tall white houses, the colour of the sun as it illuminates the street, the stretches of grass coming in and out of view according to the curves of the road.

The high street is crowded with late afternoon shoppers: couples, teenagers, mums fetching kids from school and lingering outside on this warm, sunny day. People emerging from houses, shops, supermarkets, banks, restaurants, pubs. Chelsea girls sunning themselves outside swanky cafés, chatting on mobile phones, or walking arm in arm with their designer boyfriends, scouring the boutiques for make-up and shoes. Parking attendants in their crisp white shirts slap big yellow tickets on the windscreens of sports cars parked on double yellow lines. Bikers rev their engines outside the Harley Davidson club, while top-heavy, bright red buses crawl beside the kerb, weighed down with nannies and buggies, sounding their horns at frustrated drivers trying to perform U-turns in the middle of junctions. Roadworks hold up the traffic – workmen in fluorescent jackets drilling holes in the road, filling the air with an ungodly sound that shakes the pavement. Pedestrians crowd round traffic lights, a bicycle narrowly misses an opening car door, motorbikes navigate their way painfully slowly through the crawling traffic. At the entrance to the tube station a news-seller yells and waves his rolled-up paper at the stream of bodies washing past him. Somewhere in the distance, a siren wails. The dirt, the shouts, the hurried pedestrians crossing the congested roads; the fumes, the horns – it all surrounds him in a thick web of noise.

Everything looks so normal, Mathéo thinks, and yet everything seems somehow alien too. It is almost as if he is witnessing this kind of scene for the very first time. He feels as if he is on the other side of something all those other people cannot understand. As if he is the only one who is aware of the folly of humankind: forced enthusiasm, people rushing this way and that, trying to edge ahead of each other in their urgent need to get someplace – the where hardly seems to matter. What is imperative is the need to keep going, to keep moving, to keep constantly busy – all a desperate attempt to kid themselves that they are a part of this world, that they are somehow important, that the choices they make and the actions they take and the places they go actually mean something. Guys crowding into pubs, jostling round big-screen televisions and cheering on their football teams, women trying on the latest pair of designer boots, tourists picking out useless coloured glass ornaments from overpriced boutiques . . . It all suddenly seems so utterly absurd that he wants to stop right here in the middle of the street, watching the crazy snafus of human existence, and start to laugh, or cry, or scream. What was once so familiar that he barely noticed it has turned into madness. He feels like stopping a random passer-by and asking where they are going, what they are doing and why. But although the chatter around him is all in English, it could just as well be in a foreign tongue – one that he spoke a very long time ago but has now forgotten.

His ability to remain calm is impressive. Training his eyes on the pavement in front of him, keeping his mind fixed on the one thing he feels compelled to do. Walk. Where, he has no idea. It is as if beyond that one goal he cannot think; as if the safety valve in his brain is protecting him from his own visceral thoughts, forcing him to stay rooted in the here and now.

Exhausted, abruptly unable to go any further, he stops and sits down on a low wall flanking the park, overcome by the wave of heat and noise. His phone vibrates in his pocket, startling the hell out of him. Lola's name flashes up on the screen and his first thought is to let it go to voicemail. He doesn't want to see her right now; he *can't* see her right now. But guilt forces him to answer the phone.

She is talking very fast. She sounds excited about something. She is going on about the competition, his winning dive, watching it on TV yesterday morning with Hugo and Isabel. She is just leaving school and wants him to meet her in Greystone Park. He tells her he can't right now; he is busy. But when she asks what he's doing, he can only think of saying that he's shopping in the high street. She asks him where, gabbles something about Hugo and Isabel, and then hangs up. He finds himself staring down at the phone in his hand in dull confusion, feeling trapped. He can't possibly see her right now – she sounded so alive, so animated. He doesn't recognize his own girl-friend. He doesn't even recognize himself.

Against the violent brightness of the sun, three figures clamber out of a cab and leap into the oncoming traffic, forcing a double-decker bus to a sudden, tyre-screeching halt. Dodging vehicles and laughing, they tumble across the road towards him. He gets up, steps back and tries to arrange his face into a normal expression as they come charging, Lola's arms circling his neck, her hair suddenly in his face, suffocating. She is warm and soft and sweet-smelling, yet he finds himself fighting the urge to push her away. She and Isabel are both squealing about something, their shouts and whoops shattering the air. Hugo grabs him by the shoulders and gives him a violent shake, and Mathéo quickly steps back, making a concerted effort to smile and breathe. Smile and breathe. That's all he has to do for now. They are congratulating him on the diving competition. Overwhelmed and disoriented,

103

he catches something about a gold medal, the Olympics, some stuff on the Internet, his picture in the morning paper.

'I couldn't sleep, I couldn't sleep!' Lola is yelling in his ear, her face glowing, eyes wide with elation. 'I thought I was going to go crazy, just lying in bed and staring at the clock and counting down the minutes and—'

'Me too, me too!' Isabel thumps his arm. 'My whole family got together to watch you on TV—'

'And she kept texting me every five minutes!' Hugo puts in with an exaggerated sigh. 'And everyone from school was tweeting about it at the same time—'

'We tried and tried to call you after the interviews!' Isabel adds in outrage. 'And then most of last night! But your phone just kept going to voicemail!'

'We – we went out to celebrate,' Mathéo manages quickly with a dismissive laugh. 'The pub was deafening!'

'When did you get back?'

'You said you were going to come home last night!'

'We were waiting with leftover booze from the Leavers' Ball to congratulate you!'

'How come you weren't at school today?'

Their voices merge and blur into one histrionic wave, and they all appear completely high on adrenalin, drunk with excitement, their chatter leaping in all directions as they talk over one another rapid-fire, full of so much energy he almost expects them to combust.

'What happened to your face?' Lola startles him for a moment, her hand on his cheek. 'You've got the beginning of a massive bruise on your forehead. And is that blood on your lip?'

'Oh yeah.' He pushes her hand away dismissively. 'Got pretty hammered last night with the rest of the squad. Tripped on my way back to the station.'

Hugo laughs. 'Looks more like you competed in a boxing tournament!'

'Ouch — your hands too?' Lola takes them in hers to inspect his raw and bloody knuckles, the skin grated back from the wounds, jagged white rectangles surrounding each wet, crimson laceration.

But fortunately the attention is short-lived, as Hugo and Isabel have decided that high tea is in order, and Mathéo follows them as they gather noisily around a table beneath a large parasol outside one of the French cafés, scraping the metal feet of the chairs against the paving slabs.

'Oh my God, it's all in Frog!' exclaims Isabel in horror, examining the menu.

Lola and Hugo laugh. 'Oh, no!' Hugo mocks, shaking his head. '*Croissants*, *pains au chocolat*, *café* . . . What on earth can these strange words mean?'

'Ha ha!' Isabel retorts. 'Just because I dropped out of French doesn't mean I'm stupid.'

'No, no, not stupid!' Hugo exclaims. 'Just . . .' He clicks his fingers and shakes his head. 'What's the expression?' He looks round at the others. 'Linguistically challenged?'

Isabel bounds out of her chair and goes round the table to throttle Hugo. Then she slides onto his lap. 'I could eat you – I'm that hungry!' She laughs and twines her arm over his neck and gives him a long kiss. Looking away, their intimacy suddenly embarrassing him, Mathéo meets Lola's gaze. With a jolt he is momentarily aware of her eyes scrutinizing his face, and it's a monumental effort to keep hold of the laid-back, cheerful expression. Why is she staring? Can she tell something is wrong? Elbow propped up against the table, he turns away from her, chewing his thumbnail in an attempt to calm his nerves.

They all appear to be starving. As soon as the food arrives it disappears at an alarming rate, everyone helping themselves from each other's plates: croissants, éclairs, muffins, coffees. Mathéo chews slowly so that it looks as if he is consistently eating, but only makes it through half a bun. With all the food-sharing and banter he hoped it would go unnoticed, but Lola glances at his plate while Isabel and Hugo are squabbling over the last muffin and raises her eyebrows.

'Aren't you hungry?'

'Not really,' he answers quickly. 'Had a big lunch.'

'But you told me on the phone you hadn't eaten.'

'I meant since then,' he says, meeting her concerned gaze just long enough to give her a soothing smile.

A brief moment of hesitation, and then she turns back to the others, their rambunctious enthusiasm showing little sign of waning as they tease, joke and chatter animatedly amongst themselves. They move in electric currents: their raised voices, wild gestures and constant bantering igniting the table between them, making it thrum with energy. Mathéo feels the currents curl around him, envelop his body, encircle his head, but they cannot permeate his skin to fill the icy cavern inside with heat and strength and vitality; they cannot thaw the frost, anaesthetize his thoughts or extinguish the morning's horrors. For a moment the contrast is overwhelming and he fears it will be impossible for him ever again to transmute back to his original state.

Mathéo is beginning to feel he can no longer keep up the façade, that his true feelings are about to show through. Panic washes over him; he just wishes he knew what was wrong. Maybe something to do with how pointless everything is. Why does everyone put up with the hypocrisy, the need to put on a happy face, the compulsion to keep going? He doesn't know the answer, he only knows he can't do it any more. He doesn't understand what is going on. There was a time, not so long ago, when he was delighted to be part of this group – the most popular set. But something vital seems to have changed. It is hard to identify, but somewhere inside, a part of him is desperate to get up and walk away, screaming to be set free . . . although from what exactly he cannot say. He just wants to withdraw back to his bedroom, to hide and sleep as if he were dead – as dead as he feels inside.

For a few moments he tunes them all out and finds himself sinking like a stone, turning slowly through the water towards the bottom, where he rests, staring at the surface a long way above. He is filled with a sense of being nowhere – he can forget who he is, forget everything that's happened, forget the terrible person he has become . . . Taking a deep breath, he attempts to absorb the mood around him. He knows he urgently needs to break out of this strange funk, stop analysing everything, forget the horror of this morning's trashed room as if it had never happened. He needs to be popular, fun-loving Mathéo again. Because that's who he is. That's all he is.

The girls want to go shopping; Hugo is still talking to him about the competition. It takes all the effort Mathéo can muster to engage, respond, join in with the general chatter. But he feels he is about to crack, and knows he needs to get away from the others before he does. Day yawns open like a cavern in his chest and the sun is pulsing; he can feel it burn his skin. As they pass through the market, the summer stalls are loud and bright. Suddenly the air turns thick with the overwhelming smell of fish. With bulging eyes and gaping mouths they lie there, silver and bronze scales glistening in the late afternoon sun. Tourists, as if at a show, have gathered to watch the fish being carved up, fresh on the slab. The fish-monger works his way through his produce at lightning speed: tail grabbed, razor-sharp knife slicing the soft silver bellies. Occasionally the tail continues to twitch even after a fish is split in two and tossed on the pile, the nerve-endings still reacting spontaneously for a few seconds after death. Or perhaps it's that after the brutal slice the brain remains active for just a moment longer – long enough to feel the pain, long enough to realize the struggle is over. There are other sea creatures too, of course. Seething tubs of crabs trying frantically to climb over one another, waving long, spastic tentacles in a fruitless struggle to regain their freedom. They will die far more slowly, often not until taken home and plunged into a cauldron of water, where they will continue their hopeless fight for survival, legs groping at the air in slow motion, until they eventually boil to death.

There seems to be a lot of blood; blood every-where, in fact. The others have forged ahead towards the flea market, but Mathéo has stepped in something, and there is crimson splattering the toe of one of his trainers. For a moment all he can see is red – the same red that was pulsating in front of his eyes, the same red that was running in rivulets down his legs under this morning's shower.

Suddenly Lola is by his side, her hand on his arm. 'Mattie?'

His arm shoots out of its own accord, knocking her hand away, hard. He sees her eyes widen in shock.

'Ow!'

'Sorry, I'm just . . . I didn't mean to—' He swallows hard against the gag reflex in his throat. He can taste the blood in his mouth. All that blood – where did it come from?

'Lola, I'm sorry, I'm not feeling too good. I've got to go . . .'

He sees her expression turn to one of alarm and she moves towards him, but he is already backing away, dodging the afternoon shoppers, losing her quickly in the crowds. As his feet begin to pound the pavement, a momentary flash of lightning skims through the sky and the air around him begins to buzz and shimmer. It fills his head with static, and he briefly scrunches his eyes against the sickening aura, willing it away with all his might as his stomach starts to heave. *No, not here*, he begs. *Not here, not now*. But the refracting crimson blaze at the centre of his vision slowly shatters, like sunlight on moving water. Filling his lungs to capacity, he struggles to stay focused – one foot in front of the other, and repeat, and repeat, and repeat. But the ground beneath him begins to pitch and lurch as he struggles to stay upright and not give in to gravity's dragging force. As he starts to stumble, the pavement swaying dangerously beneath him, he turns down a narrow cobbled alley, skidding over a trail of crushed cartons, fruit peel and other debris. Then, ducking behind a tall rubbish bin, digging his nails into the wall for support, he bends over double and vomits violently into the gutter, again and again, until all he is bringing up is bile and his stomach has heaved itself dry.

5

Flung back in his chair, Mathéo tries to focus on the long list of bullet points on the whiteboard and the career counsellor's dull drone through the rubble of his brain. By mid-morning, a sharp skewer seems to have entered one temple and exited through the other. His mind is slogging along, slow and sticky, trying to keep up with the monotone. Mr Mason's face is half hidden in shadow, and periodically Mathéo forgets who he is. He fears that if the dried-up fossil clears his throat one more time, he may lose it completely and hurl his notebook at the old man's pate.

His head is starting to tip on the top of his spine, heavy with the dead weight of his brain, in danger of falling off his supporting hand. His upper eyelashes yearn to meet the lower ones, and everything feels blunted, refracted through a prism of smudged glass. His mind is blank, like a board wiped clean. He takes a deep breath of sweaty, stagnating air in an effort to quell the mounting sense of frustration rising within him. It's ridiculous. All of it. Within the grand scale of things, sitting in a classroom day after day is so utterly meaningless and pointless that it actually makes his chest hurt to think about it. School is a pile of crap. School has always been a pile of crap – he had just never bothered to think about it until today. He has little hope that university, when he gets there next year, will be any different. Like right now, all these pupils taking notes as if their life depended on it. *All for what?* he wants to shout. *To get into the top university, so that you can somehow convince yourself you are better than the great unwashed? So that your parents can convince themselves that they are better parents than the great unwashed? So that Mum and Dad's fourteen-hour days at the office, paying for a fucking private education you never asked for, wasn't just a pathetic waste of a life?*

He has no idea what he wants to do as a career, cannot imagine a life beyond diving. He initially wanted to study English Literature, but as his parents and certain teachers drummed into him, he would just reappear after three years with the kind of degree that would have him trained for nothing other than bullshitting his way through a critical essay. Law, his parents said, or medicine, or finance – become a banker like Dad: yes, that was the obvious choice. So, despite having no interest in the subject, Mathéo did as he was told and applied to do economics at

Cambridge. If he stays injury-free and does well enough at the Rio Games, he will no doubt continue diving for another two or three Olympics, spending every waking moment either studying, working, training or competing. Until his form begins to dip, until his body gives out. And then he will most likely get a job in the City, at some investment firm, working fourteen- and fifteen-hour days like his father. Marrying someone, having kids he never sees, with no choice but to put them through the same educational treadmill – because at the end of the day, education is compulsory, and for a reason: without it you face a life of cleaning up other people's shit. So, if you've got the means, you try to shove your own children as far away from the shit-cleaning as possible by sending them to the best school you can afford. Even if it means spending the rest of your days working in vacuous professions such as finance or investment or law, ripping off those who can afford it or those who can't but are desperate. Like his mother, for example: a hot-shot solicitor who charges by the minute . . . He loathes it all, Mathéo realizes; the whole system. He loathes it more with every passing second.

Another fourteen minutes and thirty-five seconds before the lunch bell. Time presses down on him, slowly spinning to a stop, hanging in the air. It is an effort to move his limbs, to turn his head. The day goes on outside in the street, but in here, time moves in infinitesimal increments, or doesn't move at all. He has one of those expensive, sleek, super-accurate analogue watches – silver, with a broad black leather strap – a present from his parents in exchange for the string of As and A stars he brought back for GCSEs . . . His brain empties suddenly. He feels flattened, and it is almost an effort to breathe. He doesn't want to do anything, can't concentrate – a dull, mute pounding against his skull.

He is aware of the teacher's eyes on him.

'Mathéo, are you feeling all right?'

The squat, middle-aged man has been walking up and down the aisles and, breaking off from his soliloquy, comes to a stop beside Mathéo's desk. It isn't until he glances up into the teacher's mildly concerned face that Mathéo realizes that, unlike the rest of the class, who are now engaged in some lively debate, he is just sitting there, currently studying a chip in the wooden desk beside his unopened pencil case.

'Uh, not really. Headache. Can I go to the nurse?'

But once free of the classroom, he doesn't head for the medical room. He considers the library, but he is not in the mood for reading. Instead, he walks the corridors restlessly, passing the odd janitor or student between classes, recognizing a face here and there. He wonders if any of them can tell just from looking at him that his pain is so total, so complete, that it consumes him. It is terminal. He feels so entrapped by the horror of existence that it is hard to comprehend why the whole world doesn't feel it too. His polished school shoes squeak rhythmically against the red and white chequered lino, a lonely soundtrack to his purposeless meandering. He wishes he could describe the feeling to someone, so they could help him; help him understand what is happening. But it's something he can barely put into words. Just a heavy, over-whelming despair. Dreading everything. Dreading life. Empty inside, to the point of numbness. And terrified he is stuck down here for good.

The school canteen is a sea of white acrylic, nothing but whiteness, the vast hall buzzing with shouting, jostling, laughing students. It's so loud in here it hurts his head. The industrial-sized windows overlooking the sports fields let in too much sun, flooding the walls with brightness, turning the whole place into a giant light box. Getting through the buffet line seems to take for ever – faced by the options he cannot choose, his stomach turns over at the sight and smell of all that food. People seem to be knocking into him on purpose; faces he barely recog-nizes break into smiles of congratulation – he manages to nod and smile back, thankful for the general din drowning out his half-formed words. Standing still, tray in hand amidst the tide of passing bodies, he is lost for a moment, unsure where to go.

Until he spots Lola in the far corner, away from the throng, mercifully alone.

She is finishing off an application form with one hand while forking pasta into her mouth with the other. As he sets down his tray opposite her and takes a seat, she glances up only briefly, before returning to her paper and lunch.

'Hi,' he says uncertainly, thrown by her lack of greeting.

She continues scribbling in her barely legible scrawl without looking up, munching solidly. For one awful moment he feels like he might be invisible, a figment of his own imagination, but then she swallows her mouthful.

'Hi.' She does not look up again.

'Uh . . .' He picks up his fork and moves the salad around on his plate. 'Are you busy?'

She slaps her pen down on her notebook in a gesture of exasperation and pins him with a look. 'Not particularly. Why?'

'Well, I just—' He sucks in his right cheek, biting and pulling at the skin. 'Are you mad about something?'

She opens her eyes wide, as if amazed by his stupidity. 'Well, yeah, Mattie. And kind of confused!'

'About yesterday—' He swallows a bitter taste at the back of his throat. 'I'm sorry I took off like that. I wasn't feeling too good. Just kinda dizzy, you know?

Maybe I was dehydrated from the competition or something.'

'That's why you switched your phone off for eighteen hours? And refused to return any of the messages I left with the nanny?'

'I crashed out for the rest of the day and most of the night,' he tells her truthfully. 'I was knackered.'

'You could have called me before school this morning to tell me you weren't coming to pick me up! I nearly missed first period waiting for you. And you could have answered my texts!'

Mathéo forces himself to meet her gaze. Her eyes spark with anger, but he also detects a hint of bewilderment and worry that sets his head pulsing. He doesn't want to spike her concern further by telling her he had kept his phone switched off since yesterday, purposely leaving it unchecked so that he wouldn't be faced with the barrage of concerned voicemails from his coach, his parents, Consuela, his friends and even Lola herself.

She is staring at him, waiting for an answer.

He draws his lower lip in between his teeth. 'I messed up. I'm sorry.'

Her mouth drops open. 'You're *sorry*!' she exclaims. 'Mattie, I've been worried sick! If it wasn't for your parents I'd have come round.'

He winces against the sound of her voice, her words piercing the fragile membrane that seems to surround him. 'Look, I really am sorry, I don't want to fight. Lola, please don't be mad, I can't deal with this now. I'm just so tired—' The words catch in his throat and he stumbles to a halt.

'Mattie, I'm not mad, OK? I was just worried, that's all. I didn't – I didn't know . . .'

A big, vacuous silence: Lola as much at a loss for words as he is himself. She is worried, he can hear it in her voice. She stretches her bare arm across the table and cups her hand over his.

'Mattie, please. Please, just tell me what's going on.' Her voice is barely more than a whisper.

He shakes his head, forces a laugh and pulls his hand away. 'Nothing! I'm just – I just seem to be in this weird mood . . .'

Her eyes are searching. 'What on earth happened?'

'Nothing!' He exclaims with mock annoyance. 'I just hate it when we fight, that's all.'

'We're not fighting, Mattie.'

'OK, OK – well, good.' He takes a ragged breath. 'Because – because I've blown off training so I'm free to hang out all evening, if you'll put up with me!' He forces a laugh.

She gives him an uncertain look, as if weighing up whether to press on with the inquisition or accept the sudden change in mood. 'Cool!' she exclaims after a beat. 'That's perfect because I agreed to meet Hugo and Izzy for pizza in the park and

119

I wasn't looking forward to being the third wheel.'

His heart plummets. For the life of him, he cannot remember how he ever tolerated hanging out so much with those two when his time with Lola was already so limited.

'Are you up for that?' His expression must have betrayed him: all at once she looks uncertain.

'Of course! I'll pick up some beer!'

'It's a school night, Mattie.'

He laughs at her and shrugs. 'So?'

'Hey, that's my man!' Hugo raises a hand for a high-five as Mathéo jogs over towards them with a pack of Stella, pulling his tie down, shirt tails flapping loose. He slaps Hugo's hand and kneels down on the grass between the girls, who are busy dividing up the pizzas. The sight of the red peppers and sauce turns his stomach for a moment. He tosses Hugo a can and rocks back on his heels, angling his head into the warm breeze and taking a steadying breath. When he turns back he finds Lola's eyes on his face, the crease of concern once again furrowing her brow.

He forces a smile. 'Well, this is nice.'

She returns the smile, but the hint of sadness in her eyes throws him for a moment and his precarious veneer threatens to splinter. Quickly opening his can of beer, he takes a long swig.

'Aren't you excited about winning the Nationals?'

Isabel asks him through a mouthful of food. 'I mean, has it actually sunk in yet?'

With a monumental effort, he forces himself to engage. 'Yeah, course!' He raises his eyebrows and smiles in an attempt to reinforce the words. 'But, you know, another whole year till the Olympics. Still plenty of work to be done . . .' His voice tails off at the sinking thought.

'I think this calls for a drinking game!' Hugo declares.

'No, I want to sunbathe.' Pulling a magazine from her bag, Isabel opens it and tries to lie back, but Hugo immediately snatches it out of her hands.

'Don't be so boring, Izzy!'

'Ow ow ow!' she screeches. 'Multiple paper cuts!'

'Serves you right.'

Their banter is loud and jarring, highlighting the strained silence between Lola and himself.

'Matt, Lola – are you guys in?' Hugo shouts, swatting Isabel's bare legs with the rolled-up magazine.

'What are we playing?' Lola asks cautiously.

'*I Have Never* . . .'

'Excellent!' Lola exclaims. She glances back at Mathéo and shoots him an encouraging grin. 'You in?'

He switches on the smile and gives what he hopes is a suitably enthusiastic nod. 'Sure!' Shuffling closer to the group on his knees, he leans forward in an attempt to emphasize his willingness to participate.

Everyone settles down, falling quiet as they start thinking up statements, the first can of beer placed in the centre of their scraggly circle. After a moment of careful consideration, Hugo starts. 'I have never' – pause for dramatic effect – 'had a threesome.' He looks around hopefully.

Nobody reacts. Then, suddenly, with a dramatic sigh, Lola raises an arm and reaches for the can.

'No way!'

'I always knew!'

'Very funny!'

She falls back, laughing, leaving the can unopened.

Isabel goes next. 'I have never . . . done it in a field.' She glances at Mathéo to watch his reaction.

He glares at Lola. 'I can't believe you told her!'

'What? When?' Hugo looks outraged.

Mathéo reaches for the can and takes a good slug before passing it to Lola. The girls laugh. 'Last Easter,' they chant in unison.

'You never told me that!' Hugo protests.

'You might be my best mate, but there are certain things that I keep to myself,' Mathéo teases.

'How come Izzy knew?'

'Because they're *girls*! They talk about everything!' Mathéo laughs, genuinely, for the first time in days. It feels good. As the game continues, he feels himself begin to relax, the alcohol and superficial banter gradually quietening his raging thoughts. *This is normality*, he reminds himself. *This is the kind of stuff I should be thinking about. Who snogged who and when, who was the first to have sex, who has done the most outlandish or crazy things* . . .

Lola has a mischievous glint in her eye. 'I have never fancied my teacher.'

'Bitch!' Isabel laughs, kicking out at her with her bare foot.

'No way! At Greystone?' Mathéo asks.

Hugo rolls his eyes. 'Remember that gap-year student – Ronnie something?'

'He was really hot,' Lola comments dreamily.

Mathéo gives her a playful shove. 'What – you too?'

'Hell, yeah!' She laughs at his outrage.

'I've got one, I've got one!' Isabel shouts, alight with revenge. 'I have never' – she gives Lola an evil smile – 'been arrested.'

'I wasn't arrested!' Lola shrieks, laughing.

'OK, OK,' Isabel retracts. 'I've never committed a crime then.'

'Nicking a plastic bracelet from Claire's Accessories when I was thirteen is hardly a crime!' Lola protests.

'Uh, yes it is. Thief!' Hugo shoves the beer can towards her and Lola obediently takes a swig.

'Anyone else?' she laughs, waving the can around enthusiastically. 'Anyone else a hardened criminal like me?'

She is looking straight at Mathéo, as if she knows. As if she knows about yesterday morning, and his trashed room, the scrapes on his elbows and knees, the scratches on his arms and back; as if she doesn't believe his story about the bruise on his forehead, his cut lip, his scabbed knuckles. *Criminal.* As if she knows what he's done, what he's become.

He isn't aware of raising his arm and knocking the can out of her hand; only of the thud as his arm makes contact with her wrist, the can arcing over her head, showering her hair with beer, scattering the sunlight.

'What the hell . . . ?'

He hears their shouts of protest, voices raised in shock and alarm, calling him back, demanding an explanation, but he has grabbed his bag and got to his feet in one swift movement, and is already through the park gates, sprinting out onto the street.

He slams into the relative coolness of the house and sags back against the front door, his school shirt sticking to his skin in damp patches. Wiping his sleeve across his forehead, he attempts to catch his breath, scarlet blotches puncturing the air around him. As his racing heart begins to calm and the world swims back into focus, he gradually becomes aware of an unfamiliar hum of activity in the house around him. He kicks off his shoes in the hall and wanders into the living area. The dining table is dressed in a crisp white tablecloth and covered with plates of food: quails' eggs, caviar on oatmeal bread, eggs mimosa, oysters, wild salmon, sea bass, potted shrimps, sage-and-anchovy canapés, corn-on-the-cob, rice pudding, baked pears, meringues with strawberries and cream . . . Two restaurant waiters from Home Gourmet are still unpacking dishes and setting them out while his mother – dressed in a black cocktail dress with a large bow on the side – is in the process of turning the breakfast table into a bar. His father, in black suit and bow tie, is busy doing something with the lighting out on the lawn. The conservatory doors have been flung open, filling the whole of the ground floor with evening sunlight, the smell of freshly cut grass, and birdsong.

His mother turns to face him, eyes rendered enormous by kohl, bright red lips parting to greet him with a smile. 'Quickly, darling. You need to shower and get changed.'

He stands there, trailing his school bag, suddenly acutely aware of his damp, untucked shirt, his loose tie, his rumpled hair. 'What's going on?'

'We're having an impromptu party!' His mother gazes at him as if he's an idiot. 'Didn't you get my voicemail? It's to celebrate your win.'

He stares at her and the bustle of preparations with a mounting sense of horror. 'What? Why? Who's coming?'

'Oh, just some of our friends. A few of Papa's colleagues, a few of mine. The Winchesters from down the road. Most of the neighbours, *naturellement*. Archie and his parents—'

'So basically all *your* friends. Why do I even need to be here? I have to work out.'

She appears startled for a moment, and stops polishing the candelabra. Then her look changes to one of anger. 'How dare you take that tone with me! What's got into you?'

'I'm just not in the mood for one of your parties!'

'This is for you, Mathéo! Talk about selfish, ungrateful—'

'OK, I'm sorry,' he says quickly, sensing that her anger is at boiling point. 'I – I didn't realize.'

'Of course we've invited your friends too,' his mother continues defensively, the colour high in her face. 'The other boys on the squad, Coach Perez, even Jerry and Lola—'

She's got to be joking. 'Jerry and Lola? They're coming too? Does Lola even know about this?'

'I don't know, Mathéo, I only spoke to her father half an hour ago. Anyway, please, pull yourself together and go and get changed, the guests will be arriving any moment.'

Upstairs, Loïc's bedroom door is open. He is dressed in his summer suit – the cream one that he is made to wear for weddings and the like. It accentuates the pallor of his face. Consuela, looking uncomfortable in an ill-fitting cocktail dress, kneels in front of him, straightening his collar. Loïc shoots Mathéo an anguished look over the nanny's head. 'She's put sticky stuff on my hair to make it stand up!'

Mathéo drops his bag on his bedroom floor and leans against the doorjamb. 'It's all good. You look cool, Loïc,' he says, trying to dredge up a note of enthusiasm.

Consuela turns abruptly, looking flushed and strained, her make-up overdone, hair already falling loose from its chignon. 'Mathéo, quickly! You change? You have suit?'

He crosses over to the bathroom, if only to assuage her nerves. 'Yes and yes. I'll be down in a minute.'

He has always hated his parents' parties but usually receives enough advance warning to be able to make other arrangements or come up with an excuse to get away. After putting in the mandatory half-hour presence, shaking a few hands and answering a dozen or so questions about school, his plans for university and whether he has a girlfriend, he is normally able to slip away relatively unnoticed with the excuse of homework. But tonight clearly does not hold that option – he will be the centre of attention, with not only his coach but also his diving buddies present, and will somehow have to negotiate the congratulations and the flattery and the praise as if he is somehow worthy of it all. As if it somehow all matters; as if he gives a damn about the Nationals or the Olympics or his whole diving career at a time when his very life appears to be coming apart at the seams. Toppling, falling, splintering at his feet like the trunk of a fallen tree, its branches stirring, trembling, as if they know, in their restlessness, that something terrible has happened.

Dressed in his black suit trousers, silver-buckled belt, and a white open-collared shirt with the sleeves rolled up to his elbows, Mathéo treads slowly down the stairs. The oppressive air, sticky with the heat of bodies and food and perfume, the gentle roar of voices, music and general merriment all rise up to greet him. He sets his face into what he hopes is an expression of relaxed cordiality. A slight smile, not too forced; a friendly, open demeanour; a countenance of quiet confidence. All at painful odds with the nerves and confusion that he feels inside.

He reaches the bottom of the stairs, and the party seems to open out and swallow him whole. The ground floor is heaving with people, spilling out onto the garden patio: the men in brightly coloured shirts, the women scantily clad in the warm June evening. His father has cranked up the surround-sound and the place is almost deafening. Returning warm, sweaty handshakes, raising his voice to answer greetings, thumped on the back and clapped on the shoulders, Mathéo takes in deep lungfuls of hot, sultry air and gratefully accepts a tall flute of champagne as he tries to negotiate his way towards the relative cool of the garden. The alcohol fizzes in his empty stomach, his nostrils sting with the stench of his father's Cuban cigars, and he feels the sweat begin to congeal beneath his collar as he strives to hear what people are saying, straining his voice to answer their myriad questions, to thank them for their effusive compliments.

'Hey, it's my golden boy!' Perez catches him unawares, coming up from behind and grasping Mathéo firmly by the shoulders, giving him a playful shake.

Startled, Mathéo almost elbows his coach in the face before being swung round and given a fierce hug and several slaps on the back. People have already started to gather round. Flush-faced and with false laughter, Mathéo vainly attempts to dodge his coach's large, sweaty hand as it ruffles his hair, claps him on the back of the neck.

'You're looking at next year's Olympic gold medallist,' he announces to the gathering crowd. 'Flawless performance in Brighton, not a single dropped dive – won by a massive forty points! Twenty-five perfect tens overall, including a perfect Twister, a perfect armstand back double-somersault tuck, and finally, a perfect Big Front!' The other guests are nodding and smiling and congratulating Mathéo politely, but it is clear that Perez is already tipsy, his crimson face sweaty, brandy sweet on his breath. 'A set like that this time next year and he will send the Chinese and the Americans home in tears!'

Smiling over gritted teeth, Mathéo shakes his head in embarrassment and attempts to extract himself from Perez's grasp. He tries to make his way over to Zach and Aaron, standing in a corner, looking bored. But before he can reach them, Perez catches up with him. 'Now, you can celebrate tonight, but as from tomorrow it's back to the food plan—'

'I know.'

'And as soon as school breaks up . . . When is that again?'

'In two weeks.'

'Well, in that case, in two weeks, in two weeks the real training starts. The Olympic training. I forget – have I shown you your schedule?'

'Several times,' Mathéo replies with a tight smile.

'No holidays, no partying, no late nights, no bad foods . . .' Perez slashes the air with his forearm, as if striking items off on a list. 'And – most important . . . You know most important, Mathéo?'

Wearily, Mathéo shakes his head.

'No girlfriend!' Perez booms to the room. 'No girl-friend and no sex!'

Around them, heads turn and people titter, and

feeling the blood rush to his cheeks, Mathéo turns from his drunken coach and pushes his way through the crowd. He manages to lose Perez, only to run into the new neighbours, holding out more sweaty hands.

The evening seems to him an elaborate theatre, the sole purpose of which is for his parents to show off their son's achievement, their house, their wealth, their perfect little family. The guests are like actors, playing their part as revellers and admirers, even though most of them barely know him or have the slightest interest in diving. His father, surrounded by a posse of his golfing friends and associates, is jovial and solicitous, brandishing his cigar and knocking back the wine, laughing at his own jokes and growing more loquacious with each glass, entertaining his guests with a detailed account of his recent business trip to Cairo. On the other side of the room, his mother stands poised, hand on hip, making little smoky swirls in the air with her cigarette, tall and elegant amongst a group of work colleagues and luncheon friends in front of the bay window, their glasses of red wine luminous in the reflected evening light.

'Consuela? Consuela, more wine!' his mother calls over to where the nanny stands beside Loïc, who is grasping her hand tightly and extracting a string of *oohs* and *aahs* and head-ruffles from the stream

131

of overdressed adults who seem to be queuing up to admire him as he stands there, innocent and blond and adorable. Although used to being paraded this way at endless parties and weddings and other functions, Loïc looks none too happy, but his serious expression and doleful eyes only succeed in increasing the fuss made of him by his parents' guests. He appears panicked for a moment as Consuela disappears from behind him, and Mathéo presses his way through the throng and holds out a hand, which Loïc immediately grabs with both of his, following his older brother through the party's undergrowth and out into the deep, dappled shade of the terrace. Mathéo finds him a place to sit down on the lawn, hidden away by the rhododendron bushes, snatching him some juice and vol-au-vents along the way.

'Here.' He sits down cross-legged opposite his brother, his back to the rest of the party, and sets the plate and glass down on the grass between them.

Loïc looks up at him with a grateful smile, the relief evident on his face. 'Can you stay with me?'

'Sure. You know what? I hate these parties too.'

'But everyone wants to talk to you,' Loïc says between mouthfuls of vol-au-vent. 'Everyone likes you.'

'They don't like me; most of them barely know me. It's just because they're stupid and they've heard about the competition.' Mathéo looks across at his brother's wan face, and for the first time finds himself wondering what it must be like to be his own sibling, to be the one who is patted and petted but always overlooked – by his parents, by their friends, by Mathéo himself.

'It's not real, you know,' he tries to explain. 'Their friendliness, their questions, all the chit-chat. I just have to pretend like I'm happy or flattered or interested or whatever. It's all a game of Let's Pretend.'

'Is that why Mummy and Daddy always go out to parties? Because they like to play Let's Pretend? Is it Let's Pretend that you love diving, then?' Loïc asks.

The question throws him off guard. 'No!' he exclaims quickly. 'I love—' But then he breaks off, hesitating. Suddenly it strikes him that he doesn't need to lie to his brother. For once, he is in no rush to end the conversation, tell him what he wants to hear in order to be able to get away. 'I used to love diving,' he says quietly, cautiously, as if only just admitting the fact to himself. 'I mean, a lot of the time things ached, or the training was so intense I thought I'd pass out. But the more I trained, the better I got, and – and, well, it's nice to feel like you're really good at something. It feels kind of good to be the best. And once you become the best, you want to stay the best. You never want that feeling to go away. But then other divers come along and start training even harder, and so you keep having to work just to stay the best.'

'So are you the best diver in the whole world?' Loïc asks, his eyes widening.

Mathéo feels himself smile slightly. 'No, that's the problem. I'm *one* of the best. I'm probably the best in the country. Though once you become the best in the country, at first it feels really amazing, but then the amazingness kind of wears off. People start expecting you to win competitions, and if you don't, they get really disappointed. So you want to have that feeling of being the best again. So you train even harder, and try to become the best in the whole of Europe, and then the best in the whole world.'

Loïc holds his second vol-au-vent up to the fading light, checking for signs of tomato. 'So is that what you want to do? Become the best in the whole world?'

Mathéo chews the corner of his lip, looking over his shoulder at the throngs of people on the terrace, their voices getting louder with every sip of champagne.

'No. Not any more.'

He has surprised himself, but Loïc continues munching steadily, unperturbed. 'Why not?'

'Because—' Mathéo swallows, his throat dry suddenly. 'Because after the competition at the weekend, I realized I didn't like diving any more.'

'But you won!'

'Yeah. But I realized I didn't care about that any

more. I realized I no longer cared about what Dad or Perez thought about me. I realized that I was sick of them – sick of them always telling me what to do.'

'So you're going to give up?' Loïc looks faintly startled for the first time during the conversation. 'Dad – Dad will get angry—'

'Well, exactly.'

'Just tell him you're a grown-up now and you don't want him to boss you around any more,' Loïc suggests. 'But say it with politeness,' he adds nervously. 'In a respectly way.'

Mathéo smiles but feels his throat constrict. 'I wish I could, buddy. I wish it was that easy.'

His father calls him from the conservatory doors, looking annoyed, so Mathéo leaves Loïc to entertain himself with the games on his mobile and returns to the party. He is introduced to some new neighbours and finds himself plunged back into the heat and noise. As the Winchesters take turns pumping his hand and slapping him on the back and smiling eagerly, asking him about his Olympic preparation and informing him that their three-year-old is already showing remarkable signs of agility in the field of gymnastics, Mathéo drains his glass and accepts a refill from one of the passing waiters. He scans the crowd, but there is still no sign of Jerry and Lola, thank goodness. They must have sensibly decided to skip this circus. The volume is reaching fever pitch now. Everyone seems to be talking with strange animation, and all he is aware of is a mounting feeling of despair at the artificiality of the set-up, at the tone of his mother's voice out-shrilling her own guests, but most of all at the sensation of himself as an imposter, someone posing as a sporting hero when in reality he is a nothing, a less-than-nothing: a piece of scum on this already tarnished earth, a faulty specimen of a human being who should be wiped out, tied down to a rock and tossed out to sea, leaving the world a calmer, healthier, cleaner place. Even as he talks, drinks, laughs and greets his parents' guests, he feels himself sinking – so low that he appears to have reached rock bottom. It is not some dramatic breakdown. Rock bottom, in fact, is very mundane: it is simply an inability to see the point in anything and only wonder why on earth everything looks and feels so bad, so painful and so wrong. He feels stuck somewhere between dead and alive, and cannot imagine any place worse. All these people – how can they keep talking, keep smiling, keep laughing? Can't they feel his pain, his sorrow, his despair? Is he that good an actor? He feels so utterly wretched that it suddenly seems impossible that the whole world doesn't stop and suffer with him. On the one hand, he is desperate to keep up the façade; on the other, he is tempted just to walk through one of the conservatory walls and have the sharp, broken shards slash him to ribbons so he can finally look the way he feels. He gazes at Mrs Winchester's painted pink lips, opening and closing, opening and closing; listens to Mr Winchester's deep booming laugh, the puff-puff of his cigar and his rasping breath, and he wants to shout, *Shut up! Shut up! Shut up, all of you!* The whole world seems to have become a maze of shifting mirrors in which he wanders alone, looking frenziedly for the exit back into his real life, where people have substance, act genuine, are whole. But somewhere, somehow, ever since waking up that morning in his trashed room, he seems to have fallen into a nightmare. He wants to escape, wants to blot it all out, wants to sleep . . . No, not sleep, dammit – what he wants is to wake up!

After what seems like an eternity, he manages to escape the clutches of the Winchesters and, while his parents' backs are turned, escape back out to the garden. Dusk is beginning to fall: Loïc has been escorted up to bed by Consuela, and just a few smokers linger on the patio, the faint chill of nightfall ushering the rest of the guests inside. A large pale moth dances in the areas of light and then disappears. Breathing in the blessed coolness of the late evening, Mathéo picks up a half-drunk bottle of wine, looks about for a glass and, finding none, pinches a couple of cigarettes from an abandoned packet. For once he doesn't give a damn, suddenly reckless and self-destructive, sick of having to take care of his health during every waking moment. Moving quickly away from the patio lights into the penumbra at the bottom of the garden, he slips behind a tall poplar tree, crouches down in the grass to light his cigarette from one of the glass-cupped candles that line the lawn, and then sits back against the cool brick of the garden wall, taking a swig of wine, bringing the cigarette to his mouth and inhaling heavily.

A shadow falls over him, making him start. He freezes, hiding the cigarette's glow behind his back in the hope that whoever it is will fail to notice him and just wander back inside.

'What are you doing out here alone?'

He recognizes the voice just as Lola's silhouette comes into focus. Contrasting sharply with the suits and cocktail dresses of the rest of the guests, her legs are bare: she is wearing her favourite cargo shorts, rolled up to just above the knee, a pale yellow T-shirt, and a leather ankle bracelet above her Birkenstock sandals. Her long hair hangs down to her waist, her pale skin accentuating the smattering of freckles across her cheekbones and her bright sea-green eyes. In the eerie fading light, her appearance is more ephemeral than ever: the slight hollows in her cheeks, the slim neck, the delicate ridge of her collarbone. As usual, her face is free of make-up and her hair is unadorned – she is stunning without even trying. There are traces of violet beneath her eyes; she has an almost painfully fragile beauty about her that makes his heart ache. After having had to put on an agonizing act for the last half-hour, he is suddenly so happy to see her, he wants to jump up and hug her, feel her arms around him, reassuring him that he is still alive. He wants her to bring him back, to remind him who he once was, to make him feel real again. He wants to kiss her so much that it hurts.

'Mattie!' She kneels down in front of him. 'What the hell – you're smoking?'

'Yeah . . .' He takes a long drag, bracing himself for a lecture, but instead she just takes the butt from between his fingers and raises it to her mouth, inhaling slowly. Then she leans back, blowing smoke rings up into the darkening air. 'Is your coach here? He'd fucking kill you if he caught you!' She chuckles.

'Yeah, somewhere. But I couldn't care less. Where's Jerry?' he asks her.

'Oh, stuck in the darkroom – got a tight deadline. He sends his congratulations though.'

'I'm sorry about earlier – I don't know what got into me . . .' he tries to explain. 'And I'm sorry about this. You didn't have to come.'

She looks at him with a mischievous smile, her eyes glinting in the candlelight. 'Are you kidding me? Miss your congratulatory party, all your parents' business associates slapping you on the back and singing *For*

He's a Jolly Good Fellow?' She laughs, reaches for the bottle and takes a deep swig.

He feels the shadow of a smile cross his lips. 'So you came to mock me in my hour of need?'

'Well, yes, basically. But looks like I've missed the best part – or have you been camping out here all evening?'

'No, I only just got away. You came at the perfect time.'

'Well . . .' She hesitates, rocking back on her heels and drawing her knees up beneath her chin. 'I wasn't sure if you wanted me here.'

'Of course I wanted you here. I always want you here.' He reaches out for her, makes contact with her bare arm, slides his hand down towards hers.

'You seemed pretty mad when you took off in the park . . .' Her fingers hesitate against his, rubbing his palm gently with her thumb.

'I was being dumb.'

Over the crests of her kneecaps, her sombre eyes study his. 'What got you so worked up?'

'I don't know . . .'

She appears dissatisfied. 'You keep saying that,' she continues. 'But clearly something's going on. Was it something we said? That's the second time now you've gone charging off like that.'

He stubs out the cigarette against the damp earth and stares down at the ground, searching for the right words. 'I was being stupid,' he says slowly. 'For a moment I felt like – I felt like you were accusing me of being a—' His voice stutters to a stop. He can't say the word.

'Of being what – a criminal?' Her eyes are wide with disbelief. 'But Mattie, we were just playing a game! Why . . . Why would anyone, even for a second, think you were a criminal?' She gives a small laugh, her brow still creased in confusion.

Because I feel like one? Because I'm terrified that is what I've become? But he can't say that to Lola – he can't even make sense of it himself.

He forces himself to meet her gaze. 'Lola, I don't – I honestly don't know what's going on. I feel like – like something's happening to me. Like there's this pain, and I can't get rid of it, and it just won't stop hurting. D'you know – d'you know what I mean?' He bites the inside of his lip, a sharp point pressing against the back of his eyes. 'Have you ever felt it? It's like a feeling of depression, or – or loneliness. Like you feel separate from everyone around you, as if you no longer belong . . .'

She stares at him, her expression serious, brow creased in concern. 'But you're not alone and you *do* belong. You belong to *me*. I love you, Mattie.'

He exhales slowly, pulling her gently towards him, sliding his hand beneath her hair, cupping her cheek. His eyes close and his mouth meets hers and he kisses her gently, inhaling her warm breath, soaking up the taste of her lips, of her tongue. And he is suddenly taken over by a new fear, so violent and unexpected, it hits him like a fist in the stomach.

'Lola,' he whispers between kisses. 'Please . . . please don't leave me.'

'I would never—'

'But you will.' He kisses her almost desperately now. 'One day you will.'

She pulls back. 'Mattie—'

He tries to kiss her again, this time only reaching the corner of her mouth.

She puts a hand on his chest, gently pushing him back. 'What about the stuff you said that night by the river – didn't you mean it? I thought you wanted to stay with me for ever?'

'I do, but – life doesn't work like that—'

'Why do you say that?'

'I dunno.' He struggles to come up with some reason for this sudden, inexplicable fear. 'Because – because we're young, we're still at school.' He leans forward again, his lips searching hers. 'Realistically, how many teen relationships go on to last a lifetime?'

She puts her hand on his face, still holding him back, her eyes, full of confusion, boring into his. 'Then what's the point? If you're so sure this isn't going to last, why continue with it now?'

'I didn't mean it like that,' he whispers desperately.

'I don't want to break up. My God, it's the last thing in the world I want. It's just that I'm trying to be realistic. You will break up with me one day, I — I just know it—'

She pushes him back hard, angry suddenly. 'Stop saying that!'

He stares at her, his pulse thrumming. 'I'm sorry—'

Her eyes flash with hurt and bewilderment. 'If that's what you truly believe, then we might as well—' She starts to get up.

'No!' He grabs her by the wrist, pulling her back down hard against him.

'Mattie!' She sounds shocked.

He feels that darkness sucking him down again. 'I didn't mean to say those things. I'm just so tired—'

'So tired of what?'

He swallows in an attempt to push back the rising pain in his throat. 'Tired of feeling like this!' His voice rises. 'Like I don't deserve you! Like I've done something terrible and I'm going to lose you!'

He takes a ragged breath and holds it. Silence stretches out between them, so taut, so fragile that he feels sure it will snap. Gazing away from her into the darkness, he forces himself to take another deep breath. He inhales sharply and turns his head, trying to escape Lola's gaze as he feels his eyes sting. *I need you*, he wants to say. *I need you to stay with me and hold onto*

me and make me feel real and alive again. I need you to help me,
tell me what's wrong with me, help me get back to the person I used
to be, explain to me what the hell is happening! But he can't –
can't say any of it. He can't even move, staring down
at the grass, breathing hard. A sharp pain has risen
behind his eyes, a constriction burning his throat. As
he takes a deep breath, he feels the tears force their
way into his eyes like knives. With all the will in the
world, he cannot hold them back.

'Mattie?'

He recognizes the alarm in her voice. Presses his
thumbnail into his lower lip.

Lola reaches out a hand and touches him. With a
shake of the head, he pushes back the comforting arm.
Tears, hot and heavy, crowd his eyes. A ragged breath
escapes him as one skims the side of his cheek. He
brushes it away quickly with a flick of his wrist.

'Jesus, Mattie!' Lola is staring at him, aghast, her
chest rising and falling rapidly, as if panicked.

'I'm OK. It's n-nothing—'

'Sweetheart, how can it be nothing?' Lola sounds
breathless, almost frightened. 'What the hell's going
on?'

'I – I don't know!'

'Has your dad been giving you a hard time again?
Did something happen in training? Or – or at
school?'

He shakes his head and turns away as another tear

follows, and then another; presses the heels of his hands hard against his eyes and holds his breath in a desperate attempt to stop them.

'It'll pass,' he says frantically, wiping the back of his hand across his eyes. 'I'm – I'm going to sort it out. M-maybe I'm just going through some kind of phase.' He gives a small laugh but feels another tear spill.

'It's not a phase – you're upset about something.' She strokes the side of his face, her voice coming out softly desperate. 'Is it something you don't want to tell me about?'

'I don't know. Gah – fucking hell!' He rubs viciously at his face, using the sleeves of his shirt, the palms of his hands. 'Maybe I need to go for a walk or something to sort myself out. Maybe—'

'Shh, hold on, stay here with me,' Lola says softly, her hand firm around his wrist. 'We're going to work this out. You're going to be OK.'

'I'm – I'm scared I'm falling apart.' He presses his fist to his mouth to muffle a sob. 'All these things seem to be happening to me. And – and they're completely out of my control!'

Lola puts her fingers to his lips to silence him. 'Hey, it's all right. No one can be in control all the time,' she tells him gently. 'Right now you're just upset, that's all. Everyone gets upset sometimes. You're not falling apart. And even if you did, it wouldn't be the end of the world. I'd still be here, wouldn't I? You wouldn't be on your own.'

'I just have this t-terrible feeling—'

'About what, sweetheart?'

'That – that things have changed. That we can't stay together—'

'Oh Mattie, you're just overthinking. Maybe you're overtired because you're still recovering from Brighton.'

Recovering from Brighton . . . A chill runs through his body. No, he will never recover from Brighton, never recover from what happened there, never find his way back from the terrible person he became. A flash of red skims across the surface of his vision, the smell of blood and earth and sweat, thudding feet pounding the dry ground, ransacked breath bursting from his lungs. He presses his hand against his eyes.

'Mattie, listen to me, sweetheart. I'll always be here for you. I'll always love you.' Lola's voice is gentle, too gentle. He nods, draws the back of his arm across his face and takes a jagged breath. Then looks at her and manages an embarrassed smile.

'Come here.' She leans forward and breathes the words against his shoulder, puts her arms around him and pulls him close, holding him tight as he disintegrates beneath her touch, covering his face with his hands. Rivulets form down the cracks between his fingers; the tears hurt, his head hurts, everything hurts. He presses his face against her, trying to halt the onslaught, trying to stem the flow, but it's as if his body has a will of its own, forcing him to communicate with Lola, show her how bad he feels, even though it's the last thing he wants to do right now . . . But gradually, after several minutes of silent, painful tears, he senses an easing of the pressure in his chest, of some of the pain in his mind. Lola just holds him quietly, her head resting against his, and slowly he begins to pull himself together, firmly burying the pain – still present, but weaker now – deep down inside him. Deep down, back down where it belongs.

6

He has found the answer. He might be unable to
suppress his feelings, he might be unable to go back
to his carefree life, he might be unable to return to the
person he was before that night . . . but he can pretend. He remembers enough of his old self to be able
to summon up a pretty good impression, so long as he
keeps busy. Filling his days with training – pool diving, dry diving, acrobatics, gymnastics and home
workouts – as well as spending time with his friends
and, most importantly, Lola, allows him to pretend to
everyone, including himself, that everything has
returned to normal, that the black wave has subsided,
the thick veil has lifted; that the suffocating bubble
has burst, allowing him once more to step back into
the real world. A world where the most he has to
worry about is perfecting The Big Front, putting in
extra hours at the pool to satisfy his parents, finding

excuses for coming home late in order to hang out with Lola. And, for the moment, it seems to be working. He is careful to spend as little time alone as possible – he works out with the music blaring, Skypes Lola late into the night, even starts spending time with Loïc before his parents get home. Nearly two weeks have passed since Nationals, school is almost at an end. The dark thoughts are still there, the black waters are still simmering, but they are kept below the surface, deep below the surface, forced down into the darkest recesses of his mind.

Jerry has an overnight photoshoot in Paris, and Lola decides that having the house to herself calls for a sleepover.

'Aren't we a bit old for sleepovers?' Mathéo protests as she brightly springs the idea on him across the canteen table.

'No, it'll be very grown up!' Lola giggles. 'I'm going to cook!' She throws her arms out in an expansive gesture and knocks over the pepper shaker.

Mathéo begins to laugh. 'You – cook? You can't even eat without sending things flying.'

She takes a large mouthful of yoghurt and sticks out a white tongue.

'Very mature, Lola!'

She starts to laugh, spattering yoghurt across her tray. He ducks beneath the table. 'Look at you! You're a public health hazard!'

She scrunches up her eyes in a desperate effort to swallow before bursting into guffaws. 'Stop making me crack up, then!'

'I'm not doing anything. You're the one flinging pepper about and showering me with yoghurt!'

'Mattie!' She wipes her streaming eyes. 'Stop mocking me, you bastard, and listen!'

'Are you sure you want Hugo and Isabel copulating on your new sofa-bed—?'

'Will you just listen? There isn't going to be any copulating!'

'At all? Then I'm rapidly losing interest in this—'

She whacks him on the arm. 'Stop it! I thought we could all spend the night in the living room, drag some mattresses down and have a movie night.'

'And paint our nails and braid each other's hair?'

She starts spluttering again.

'Can you try swallowing before cackling like a demented witch?'

'I swear, Mattie. Your hair may be too short to braid, but I'm going to paint your nails if it's the last thing I do!'

Fortunately, by the time the day comes round, Lola has things other than nail-painting on her mind. Namely trying to salvage the dinner she is busy incinerating. After a morning of acro and an afternoon of diving, Mathéo goes home to change, leaving a note for his parents in the hope of avoiding a row. Famished, he joins Lola in the kitchen as soon as Jerry departs.

'Are you actually cooking, Lola?' Isabel exclaims in disbelief as soon as she and Hugo arrive.

'*We* are,' Mathéo points out, sitting at the kitchen table and wrestling with the bottle opener. 'Although I had no part in that evil burning smell.'

'Shut up, everyone!' Lola yells from the cooker. 'Of course, Izzy. What did you think? That I was going to feed you hot dogs?' One of the saucepans begins to bubble over and she quickly snatches off the lid. 'Ouch! Fuck!'

'D'you want some help?' Hugo asks, suppressing a laugh.

'No! I can do this! Now will you just leave me alone and – and chat amongst yourselves or whatever!'

'All right, keep cool, Lola.' Isabel turns to Hugo. 'I think the hostess is getting a touch stressed, so perhaps we should act as if everything's under control and—'

'It *is* under control!' Lola shouts.

'We're ignoring you, Lola!' Isabel shouts back.

Mathéo opens the bottle of red and turns his attention to the white. 'Right, what's everyone drinking?'

'Whisky!' Lola declares, dropping a spoon.

'Uh-uh – no alcohol for you until dinner is sorted

or the whole house is going to go up in smoke,' Mathéo tells her.

Lola swears. Isabel laughs and holds out her glass for some red. Hugo goes over to fetch the beers from the fridge.

'So, what's it like making dinner together like an old married couple?' he asks, a mischievous glint in his eye.

Mathéo accepts a can of beer, opens it and props his bare feet up on the corner of the table. 'Incredibly stressful,' he replies, taking a deep swig.

'Yeah, we can see you're right on the edge of a breakdown there, Mattie!' Isabel laughs.

'I'm not kidding! She actually hit me with a spoon.'

'A wooden spoon!' Lola calls over her shoulder, still juggling pans. 'He kept trying to eat everything.'

'Well, I was starving. I've been training all afternoon!'

Lola summons Mathéo to help her dish up, and finally the four of them gather round the kitchen table.

'So, what is this exactly?' Hugo looks down at his plate, an eyebrow raised in mild concern.

'I don't think it has a name,' Mathéo puts in.

'Bangers and mash?' Isabel suggests helpfully.

'But there are baked beans,' Hugo says doubtfully, forking up a spoonful of sausage and beans and observing it warily.

'I made it from a Nigella recipe!' Lola exclaims in outrage.

'Uh – babe . . . ?'

She turns towards Mathéo in annoyance. 'What now?'

He fights back a laugh. 'Is the mash *supposed* to be orange?'

'Some of the baked beans fell in, OK?' Lola yells in mock annoyance. 'Just leave me alone, you ungrateful pigs!'

'Wait, wait, I think we should make a toast,' Mathéo says tactfully, shooting Lola a reconciliatory smile. He raises his can. 'To the world's most well-meaning cook!'

'Absolutely!' Isabel agrees.

'And to the end of fucking Greystone!' Hugo adds.

'Jeez, yeah. Less than one week left!' Isabel exclaims.

'Hey, I think we're going a bit off topic,' Lola protests.

They all laugh, raising their glasses to her. 'Cheers!'

A warm fug of love and camaraderie seems to envelop the room. Despite the mattresses waiting for them in front of the television in the living room, this all suddenly seems quite grown up and exciting.

Hugo is talking animatedly about the upcoming holiday. 'First time without the parental unit – it's going to be wild!' he exclaims. 'Matt, please tell me you've managed to persuade your parents to let you come for at least a few days.'

'No, I've really got to get stuck into this new training routine,' he answers quickly. 'But next year, after the Olympics, definitely!'

'Oh, bugger,' Hugo complains. 'Not even for the weekend?'

'No, but Lola's going to go,' he informs Hugo lightly.

'Really?'

Lola's gaze meets his across the table. 'I said I'd think about it.' Some of the brightness suddenly leaves her face.

'Persuade her, guys!' Mathéo turns to the other two. 'She's never been to the South of France before and it's her only chance to go on holiday this summer—'

'Oh, come on, Lola! Lola, please!' Hugo and Isabel instantly pitch in.

But her eyes haven't left his. 'But I'd rather spend time with—'

'There won't be any time,' Mathéo says, forcing himself to keep his tone light. 'Perez will have me training eight hours a day.'

'You're coming, then,' Hugo declares.

Lola glances back at Mathéo. 'Are you sure?'

'Yes! I want you to go – it's wonderful there!'

Lola begins to smile and turns back to the others.

'OK, then. I'd better hurry up and book my ticket.'

'Yay!' Whoops and cheers from Hugo and Izzy. Mathéo forces himself to join in.

The conversation soon turns to other things, like Lola's show and the final inter-school cricket tournament. Hugo gets up and grabs a broom to demonstrate a particularly tricky cricket stroke, narrowly missing decapitating Isabel in the process, and laughs at Lola's warning that if he doesn't start being more careful, he will eventually find himself on trial for manslaughter. Everyone is chatting, but as they do, Mathéo feels himself – at first gradually, and then suddenly – slipping out of the conversation. It is as if something inside him has shifted, a thought or memory has returned, and he suddenly feels out of sync with the group, as if they are all part of a play and he has forgotten his lines. He doesn't even feel left out of their holiday plans: he is used to such sacrifices. Yet out of nowhere, he is back to being the perennial outsider with his nose to the window, looking in on a world from which he is excluded. The others are in high spirits and increasingly talkative, but he starts having to make a concerted effort to focus on the conversation and try to chip in whenever he can, a task not made any easier by the fact that the girls are becoming shrill and Hugo never seems to stop talking. Their words cannon through his brain, making his head hurt. He feels heavy with thoughts, weighed down by them; and terribly tired – tired of wit and intellect, everybody's little displays of genius. Tired too of misspent and knotted energies, tired of the hypocrisy, and tired of feeling he has something to hide. Yet he does, he knows he does, even though he still can't remember what it is. Can't remember or won't remember? It is almost the same thing. Brighton. A cool night and a sky full of stars. The crunch of twigs and the crack of his fists against skin, his fists against bone. And the blood – always, always the blood, so bright and red beneath the light of the moon . . .

Appearing to notice his flagging social skills, Lola flashes him an encouraging smile, and suddenly he wishes the other two would simply disappear and he could just be alone with her. As the conversation turns to the evening's movie schedule, Mathéo reaches for her hand beneath the table, slipping his fingers between hers, gently squeezing them. The kitchen seems to have become very small, overheated and claustrophobic. Even though the food actually turned out pretty well, he finds he has no appetite. Talking and gesticulating, Lola withdraws her hand from his and the brief moment of solidarity between them instantly evaporates. He aches to reach back for her, but she has picked up her knife again. He pushes his fingers into the cool hollow of the chair-back. Fatigue, both physical and emotional, presses down upon him like an invisible force. As the other three wax ever louder, his own silence appears increasingly pronounced, and the more aware he grows of his reticence, the more paralysed he feels by it. Lola is making stalwart efforts to draw him into the conversation, but he keeps missing the bait. Perhaps because he suddenly feels painfully attuned to what the others must think of him as he just sits there in silence. Moody, strange, crazy even. And that's the thing. They are right. Of course, they are absolutely right.

Isabel produces brownies for dessert, and Mathéo slips his hand around Lola's again, curling his fingers round her thumb and pressing the heel of his hand against her palm. *Don't pull away*, he wants to say. *I don't know what's happening to me, but suddenly I need you, I really do.*

After dinner they load the dishwasher and pile into the living room, fighting over mattresses, still arguing over which films to put on. Mathéo feels as if he is watching it all from a very great distance. He wishes he could just find some excuse and leave, but knows that Lola wouldn't buy it, would be really upset if he just walked off yet again. With a concerted effort, he manages to dredge up answers when addressed, but otherwise feels completely incapable of initiating any kind of conversation. Fortunately Hugo is too tipsy to notice, but Isabel asks him if he is feeling OK more than once, and Lola keeps shooting him looks of alarm that set his pulse racing.

Collapsed in front of *Skyfall*, a relative calm descends as the evening draws to a close behind the curtain-less windows. Sprawled out on his front, propped up on his elbows and staring blankly at the television screen, Mathéo is aware of a rising pain within him. Everything hurts. He can barely lie still. He feels caught. He wants to run, but where? He feels certain he will always remain like this – trapped within his own body, his own mind. The emotional pain is so strong, it becomes physical. He feels it knotting and twisting inside him, ready to crush him, suffocate him. He is losing his grip, he is losing his mind. He thought he had it all back under control, but suddenly nothing makes sense any more. Does anyone else know what it's like to be stuck somewhere between dead and alive? It is a half-world of incoherent pain where emotions you put on ice start slowly thawing again. A place where everything hurts, where your mind is no longer strong enough to force your feelings back into hibernation. His arms suddenly feel unable to support him and he drops his head between them, resting his face against the mattress. He is coming undone. And he is trapped, literally – there is nowhere he can go without making a scene. A caged animal with nowhere to run.

'I think Mattie's asleep,' Isabel says suddenly.

Mathéo presses his face into the pillow and slows his breathing down to a deep, steady rhythm. Yes, let them think he is asleep. At least like that he won't have to join in the conversation, pretend to be interested in their chatter, force laughter at the comedy the others are now enjoying.

'Matt?'

'Leave him, Hugo. He's knackered from training.' Lola's voice, coming from the mattress beside him.

Moments pass. Hugo and Isabel go back to their running commentary. Mathéo is aware of the brush of Lola's hair against his arm, her warm breath on his cheek. It takes all the willpower he can muster to stop himself from responding when he feels her lips against the corner of his mouth. 'Love you,' she whispers.

He holds his breath. Does she know he's faking? But then Hugo makes some coarse remark, Lola laughs and threatens to thump him, more alcohol does the rounds. The second film comes to an end, chatter becomes interspersed with periods of silence, and gradually they all fall quiet beneath the darkened glow of the television, and someone begins to snore. He sinks into the mattress, overwhelmed with sadness, the feeling so strong it seems to be in his bloodstream, like a drug. The weight of it fills him up, pins him down . . .

She starts screaming. Really screaming. The kind of scream that comes from more than just fear. It's a scream of horror; it's a scream of someone who knows what lies in store. She is trying to get away, bleeding from a blow to the head, crawling over the hardwood floor. She reaches a white wall – reaches up. But she is cornered, trapped as the shadow falls over her. She is grabbed by the hair and dragged down the corridor to a bath – it is deep and full, and water spills over the edge as she is plunged inside. She fights and kicks and thrashes, splashing up water, soaking his shirt, but his grip on her neck is too strong. Gradually her attempts to free herself begin to weaken – she is slowing down, deprived of oxygen, lungs filling with water. The last few bubbles escape from her nose and rise to the surface and she is still, face white, lips blue, staring up at him, her eyes wide with horror and disbelief.

He can still hear the screaming, still hear her screaming, but now there are other sounds as well. Shouts and yells and hands pulling him this way and that, shaking him by the shoulders, and he sees eyes and faces and heads swarming above him against the bright yellow glow of the ceiling. The yells are now coming from him, bursting from his lungs and into the chaos of the room, rising above the voices.

'Matt, Matt, stop it, you're dreaming!' Hugo is the one gripping him by the shoulders, shaking him, pulling him up and shouting in his ear.

'Wake up, wake up!' Isabel looks distraught, eyes huge in her face.

'Mattie, come on. Look at me, look at me!'

He is sitting on a mattress in the Baumanns' living room. He turns to look at Lola and tries to stop the anguished yell of terror erupting from his mouth. He tries to hold his breath, covers his mouth with his hands, tries to stop, manages to stop – leaving in its place a gasping, choking sound.

Hugo and Isabel shrink back, still staring at him in shock. He feels Lola's hands on either side of his face, holding him still, trying to stop the rocking, forcing him to look at her.

'Mattie, look at me. It's just me. It's Lola. You're all right,' she says. 'You're all right.' Her tone is hushed but her eyes betray her distress. She begins to gently stroke his back, and he is aware that his T–shirt is drenched in sweat.

'No!' The word bursts from him like a bullet. 'No!'

'No, what?'

'She's all right! She's all right!'

'Yes, she's all right,' Lola nods earnestly. 'She's all right. You're all right. Everybody's all right.'

He hears his breathing grow ragged, feels himself shake. His cheeks are wet. He seems to be crying, muffled sobs breaking the taut, shocked silence.

Hugo is saying something. 'Hey, buddy, it was just a dream!'

'You're awake now,' Isabel informs him. 'You're awake, Mattie! It's OK!'

'Jesus!' Hugo sounds vaguely appalled. 'What the hell's happening to him?' He looks at Lola. 'Do you think he can hear us?'

'You can hear us, can't you, Mattie?' Her eyes are still fixed on his as if willing him back to the present. 'You know you're awake, don't you?'

He nods, still trying to quell the gasping, sobbing sound.

'Jesus,' Hugo says softly, again. 'Should we call someone?'

'You just need to calm down, sweetheart. You just need to calm down . . .' Despite her wide-eyed expression, Lola's voice is soothing. Sitting on the mattress beside him, she strokes her fingers up and down his cheek, holding him close.

'I – I want—' He takes a deep breath in an effort to steady his voice. 'I want . . .'

'What do you want?' she prompts him quietly.

'I just want to f-forget—' He reaches out for her. 'I just need to forget. Lola, you've got to help me forget!' His voice sounds strange: brittle and panicky.

'What the fuck . . . ?' Hugo asks, his voice rising again.

'Is he still dreaming?' Isabel sounds bewildered.

'Mattie, we can do that,' Lola says earnestly. 'I can help you forget.'

He looks around at the three blank faces. Realizes they have no idea what he is talking about. He rubs his cheeks hard and takes a deep, steadying breath.

'It – it was just a nightmare.' Breath. 'I was just imagining things, as usual.' Yet he can't remember ever having a nightmare as vivid as this before.

'We know!' Isabel exclaims.

Mathéo swallows, forcing himself into some semblance of calm. 'I'm sorry I woke you,' he says, trying to keep his tone off-hand. 'But I'm fine, OK?' A certain hardness enters his voice and it comes out defensive.

'You don't look fine.' Hugo still sounds deeply shocked. 'What the hell was the nightmare about?'

He finds himself sliding back on his mattress, wishing Hugo and Isabel would just disappear. 'Look, just give me some space, OK? I'm fine – you don't all need to make such a fuss. Jesus!' He is no longer speaking in measured tones, the anger burning in his cheeks. He wishes they would all disappear. He wishes he could just disappear. They don't need to see him like this. They don't need to act all concerned. They are driving him mad!

'Dude, come on. We're just trying to help!'

'I don't need your help!'

'Mattie . . .' Eyes sharp and watchful, Lola raises her palms in a peace-making gesture. 'No one's making a fuss, OK?'

'Fine. Then just go back to sleep!' He registers the hurt in Lola's eyes and it makes him want to scream. 'I'm going to get a drink of water. Goodnight.'

He exits the room, flipping off the light switch as he goes and banging the door behind him. Immediately, the voices start up again from behind it: Hugo saying he has never seen Mathéo like this before, insisting they should call someone. Lola responding that it would only make things worse . . . In the privacy of the kitchen, he leans heavily against the closed door and bends down, hands on his knees. He bites down hard on his lower lip and screws his eyes shut, fending off a deep, dark desire to fall to the floor and weep. He is starting to feel he must be going insane. His mind seems to be full of angry, red, spitting sparks, making him want to hurl things, smash plates, hurt someone: punch Hugo, smack Isabel, hurt Lola badly so that she understands how he is feeling. He straightens up and wipes the sweat from his face with the back of his hand. He is going crazy. He is evil, truly evil, evil and dangerous. He shouldn't even be here.

He starts violently, jumping away from the door as he hears the handle turn behind him. He goes over to the counter and tries to pour himself a glass of wine, but little goes into the glass and the alcohol forms a small crimson pool around the base, like blood against the white tiles. His fingers are trembling, casting shaky shadows on the table. His breath catches in his throat as he feels Lola approach from behind, sliding her arms around him.

'Don't—' He starts to move away, trying to prise her arms from around his waist.

She holds on resolutely, pressing her mouth into the dip between his shoulder-blades, her breath hot against his skin. 'Please tell me what's going on. You've been in this strange mood for weeks, and it's getting worse.'

He reaches for a sponge to mop up the spillage, drops it and presses the back of his hand to his face. 'I don't know—' His voice cracks. 'I feel like I'm going crazy!'

She hugs him tighter, her cheek pressed against his back. 'Jesus, you're trembling!'

He lifts the wine bottle to his lips and takes a deep slug, the liquid burning the back of his throat, rivulets running down the side of his chin and onto his neck. He gulps – spluttering, choking.

Lola releases him and tries to prise the bottle out of his hands. 'Come on, Mattie. What are you doing?'

He steps back, holding the bottle out of reach, and a bark of laughter escapes him. 'What does it look like? Getting wasted. I wanna pass out, forget all this shit—'

'What shit?' Lola's expression turns from one of concern to one of anguish.

He winces and moves away, leaving the kitchen and opening the door into the garden, trying to lose her in the damp cool of the night. He waves the question

away with the back of his hand, aware of her following him, rubbing her lower lip with the tip of her
index finger the way she always does when worried.
He wishes she would go away, leave him alone, sick of
being the cause of her anxiety.

'Where are you going?'

'I don't know!'

Silhouetted against the heavy, dark sky, the neighbouring rooftops have the unreal, one-dimensional
look of figures pasted in a collage. He stops at the end
of the garden, leans against the damp of the brick wall
and slides down to sit against it, elbows on knees, his
torso limp and yielding. He swigs wine from the
bottle as if it were water, hoping it will anaesthetize
him. Lola sits down on the grass and hugs her knees to
her chest, her white nightie ghostly in the moonlight.

'Is getting drunk really going to help?'

He takes another long swig, half laughs, half
chokes. 'Yes! Especially if after I've finished you hit
me over the head with this bottle!'

She doesn't smile. Instead, stays huddled with her
knees under her nightie, the whites of her eyes
luminous in the darkness. He finishes off the wine,
tips back his head and watches the stars expand and
retract above, aware that a chill has risen around
them, a cold breeze carrying the promise of cooler
days. Goosebumps rise beneath his damp clothes and
he seems to drift in and out of consciousness. It lasts

for ever, or only a minute, or it passes so quickly that it barely happens at all. That it's the middle of the night makes little difference. If there is no real beginning, and no real end, what does time really mean?

Silence has enveloped them. The words continue to hang unspoken in the air, creating a vortex of unasked and unanswered questions swirling between them. He can tell that Lola has run out of words, is at a loss over what to do next. He feels consumed by the terrible feeling that he is losing her, that the gulf of misunderstanding between them is widening by the minute, washing her away from him, out to sea. Like the girl in the bath, her eyes are locked onto his, desperately trying to hold on. But it's no use, he sees that now. Whatever efforts he may make to hold on to her, she will ultimately be swept away from him. They do not belong together any more. He feels it with such earth-shattering certainty that it takes his breath away. He wants to scream at her not to abandon him here but knows that it's useless; that despite her efforts, she cannot reach him now. Her face, bleached in the moonlight, appears before him as if sunk in deep water – as in his nightmare. Gradually her attempts to reach him begin to weaken – she is slowing down. The last few bubbles escape from her nose and rise to the surface, and she is still, staring up at him, her eyes wide in horror.

7

He skips school the following day. Texts Perez with the excuse of a bad cold and persuades Consuela, after his parents have left for work, to phone Greystone. She seems to believe him and tries to bring him soup, but he keeps his bedroom door firmly locked and only goes down to gather snacks from the kitchen after everyone has gone to bed. He tries listening to music, tries reading, tries playing computer games, but cannot concentrate on anything. Most of all he tries to sleep; he craves oblivion – the absence of thought, of fears, of memories that constantly threaten to pierce through the fragile membrane of his sub-conscious. He no longer wants to recall what happened that night in Brighton. He knows he did something terrible, and that is as much knowledge as he can bear. At times he thinks he has some idea of what it might have involved, but whenever he tries to face it, his thoughts go skidding off in another direction, terrified of the images that lie buried deep down in the darkest recesses of his mind.

That morning he'd left Lola's sleepover early with the excuse of training, and texted her later to apologize for his behaviour, using an excess of alcohol as his excuse. He senses she doesn't believe him, though, and she calls to check up on him in the evening. He presses the handset hard against his ear, as if trying to bring her closer to him, absorb the sound of her voice, fill his empty chest with the warmth of her words. He already misses her desperately – clenching his hands into fists and biting his knuckles to stop himself from jumping up and going round to see her. There is a gaping hole inside him, a yawning void where she should be – at his side, in his arms, snuggled up against him. Yet she fills his night with terrors: obscure, twisted dreams of her trapped underwater and drowning.

The next day, however, he has no choice – his mother is going to work late and, despite his protestations, decides she will drive both sons to school on her way. Loïc is delighted at this unusual turn of events, and chatters non-stop until they reach his school gates. As they pull away, however, leaving him still waving on the pavement, their mother turns to Mathéo with a sharp crease between her thin, perfectly plucked eyebrows.

'Perez called last night. Said you took yesterday off.'

'Had a cold. Didn't want to risk it affecting my balance.' Mathéo turns away quickly from his mother's stare, propping his elbow against the edge of the open window and chewing his thumbnail. He can tell from her silence that she is unconvinced. 'Did – did you tell Dad?' He cringes inwardly at the note of anxiety creeping into his voice.

'No,' she answers slowly. 'I expected you to.'

'I didn't want to worry him.' His voice comes out brittle and defensive. 'You know what a fuss he makes if I ever miss a session.'

'I think he'd have been sympathetic if you weren't feeling well.' Her voice softens slightly. She sounds disappointed, hurt even.

He tears at a hangnail.

'You seem kind of . . . distant, lately,' his mother continues quietly, turning the wheel with a soft, velvety sound beneath her perfectly manicured hands. 'Is everything all right?'

It throws him, this unexpected display of concern, and for a moment he is unable to reply. Perhaps, despite her workaholic lifestyle, she notices things more than he gives her credit for.

'Mattie' – she hasn't called him that for ages – 'if there's something bothering you, I'd like to think that, as your mother, I'm someone you'd trust enough to tell about it.'

'There – there isn't,' he says too quickly, hating his giveaway stammer. 'I'm just a bit tired after the, um – the – the, you know . . .' His mind goes blank suddenly. He is overcome with the strange feeling of falling through space, like a dive with no form. 'Mum?' He looks at her, breathing hard. Suddenly he wants to tell her – all of it. The blackout the night after the competition, the overwhelming feeling that something terrible occurred, the nightmares, the certainty that something within him has irrevocably changed.

'*Qu'est-ce qui ne va pas, mon chéri?*' She has pulled to a halt outside the emptying school grounds. He feels himself flush, his throat constrict. Perhaps if she hadn't used that term of endearment, perhaps if she hadn't looked so very unusually . . . caring for a moment, he would have been able to tell her.

'No, it's – it's nothing. Thanks for the lift. See you tonight.'

She reaches out to touch his cheek, but he grabs his bag and ducks out of the car before she has a chance to make contact, slamming the door behind him and giving her a reassuring wave before jogging across the asphalt to class.

Although it has only been a couple of days, Mathéo feels as if he has not seen Lola for weeks, and spends the first half of the morning counting down the minutes until break. But Lola is nowhere to be found.

Despite having arranged to meet her at their usual hangout before saying goodnight to her on the phone last night, he ends up spending the whole of morning break sitting on one of the benches at the bottom of the cricket pitch alone like a fool, pretending to watch the inter-school match while calling her mobile and repeatedly getting her voicemail. He goes in search of her at the auditorium and then the school gym, but no musical rehearsals appear to be taking place today. He walks past the cell-like window in the door of the drama department more than a dozen times, until some of the pupils begin to notice and turn their heads. With a sigh of exasperation, he checks his mobile for a reply to his text, a missed call – but still nothing, and he is beginning to get antsy now. Lola always has her phone on her – if for some reason she wasn't able to come in to school, she would let him know. Anyway, she sounded perfectly fine when they spoke last night. Something must have happened this morning. Something serious enough to stop her from even answering her phone. He is beginning to feel sick, filled with a terrible sense of foreboding, as if he will never see her again.

When lunch finally comes around, Mathéo grabs his tray and hurries towards their usual table at the far end of the canteen, but finds only Hugo and Isabel seated there. He drops his tray onto the table with a clatter and performs a thorough scan of the busy hall before scraping back a chair and throwing himself into it.

'Where the hell is she?'

'Well, hello! Good to see you too!'

'What?' He forces himself to meet Hugo's questioning gaze, his voice coming out sharper than intended.

He is aware of Hugo and Isabel exchanging glances. 'Earth to Matt . . .' With a highly irritating noise, Hugo clicks his fingers in front of Mathéo's face in an overblown attempt to get his attention.

'We're right here – can you see us?' Isabel laughs. 'Lola's not in today.'

'What? Why?'

They both look so startled that he realizes he is no longer speaking in measured tones.

He takes a deep breath. 'Sorry. I – I just need to talk to her about something important. Have you got any idea where she is?'

'Whoa – a very important question?' Hugo performs his infuriating eyebrow wiggle and Isabel snorts.

'Look, do you know where she is or not?' Shouting was a mistake: a couple of students at the next table turn at the sound of his raised voice.

'Mate, what's going on?' Hugo's expression merges into a mixture of annoyance and concern.

'Nothing, I – I'm just trying to ask you a simple question—'

'We don't know,' Isabel cuts in swiftly. 'We haven't seen her today. She's probably just got a dental appointment or something and forgot to let us know. Have you tried her phone?'

'Of course I've tried her phone!'

'Hey, c'mon – chill, man!' Even usually laid-back Hugo is beginning to look discomforted by the unwanted attention. 'What's the emergency?'

Mathéo empties his lungs, trying to bring his tone back down to a more acceptable register. 'I thought you were supposed to be her friends! Don't you give a damn about her?'

Hugo's head jerks back in surprise and he stares at him, stung. 'Whoa, whoa, whoa. Back off there, buddy. You're being a dick!'

'Why?' He finds himself shouting again, despite his efforts to stay calm. 'Because I'm the only one who is concerned about Lola's whereabouts when she doesn't turn up at school and switches off her phone?'

'She often skips school at the last minute to go on one of her dad's shoots, you know that—'

He feels his heart skip a beat. 'Jesus, how can you just say that? Something could have happened to her!'

Hugo stares at him. 'Don't you think you're being a bit paranoid, mate? Not to mention possessive?'

Mathéo stops breathing for a moment, feels the blood rush to his face. He pins his friend with a look of undisguised fury. 'Possessive?' He takes a painful breath. 'Fuck you!'

Before he has a chance to think, he has jumped to his feet, kicking back his chair and sending his fork clattering across the table, overturning Hugo's glass. There is a sudden hush around them as pupils at neighbouring tables turn to watch the commotion.

Hugo's eyes widen and he takes a breath to reply, but before he has the chance, Mathéo grabs his bag and strides out of the canteen.

Damn them, damn them, damn them! He paces the empty classroom, fist pressed against his mouth, knuckles pushing his lip hard against the ridge of his teeth. He breathes in slow, rhythmic breaths, trying to calm down. He is not going to get upset over Hugo's stupid big mouth and mocking banter. But in spite of his efforts, the irrefutable knowledge slowly sinks in that he has only succeeded in cutting himself off from his friends even further. They have been talking about him behind his back ever since he returned from Brighton – of that he is sure. They even treat him differently now – as if he is a little fragile, a little unstable, a little broken. It's almost as if they *know*. And yet that is impossible. Who would have told them? Unless they have guessed; unless he has betrayed himself with his own demeanour and they have read the guilt in his eyes . . . Perhaps that's it. Perhaps Lola has found out what happened and . . . If she has, it's not surprising she's not answering her phone and is skipping school. She won't want to see him again. Not ever. She won't be coming back. Oh God!

'Hey—' Mathéo turns from the window with a start at the sound of Hugo's voice in the doorway. 'She's just started rehearsals in the gym.'

'What?' He takes a step back in surprise, banging his hip against the windowsill. 'How – how do you know?'

'A couple of Year Sevens in the canteen just told me. They had a late start.'

Draining his lungs, Mathéo sags back against the sill, the anger suddenly ebbing from his veins, his body weak with relief. 'Oh . . .' He feels the blood rise to his cheeks. 'Oh, OK . . . Um, thanks.' He tears at a hangnail, stares at the floor, breathing hard.

Hugo is watching him carefully, eyes narrowed in concern. 'Are you OK?'

Mathéo takes a sharp breath, attempts a conciliatory smile. 'Yeah, yeah. Sorry I snapped. I just – I just . . .' He shakes his head, his voice tailing off as he finds himself unable to come up with a reasonable explanation for his earlier outburst.

He is aware of Hugo closing the classroom door and slowly crossing the room. 'Matt, what's going on?'

'Nothing! I – I just . . . Nothing!' Keeping his head lowered, Mathéo raises one arm slightly to keep Hugo at a distance.

Hugo stops. Leans against the whiteboard. 'Come on. We've been mates for years, but suddenly I feel like I don't know you any more. You storm off in the middle of conversations; there was that crazy nightmare; you look like shit—'

'Thanks!' Mathéo forces himself to meet Hugo's gaze and manages a brief laugh.

But Hugo's expression remains serious. 'You know what I mean. You look like you haven't slept properly in ages. Don't tell me you're already stressing out about our A-level results! Or are things not working out between you and Lola?'

Mathéo feels himself flinch. 'No!'

'Jeez, come on – it's Lola, isn't it? I tell you everything about Izzy—'

'It's not what you think, Hugo.' His voice has begun to rise again, he can feel the constriction in his throat. 'It's – it's fucking complicated, OK?'

'Then tell me. I'm not gonna blab.'

He winces as if struck, sucking in air through his clenched teeth. For a moment he thinks he's going to lose it completely, break down in front of his oldest friend.

'Damn it, Hugo!' He slams his fist against the windowsill behind him. 'Just – just stop asking me fucking questions I can't answer.' He feels his voice catch, tears swarm into his eyes. 'Please! Jesus . . .'

Hugo looks suitably stunned. 'Hey, buddy, come on. I didn't come here to make it worse—'

'Then stop it, OK?'

Hugo holds up his hands. 'Fine! Take it easy, Matt. I'm sorry, I didn't mean to upset you.'

With ragged breaths, Mathéo turns back to the window in an effort to recover his composure. Biting the corner of his lip, he stares down at the cricket match on the pitch below, blinking rapidly.

'Do you want me to go?' Hugo asks after a long moment.

Mathéo nods, not trusting himself to utter another word.

'Fine.' Hugo sounds defeated. 'But look – if you ever just wanna talk, I'm here for you, mate, OK?'

Holding his breath, Mathéo nods his head and closes his eyes.

He has nothing on at school for the rest of the afternoon so, in an effort to avoid Hugo, hangs around outside the gym until Lola is done with rehearsals. She finally emerges just after two and, as his parents are still at work, he persuades her to come back home with him for the afternoon. He is desperate to wipe the conversation with Hugo from his mind; he has missed Lola so much during the last couple of days, wants to put all that behind him, aching to feel that connection with her again. Still painfully aware of

Hugo's comments about his demeanour, he makes a concerted effort to act laid-back and cheerful in an attempt to recapture their carefree banter of the past.

Consuela won't stop fussing around them, so in the end they manage to get rid of her by going outside to sunbathe, snuggled behind the rhododendron bushes at the end of the garden. They chat about stuff Mathéo missed the day before – Hugo getting blind drunk and Isabel going ballistic when he 'accidentally' kissed an ex at someone's end-of-school party. After a while, the two of them lapse into companionable silence in the heat of the sun.

Eyes half closed, Mathéo suddenly remembers something that tickled him that morning on TV and starts to laugh. 'Hey, listen to this . . .' But Lola doesn't move and, looking down, he sees she has fallen asleep against his chest. She lies face down, arms wrapped loosely around his neck, her only movement the steady rise and fall of her shoulders. Her pale eyelashes are still against her cheeks, her nostrils constricting slightly with each intake of breath, her face gently flushed with the warmth of the late-afternoon sun.

Carefully reaching for her discarded bottle of water, Mathéo tilts it gently over her face, letting fall a few drops onto her cheek. She twitches and wipes them away, but then he catches her nose, and finally her ear.

'Hey!' She raises her head and squints up at him, holding out a hand to deflect the stream of water now aimed at her eyes. 'What the hell . . . ? Aargh!' She pulls herself into a sitting position and wipes her face with the back of her hand, shaking her head in an attempt to get the water out of her ear. 'You bastard!'

She makes a vain grab for the bottle, but Mathéo rolls away, holding it just out of her reach and squeezing it like a water gun, spraying the back of her neck.

Half laughing, half cursing, she jumps to her feet and lunges for him. 'Oh, you are *so* dead!'

Lola grabs the bottle and attempts to dodge past, but he is too quick and catches her round the waist, wrestling it out of her hand. She attempts to get it back, but is instantly blasted with water and dashes away shrieking, heading towards the large tree in the hopes of swinging herself up into its branches. Mathéo gets to her just as she reaches it, however, drenching her head and shirt as she shrieks and struggles. Finally she escapes his grip and races back into the house, slamming and locking the conservatory doors behind her with a triumphant whoop.

After a considerable amount of banging, Consuela finally lets him in, looking mildly horrified, Loïc trailing in her wake. Mathéo takes the stairs two at a time and eventually catches up with Lola in the top-floor bathroom, where she is attempting to dry herself off with his flannel.

'Your shirt is transparent,' he laughs, slinging her over his shoulder and carrying her into his bedroom. He throws her unceremoniously down on the bed. 'Look at you! You're a disgrace, Miss Baumann!'

'Not funny! Gimme one of your T-shirts right now!' she growls, kneeling up on the bed and lowering her head to unbutton her top; her wet, tangled hair falling forward, obscuring her face.

He jumps onto the bed beside her, almost knocking her over. 'No.'

She looks up at him as he helps her out of her sodden top. 'What d'you mean *no*, you filthy rat-bag? You want me to walk around in my underwear for the rest of—?'

His mouth meets hers with a jolt, cutting her off. 'No,' he gasps between kisses. 'Personally, I think you should wear nothing at all.'

She starts to laugh, but he bites her bottom lip to silence her, and suddenly they are kissing hard, almost frantically, so fiercely they hardly have time to come up for air. His hands grip the sides of her face, then slide into her hair, her mouth hot and fierce against his. As their kisses become stronger, more urgent, almost painful, he wraps his arm around her waist, pulling her towards him so that their bodies are pressed tightly together, his hands pushing against the back of her neck, her head. He is kissing her so hard, they barely have time to surface for breath. She smells of grass and earth and peppermint, her lips salty and her hair soft and damp. And he never knew a kiss could be filled with so much emotion – passionate, yet somehow also desperate, as if it were both the first and the last kiss in the world.

He divests her of her top, leaves her to do the rest, and pulls his T-shirt over his head, kicking off his trainers and stepping out of his jeans. Then, suddenly, they are both naked on the bed, sending the duvet tumbling to the floor, their bodies meeting instantly. He can feel a current slide under his skin, crackling with electricity; it is the first time they have had sex since they got drunk by the river, and he is so turned on she has to remind him to use a condom. He sits up, cursing, and then presses down on her again and moves his mouth over her breasts, kissing her from her navel to her neck, then making contact with her mouth with a gasp, the sudden press of her lips against his almost making him come.

She circles his torso with her arms, wraps her legs around his, her grasp so fierce, so urgent, he can feel the edges of her nails against his back. She is holding on so tight that for a moment he feels trapped: trapped within her grasp, trapped within her body, trapped against his will. And suddenly he knows there is no escape, nowhere to run, nowhere to hide. He can only freeze and lie still and try to disappear, evaporate into the air around him.

'Hey!' The voice, not one he recognizes, calls to him as if from outside a nightmare. 'Hey!' A breath, a silence. 'It doesn't matter. You're probably just tired or – or . . .'

It takes him a moment to recognize the voice, the surroundings. Lola. But something has changed. He is cold; so cold he has to hold himself tight to stop himself from trembling. Something is very wrong: he hasn't come, all earlier arousal completely sapped from his body. He has retreated, his penis limp and useless in the sudden cold, the sudden fear, the sudden emptiness of the room.

'Fucking hell . . .' He rolls away from her, quickly removing the empty condom and reaching for the duvet on the floor. Drags it back over them both, then rescues his T-shirt and boxers and pulls them on hurriedly. He looks up into a face that is almost as shocked as his. 'Damn, I'm sorry, I – I really don't know what happened!'

'It's OK.' Pulling the duvet up to her chin, Lola is flushed, her lips stained red with the strength of his kisses. But she is looking at him with a look of nervous uncertainty and he presses his fist against his mouth and realizes he is trembling. 'Sweetheart . . .'

He starts, the touch of her hand like a burn. He raises an elbow as if in self-defence. 'Wait – just give me a second here!'

She recoils immediately, huddling against the pillows. 'Sorry—'

'No, it's OK. It's not your fault. It's just – it's just—' His heart is racing. He can't seem to catch his breath. He bites the knuckles of his fist in an attempt to stop himself shaking. *OK, get a grip*, he tells himself. These things happen. Except that he is overcome with a feeling of horror, of utter certainty. He will never be able to have sex again. He will have to leave Lola. It wouldn't be fair not to. He will lose her for ever because he will never be able to make love to her again.

Through blurred vision he is aware of Lola pulling on her underwear, going over to his drawers to fetch a dry top, then sitting down beside him on the edge of the bed, reaching out to take his hand and wincing as he instantly pulls back.

'Lola, I've – I've got training. I'm late—'

'Mattie, don't be like this. Please don't be upset!'

'I'm not!'

'You're angry, then—'

'No, I'm just late, I have to go.' He swings his legs off the bed and stands up, pulling away from her attempted embrace.

'I don't care about what just happened. But I care about *you*!' Tears spring into her eyes. 'Something's wrong. Something's been wrong for weeks now. That's what I care about. And it kills me that you won't tell me!' She bites her lip, tears spilling over the edges of her lashes. But he forces himself to turn away, cross the landing to the bathroom and get ready for training.

There is a red exclamation mark next to today's date on his iPhone calendar. It's been there for several weeks now – Perez knows better than to spring things on him at the last minute. This particular red exclamation mark has only ever meant one thing to Mathéo: a new dive. This afternoon, for the first time, he will attempt the reverse handstand triple tuck off the ten-metre board. He has been practising it for several weeks now as a dry dive, into the foam pit down at the gym. He has spent several sessions practising it off the five-metre board in the safety harness. But today there will be no rig to control his fall, no pit full of soft foam to absorb the shock of entry. Today he will be launching himself backwards from the handstand position off the highest board – higher than two double-decker buses – and twisting and somersaulting through the air, legs flexed, toes pointed, then knees bent, hands gripping his ankles before straightening out and hitting the water like an arrow.

Mathéo knows only too well by now that thinking about what could go wrong when diving is always a recipe for disaster. But after what happened with

Lola, his mind only seems capable of dwelling on the negative – dark, self-destructive thoughts he can no longer relegate to the side-lines of his consciousness. Arriving for training ten minutes late, he takes his time getting changed, spending longer than necessary strapping up the wrist he injured back in January, lingering for a while under the hot shower and going through his stretching routine and warm-up dives with a thoroughness usually reserved for competitions. The session is already well underway and the other divers are already going through their sets. His father, who always comes home early to watch him perform a new dive, is striding impatiently along the bottom row of the bleachers, looking typically out of place in his business clothes, despite having removed his jacket and loosened the knot of his tie. His face glistens with sweat. Now he is leaning over the rail of the bleachers, talking earnestly into Perez's ear, forcing the coach to stand back against the wall with his head half turned to listen, while simultaneously keeping an eye on the squad's three other divers, shouting out the odd instruction and blowing into his whistle to let each one know when the pool is clear. Mathéo already knows how the conversation is going: his father will be badgering Perez to tell Mathéo to hurry up; Perez will be trying to persuade Mathéo's father that it is safer to let Mathéo take his time. But after a while, even Perez's patience begins to wear thin; he emits three sharp blasts from the whistle around his neck and everyone stops.

'Right, let's get moving! Aaron, in the warm-up area loosening up your lower back! Zach and Eli, go through your sets on the lower boards! Matt, get started on the reverse triple tuck from the ten-metre right now, please!'

However, as is the custom when one of them is attempting a new dive, the other squad members hang back to watch.

'Good luck, man,' Aaron says with a lopsided grin as he goes over to the warm-up area and stretches out on his towel at a strategically positioned angle. Zach and Eli come over, as is customary, to give him high-fives before going to sit down on the ends of the lower boards and lean back on their hands, getting comfortable. A group of girls from the synchronized swimming club cut the music to their routine and gather to sit with their coach in and around the hot tub. Several lifeguards appear as if from nowhere to join the two already on duty – Mathéo senses rather than sees them in their matching tracksuits, gathered on the far side of the diving pool. Even the recreational swimmers pause for a break, hanging round the ladder in the shallow end for the best view. The regulars all know him by sight, recognize his name, and those who don't know him stop anyway to see what all the fuss is about. All it takes is for Perez to raise the megaphone to his mouth, go through the standard safety procedure of announcing his name and the fact that he will be attempting a new dive for the first time, and everyone stops to watch. There must be at least thirty pairs of eyes on him as he steps out from beneath the poolside shower and briskly shakes the water from each ear. Thirty pairs of eyes follow him as he picks up his chamois cloth, walks over to the boards, and begins his ascent.

It might be a scant audience compared to competition days, but here almost everyone either knows him by name or knows him personally, having watched him train and dive over the years. They know his idiosyncrasies, are familiar with his body language, can tell in an instant whether he is feeling confident, cautious, or downright terrified. Some have even witnessed his meltdowns as a kid, when he would run from the pool, sobbing in fear. But over the years he has learned to control his emotions – is known on the team for never bottling out of new dives. So the focus here feels much more intense, much more direct, much more personal. In many ways, when attempting a new dive for the first time he is at his most vulnerable, his most exposed, his most defenceless. Even though he is well-liked by most of these onlookers, he knows only too well that their bated breath stems as much from speculation that he may crash and burn as from a desire to see him nail the dive. Much like watching a stuntman attempt a crazy feat, they hope either for a spectacular dive or a spectacular catastrophe.

Usually he doesn't give this quite so much thought, but usually he feels prepared, confident, in charge. Not since he was a child has he ever felt this goddamn nervous. But today, as he climbs the long chain of ladders, he feels his pulse increase with every rung. He can sense the muscles in his legs beginning to shake; when he reaches the top, it's as if he has already scaled a mountain. The air seems thinner up here, less oxygen; his breathing is fast and shallow. He knows his body is reacting to stress and that, if he is to stand any chance of completing the dive without incident, he must turn that stress into determination, turn the nerves into adrenalin. He knows all the techniques, has been through them countless times over the years with the sports psychologist, but today he struggles to bring them to mind. The nerves and synapses in his brain are coping with a much bigger problem, trying to fight back a very different kind of memory, although the two seem somehow interwoven – as if performing this dive were symbolic of another, far more harrowing experience. But he can't think about that now. He *won't* think about that now . . .

He forces himself to walk over to the edge of the platform, to look down at the pools and miniature Lego figures below. Today, the ten-metre seems higher than before, the water a long way further down, and the board feels slippery and flimsy beneath the soles of his feet. He takes a deep breath and conjures up the image of the dive the way he is supposed to, trying to feel each twist and turn in his body, mentally going through every little movement in his mind. But there is something blocking it, something in the way, and sweat rises to the surface of his skin and his lungs feel ready to burst. He wipes his face with his cloth, pressing the soft fabric against his closed eyes, willing himself to visualize the dive. But he is pacing the board now and breathing too fast, twirling his cloth frantically between his hands – ten times one way, ten times the other; another ten times before he reaches the end of the board and he'll be OK; another ten times before he walks back to the wall and he'll nail it. His heart is pumping like machine-gun fire, shooting blood around his body as if he were already flying through the air. He can hear his half-whispered affirmations as he mouths them frantically to himself – faster and faster, until they all blend into one word and make no sense at all. His whole body is buzzing with uncontrolled energy now, the electric grid of his nervous system firing at random. He can feel the electricity in his veins: he is a live wire, he is alight and on fire and shaking. Shaking!

Shouts of encouragement rise up to greet him: his

squad mates, the synchro girls, the lifeguards, even the recreational swimmers.

'Go for it, Matt!'

'You can do it, mate!'

'We know you can do it, Mattie!'

'We love you, babe!'

Giggles from the synchro girls, but Perez's voice echoes above them all.

'Switch off the thoughts now, Matt,' he booms into the megaphone, 'and count yourself in. Get yourself into position and just count yourself in. You've practised it more than enough. Your body knows exactly what it has to do.'

Your body knows what it has to do, your body knows what it has to do. But no, no, no, he doesn't want to do it! Didn't they hear him the first time? Didn't he shout? Didn't he fight? Didn't he beg and plead, beg and plead, like a little child. *No, please no. Don't make me do it. I'll do anything else. Not that, please not that, please stop it. Please, God, please!* . . . They are all looking at him. At his body. High up here, in full view of everyone. Naked, apart from his Speedos, his body exposed to them all. He can feel their eyes on him, willing him to obey. Yes, his body knows what it must do. *After you've done it once, you never forget, never forget, never forget.*

'Mathéo, for God's sake, just do the bloody dive!' His father now. He has left the bleachers in frustration and has joined Perez at the side of the pool, both men with arms folded and heads tilted back, united in their frustration. 'You're over-analysing it, you're winding yourself up! Just get a move on, for chrissakes!'

He spins his cloth, pacing, still pacing. Every time he reaches the end of the board, his mind screams, *Not yet!* and he turns and makes his way back to the wall. Just one more time and then he'll do it. Just one more time, just one more second, and then he'll be OK, then he'll be ready. He runs his fingers through his hair, scraping his nails against his scalp. He can hear the sound of his panicked, shuddering breathing. *Oh God oh God oh God oh God* . . .

It's gone very quiet down on the ground below. The audience holds its collective breath, waiting to see if he is going to bottle out of it – come back down the ladders and disappear off into the changing rooms in shame.

'Deep breath, buddy.' Perez's voice is gentler now, clearly aware he is at breaking point. 'Shut out the thoughts. Take it nice and easy. As soon as you've done it once, you'll know you can do it again.'

You'll know you can do it again. The first time, you think you'll die. The pain is so great, you *hope* you'll die. But you don't, and it happens again, and then again, and then again . . .

They are all watching him, feeling for him, willing him to go for it, and he knows now that he has no choice, he never did have a choice, his body is no longer his own. Others tell him what to do and he obeys; he obeys or they get frustrated, they get angry. So angry. Yes, he will do it and he will get hurt – so badly that to others it will be unimaginable; so badly he may never recover.

Slowly he makes his way to the edge of the platform. Finds his spot, takes a deep breath. He slides his feet apart, lowers his arms and searches for the perfect grip on the edge of the board. Gradually he transfers the full weight of his body onto his hands, his wrists, his arms, his shoulders. His ankles begin to loosen, and with great care he raises his feet off the ground. No wobble, no fall. Slip now and it's all over. With flexed legs and pointed toes, he brings his feet together straight above his head. His body is stretched upwards by his toes – he is taut, he is tight, he is strong, he is all muscles and sinew. His back to the water, he prepares to launch himself into the void. Ready? Never, but it's time to count himself in.

One: he is hit from behind, sent sprawling to the ground. His body tightens, he does not move.

Two: he is grabbed by his hair, face smashed against the damp-smelling earth. He takes a deep breath, stretches himself up as high as he can go.

Three: he is pinned to the ground, crushed by a weight from which there is no escape. But this time he can get away – he can fly. With a flick of his wrists, he launches himself away from the board and into the air. Away, away, away. He doesn't care where, as long as he is free. And then he remembers: begins his first somersault, eyes searching for the slash of blue. But it's not where it's supposed to be: he finds the platform edge instead. And he is rotating straight towards it. Close, too close! *Too. Damn. Close . . . BANG!*

And just like that, he's dead. This time it's easy. Why wasn't it before? He had wanted it, begged for it, prayed for it even. But no, just the pain, again and again. This time, however, as he spins down ten metres in freefall, he feels the world just skid away. He hits the water. Sucked into darkness. Plummets down, down, deep down. Feels only relief. Absolution. It's all over. Never again. He is free, he has flown. At last he has found what he was looking for. He has found peace.

8

Down, down, down. Deep beneath the surface. He is trapped underwater, drowning, but has neither the energy nor the desire to pull himself free. Echoes in the distance: the sound of people talking, the rattling of a trolley, rhythmic bleeping of machines, strains of music interspersed with laughter, someone crying out in a low plaintive wail. Like radio static or inter-ference, voices cut in from a distant, foreign station. He is rocking on the surface of life. Someone is saying his name; he tries to open his eyes but they seem held down by weights. No, no, no. He doesn't want to wake up. He will stay down here for ever, adrift in a time-less ocean. The world can go on without him; he wants no part in it any more. But words and phrases and snatches of conversation are seething all around him. Voices that tear at his ears, reverberate in his skull; he feels he will scream if they do not shut up.

The world is garish, sharp; it cuts at his brain. He tries to slide back under, but his mind is spitting and fritzing, its wires burned out. He can feel the proximity of oblivion, can touch it, can taste it even, yet his mind insists on turning this way and that, slogging in and out of consciousness.

He is beginning to rise, to struggle, blinking and gasping, to the surface. Blotches of life and fury. He opens his eyes to a harsh white room, and a light that screams in agony. He is in a world of hurt, his head pounding, full of static and cracking pain. He gets a hint, a glimpse of his surroundings; a blurred image, like a poster seen from the window of a speeding train. He is aware of a poorly defined human shape hovering nearby. A pulse of fear runs through him: the shadow's edges are splintered, ragged, like something lost at sea. He is struggling to open his eyes now, to move his head. A crackling, fiery bonfire flares up in front of him, illuminating whatever he looks at. He is disorientated and confused, his senses overstretched, aching.

He is aware of another sound now, something between a groan and a whimper.

A placatory hand pats his arm. The sound of a woman's voice. 'Mateeo?' She mispronounces his name. 'You're OK. Can you look at me? That's it. Good! Look at me, right here. Do you know where you are?'

His eyes slowly focus on a woman in nurse's uniform. He is lying in a bed, a machine bleeping to his right. His hand feels fat and heavy – he looks down to find several tubes running into the back of it, taped down and bandaged up; a plastic clip is attached to his finger and a blood-pressure cuff is wrapped around the top of his arm. There seem to be an awful lot of wires.

'Hospital?' His voice sounds cracked and feeble; his lips are sore and dry.

'That's right. You're in Duke's Memorial – you were brought in about an hour ago with a head injury. Do you remember how that happened?'

He tries to nod. Winces sharply. 'Training.'

'Come again?'

'Diving. I mistimed the – the . . .' He makes a circular motion with his finger. Such an effort to speak. 'The rotation,' he manages. The pictures seethe and swing in front of him: shards of memory that he has to reconstruct from the mayhem in his mind. He can't seem to go back in time, but neither can he move forward, his memory too capricious to trust. There is no chronology inside his head. Instead, it is composed of myriad images which spin and mix and part like sparks of sunlight on water, then vanish entirely, no more substantial than a dream.

There is a fold in time because suddenly another person is in the room – a man in a white coat, shining a light in his eyes. He is asking Mathéo to follow his finger. So Mathéo stares at it, then beyond, through the late afternoon sun that fills the window, to somewhere so far away that he seems to disappear . . .

The doctor moves away. Dark spots dance before Mathéo's eyes. The spots seem to elongate, turning into shadows, turning into trees. The flash of trees rushing past him. Trees, tall and threatening in the dark, stretching up into the night sky. He closes his eyes to get rid of the image, but it only makes it clearer, and now he can hear the crunch of twigs beneath his trainers, the panting, retching sound of his breath tearing at his lungs. He is running. Running away from the scene of the crime, running away to escape what he has done, running away to escape what he has become. And suddenly he remembers. Remembers it all. That night in Brighton. That night he transformed into something horrific, despicable, became a different person, and he has been trapped in this different body ever since . . . He holds his breath, willing the memories away, pushing himself back down into oblivion, back into a place where he no longer exists . . .

He hears his name being called, over and over again, and finally he forces himself to open his eyes a crack, blink groggily at the blurred shape beside him. He recognizes his mother, sitting on the edge of his bed and patting his tube-free hand. She is talking to him about brain scans, although he can't remember how the conversation started. His father and the doctor are somewhere nearby, bulky shadows by the window, their voices low and resonant, filling the room with unwanted sound. Perez also seems to have appeared and he learns from the conversations that swirl around him that he has a ten-centimetre gash on the side of his forehead and twelve stitches, that he has concussion but that his skull is intact and the EEGs show no sign of internal bleeding or bruising. He also gathers that, between falling unconscious into the pool and being dragged out by Aaron and Perez, he managed to inhale a lungful of water, stop breathing for over a minute, and had to be resuscitated by one of the lifeguards.

They all keep talking: his mother, his father, Perez and the neurologist. Their words are like bullets, ricocheting off the walls. Sometimes they are aimed at him and he does his best to answer. But when he closes his eyes to try to escape, they just seem to grow louder. He wants nothing more than to go home. He hates hospitals – the last time he was in one was when he fractured his wrist after an awkward landing in the foam pit; he was discharged with a plaster cast only a few hours later. But this time, when he tries to get out of bed, everyone gets very agitated and he finds himself pushed firmly back down against the pillows, dizzy with pain.

'We need to keep you in for a night or two, Mathéo,' the doctor informs him firmly. 'Just for observation. You've suffered concussion and inhaled quite a bit of water and stopped breathing.'

Mathéo closes his eyes again to hide his distress; the conversations continue without him and gradually fade out into the corridor. Sometime later his parents come back in to say goodnight.

The evening seems to go on for ever. His head feels ready to explode. He dozes fitfully – waking with a start when he feels himself falling again, only to find himself stuck in a hospital bed covered with a thin white sheet, soaked in sweat and shivering. Each time he closes his eyes he sees the edge of the platform rushing towards him, the world spinning at all angles. He feels trapped and crushed by an invisible weight that presses down over the whole of his body. He just wants to move, get comfortable, kick off the clammy sheet and run outside for some fresh air. But the room is heavy with the smell of medicine, the lights blaze down from a pale blue ceiling, and all Mathéo wants to do is scream. He asks for a drink but the nurse insists he can have nothing until morning. The empty saline drip is replaced with a fresh one but does nothing to quench his thirst. He tries to sit up, but dizziness forces him back; he is overcome by a feeling of utter uselessness when he realizes he can't even get out of bed. Different nurses come in at regular intervals – to check his temperature, his pulse, his blood pressure. At first he is too hot and then he is too cold; he feels exhausted but sleep eludes him. At some point he must have said something because a nurse starts patting his hand, telling him he'll be OK, that he can go home soon. He wonders what that means. Wonders if he cares. Life has dug itself out of him and he feels himself sinking, his desperation too big and empty for any one person to contain. Fear has run its course and depression has whittled him down to nothing.

He must have drifted off for a while because when he next opens his eyes, the light has changed. Through the window opposite his bed he can see that the sun has turned golden, beginning to dip in the sky. He takes a breath and feels something move against his face. Someone is stroking his cheek, holding his hand. With a startled gasp, he turns his head.

'Sorry, sweetheart, I didn't mean to wake you.'

He follows the voice and meets Lola's eyes, full of tenderness and concern, her hair hanging loose over her shoulders, touching and brushing his bare arm. She is sitting on the edge of his bed, leaning over him, her fingers warm on his face. 'Hey, you!'

The tears prick at his eyes. Seeing her is too intense, too direct an emotional hit, and one he fears might break him. He can hardly believe she is here, is scared it could be a dream, that he'll close his eyes and wake up only to find her gone again.

'Hey . . . It's all right, Mattie, you're going to be fine!' Despite the reassuring smile, her bottom lip quivers and she rubs it with her finger. 'Mattie, don't – you're going to get me started now!' She scrunches up her eyes for a moment, takes a steadying breath and then opens them.

'I asked for it, didn't I?' She lets out a dramatic sigh. 'Falling in love with a crazy daredevil whose idea of fun is throwing himself off diving boards and spinning about in the air like some kind of superman on speed!'

He chokes back a sob and manages a small laugh instead, pressing the back of his bandaged hand against his eyes. A moment passes. He swallows what feels like a fireball in his throat.

'I'm sorry, about – about this afternoon . . .'

Gently she pulls his hand back down. 'Don't be silly. You don't need to apologize. And that's the last thing you should be thinking about now.'

'I'm sorry I just walked off like that—' He takes a deep breath and reaches up to wipe his eyes.

'You were late for training,' she reminds him gently. 'And guess what? I got to be a model for a top magazine!'

He blinks at her.

'Yeah,' she continues blithely. 'Dad took me along

to a photoshoot this afternoon and the editor took one look at me and decided I was just perfect for the cover of *Vogue*!'

'Oh.'

A beat, the hint of a smile, then she starts to laugh. 'Oh sweetheart, that's some concussion you've given yourself!'

He sniffs and finds himself smiling too. 'Hey, but I've always said you'd end up being spotted!'

'To be fair, it is for a cover. But sadly not *Vogue*. They needed someone who could ride, so you're looking at next month's cover of *Horse and Hound*.'

'So—' He closes his eyes for a moment to gather his thoughts. 'They – they had the horse but needed a hound?'

'Bastard!'

She mimes a punch to his nose. She has returned to her usual teasing, cheerful self, but suddenly the gap between them seems to widen again. He needs her back, needs something – a hand, a kiss, a hug – anything to keep him from drifting off the edge of the world.

'Lola?' He hears the note of anguish in his voice.

'It's all right, Mattie, I'm right here.'

He is aware of her shifting on the bed to lie down beside him, resting her head gently against his chest, just below his chin.

'They say you'll most likely be discharged tomorrow but that you shouldn't go back for the last week of school, so I was thinking . . .' She looks up at him, curling the tip of her tongue over her upper lip and rolling her eyes to the side in an expression of extreme mischief. Then, abruptly, her expression changes. 'Hey—'

A tear escapes down the side of his face; he takes a deep breath and holds it. He sucks in his right cheek, biting down hard, and stares at her, unable to utter a word.

'Sweetheart, what is it? Are you in pain? Do you want me to call the nurse?'

The air exits his lungs in a rush, and he presses his fingers and thumb against his eyelids in an attempt to keep himself from sobbing. 'There's something I need to tell you . . .'

Her hand wipes the tears from his cheeks as they fall. 'What is it you need to tell me?' Her voice is low and urgent, almost a whisper. 'Oh God, darling, try. Please try and tell me what's happening to you. I love you, I want to know!'

'I'm scared.' The words come out of their own accord, bypassing the filter in his brain. He presses his hand down against his eyes to avoid seeing her expression.

There is a long silence. She lets the pause sit and then grow. He knows she is struggling to make sense of the word, of his erratic behaviour. She is trying to understand. 'Of diving?'

'No!'

He senses her shock through the air-conditioned, sterile air between them. Her shock, and then a new emotion – a fear of her own. 'Of what, Mattie?'

'Of – of—' He fills his lungs, then empties them slowly in an attempt to force himself into a state of calm. 'Of remembering . . .'

'Remembering what?'

'Something bad.' He closes his eyes. 'It was a nightmare – I was sure it was a nightmare. Or maybe I just really wanted to believe it was a nightmare. But then, when I was counting myself in to the dive, I began to remember: it all started coming back—'

'The nightmare?' Worry and confusion sounds in Lola's voice. 'Or the thing you thought was a nightmare? What happened, sweetheart?'

An image flashes through his brain. A man, just slightly out of focus. The crack of his own fist meeting bone. And blood, lots of blood . . .

'Mattie?'

He forces himself to open his eyes, forces himself to look at her. 'I'm scared of losing you . . .' His voice rises. He holds his breath. Articulating the words seems to somehow magnify their power so that they take on a whole new meaning of their own. It's almost as if he has foretold the future, cursed them both with a prophecy that cannot ever be unsaid, cannot ever be undone.

'Why?' A breath. She pauses as if to gather her thoughts. Strokes his hair rhythmically, gazing out of the darkened window at the distant lights of the city.

Mathéo takes a deep breath, trying to steady his heart. The morphine is acting like some kind of truth serum, of that he feels sure. The pain in his head and the shock of the fall has skewed his thought processes, knocked down his defences, and he no longer feels in control, either of his emotions or of the words coming out of his mouth. A different type of fear begins to grip him – the one that he might fall apart completely, right here, right now, and tell Lola everything. Everything his brain spewed out from the darkest recesses of his mind as he stood atop that damn diving board. Ruin their relationship with just one sentence, shatter her image of him in the space of a second, destroy every memory, every kiss, every secret, every shared moment of intimacy, every good thing that has happened between them from the moment they first met.

Her voice, oddly disembodied in the gathering gloom, propels him out from the vortex of his mind. 'Did you – did you cheat on me, Mattie?' It is barely phrased as a question, much less an accusation; it is simply the agonized gasp of someone searching for some kind of explanation.

He feels himself go completely cold; cold and then numb, as if his body has suddenly been sucked dry of all substance, of all feeling, of all emotion. For one insane moment he thinks he is going to tell her: absolve himself of all this guilt, clear his conscience and free himself from the weight of this hellish, secret albatross. But then he imagines life without Lola: the guilt still present but not just his life in tatters, hers as well. He imagines never seeing her again: that vibrant, expressive face, that mischievous smile. The way she bites the tip of her tongue when she is teasing, the way she rubs her finger against her lip when she is worried. He imagines never again seeing the spark of mischief in those gold-flecked eyes, never again feeling the caress of her hair against his cheek. He imagines gradually forgetting the feeling of being held, of being stroked, of being kissed by Lola — and he cannot do it. Cannot utter the one word that would wipe out her love for him for ever. So he shakes his head and closes his eyes.

9

He is discharged the following afternoon and spends the next couple of days knocking around the house, bored, while his parents are at work and his brother at school. Consuela fusses around him like a pestering fly and he attempts to drown out her whine with daytime TV and naps on the living-room sofa. Lola is busy with the musical and so their interactions are restricted to late-night Skype calls and sporadic texts throughout the day. Every morning, however, with a look of confusion, Consuela hands him an origami crane from the letter box, the paper bird bearing only his name, its wings tightly folded around Lola's message. Sometimes it's a little anecdote from school, other times it's a comment about her day. Just a few lines in that neat, slanted handwriting of hers, but always ending with something romantic, or an expression of her affection – anything from something as simple as *I miss you* to a declaration of something stronger.

Aaron, Zach and Eli have all been in touch, wishing him better. Perez has been calling him on his mobile two, sometimes three times a day, but Mathéo has just been letting it go to voicemail. He returns to the hospital for some tests and is almost relieved when he is told that normal service can resume. Normal service, except for diving – much to his father's annoyance. The neurologist is clear, even gives him a copy of the medical report: training in the gym is fine, but he will need a good fortnight away from the pool – to keep the wound dry as much as anything else.

Mathéo texts Perez the news with some satisfaction. He pretends to be fed up when telling his parents, but deep down feels nothing but relief. He doesn't want to think about the new dive, or anything to do with diving. Maybe now that he is being allowed time off he will be able to put some distance between himself and the horror of what happened in Brighton. Now that he's remembered, he desperately needs to forget about it again, blot it for ever out of his mind, take it with him to his grave. No one can ever, ever know, or his life – his life will be over. He just needs to wipe his mind completely clean, wash the blood from his hands and return to something of his former self.

After seeing the specialist, he has to wait an

agonizing six hours before he can speak to Lola. It's the very last day of school and the final night of the show: he has specific orders not to call or text, in case the unimaginable happens and she forgets to turn off her phone. But after being parted for two days, and effervescent with the news that he will no longer be under Consuela's surveillance or immersed in his usual intensive training schedule, he feels unexpectedly heady with freedom.

'Meet me tonight outside the school hall?' Lola sounds rushed but excited. 'Promise?'

He laughs. 'I promise.'

'Two weeks off training? That's going to be so cool. We can— Hey, that means you can come with us to the South of France!'

He gives a sardonic laugh. 'Yeah, right. Just because I can't use the pool doesn't mean Perez is going to give me any time off training.'

But he can't help but feel a real pang of jealousy now that Lola has agreed to go, at his insistence, without him. Hugo's parents' villa is a place of glorious, hedonistic freedom, in the middle of nowhere, right by the beach. Until training got serious and even holidays stopped, he spent time there every summer. After hanging up, he flops back against his bed, picturing the glorious cliff-edged house, the enormous stretch of sandy beach, and the three of them, alone save for the housekeeper, free to do whatever they pleased.

* * *

'Consuela, can I give you a hand with dinner?' The kitchen is cool and smells of disinfectant. It is already gone six, and he wonders for a moment if she has maybe forgotten, busy testing Loïc on his times tables.

'No dinner tonight.' She looks up from Loïc's textbook. 'Mrs Walsh, she call.'

Helping himself to a can of iced tea from the fridge and taking the biscuit tin from the cupboard, Mathéo trails over to the breakfast bar and sits down with his snacks. 'She called to tell you we weren't having dinner?'

'Yes,' Consuela replies with no attempt at further explanation. 'Loïc, now we try the seven, yes?'

Head threatening to fall off his supporting hand, Loïc puffs out his left cheek in boredom. 'The seven what?'

'The seven!'

'Mattie, I don't know what she's talking about.' He looks over plaintively and his eyes alight on the biscuit tin. 'Can I have one?'

Mathéo flashes his brother a warning look. 'Your seven times tables. Don't be rude, Loïc.'

'But can I have one?'

'All right. Ready?' He tosses a Jaffa Cake over to his brother and, with a whoop, Loïc jumps up from his chair and just makes the catch, cramming the biscuit into his mouth. 'Another one, another one. Come on,

211

make it harder!' He claps his hands together and, hands on bent knees, takes up a goalkeeper's stance.

'No. Mathéo, please! Loïc, we must study and Mrs Walsh say no eat before dinner.'

Loïc ignores her entirely, rubbing his hands together, hopping from foot to foot.

'OK, but last one,' Mathéo concedes.

'Whoa! Yeah, what a save!' Loïc cries triumphantly, skidding across the floor in his socks.

'Loïc, you sit down, please!' Consuela's voice is inching towards a tone of mild hysteria, so Mathéo points to the chair and Loïc slides back onto it, the animation on his face fading back to resignation.

'Sorry.' Mathéo flashes Consuela an apologetic look. 'But about dinner – I can make us some pasta if you want.'

Her eyes widen in alarm. 'No, no. Mrs Walsh, she said no dinner.'

Taking a swig from his can, Mathéo moves the biscuit tin out of view of his brother. 'She told you not to make dinner because she's bringing home a take-away or something?'

Consuela's eyes widen further. 'No, no, Mathéo. No allowed takeaway.'

'No, I don't want – I'm not—' He takes a deep breath, trying to keep the mounting frustration from showing on his face. It is imperative he finds out what is going on with dinner in order to make sure he can get away in time to meet Lola after the performance. 'Did my mother say why she didn't want us to have dinner?' he asks slowly and carefully.

'Yes. No dinner.'

Loïc gives a small snort as he writes out sums in his exercise book. 'No dinner, no dinner,' he mimics, chuckling softly to himself.

'Did my mother say she wanted to make dinner herself?' Mathéo tries again.

'No! No!' Consuela shakes her head earnestly, looking horrified at the idea. 'Mrs Walsh no make dinner!'

Mathéo fights back a sigh of exasperation. 'So tonight, no food?'

Loïc presses his hand over his mouth to suppress a giggle.

'Yes, food!' Consuela exclaims almost angrily. 'Tonight food. Of course food.'

'But no dinner—'

Loïc snorts from behind his hand. 'This is like something out of—'

'Hey!' Mathéo pins him with a warning look. 'Food but no dinner,' he repeats in frustration. 'Food tonight?'

'Yes! Of course food tonight!' Consuela looks at him as if he is a moron. 'You must eat food tonight, Mathéo!'

'Yes, fine – believe me, I want to eat some food

tonight,' Mathéo mutters as much to himself as to anyone else. 'Where are we eating this food?' he tries a final time.

'Outside.'

'A picnic?' Loïc looks up hopefully.

'No! No!' Consuela almost shrieks. 'You finish work quickly, Loïc. Mathéo, you get ready please!'

'But get ready for what?' His voice begins to rise despite himself.

'For eating out! Good place. You wear good clothes, Mrs Walsh says.'

Loïc puts down his pencil and looks up at Mathéo. 'Oh, we're going to—'

'A restaurant,' they both say, solving the riddle at last.

Their father is celebrating some big deal he closed at work today, and he has booked a table at their favourite French restaurant, which overlooks the Thames and serves four-course meals with food that looks like modern art and takes for ever to arrive. Loïc is overtired and sulky, unwilling to try anything on the menu, their parents keep ordering more wine, and Mathéo begins to despair of ever getting away in time to meet Lola after her last show. When they eventually get home, he has to wait until Loïc is sent to bed, Consuela has left for the night and his parents have gone into their room, before pulling on a jacket over his faded T-shirt and worn jeans, creeping downstairs, slipping on his trainers and letting himself out through the conservatory doors towards the golden pools of artificial lighting that line the lawn. He reaches the school car park just as the younger pupils are streaming out in their costumes, talking animatedly to proud parents wielding camcorders – the school hall lit up like a beacon from the outside, disgorging teachers and pupils and parents and siblings; whole families, all bursting with high-octane chatter. The musical was clearly a great success and he feels a surge of pride that it was his Lola who was behind it all. She is incredible.

As the crowd thins, he retreats into the shadows, holding the roses behind his back, but when Lola appears, she already has an armful of flowers. Squealing in fright, she drops the lot as he jumps out from behind her and grabs her round the waist, twirling her round.

'Oh my God, you crazy idiot! You nearly gave me a heart attack! Are you trying to kill me? Shit, you gave me such a fright!' But she is laughing, turning the heads of the last members of staff to leave the building. Amongst the scattered bouquets he pulls her into a long, hard kiss, despite the presence of his maths teacher, who is locking up.

'I'm so sorry I couldn't come. I had to spend the evening with my parents at this horrible restaurant—'

'It's fine. I'd have been even more stressed out if you'd been in the audience!'

He smiles down at her beaming face, eyes still aglow from her triumph. 'So it was a success?'

'It was, it was! But I'm so glad it's over. No more teaching dyspraxic kids the difference between left and right, or trying to get tone-deaf Year Eights to sing in tune! And you're out of the house at last!' Her words are like a stream of effervescent bubbles, rushing towards the surface; he can feel the energy and excitement beaming out of her like a bright, white light.

'You've *got* to come to France with us!' Lola exclaims, picking up her bouquets and piling them into his arms. 'I want — no, I *demand* at least one week away with you before you start your crazy training again. So I dunno — cheat on the MRI scan—'

'How can I cheat? It's not a lie-detector test, you silly moo!'

'I don't care! Think crazy thoughts, or don't think of anything at all. Pretend you're brain dead — after all, that shouldn't be too hard. I'm sure when you hit your head on the board you lost a few dozen IQ points!'

'How much champagne did you have? You're so pissed,' he teases her.

She thumps him. 'Two glasses. If that!'

'Then it's just insanity talking.' He pulls her to a

stop in the street and kisses her again. 'You're crazy and hyper and deluded – and you haven't even thanked me for the roses!'

'What, these squished things?'

'They're only squished because you trampled on them!'

She laughs again, the sound sparkling up into the night air. 'I'm joking, they're beautiful. I love you – come here.'

They have arrived outside Lola's house and she reaches up for him and kisses him again so fiercely that the bouquets go scattering back down onto the pavement. She leaves him to pick them up while she goes to unlock the front door, loudly informing him that now she is a hotshot director, she will need an assistant to help her with things like bouquets and awards and—

'Shh, it's almost twelve! Your dad will be asleep! Let's go back to mine: my parents are in bed, we can creep in—'

'Dad's not here! Thank God, or he'd have come tonight and embarrassed me with a speech or some-thing at the end of the show.'

'He didn't see it?'

'He came to yesterday's performance. Still managed to be massively embarrassing by chanting for me to come on stage at the end.' She gets the front door open and is almost knocked over by Rocky, jumping up at her and yapping in frenzied excitement.

'But when is he coming back? Come on, Lola, I really think we should go back to my house.'

Lola looks surprised. 'Why risk it when we've got this house to ourselves? I know your bed is a hundred time more comfortable but—'

'What if your dad walks in?'

'He won't. He's not back till tomorrow night. He had a booking for this big-deal Calvin Klein photo-shoot and said he just couldn't get out of it. So it's your job to keep me company till then.' She plonks the bouquets unceremoniously on the kitchen table.

'Are you sure he won't be back tonight?'

'Yes! Anyway, Dad loves you. When has he ever complained about your staying over?'

'OK . . .'

'Down, Rocky, down, you crazy dog. I feel like I haven't seen you for years, Mattie, so you're *definitely* not going anywhere!'

She reaches for the light, but before she can turn it on, Mathéo lifts her up and seats her on the edge of the kitchen table. 'Good, because I wasn't planning to!' Shrugging out of his jacket, he takes her face in his hands, starts to kiss her seriously now.

'Wait. I need to put the flowers in water—'

'Oh no, no, no. No waiting.' He is kissing her

harder and faster. 'Waited too long already, can't believe I haven't seen you for so long!'

'Only two days!' she chuckles, pulling back for air.

'Shush.'

He is trying to kiss her, but she keeps bursting into laughter. 'We don't' – kiss – 'have to shush. Dad's away, so for once you can be as loud and as *ooh* and *aah* as you—'

'Will you shut up?' He kisses her fiercely, but the laughter vibrates from her mouth to his, rendering further kissing an impossibility, so he hoists her over his shoulder and, with difficulty, negotiates the narrow staircase with Lola squealing and Rocky yapping hysterically at his heels.

The light of the streetlamp outside her window falls through her open curtains, bathing her bedroom in a soft orange glow. As usual, her bed is unmade, and discarded clothes and books litter the carpet. As soon as he puts her down, Lola's fingers slip beneath his T-shirt, pressing against the ridges of his stomach, sending a swift, pure thrill racing through his muscles, goosebumps rising on the backs of his arms. Her hair hangs tousled, her face hot to the touch; she is flushed and dishevelled and beautiful and perfect. Mathéo kisses her cheek and neck and breasts, pushing down her skirt with rushed, fumbling fingers. Then Lola pulls the T-shirt over his head, unbuttons his jeans, and slips her hand inside, beneath the waistband of his boxers . . .

Suddenly he is struggling: twisting and writhing against her, grappling with her hands, grabbing her by the wrists, holding her back. 'Lola, stop! Wait, stop!'

She laughs. 'Mattie, if this is your idea of playing hard to get . . .' Her arms circle his neck and she pulls him back towards her.

'No, I'm – I'm serious!' He feels as if he is suffocating. Lola's hands are still on his skin – touching him, stroking him.

'Lola, stop!' he hears himself shout. 'I said *stop!*' Grabbing her tightly by the arms, Mathéo shoves her away as hard as he can. There is a thud, and she goes sprawling across the carpet, crashing hard. He hears the whack as her shoulder makes contact with the wall, and then she falls back against it, tangled hair hanging in her eyes, lips kissed sore, an expression of wild, undisguised shock on her face.

Mathéo takes a couple of stumbling steps back, arms at his sides, panting. His hands shake as he struggles to do up his jeans, to rescue his T-shirt from the floor. Lola sits up slowly, gingerly reaching for her top and threading her arms through the sleeves. She is staring at him with a look he does not recognize: a mixture of hurt and shock and bewildered astonishment. But most of all, of fear. She is clutching her left arm against her chest protectively, cowering back against the wall, shivering, as if terrified of him.

'Shit, I didn't mean . . . Oh fucking hell, I didn't –

I didn't hurt you, did I?' His voice is unrecognizable to his own ears, as if he is being brutally shaken. Breathing hard, he moves towards her, reaching out for her, but she shrinks back with a startled gasp, a look of pure horror in her eyes.

'L-Lola, speak to me! Are – are you all right? Did – did you hurt your arm?'

Her hand moves up to grip her opposite shoulder and she tries unsteadily to get to her feet, wincing in pain.

'Wait. No, wait! Don't move. Let me see!'

He tries to touch her arm, but she holds out a hand to keep him at bay. Her breathing is sharp and shallow. 'I think—' A strangled sob. 'I think you should go.'

She moves round him to reach the door, but he restrains her. 'Lola, no, wait, d-don't. Please don't. Listen to me: I'm so sorry – I mean it. It – it was an accident. It was just an accident, Lola, you've got to believe me!'

'An accident?' She gapes at him. 'You slammed me against the wall!' Her eyes fill with tears and she pushes him away, trying to get to the door.

'You don't understand—' His voice begins to rise. 'I didn't mean to. Lola, I'm so sorry – I didn't know what I was doing. I just panicked!'

She stares at him as if he is crazy. 'You *panicked*?'

'I thought—' His mind scrabbles around desperately for some sort of explanation. 'It was just that I thought – I thought I heard an intruder!' His excuse sounds pathetic, even to his own ears.

Lola just stares at him, her eyes like those of a frightened animal: wild with fear, glistening with pain. 'I need you to go.'

'Lola, please—' Careful not to touch her, he tries to block her path. 'Can – can I just have a look at your arm? Please. Please, Lola. I have to know you're OK!'

Her hand shoots out, keeping him from touching her. She stands there, shaken and bedraggled, still holding one arm protectively against her chest. 'Mattie, I mean it, don't touch me. Just go!'

He steps back, sagging against the wall, banging it with the back of his head as he raises his face to the ceiling and closes his eyes against the threat of tears. 'Lola, I'm so sorry. I'll do anything—!'

'If you really are sorry, then go.'

He tries to say something, anything, but no sound comes out. Rising suddenly, he turns and leaves Lola's room, treading swiftly down the stairs and letting himself out into the darkened street.

He lies awake deep into the night, feeling sick. Sick with shame. Sick with self-loathing, self-hatred, self-disgust. He should have died when he fell from that board. It should have all ended there and then. Lola, his friends, his family would all be better off without him. There isn't a single part of himself that he doesn't hate. Everything hurts. Everything has gone so terribly wrong. Why on earth did he push her away like that? He has truly gone insane. He is dangerous – not just to himself but to others. Maybe he'll never recover from what he did in Brighton. Maybe he really has become a monster. Maybe this is his punishment. Maybe, maybe . . .

After several hours of this torture, he can no longer lie still. Climbing out from beneath the sheets, he pads out of the bedroom. Treading softly downstairs, he makes his way through the darkened house, across the hall, into the living room, the furniture around him ghostly in the moonlight. He circles the place like some kind of predator, his hands brushing the walls. He feels trapped. He wants to run, but where? However far he goes, he will not escape, *cannot* escape his own loathsome self. He will always be trapped within his own body, his own mind. The emotional pain that comes with this realization is so strong, it feels physical. He senses it knotting and twisting inside his body, ready to destroy him from within. He is losing his grip, he is losing his mind. Does anyone else know what it is to be dead yet still alive? This is it. *This is it.* A half-world of torment, where memories frozen into oblivion slowly begin to thaw. A place where everything hurts, where your conscious mind has neither the strength to let you function in the real world, nor the power to return you to hibernation.

Crouching down on the carpet, he drops his head to his knees and begins to cry.

How will he ever get Lola to forgive him? How can he explain to her what came over him when he barely understands it himself? One moment he felt as if he couldn't get enough of her – yearned for the touch of her hands over his body, craved her naked form pressed against his, longed to be as close as two beings could ever be, to inhale her mouth, her lips, her tongue – feel himself inside her, so aroused he felt overcome with a kind of madness, overwhelmed by a passion and an urgency only sex could relieve . . . Then, the next moment, he felt trapped – caught and propelled into a nightmare of distortion, horror and disgust. He felt dirty and exposed and loathsome, wanting only to cover his nakedness and get as far away from her – from him – as possible . . .

He can't believe it, can't believe it has come to this. That night, that night in Brighton, that *one* act is destroying his entire life, besmirching the one pure, untarnished thing he has to hold on to: his love for Lola. Beautiful Lola, with her sense of mischief, humour and fun, with her talent, kindness, affection and sensitivity. Lola and her love for him – so strong and bright it is like the sun on a cloudless day. It carries him, sustains him, feeds him and energizes him – through his parents' absences and his academic pressures, through his gruelling training and competition fears. Through every new dive and every expectation, through fears of accidents and failures, through to anxieties about the Olympics, his future. All those small yet weighty worries, like gravel chips that scrape and wear away at him each and every day. Lola gives him the strength to stand up to them, pick himself up after every fall. She gives him the strength to keep wearing all those different masks: the mask of the popular, cute, beer-drinking jock around school, the mask of the dutiful, charming, academic son at home; the mask of the prodigal, awe-inspiring, championship diver he is expected to epitomize, not just in daily training but at every competition, in every interview – on television, the web and even in the papers. So many roles to fill, so many duties, so much fucking, goddamn, constant expectation.

With A-level results out in just over a month's time, with competitions ongoing throughout the summer, with a deferred university place hanging in the balance, and with the Olympics now only thirteen months away, he is not only under the scrutiny of his peers, his closest friends, his diving team and his family, but of an entire nation! The pressure in his life has never been so great, the stakes have never been so high, and his emotions have never been so stretched, so deep, so volatile and so precarious. He *cannot* let that one stupid night in Brighton get to him; it was a terrible mistake that he should never have let happen. But he did, so now he *must* purge it from his mind! Purge it from his soul as if it has never been, forget about its very existence and just get back to the overachiever he always was – still *is!* But none of that, none of it is possible without Lola at his side. Lola – his rock, his jewel, his pearl, the other half of him, the figure of strength and compassion and love that she epitomizes. Lola, the one person he has never had to wear a mask for, the one person who knows him in all his imperfections, with all his fears – and loves him all the same. He cannot lose her, because without Lola life is simply devoid of all meaning, all worth, and he is whittled down to nothing. Less than nothing: an actor, an imposter, a shell. Dead inside.

Only when he hears the sound of footsteps does he become aware of his own physical presence, curled up on the living-room floor at the foot of the sofa, knees pulled up to his chest, shivering in T-shirt and pyjama bottoms, clutching a cushion for warmth and comfort. He thought he had been quiet, crying silently with his face pressed into the sofa cushion, but when he lifts his head he is startled to see Loïc standing there solemnly at the far end of the room, at the foot of the marble staircase. With his fine, white-blond hair and pale complexion, he resembles a small ghost in the vast room, illuminated only by the moonlight falling through the large bay windows. If not a ghost then a statue, standing there unmoving, fitting in perfectly with the sparse but expensive furniture that surrounds him.

Shocked and humiliated, Mathéo is lost for words – he has no way of disguising his tears and can think of no other reason for his brother's unexpected appearance. Loïc has a phobia about ghosts and never normally ventures downstairs on his own at night, and certainly not without switching on the lights. Mathéo realizes he has no idea how long Loïc has been standing there, witnessing his big brother's meltdown: he cannot remember ever crying in front of Loïc before . . . Shame makes him want to snap, tell Loïc to go away and leave him alone, but he has been sobbing so hard he does not trust himself to speak. He is still gasping in that juddering, uncontrollable way that only ever accompanies a massive crying jag, and the tears are wet on his cheeks. He presses a clenched fist to his mouth and attempts to hold his breath, but the air only bursts from his lungs with a choking sound. For some reason, Loïc's silent, stricken presence seems to upset him still further. He tries again to get a handle on his breathing, rubs his face hard with the heels of his hands, clamps a hand over his mouth and frantically tries to gather enough breath to tell Loïc to go back to bed. But every time he attempts to speak, the words are punctuated by sobbing gasps.

Loïc's eyes have not left Mathéo's face. He appears subdued, his usually plaintive gaze replaced by one of deep sorrow, but with no discernible trace of shock or fear. He takes four measured steps towards Mathéo, his bare feet silent against the marble, and then slowly kneels down a couple of metres away, as if approaching a wild animal. Gingerly he holds out a hand. It takes Mathéo a moment to realize that his little brother is holding out a crumpled tissue and, still unable to speak, Mathéo has no choice but to nod his thanks, reaching out to accept it. He rubs it against his cheeks, the breath still catching in his throat, then empties his lungs slowly and lowers his eyes to the gap on the floor between them.

A couple more steady breaths, and then he whispers, 'Thanks.'

'You're welcome.' Loïc's voice is barely more than a whisper, but calm, more mature than usual. 'Do you want me to go away now?'

Fixing a point between them on the ground, Mathéo breathes slowly through his mouth, concentrating on staying as calm as possible. 'N-no. Of course not.'

'I don't think anyone else heard,' Loïc says, as if reading his brother's mind. 'I woke up to go to the loo and your door was open and I saw you weren't in bed. So I came to find you.'

'Why—' Gasp. 'Why did you come down?' Mathéo asks thickly, in an attempt to make conversation.

'Because I was worried you might of ran away.'

Mathéo's eyes flick upwards, startled, to meet his brother's steady gaze. 'What – what makes you think I'd do that?'

''Cos you been sad for a long time now. And sometimes, in books, when teenagers get sad, they run away.'

The whispered words hang there in the silence, slowly forming themselves into a question – a question of such magnitude that Mathéo can actually sense its presence in the air between them. He wipes his cheeks. 'But who – who told you I was sad?'

'No one. I just could see by your face. After the big competition you won on TV, when you came home, you were sad. And then you got more sad. And then you had nightmares.'

Mathéo is staring at Loïc now, his pulse beginning to race. 'What? What nightmares? How – how do you know?'

'Don't you remember? You talked and shouted, and sometimes you cried a bit too. I came into your room and said your name louder and louder till you waked up. Then you told me to go to bed and fell back asleep.'

'Shit . . .' He breathes deeply, rattled by this revelation. 'How often?'

'Twelve times,' Loïc replies without missing a beat. 'I was thinking tonight was thirteen, but this time wasn't a nightmare 'cos you were awake.'

Mathéo finds himself staring at his brother in shock. 'Did – did anyone else hear?'

'No, just me, 'cos I have very good hearing. I always wake up straight away if there's a noise, even when other people can't hear it. I didn't go get Mummy or Daddy in case they asked you lots of questions and you didn't want to answer.'

Hugging the cushion tighter to his chest, Mathéo tries to imagine Loïc coming into his room to wake him from a nightmare, and fails. But his brother is not one for making things up. 'You – you said I was talking – what kinds of things was I saying?' Fear grips him suddenly; fear of what he might have said.

'It depended. Sometimes you shouted, or sometimes you sounded very sad. I can't remember everything, but lots of times you said, *Why me?* and *You've always been kind to me*, and *Please don't – you're a good person*. And one time—' He hesitates, biting his lip and looking down as if afraid of getting into trouble. 'Um – you said the f-word. But it wasn't your fault because you didn't know you was saying it because you was sleeping!' He shakes his head earnestly, as if to reinforce this fact. 'It wasn't your fault, Mattie.'

Unsteadied again by Loïc's touching concern that he should not blame himself for swearing, Mathéo quickly changes the subject: 'Did I ever say what – what was happening in the dream?'

'No. But you always sounded like you were angry

and scared. Lots of times you shouted, *I swear on my life I won't tell.*'

Mathéo feels his heart rate accelerate. 'Did I ever—' He swallows. 'Did I ever say a name? Anyone's name?'

Loïc shakes his head, and Mathéo momentarily closes his eyes and breathes deeply in relief.

'Loïc?'

'Yes.'

'Can you promise me something? Can you promise you'll never tell anyone about this – about those things I said?'

'I promise.' Loïc levels his unblinking gaze, and for the first time in the conversation, Mathéo recognizes real fear in his brother's eyes. 'Did someone hurt you, Mattie? Is that why you have nightmares all the time and you're always sad?'

The interrogation behind his little brother's gaze unnerves Mathéo. The question is so simple, so straightforward. And that it should come from his eight-year-old brother, from Loïc – the kid brother he leaves to the nanny while he concentrates on pursuing his busy, action-packed life – just knocks the breath from his lungs. All those days, all those evenings, when he'd get back from school or training, take the stairs two at a time to change and call Lola, or rush through his homework before hitting the gym. All those evenings he'd contrived to ignore Loïc – his

231

own brother, for ever stuck downstairs with the nanny. His own brother, who was always so desperate to hold him up with questions about his day, or his diving, who'd even pretend to be stuck on his homework in a frantic bid for a few minutes of his big brother's time. All those delaying tactics just to get a tiny bit of attention. Attention he craved but got from no one other than a string of nannies with poor English, while his parents were either working or socializing, playing golf or tennis or keeping fit at the country club. Parents who pretty much ignored their younger son every meal time to discuss Mathéo's training, Mathéo's competitions, Mathéo's new dives, Mathéo's grades, Mathéo's accomplishments, Mathéo's future. And even so, despite barely exchanging more than a few words a day with his big brother, Loïc had been the only one to pick up on the fact that there was something wrong, that something had happened, that something had changed, and that Mathéo was 'sad'. Unbeknownst to anyone, even to Mathéo himself, Loïc had been regularly coming into his big brother's room at night to wake him from his nightmares – without any thanks, and without mentioning it to their parents in case Mathéo didn't want them to know . . .

'Loïc?'

'Yes.'

'Someone . . . someone did hurt me.' Pause. 'But –

but it's OK now. I'm OK now.' He attempts a reassuring smile, but the breath catches in his throat. 'Thank you for – thank you for not telling anyone. Thank you for coming down to check on me. Thank – thank you for waking me up from the nightmares.' He takes an unsteady breath. 'I know I'm always busy with stuff, but – but I love you a lot, you know.'

Loïc looks up with a shy smile. 'I love you too.'

With a grin, Mathéo chucks the cushion at him and holds out his arm. 'I forget: are you too old for hugs?'

Loïc's face lights up. 'I'm only eight, silly!'

'Get over here, then!'

His smile broadening, Loïc shuffles over on his knees and giggles as Mathéo pulls him onto his lap. For the first time in years, Mathéo feels the fragile body of his kid brother pressed up against his own. Loïc is small for his age, as light as a bird, and feels almost insubstantial, but his hug is fierce. He smells of soap and kiddie shampoo. And for a while they just sit there, Loïc warm and floppy with sleep, until eventually his arms loosen around Mathéo's neck and his head grows heavy. Careful not to wake him, Mathéo stands up, shifts him gently against his shoulder and carries him upstairs. At the door of Loïc's bedroom, he hesitates. Loïc's king-size bed seems ridiculously large for such a small child. Crossing over to his own room, Mathéo lowers his brother carefully down onto the mattress, tucking the duvet in around him. Then he pads round the bed to climb in beside him. If he has a nightmare tonight, at least Loïc won't have to get up again. It even seems conceivable that having his little brother sleep beside him might keep the nightmares at bay . . .

10

The following day he wakes late. Loïc is gone from his bed, no doubt summoned to breakfast, so Mathéo spends most of the morning holed up in his room, doing his best to contact Lola. He tries calling her mobile, texting her, emailing her – but nothing. Whether at home or not, she is never without her mobile, so she must know he is trying to reach her. He leaves a couple of voicemails, imploring her to call him back. It's not like Lola to go cold like that, refuse to talk, cut off all contact – but this is uncharted territory for them both. What terrifies him to the core is the thought that he may have wounded her feelings beyond repair, that the gulf between them may be non-negotiable, unbridgeable, may end their relationship for ever . . . But he can't allow himself to go on thinking this way or he'll go insane. He worries she may have spoken to someone about what happened, to Isabel or Hugo or, God forbid, Jerry, and that news of his actions may well have spread, misinterpreted no doubt as deliberate violence. But above all, he worries desperately he might have seriously injured her. Even though it was a reflex action, he'd still pushed her so hard that she'd slammed into that wall.

He thinks back to last night: it had started off so great. One minute they were messing around, laughing, having fun; the next they were in her bedroom, kissing hard. His whole body craved hers – they hadn't slept together in so long – but then, all of a sudden, the sensation of being touched became horrific, repulsive. He closed his eyes and she'd morphed into someone else – someone who wanted to hurt him, who enjoyed his pain. Someone he had once trusted, transformed suddenly into a monster . . . But Lola had no idea about it all: as far as she was concerned, one moment her boyfriend was initiating sex, the next he was pushing her away – and brutally at that: throwing her against the goddamn wall! Surely she can't believe he'd meant to push her away like that! Surely she doesn't believe he did it on purpose! Yet how can he know?

Pacing his room, phone in hand, he feels increasingly desperate as the morning wears on. He wants to go round to her house, face her in person, so he can tell her the truth, tell her what happened, confess to everything in the hope she might understand. But that would mean having to face Jerry, and he is sure to know by now – Lola tells him everything. Jerry is bound to have asked questions; he always senses when his daughter is upset. To make matters worse, Mathéo has a pretty strong feeling he won't be able to leave his own house without a grilling – whatever excuse he thinks up. For once his parents are lingering over breakfast . . . he can hear them through his balcony's open windows.

It is a bright, warm day, at painful odds with his countenance, the sun beaming down from a china-blue sky. A warm breeze floats in, ruffling the white mesh curtains. The clink of glassware and crockery from outside indicates that breakfast on the terrace is still in full swing. Consuela's nasal tones contrast sharply with his father's pontificating drawl about the Eurozone crisis, while his mother talks over them both, fussing in French over Loïc's lack of appetite and shooting orders at Consuela in perfect Spanish. Only Loïc's voice is missing from the chatter and Mathéo worries that last night's episode may have rattled him enough to induce him to finally confide in his parents about the nightmares, despite the promise of the night before. It must have shaken Loïc up seeing his big brother, almost ten years his senior, collapsed on the living-room floor, sobbing like a child. Mathéo feels himself flush at the memory. But then again, all this time Loïc has known far more about Mathéo's distress than the other three combined . . . and, though on the one hand it causes Mathéo pangs of guilt, on the other hand there is no denying that the realization also brings him some relief – relief that there is at least one person who knows, one person who cares, one person who has some idea, however small, of the torment he is going through.

'*Chéri*, come out and sit down with us. Have some breakfast.' His mother manages to intercept him before he can even reach the front door.

'It's OK. I'm not hungry. I'm just going out for some fresh air.'

'You can get fresh air right here in the garden.' She pulls out a chair and directs Consuela towards the coffee pot with the tip of one immaculately manicured finger. Too tired to argue, Mathéo leaves the relative cool of the kitchen and joins them on the terrace, the sun-drenched decking warm under his bare feet. His favourite jeans seem to have stretched since the last time he wore them and, beltless, slip down to rest on his hips beneath the faded grey T-shirt. Despite the giant parasol, the light strikes him painfully in the eyes, making him squint. Already he feels exhausted, flattened by the sheer brightness of the day. Stirring sugar into black coffee, he sags back in his chair and watches the familiar weekend breakfast unfold. Everything is so . . . devastatingly predictable. He doesn't know why this upsets him, but it does — to the point where it feels almost tragic. The day is already turning out to be another scorcher: the sun beating down from high up in a seamless blue sky, a single blackbird warbling away as if nothing is wrong. Loïc is clad only in pyjama bottoms, his top half bare and fragile-looking, bed-tousled hair hanging like an untidy straw thatch in front of his eyes. He appears bored and sleepy, his eyes listlessly following Consuela as she spreads unwanted jam on his croissant, his narrow shoulders slumped, as if in defeat. His father, dressed for golf and immersed in the *Financial Times*, swats ineffectually from time to time at a large bluebottle, determined to get at his plate. His mother is dressed for the gym but still manages to look elegant in leggings and an oversized T-shirt that slips off one tanned shoulder, hair pulled back into a tight chignon. Come eleven o'clock, his parents will get into their respective cars and drive to their respective leisure centres, Consuela will walk Loïc to his tennis lesson, then later to a play-date or the park, and in the evening his parents will go out to one of their cocktail or dinner parties. The following day will be more of the same, and the family will continue the treadmill of separate weekend leisure and social activities before regrouping for Sunday dinner to mark the end of another meaningless week.

'You look tired, *chéri*.' His mother's voice breaks through the fragile web of tinkling cutlery, rustling paper and buzzing fly. 'Haven't you been sleeping properly?'

'I'm fine,' he says firmly, levelling his gaze with hers.

'You're dreadfully pale and you've got huge shadows under your eyes. Mitchell, don't you think our son looks pale?'

His father lowers his paper and pins Mathéo with a frown. 'Too much lounging around. His body's not used to it – Perez should have him training at the gym at least.' He swats at the fly in irritation. 'What date did the doctor say you could start diving again?'

'After I get my stitches out and depending on the results of the EEG scan.'

'And when's that?'

'In two weeks.'

His father sighs in frustration. 'Perez isn't suggesting you stop training completely until then, surely?'

'It really doesn't matter.'

He sees his father's eyes widen. 'What are you talking about?'

Mathéo takes a deep breath and gets to his feet, ready for a quick exit. 'I never want to see Perez again in my life!' he declares, leaving the table. And then finds himself articulating words he never thought he'd ever say: 'I'm giving up diving, Dad.'

'Lola, let me in. Please, I just want to talk to you. I *have* to talk to you. It's really important – you have no idea!'

After leaving the house, he decided to wander over to see if Jerry's van was still missing from the driveway – thankfully it was – but there was no telling when he'd be back. Mathéo has been hammering on the door for the last five minutes, has already heard Lola's voice from inside, firmly informing him that she is not in the mood to talk and that he should get lost. He sags forward against the solid wood, hanging onto the knocker for support, pressing his face against the crack between the door and its frame, aware from the proximity of her reply that Lola is just behind it, most likely sitting on the stairs.

'Lola, everything's falling apart. If – if you never want to see me again after this, then that's fine. Well, not fine. God, no, not fine, but – but I'll understand. I promise I'll leave you alone. But I want to check you're not hurt and . . . and I want to tell you, Lola! I *have* to tell you. I owe it to you now, and – and if I don't tell someone soon, I think I'm going to go truly insane! I need – I have to – I think I need help. Lola, please!' His voice cracks: he has run out of words, run out of time. She has already decided to leave him. He will have to spend the rest of his life without her, try-ing to find a reason to stay alive. He closes his eyes and presses his forehead against the archway, utterly spent, the soft fabric of his T-shirt sticking to his back. Suddenly the door opens and he half stumbles, half falls into the hall.

'Jesus!' She steadies him with her arm.

Blood-red blotches puncture the air around him. He feels the cool touch of Lola's hand against his, tries to keep hold of it. Briefly it is as if there is another person there, hovering just behind her, and a frightened, prickling sensation begins to spread all over his skin. He tries to straighten up, tries to still his galloping heart, but the fear is so real he can almost taste it.

He kicks the door shut against the harsh light of the encroaching afternoon and slumps against the wall of the narrow hallway.

'What is it you wanted to tell me?' Lola asks, keeping an unnatural distance between them. Her arms are folded round her waist, as if hugging herself against a cold wind that only she can feel. She looks frail and wan, her eyes enormous in her pinched face, violet shadows under pink-rimmed eyes, the sleeves of her blue cardigan pulled down over her hands.

'Did I hurt you, Lola? I – I mean, physically?'

She doesn't reply. Instead she turns her head a little and he sees the deep, heavy sadness in her eyes.

'I thought you had something you wanted to tell

242

me,' she says after a pause, stepping back and hugging herself more tightly now.

There is this terrible void between them and he doesn't dare reach out to try and bridge it for fear of her reaction. They are like two beings on opposite banks of a torrent, gazing across at each other while the waters rage between them.

'I – I do,' he falters. 'But first I really need to check your arm; check I haven't hurt you.'

She seems to shrink back further again, as if fearing his touch. 'As you can see, I'm fine,' she says coldly. 'Nothing broken or anything.'

'But – but your arm. Your shoulder. It hit the wall. Does it — I mean, did it really hurt?'

She hesitates for a moment, then sucks in her lower lip in an attempt, he can tell, to hold back tears.

His voice bursts out of him with a will of its own. 'Oh dammit, Lola, please just – just let me see!'

Instinctively, he reaches out a hand and she moves back immediately. 'It's just bruised,' she says quietly.

'Can – can I have a look?'

'No.'

'You – you've got to believe me,' he says, cupping his hands over his mouth, his voice softly desperate. 'I *never* meant to hurt you. It's the last thing in the world I'd want to do.'

'Look, just tell me why you threw me against the wall and then go,' Lola says, tears pearling on her lashes. 'I just really need some time alone right now.'

'OK,' he says desperately. 'OK. That's why I've come. I – I—' He fills his lungs, empties them slowly, wipes the back of his hand across his clammy face, runs his hands through his hair. His knees suddenly feel dangerously weak. 'Can – can we sit down somewhere?'

Silently she turns, leading the way into the small front room. Rocky is stretched out on the sofa, so Mathéo sits down on the carpet, leaning his back against the armrest and drawing up his knees. Lola curls up on the armchair beside the window.

The room hangs heavy with silence. As much to escape Lola's expectant gaze as to gather his thoughts, Mathéo finds himself pressing his hands against his face, pushing his fingertips over his eyelids, the vision inside his head filling with exploding, blood-red stars. *You have to tell her*, he reminds himself. *You will probably lose her anyway, but if you want even the slimmest chance of getting her back, you have absolutely no option but to tell her. And it has to be now. Right now. This very minute. Because Jerry could come back at any moment. And because if you sit here in silence a second longer, she will imagine you tricked her into letting you in and will demand that you leave. And she's already angry. Angry and upset and confused and . . . Do it now! Speak, for fuck sake!*

'Mattie, if you're not—'

'I am, I am!' His voice is almost a shout, and he sees her start. 'I'm just . . . Shit, I should have worked out

244

how I was going to say it before coming here—'

'To make the story more convincing, you mean?'

'No! So that I knew what words to use to describe this – this fucking dreadful—' A pain grips his throat, forcing him to stop, and he claws at his face in despair. *You've got to calm down. You've got to tell her. With every passing second she is slipping away from you. Like the girl in the bath. She is starting to disbelieve you and you haven't even begun. Any moment now and you'll lose her for ever!*

'Mattie, I can't deal with all this right now. Just go, please.'

He forces his hands away from his face. His fingers are wet. 'Lola, please – you've got to let me talk—'

'Talk, then!'

'I'm trying! Just promise me you won't hate me!'

She stands up and steps tentatively towards him. 'You cheated on me.'

'Yes . . . No!' Cheating – suddenly he can't quite fathom the meaning of the word. 'Oh God . . .'

'Jesus.' She winces as if from a blow. Turns her head away and closes her eyes. 'Get out.'

'I didn't cheat!' He jumps to his feet, grabs her by the shoulders and hears her gasp. 'I didn't cheat, I didn't, I didn't! At least I didn't *want* to!' He presses a fist to his mouth to strangle a sob.

'Let go of me, Mattie! Let go of me right now!' She is shouting.

'No! You've got to hear this – you've got to know, you've got to understand!'

'Let go of me!'

'Just listen!'

'I don't want to hear it!' She grabs his arms, tries to push him away.

'You have to!'

'No! Get off me, Mattie, or I'll scream, I swear!'

'I was attacked!'

'What?'

He shakes her by the shoulders. 'I was attacked, OK? I was forced – I was forced – I was forced . . . Oh shit!'

She stops struggling, stares, quiet suddenly, and very, very still. 'Forced to what?'

He commands his gaze to meet hers, gasping, heart pounding, trickles of sweat running down the side of his face. 'To – to . . . Oh fucking hell, Lola . . . to – to have sex . . .'

She pulls back angrily. 'Oh, you were forced to cheat, were you?' Her voice is mocking now, heavy with sarcasm. 'Some girl just threw herself at you?'

'It wasn't a girl. It – it was a guy. He was bigger. A hell of a lot heavier. I fought as hard as I could, but he had . . . Lola, I'm sorry. He beat the crap out of me, he threatened to kill me: he had a knife and so I believed him. I got scared, so scared. I couldn't fight any more, so – so I let him!' He feels the tears

246

puncture through his eyes. A harsh sob escapes him.

There is a terrible silence. He lets go of Lola's shoulders and she almost falls backwards, stunned. 'You were . . .' She struggles to finish the sentence. 'You were raped?'

He nods, holding his breath, silent tears spilling down over his cheeks, hot and heavy, dropping from the edge of his jaw and onto the collar of his T-shirt.

'When?' Lola gasps.

'At – at the Nationals in Brighton. The n-night after the win. I was walking back to the hotel and – and this guy said he needed help. So I followed him!'

He sees her face change: first shock, then horror, then a mixture of fear and despair. 'Mattie! Oh no – oh God . . .'

He sags back against the wall, but feels little relief. Now that he has uttered the words, now that his horrific secret is out, he realizes he can never retrieve it, never erase the confession. Just as, try as he might, he has never been able to erase fully the events of that night from the deepest recesses of his mind. They were always present, lurking like shadows, but he'd never been able to unveil them, or perhaps had just been too afraid – until the diving accident had forced him to crash back in time and face the truth of that night . . . that night he'd been such a coward he'd let the unthinkable occur, then come home, got drunk and trashed his room in fury – fury at himself for allowing it to happen.

Lola keeps standing there, frozen, staring, and he realizes that she will never again see him in the same light. From now on, for the rest of his life, he will always be *that guy who was raped*, for ever defined as a victim.

'Oh Mattie, no . . .'

The sight of the tears in her eyes hits him like a fist in the stomach. He sees her pity. Senses her pain for him. It makes him feel so dirty, so ashamed, that he wants to scrape off his own skin. He wants to run, but is trapped. Taking a step back, he hits the bottom stair tread with his heel, his legs buckle abruptly beneath him and he slides down against the banister, muffling a sob with his clenched fist.

'Mattie . . .' She approaches gently, tears tracking down her cheeks. She kneels down in front of him, tries to take his hand.

He pulls away. 'Don't!'

She reaches for his cheek.

He turns away. 'Please don't!' He is crying hard now, both hands cupped over his mouth as if to prevent himself from ever speaking again.

'Mattie – oh God – just tell me – tell me what to do.'

He cannot answer her, sobbing silently.

'Let me touch you. Can I touch you? I just want to hold you—'

He tries to fend her off with a raised elbow.

'Please!' Tears spill down her cheeks. She puts her hand over his, gently squeezing his fingers. 'Let me hold you. You'll get through this, I promise! I'll do anything. You just have to tell me . . .'

Exhaustion begins to press down on him. He allows Lola to push away his arm, slide over beside him, circle his neck with her arms and hug him tight. He can feel himself crumbling, breaking into minute pieces, and only the strength of her embrace seems capable of keeping him from falling apart for ever.

11

As soon as he manages to bring himself under control, he tries to leave with the excuse that his parents are expecting him home for lunch and that he doesn't want Jerry to come back and see him in this state. The truth is, Lola's shock is beginning to fade just enough for her to start asking questions. She wants him to go to the police; she wants to know whether he got a look at the man's face, whether he could describe him, or pick him out in a line-up. She starts asking whether he thinks the man could have been a fellow competitor, or a spectator, or a crazy fan, or a stalker.

He has already said too much.

'I can't talk about it right now. I need to go,' he informs her, rubbing his face viciously with his sleeve, heading resolutely for the front door. The relief he expected to feel when he told her has failed to materialize. He should never have done it. But what choice did he have?

She holds him back in the hall. 'But Mattie, you've waited too long already. We've *got* to go to the police—'

'You're not listening to me!' He shakes her off. 'I said I'm not going to the police – not now, not ever! Too much time has passed, and there is no way I'm going through the interviews and statements and – and medical exams and—' He gasps for breath. 'Can you imagine what it would be like to have to describe every second, every detail to a courtroom of strangers? Describe what happened? How he – he . . .' He shuts his eyes tight for a moment.

'OK, Mattie. OK, sweetheart. But maybe they could interview you in private and film it for the court case. I've heard they do that for minors—'

'By the time it got to court I wouldn't even be a minor any more! And the psycho could try to turn it on me! Say I agreed to it, or something. Or that I was making it all up because I was angry at him for – for – anything . . . I don't know!'

'But no one would believe you'd willingly have sex with some random stranger in a wood!'

'But what if he wasn't a stranger! I – I mean, what if he *claimed* he wasn't a stranger?' He feels a sharp pain in his chest, as though he's been stabbed. He is losing it, needs to keep his thoughts in order. 'I mean, *of course* he was a stranger! But – but—'

'Shh, shh.' Lola strokes his face. 'Sweetheart, why on earth would he pretend he knew you? What difference would it make?'

'He could make out I did it willingly! And – and do you have any idea what would happen if word got out? The media would have a field day! I'd become better known for – for *that* than for my diving. I could never go back to it. The press would ask questions at every interview. My fans, my supporters – the whole diving world would know!'

'OK. Shh. OK . . .' Lola runs her fingers softly up and down the side of his face. 'But sweetheart, you're going to tell your parents, right?'

'No!' He shouts in desperation. 'They'd force me to go to the police!'

'But Mattie, you need some support – you need some kind of help. What happened to you was traumatic! You can't just keep it a secret and carry on as if nothing's happened!'

'I can.' With great effort, he forces himself into a semblance of calm. 'I have been for weeks already. It was tough at first, but now I'm fine. As long as I've got you in my life and you understand why – why some things are difficult right now . . .'

'But Mattie—'

'No! Listen, if – if you still love me, if you want

to help me, just promise you won't tell anyone, Lola!'

Her bottom lip quivers. 'Of course I still love you.'

Tears of relief crowd in his eyes. 'Then you promise?'

'OK.'

'You won't tell anyone, ever?' he insists. 'Not even your dad, or Izzy?'

'I promise. Not anyone. But Mattie—'She reaches for his face again, but he dodges her, terrified of what he might say, what he might do.

'I've really, really got to go.' He presses his fingertips to his eyes for a moment, takes a deep breath and opens the front door. 'I'll speak to you later, OK? I'm – I'm sorry, Lola!'

She shakes her head and swallows, eyes brimming. He squeezes her hand and ducks quickly through the door before the sight of her stricken face can unhinge him further, braving the remorseless sunlight of the early afternoon.

Back home, in the safety of his bedroom, he locks his door, closes the curtains, and gets into bed fully dressed, pulling the duvet tightly around him. Despite the warm breeze drifting in through the net curtains, he is shivering hard. So now Lola knows. How long before she realizes she doesn't want to have sex with a rape victim, let alone be in a relationship with one? How long before she actually starts picturing the attack for herself? How long before her pity turns to disgust . . . ? He burrows his face into the pillow, silent tears soaking the fabric. He tries to console himself with the thought that now at least she understands why he pushed her like that; now at least she realizes it had nothing to do with her; now at least she has an explanation for his erratic behaviour over the last few weeks – but it is of little comfort. Lola won't leave it at that. Gradually she will ask more questions, require more details, request answers he can never provide. Images, sounds and smells flash through his mind, swirling, snaking, churning like snatched visions from the seat of a roller coaster. He feels wildly sick and tries to force himself to breathe slowly, to think calmly, to bring the spinning memories to a stop and purge them from his mind. No one else will ever know, he reminds himself. He can trust Lola. He will *never* have to go through that confession again.

He spends the next forty-eight hours holed up in bed, dozing fitfully, plagued by nightmares that leave him gasping and shivering, bathed in cold sweat. He turns off his mobile and informs Consuela that his head hurts whenever she calls him for meals or tells him Lola or Hugo are on the line. He even ignores Loïc's worried voice, calling through the door to ask him if he is all right. Mercifully, his parents have a busy start to the week . . . But then, on Monday evening he is roused by a short, sharp rap on the door, which he recognizes instantly as his mother's.

'I'm in bed,' he calls out quickly. 'I've got to get up early tomorrow.'

'Open this door right now, Mathéo, or I'll call your father.'

'Wait! No, Mum, don't—' He throws back the duvet, pulls on a T-shirt and pads across the room. The moment he turns the lock, the door swings open. Mathéo retreats to the safety of his bed, hunching up against the headboard, knees clasped against his chest. His mother closes the door behind her with a sharp metallic click, snaps on the light, hesitates for a moment, then comes to perch on the bottom corner of the bed. She smells of expensive perfume and red wine. Her hair is done up in an elaborate chignon and he can tell by her kohl eyes and dark red lipstick that she has just come back from an evening function. Wearing a sleeveless black dress embroidered with sequins, a burgundy chiffon scarf and three-inch heels, she looks awkward and out of place in his bedroom. He cannot remember the last time she has been in here, and he senses her taking in the clothes on the carpet and the collection of empty coffee cups on his bedside table with a disapproving crease of her brows. Her wandering gaze finally settles on him, and he is suddenly painfully aware of his crumpled T-shirt and unwashed appearance. He presses his back against the wall, wishing it would swallow him up, and avoids his mother's eyes by picking at a loose thread on the knee of his pyjama bottoms.

'So, what's going on?' As usual she is short, sharp and to the point. But despite her brusque tone, he is aware of something else – a note of genuine concern. He feels it threaten to pierce the fragile bubble with which he has attempted to seal himself off from the rest of the world.

'Nothing, I'm just tired. I was trying to have an early night!' His voice comes out shaky and defensive, belying his apparent calm.

His mother lets out a quick sigh. 'Consuela says you've been in your room since the weekend. She's worried you're not eating.'

'Well, if *she's* the one who's worried, you can tell her she's wasting her energy.'

'Mathéo, stop it. Obviously I'm worried too. Your father and I both are, especially after the argument at breakfast on Saturday.'

'Oh, so Dad sent you up to check I'm not really planning to quit diving?'

She purses her painted lips in a gesture of annoyance, but her eyes give her away. 'That was *one* of his concerns,' she replies.

'Did he go ballistic?'

'A bit – you know what he's like. And Perez warned us you might go through a phase of not wanting to dive after such a nasty accident. But it's not like you to let that stop you. Diving has always been such a big part of your life. Why would you want to throw away all that hard work and training, all the sacrifices we've made? *You've* made? What's going on, Mathéo?'

He cannot look up. Cannot answer.

'I know your father pushes you – he is very ambitious for you; we both are,' his mother continues, undeterred. 'You have an exceptional talent and we would hate to see it go to waste. But believe it or not, we only want what's best for you. Yes, I know when you were a child your father pushed you too hard, especially when you were scared of trying a new dive. But that was only because he saw how talented you were and how much you loved winning! These last few years though, you've been allowed to work out your own schedule with Perez. Your father respects that. Yet you have chosen to train harder than ever until – until a few weeks ago. Then something seemed to change.'

'So? People change. I've been diving most of my life; maybe I want to do something different!'

'But it's all been so sudden,' his mother says, her tone carefully measured. 'What on earth prompted it? Up until a few weeks ago you were your usual competitive self. You were really excited about next year's Olympics. Now, all of a sudden, ever since you won that medal in Brighton, you're pretending to be sick all the time. Perez said you had a panic attack on the diving board and that's why you hit your head—'

'I didn't have a panic attack. It was just an accident!'

'OK.' His mother emits a sigh of exasperation. 'I haven't come to argue about that. What I've come to say is that your father and I are worried about you. Something's clearly upset you. Consuela says this is the third time in a month you've locked yourself up in your bedroom like this. Your friends keep ringing the landline sounding upset. You refuse to take their calls. Even Loïc seems worried—'

'What did he say?'

'Nothing. But he keeps asking where you are. Consuela says you haven't been eating properly and I noticed on Saturday that you've lost a lot of weight – those jeans were practically sliding off you. And you look like you haven't slept for a week.'

'I told you, I'm just tired—'

'You're also clearly upset.'

He flinches and feels the blood rise in his cheeks. Pulling out another thread from his pyjamas, he starts picking at the small hole he has created above the knee. 'I'm not . . . It's not . . .' His voice quavers and he takes a steadying breath.

Silence. It hangs in the air between them, heavy and opaque. After a while his mother tries again.

'Are you worried about hurting yourself during training?'

'No.'

'Hitting your head like that must have given you a fright.'

'It's nothing to do with that.'

His mother shifts further up the bed and reaches for his hand. '*Chéri*, what's happening?'

For a moment he pictures telling her. Imagines offloading the whole sordid weight onto her shoulders and shouting at her: demanding to know why she has never been there to watch over him, why she has always just let him go off to diving competitions here and abroad with Perez and his father, why she has never come too – if not to support him, then at least to protect him, to look after him, to make sure nothing like this could ever happen. But he knows it's no use. Instead, he just shakes his head and looks away.

'You don't want to talk to me?' He hears the hurt in her voice.

'It's – it's not that. There's just nothing to say. I'm not saying I definitely want to give up diving for good. Maybe I just need a break, and a new coach.'

'OK, that's your decision. But why now? And what have you suddenly got against Perez?'

'He's just a fucking maniac, OK? He knew I wasn't ready to attempt that dive, but he kept pushing and pushing!' His voice rises abruptly and he sees his mother flinch in surprise.

'But he's been your coach for nearly six years now. Everyone says he's the best in the country. That's why we sent you to him. He says you're like the son he never had. He really cares about you, Mathéo. He's confident you could do really well in the Olympics – that's why he always gives you so much extra time, much more than to the others on the team—'

'Well, maybe I don't want the extra time!' Mathéo finds himself shouting.

His mother just looks bemused. 'Have you and Perez fallen out?'

'No . . . I don't know. I'm just sick of constantly being told what to do.'

His mother sits back, inhales deeply. He can tell she is just longing for another glass of wine and a cigarette.

'Maybe what you need is a break,' she suggests finally. 'A holiday. Go away for a while.'

Suddenly she has his attention. Maybe that wouldn't be such a bad idea. Get away from here – from the people, the memories. Get away from this house, his father, Perez. He wishes he could leave and never come back. Run away from this life – the sordid mess of that one night, the broken, pathetic shell of the person he has become – and start anew.

'Maybe you could spend a week or so with that friend of yours – the one whose father works in the City.'

'Hugo?' He looks at her in astonishment. 'Go to the South of France with Hugo and the others?'

'Yes, you've always enjoyed it there in the past. Go and spend the week with them, *chéri*. Have a proper break this time.'

'But Dad—'

'I'll speak to Dad. He's worried about you too, you know. He was really quite shaken by your accident.'

'But a whole week? Perez will go nuts.'

'It's not up to Perez. We're your parents. We make the decisions.' She stops for a moment, reaches out and touches his cheek. 'You need a break, *mon amour*. Speak to Hugo and arrange it tomorrow, OK?'

He nods, something akin to relief finally spreading through his body. 'Thanks.'

12

The day of departure dawns clear and bright. Sometime during the night, a sense of immense relief has crept into Mathéo's veins. Relief that he can finally get away from all this – from his father, from Perez, from the treadmill of training. For a few moments he just lies there, watching the sun knife in through the gaps in the curtain. He feels as if he has been waiting for this day, this moment, pearling on the horizon like a mirage, always just out of reach. And now that it's here, nothing can take it away from him: the only way is forward, life's velocity only ever sweeps in one direction and for that he is infinitely grateful. He will move on with his life, put all that sordid mess behind him. He stretches and yawns and closes his eyes and opens them again. Splayed out across the bed, he gazes sleepily around at his book-laden desk, his clothes-horse chair, the framed Van

Gogh prints hanging from the white walls and his open rucksack on the shag-pile carpet. He will go to the sea, wash himself clean, wash away the past month and come back a new person.

After showering and shaving and inspecting his face for signs of spots, he dresses in his favourite jeans – the faded, stonewashed ones his mother always complains about because they are so old and worn, the denim thin and soft from years of use, the ends scruffy with loose threads and rips in both knees. Although they are slightly long in the leg and the bottoms have always crumpled over his ankles, like the others they feel looser than usual, and he has to thread a belt through the loops in order to keep them from slipping down past his hips. He pulls on a faded grey T-shirt and realizes that it too seems to have stretched, the short sleeves baggy round his biceps, the thin material revealing the outline of his collar-bone. Faced with his reflection in the full-length mirror of his room, he cannot deny that he has indeed lost a great deal of weight; his skin is pale and anaemic, the only colour in his face emanating from the scarlet crack in his chapped lips and the violet shading beneath his eyes. He looks frail, sickly almost, and badly in need of a tan. Slipping his feet into Birkenstock sandals, he exchanges his expensive, heavy silver watch for a plain waterproof one and fastens the leather friendship bracelet from Lola around his other wrist. His shaggy mop of dark blond hair, hanging down over his eyes, is so overgrown it is beginning to curl, lending him, he notes briefly, a somewhat bohemian look that his parents will hate. The knowledge gives him an odd sense of satisfaction.

He finishes packing, performs a quick scan of his room and then heads downstairs with his large ruck-sack. The kitchen, with its gleaming chrome, smells of disinfectant – empty and sterile like a showroom. Consuela hasn't arrived yet and the others are all still in bed. He glances around for a note from his parents but there is none, though the holiday cash they gave him last night was generous. So he goes in search of a piece of paper and starts writing a message to Loïc:

Hey buddy,

See you in a couple of weeks. Give me a call whenever. Hope tennis camp is a blast. Don't get too good cos I don't want you to embarrass me when I get back. Try to chat to some of the other kids even if you don't feel like it. I know it can be tricky, but you're such an ace player I bet everyone will want to be your mate. And at least you'll be getting away from CERTAIN PEOPLE and can do what you want for a change. Here's £10 for snacks, etc. Don't tell Mum and Dad – that way you'll get more. Left iPad and charger on my desk for you but remember to sneak them into your bag at the last minute. Gimme a call sometime if you're not too busy with your new friends. Will miss you loads but

look forward to thrashing the new tennis champ when I get home.
Don't worry about anything, I'm fine now.

M

Clambering out of the cab at Heathrow Airport, he and Lola make their way quickly to the prearranged meeting point in the main hall, where squeals from both girls and a cheer from Hugo cause a group of Japanese tourists to look round in mild alarm. In the absence of any vacant chairs, the four of them sit down on the floor together, forming a little island in the sea of passengers eddying back and forth. The departure hall is brightly lit, the walls so bleached out with artificial whiteness that it feels to Mathéo like he has stepped into another world. A homeless man dozes in a corner. A janitor, shrunk down by the flickering departure screens above, creates a glistening path with his broom. Most of the columns on the screens are black and silent, but two are ablaze with green neon letters and numbers. Lola and Isabel are both talking at once, fuelling their own excitement, their voices shrilling in the giant atrium that surrounds them. Dropping his rucksack, Mathéo hugs Isabel, gives Hugo a slap on the back, their excitement contagious, and for a moment he feels almost normal again. Lola and Isabel continue their high-pitched chatter until finally, exhausted, they flop back against rucksacks and rolled-up jackets as makeshift pillows.

'I couldn't sleep, I couldn't sleep!' Lola informs them, her face glowing, eyes wide with elation. 'Dad insisted I went to bed at ten but I couldn't lie still, and every time I got up he sent me back to bed again until I thought I was going to go crazy, just lying there, staring at the clock and counting down the minutes and—'

'Me too, me too!' Isabel thumps Lola's arm. 'I tried to sneak out of the house but Mum caught me—'

'And so she kept me awake all night by texting me every five minutes!' Hugo puts in with an exaggerated sigh. 'And she kept on sending me the links to all these places on YouTube which she suddenly decided she had to visit!'

'Yeah, and then we ended up on Skype,' says Isabel. 'And Hugo kept saying we had to go here and here, and finding all these new places!'

'I tried texting you, Mattie, but you never answered!' Lola adds in mock outrage. 'How did you actually manage to sleep?'

Despite being relieved by her tone and demeanour, Mathéo cannot ignore the strain of forced ebullience in her behaviour, her desperate effort to act as if nothing has happened or changed between them.

'I was wiped out!' he admits, forcing a laugh, playing his part. 'But I kept having these horrible dreams where I woke up and found I'd overslept and you'd all left without me.'

'Aw, we'd never do that!' Lola slings an arm around him and pulls him into a hug, almost tipping him backwards. 'We'd drag you from your bed if we had to and put you in a giant rucksack and—'

'Ow!' he exclaims, laughing at the same time as a strand of his hair gets caught in Lola's watch. 'But seriously, guys, it was horrible. I kept waking up with a jolt and hurling myself out of bed!' He exaggerates for the benefit of a good story and they all laugh, far more loudly than necessary.

'I can just imagine Matt going like this . . .' Hugo impersonates him springing in and out of bed, and Mathéo realizes they are all completely high on adrenalin, drunk with excitement, their conversation ricocheting from peak to peak as they talk to one another, past one another, over one another with so much energy they appear about to combust. It is a monumental effort to keep up and only gradually do they slow to a more acceptable pace, ratcheting their voices down a level to turn to more practical matters, such as checking in and making their way through the long queues at security.

'Gate twelve, gate twelve!' Isabel suddenly squeals excitedly.

All eyes swing to the board.

'Shit, that's all the way down at the bottom. Hurry up!' Hugo shouts.

A massive scramble to retrieve jumpers, jackets,

bags and rucksacks ensues. They race down the long carpeted corridors in an attempt to avoid the boarding queues, but Isabel drops her sunglasses. Then Lola nearly loses her sandal and ploughs, headfirst, into Hugo's rucksack as he stops dead.

'It's this one, it's this one!'

'No, that's gate eleven!'

'On this side it's twelve – are you blind?'

'Oh, shut up, you!'

'Come on, come on!'

'Shit! Where's my boarding pass?'

Amidst much laughter and hysteria, they finally locate the right gate, manage to get to the front of the queue and follow the suspended tunnel into the mouth of the plane.

Hugo almost knocks himself out as he tries to heave Isabel's rucksack into the overhead lockers.

'Jesus, what have you got in here? Rocks?'

Mathéo reaches across to give Lola a hand.

Eventually the rucksacks are stored and they collapse into their seats – Mathéo and Lola on one side of the narrow aisle, Isabel and Hugo on the other.

As the plane begins to fill up with more and more passengers searching for their seats, squeezing and jostling and struggling to load hand luggage into the lockers, Mathéo falls quiet, staring out of the window. Beside him, Lola is watching him anxiously out of the corner of her eye. Even though he is painfully conscious of her scrutiny, he pretends not to notice, trying to keep his expression as neutral as possible. Since telling her about Brighton four days ago, he has managed to make her promise to leave the subject alone so that he doesn't have to think about it – at least for the duration of the holiday. But as both the excitement and adrenalin begin to ebb, it's a monumental effort to keep hold of the laid-back, cheerful expression. Elbow propped up against the window ledge, he chews his thumbnail in an attempt to calm his nerves, eyes trained on the small porthole of grey runway, long, low buildings stretched out along the morning skyline. On the other side of the aisle, Hugo and Isabel's rambunctious enthusiasm shows little sign of waning as they tease, joke and chatter animatedly. Glancing across at them for a moment, Mathéo is painfully aware of the contrast between their two states of being, his and theirs, and how hard it is to transmute back from the outer darkness.

'Aren't you excited?' As the other passengers begin to settle down, Isabel glances across at him under the thin braids she is plaiting into her overgrown fringe. She is chewing her gum with great gusto, snapping it with her tongue, making an irritating sound. But the tone of her voice holds a faintly resentful edge, as if suggesting he is not making sufficient effort.

'Of course!' Dragging his eyes away from the window, he forces himself to engage, shooting her a bright smile and raising his eyebrows in an attempt to reinforce the words. 'How about you?'

'What do you think?' She laughs. She seems louder than usual, tanned and busty, her tight red top barely concealing her bra, her short skirt adorned with tiny beads sewn on in the shape of hearts. Looking away, Mathéo's gaze meets Lola's, and her lips twitch upwards, almost like a question mark, as if asking him if he is all right. He manages a reassuring smile in return.

As their plane slowly begins to move, taxiing towards the runway, the airport buildings fading into the morning mist, he feels his precarious veneer splinter for a moment, and has to take a long deep breath, fixing on the trail of runway lights that smear and blur beneath the window. Drawing his bottom lip between his teeth, he bites down hard and keeps his head turned away, sensing Lola's eyes still lingering on his face. She's about to say something when, across the aisle, Hugo interrupts with, 'Hey, come on, you two, we're on holiday! School is out for good! We'll never have to sit through one of Croaky's assemblies again!'

'Unless I have to re-sit my history A-level!' Lola quickly switches on her smile and pulls a face. 'I can't believe our results are coming out in less than a month!'

'OK, no exam talk for the duration of the holiday,'

Hugo declares triumphantly. 'We're not even going to think about results – OK?'

'Definitely!' Isabel chimes in.

As the air hostesses go through the safety demonstrations, Mathéo lets his breath out slowly, grateful to Lola for diverting Hugo's attention, and soon the noise of the engines becomes too loud for conversation. It's a relief to be moving and, even though they haven't left the ground yet, Mathéo is thankful the journey has begun. As the announcements finish and the seatbelt lights go on, the roar inside the cabin intensifies. The plane begins to gather speed, preparing for takeoff. Beneath the window, the runway blurs and bumps and rattles. With every passing second he is putting more distance between himself and home, between himself and everyone back in London; with every passing minute, he is sloughing off more of his old skin, leaving the damaged Mathéo behind.

Montpellier is sizzling, blinding and packed. The others are all fizzing with excitement again; even Lola seems to have perked up. The hustle and bustle, the traffic, the shouts, the crowds of tourists posing for photos and blocking congested roads; the heat, the braying of horns all encompass him in a thick, chaotic web. Fortunately Ana, the housekeeper, is there to pick them up in an air-conditioned people-carrier, and they jolt their way through stop-start traffic and out onto the motorway, until finally, a good forty-five minutes later, they find themselves on one of the narrow roads that wind down to the coast.

Leaning his forehead against the cool inside of the window, Mathéo watches the exotic scenery flash past. Like most Basque drivers, Ana barely touches the brakes as she rounds the sharp, cliff-edge corners. On one side the forest blooms with colour – thousands of different shades of green, interspersed with red and purple flowers erupting from the branches like mini fireworks. On the other side, a river curls out under the sheer cliff-face of the gorge towards the sea. They can smell it now, glimpse it even, beyond the cedar trees and the red-roofed villas: a sparkling, frothy white line in the distance, separating the earth from the vast expanse of deep blue sky. Muggy London seems a million miles away – here the scenery is breathtakingly dramatic, the landscape lit up by a sun so strong, so sharp, so white, it overpowers everything.

The car crawls steeply up a narrow road towards the centre of a pretty village full of quaint cafés and postcard shops, before dropping back down again into the thick, lush countryside, hedgerows drooping with flowers. Ahead loom the silhouettes of low hills, dappled green and purple against the light. As the ground beneath the wheels grows rougher, the car swings off the road before meandering gently downhill along a farm track towards the sea. They reach the very edge of the cliff, the plateau jutting out over a concealed private beach, and turn sharply into a tunnel of trees. And as they emerge, the house comes into sight.

It is every bit as glorious as Mathéo remembers. Isabel has been to stay before, but Lola is seeing the house for the very first time. He has prepared her for it but knows she will still be bowled over, just as he was that first time he came to stay when he was twelve – even though by then he'd already been taken by his parents to several luxury holiday resorts. But this place is different from any other holiday villa. A curved driveway of white stone leads up to the front of the house, flanked by enormous stretches of grass where, in the past, he and Hugo played games of football, badminton and table-tennis. The freshly mown lawn is bordered by brightly coloured plants and bushes trimmed into geometric shapes. To the far right is the swimming pool, steps carved into the concrete of the shallow end; it stretches all the way to the very front of the garden, where it overhangs the beach. From the deep end you can look down onto the sand below, and when the tide is high, the end of the pool appears to merge with the sea. There is a hot tub on one side, a row of white sun loungers and parasols down the other, and a covered wooden terrace at the bottom, which houses the barbecue and bar. The house itself is vast: a mixture of white concrete, cream sandstone and pearl marble. It is just two storeys high, but stretches out in all directions. The upper floor consists of four large ensuite bedrooms, as well as a separate bathroom and laundry room. The ground floor is a palatial open-plan area: the main hall separating the living room and games room on one side, the kitchen and dining room on the other. Each room has French windows opening out onto the marble terrace that surrounds the whole house, and upstairs, supported by thick columns, the bedrooms are all connected by an outdoor gallery, just the right height for a breathtaking jump down onto the grass, and wide enough for sitting out on sun loungers or even for kicking a football around.

Lola almost trips as she heaves her rucksack from the boot, busy squinting up in amazement at the house, framed by the hills behind it, resplendent in the sun.

'Oh, no way!' she exclaims, as much to herself as to anyone else, her wide-eyed gaze soaking up the lawns, the pool, and finally the sea just beyond. 'Mattie told me it was amazing, but this is – this is just—' She comes to a halt, uncharacteristically lost for words.

'Not bad, huh?' Hugo smiles, lowering the sunglasses from the crown of his head. 'My parents are planning to retire here, but I don't see that happening any time soon. Dad doesn't trust anyone else to run the company.'

'You have to try out the pool, Lola,' Isabel pitches in with excitement. 'It's always at the perfect temperature, and it's huge, and the hot tub is amazing, especially at night.'

'Why don't you give her a tour?' Hugo suggests with a grin of pride. 'Matt and I will take the bags in.'

Isabel is already galloping over the grass. 'Come on, I'll show you the secret path down to the beach!'

Lola relinquishes her rucksack, moves to follow, then looks back at Mathéo, appearing to hesitate for a moment. In her white cotton top and cargo shorts, she appears fragile and coltish, her long bare legs and slender arms alabaster white, unruly chestnut hair pulled back into a dishevelled knot. Mathéo finds himself engulfed in a tidal wave of guilt. She should be as excited and carefree as the others, relishing the beginning of the holidays and celebrating the end of school, the beginning of a new chapter. Instead, she looks anxious and vulnerable, her pinched face white from too many sleepless nights, weighted down by his own dark, dirty secret.

'Go on!' he urges. 'I'm dying of thirst so I'll see you inside.'

For a moment he fears she will refuse, but then Isabel calls her and she turns, loping across the grass, flip-flops slapping against the soles of her feet, to join her friend.

Mathéo takes the remaining rucksacks from the

boot, thanks Ana and follows Hugo across the terrace, through the porch and into the echoing, air-conditioned cool of the hall.

'Which room do you want us in?'

'Ana will take the bags up,' Hugo replies. 'Come and have a drink – you look knackered.'

'But I can do it—'

'Don't bother with that now. Come on!'

In the kitchen, Hugo hands Mathéo a cold beer from the fridge and they amble out onto a shaded part of the terrace and sit down on the sun loungers over-looking the pool.

'So – everything OK?' Hugo has an air of pre-occupation, his eyes narrowed on his beer can, taking longer than necessary to open it.

'Yeah. Why?'

Hugo lowers his shades back down over his eyes and takes a deep swig. 'You and Lola seem kinda – I dunno.' He turns to look at Mathéo cautiously.

'We're fine.' Mathéo's voice comes out more hesitant than he would have liked. He wipes his damp forehead with the back of his hand and squints out over the glassy surface of the pool. 'Why? Has – has she said something?'

'Not exactly . . .'

He feels his heart skip a beat. 'What do you mean?'

Hugo shrugs with exaggerated nonchalance. 'Nothing much. Just that Izzy mentioned Lola was

276

upset about something. And you've been pretty quiet so far.'

Heart pumping now, Mathéo turns away, clears his throat. 'Did – did Lola say what she was upset about?'

'No. We figured you'd maybe had an argument or something.'

'Why would we have had an argument?'

'I dunno!'

'Well, we didn't. We're fine.' He swallows, his mouth suddenly dry. 'Everything's fine, OK?'

'OK.' Hugo raises his eyebrows briefly in response to Mathéo's defensive tone but lets it pass. 'So – does that mean you're feeling better?'

'Better than what?' Careful to keep his voice light, Mathéo settles back against the sun lounger and puts on his sunglasses in an attempt to avoid Hugo's questioning stare.

'Well, you know – what we talked about before.' Hugo looks uncomfortable but presses on. 'You have been acting kinda bummed out—'

'Nah.' Mathéo turns his face away to squint into the sun. 'Just tired. You know. Straight back into training after exams . . .'

Hugo looks sceptical, but any further questioning on his part is abruptly cut short by laughter from the girls as they come running across the grass, legs streaked with wet sand.

'No, no!' Lola is shrieking over her shoulder at

Isabel. 'Don't you dare – my watch isn't waterproof!'

Hugo's face cracks into a smile. 'Let's get it off her, then!' He puts down his beer, leaps up with an evil grin, and sprints over towards them, his earlier concern quickly forgotten.

They spend the rest of the afternoon in the pool, messing around with a ball and Frisbee and a couple of lilos. As the sunlight turns from blinding white to pale gold, Ana brings dinner out to them on the terrace, where in swim shorts and bikinis, still damp from the water, they gather around the table to devour seafood paella. Hugo digs out more beers, Isabel breaks open the wine and Mathéo does his best to join in with the noisy chatter.

Later that evening, after the sun has almost set and the other three have gone inside to play Cheat, Mathéo returns to the garden. A blue-grey dusk is stealing over the lawns, darkening the water in the pool. The candles on the table flicker wildly, casting jagged reflections on the wall behind before guttering out in the sudden breeze. The light slips away from the hills behind the house like sand through a timer. The sun is almost gone now – only its reflection remains, its glorious colours fading on the underside of the clouds. Walking over the grass to the pool's steps, Mathéo slides beneath the water, ripples slithering across its surface. Its cool, comforting familiarity is silky against his skin. He swims a full length before surfacing and wiping his eyes with his fingers. Then, resting his folded arms on the concrete lip of the deep end, he gazes out across the sea at the hazy coastline of the bay and tries to lose himself in the changing colours of the distance. The beauty of it all, the contrast with human existence, fills him with a sadness so strong, he feels himself sinking beneath the weight of it. He can run as fast and as far as he wants, but nothing, he realizes, will ever be able to return him to the person he was before the night of the attack and, as a result, nothing will ever seem quite as beautiful and unspoiled again. You cannot undo the past; you can only learn to live with it, find some way of making peace with it, and move on. And he wonders how that can ever be possible, how anyone can ever truly accept being brutalized in the way he was. Is it really possible to learn to forgive? And in doing so, are you offering up an absolution? He closes his eyes and rests his forehead on his arms, the water lapping gently against his mouth, and wonders how he can go on existing, so used and so dirty and so damaged, while surrounded by so much beauty.

He lifts his head at the sound of footsteps and sees Lola clipping across the paving stones set in the lawn. She is wearing a sleeveless cotton dress over her bikini, her long hair still damp and her shoulders pink from the sun. Sitting down at the pool edge beside him, she turns to follow his gaze out over the rising tide and towards the twinkling lights of the distant coastline.

'I was thinking of heading off to bed soon,' she says quietly. 'Are you going to come?'

He nods, sucking in his left cheek.

'Hugo has given us a double room,' she says, her voice low, still not turning to look at him. 'Shall I ask if I can sleep somewhere else?'

'Of course not!' Mathéo feels his heart accelerate and the blood rush to his cheeks, stung by the mere suggestion. 'Just because of what happened doesn't mean – doesn't mean I want you to – to—'

'It's OK, that's what I thought, but I just wanted to double check.' She turns to him now, wiping the wet hair back from his forehead. 'Sweetheart, you're shivering. Shall I get you a towel?'

'Wait!' He circles her wrist with his hand to retrain her. 'It's – it's so . . . Don't you think it's beautiful?'

'God, yeah!' she exclaims. 'I was telling Hugo if my dad had a place like this, I'd never leave.'

'I mean the sea. And the sky. And the light. It's – it's just all so beautiful and—' He hears the tremor in his voice. 'And I feel like I never really appreciated it before.'

Lola looks down at him, her expression serious now. 'You've needed a holiday for ages, sweetheart.' She strokes his wet cheek.

'I dunno . . .' He sucks in his lower lip and bites

down hard. 'Me – being here, after what happened. It all feels wrong somehow.'

In the main guest room at the front of the house, he stands gazing out of the floor-to-ceiling windows, clad in just his pyjama bottoms, waistband pinching and nipping at the beginnings of sunburn, face flushed from the hot shower. Pulling open the heavy glass door, he walks onto the balcony and gazes out at the last remnants of sunset stretching across the sea. He hears Lola emerge from the bathroom and pad out to join him. She rests her hand on the bare skin at the small of his back: it feels like a small gesture of solidarity. It is only a tiny movement, like a petal falling to the ground, but it moves something within him.

For a while they just stand there, quiet in their own space. Then Lola breaks the silence, her voice barely more than a whisper. 'Do you want to talk about it now?'

'No.' The word holds no anger, but nonetheless it's a kneejerk reaction, uttered almost before she has finished her question.

There is a pause before she exhales. 'OK.' Running her finger down the inside of his arm, she slides her hand down until it meets his, and holds it gently. 'But then, Mattie, you need to tell me. Tell me what I should do . . .'

He fixes a spot on the horizon where the sea meets the sky. Takes a shaky breath. 'Pretend it never happened.'

'Is that really what you want?' He hears the catch in her voice.

'More than anything.'

'OK . . . OK, then all I can do is promise to try. But only as long as you know that I'll always be here – if ever you change your mind and do want to talk, or if ever you want to tell your parents or anyone else, or decide to go to the police. I'll always be here by your side, Mattie. Do you understand that? Do you believe me?'

He bites his tongue and nods. Keeping his eyes fixed resolutely on the horizon, he squeezes her hand, and watches the lights blur and refract in the distance.

After a while Lola goes back into the room, chilly from the cool air coming in off the sea, and turns off the light, rolls down the duvet and slides under the thin cotton sheet. Hair spread out across the pillow, she seems to be waiting, curled up on her side, waiting and watching him, her eyes wide and bright in the moonlight.

'Mattie?' she says softly after a while. 'Aren't you tired?'

'Yeah. I'll come in a sec.'

He feels her pause, feels her mind working. 'You mustn't think we have to . . . I mean, I'm not expecting anything. We don't need to – you know –

do anything. Not until you're ready, or – or *ever again* if you don't want to—'

He turns to look at her, his breath accelerating. 'What?'

'After what happened, I totally understand if you never want—'

He comes in swiftly from the balcony, shutting the doors firmly behind him, and takes a shaky breath, leaning back against the glass. 'You – you don't want to have sex with me any more? I haven't caught anything, you know. The first thing I did when I remembered was get checked out.'

Her expression changes and she props herself up on her elbow. 'Of course I want to have sex with you! I just thought, after the last couple of, uh – tries, that maybe you'd prefer to wait a while.'

He turns back to look at the gathering darkness, his heart hammering, the blood pulsing in his cheeks.

'Mattie?'

He doesn't reply.

'All I'm saying is that it's entirely up to you.'

'It's not like I can't – I can't do it any more, you know!' His voice comes out loud and shaky with humiliation and fear. The truth is, he doesn't know. Maybe he can't. Both attempts after that night – the night he was raped – had ended in disaster. Maybe his body will reject all forms of sex from now on for its own protection. Maybe he will never be free of the memories; sex will for ever be inextricably linked with pain and helplessness and anger and terror, and he will have to spend the rest of his life alone, locked into his painful secret.

He turns to half face her, fiddling with the net curtains. 'I know what happened was pretty gross. So – so if you don't want to, that's – that's perfectly understandable.'

The look on Lola's face makes him flinch and he feels his throat contract.

'Oh Mattie, of course I do. You're still you.'

'I just really don't want you to stay with me out of pity or – or something!' he says raggedly. 'We – we could still stay friends. Best friends.' He gives a short laugh in a desperate bid to lighten the atmosphere.

Stricken, Lola gets out of bed and moves tentatively across the room towards him. 'You already are my best friend,' she says quietly. 'But nothing's changed, Mattie. I still love you just as much as before. More, if that's even possible.'

She moves towards him, but he holds out a restraining hand, terrified that if Lola so much as touches him, he will crumble. 'But – but how can you, now that you know what happened? What – what I've done. Doesn't it disgust you?'

'God, Mattie, no! *You* didn't do anything wrong!' She stops a couple of metres away and stares at him with pink-rimmed eyes.

Jokingly, he waves his index finger at her. 'Don't you f-fucking start!' He tries to laugh again but manages only a jagged gasp.

'You shouldn't have felt you had to keep it to yourself for so long.' Lola's voice quivers. 'All that time you had to pretend—'

'Stop it, it was fine. For ages I just couldn't remember. I knew I'd done something terrible, but it wasn't until I woke up in hospital after the diving accident . . .' He shakes his head at her in mock exasperation, but as he attempts a reassuring smile, a tear escapes, skimming the edge of his cheek.

'*You* didn't do anything, Mattie! It was that sicko who—' She breaks off and he sees her wince, reaching out for his hand which he quickly moves away.

'Don't. It's in the past. I'm OK now.' He takes a ragged breath and feels a second tear fall from his lashes, hot and heavy. 'At least I think so . . . Damn!' He wipes the tear away with an angry flick of his hand.

'Mattie—'

'It's OK.' His voice cracks despite his attempt to reassure her. 'It's just that I feel so – so dirty, you know? And however many times I shower, however hard I scrub myself, I'm scared I'm always going to feel this way.'

'But that's a normal reaction, sweetheart. I've read up about stuff on rape, and they say it won't last.' She steps towards him, reaching out for him, but he moves away quickly, banging his elbow against the balcony door.

'Lola, don't! I'm fine. Look, it's – it's just been a long day!' He scrapes at his cheeks with his fingertips and presses his fist against his mouth, afraid that if she touches him he will fall apart completely.

'I know, sweetheart. I just want to hold you.'

Cupping his hands over his nose and mouth, he presses his forehead against the glass, sliding just out of reach. 'Just – just give me a sec!'

'Mattie, what you went through was terrible! Anyone would be upset!'

'You don't understand . . .' He claws at his cheeks. 'I was such a – a—' He takes a frantic gulp of air. 'A fucking coward—'

'Mattie! How can you possibly think that?'

'I was so scared of dying that I let him – I *let* him, Lola!'

'You didn't! He gave you no choice!'

'I – I asked for it!'

She looks almost angry, her eyes very wide. 'Stop it, Mattie!'

'But then, once he started, and – and after it was over, I wished – God, I wished so much he'd just killed me instead!' A sob escapes him and, hands over his face, he presses his forehead even harder against the balcony door, imagining the glass splintering all over him, cutting him to ribbons. 'Why – why did I let him?'

Lola suddenly seems possessed by an unworldly strength, her arms around his torso, pulling him away from the window, manoeuvring him firmly towards the bed, despite his efforts to push her away.

'Mattie, stop – look at me.' Her voice is calm but her tone is firm, laced with anger, and she firmly grabs his wrists and pulls them down from his face, her hands on either side of his head, forcing him to meet her gaze.

'You weren't given a choice. It would have happened whatever you said or did. None of it was your fault, Mattie. None of it! Do you understand?'

'I should have—'

'No. Look at me, Mattie!' Her voice rises again. 'None of it was your fault. *None of it was your fault!* Are you hearing me?'

She is shouting now, her face flushed with a mixture of fury and desperation, and for a moment it catches him by surprise and he finds himself staring at her, startled by the absolute certainty of her words.

'None of it, Mattie! I want you to say it: *It wasn't my fault.* Say it, for chrissakes!'

'Shh, we'll – we'll wake the others—'

'Then say it!'

'It wasn't . . .' A tremor runs through him, and

suddenly he feels exhausted, barely capable of speech. 'It wasn't . . .'

'Say it, Mattie.' Her voice drops slightly. 'Deep down, you know it's true.'

'It wasn't' – he closes his eyes and inhales deeply – 'my fault.' He scrunches up his eyes and holds his breath as a silent sob shakes him from the inside. 'Fucking hell, that bastard! It wasn't my fault! It wasn't my fault!'

The anger and the shame, the guilt and the fear have run their course – for now, at least – leaving him empty and vulnerable and exhausted: so exhausted in fact that he can barely sit up, slumped against Lola, his head on her shoulder. His face is pressed against her hot, damp neck – her hair in his face, his tears soaking the shoulder of her nightie. He is kneeling close to her and she has one hand against the back of his head, keeping it from slipping off her shoulder, and the other pressed against the clammy skin between his shoulder-blades, stroking his back in small rhythmic circles. Slowly his breathing stills and the night regains its calm, the steady rush of the waves on the beach outside soothing the hurt, washing him clean. Lola's breathing is quiet and rhythmic too, and barely perceptibly they sway back and forth, as if the bed were a small boat far out at sea.

13

He is falling. Free falling through the air. He jumped from the plane without his parachute. The sky is bright above him, and when he hits the ground, he knows it will be hard. Hard enough to shatter every bone in his body. Hard enough to crack open his skull. His only hope is that it will be quick. That there won't be a brief moment of consciousness when all he can feel is intolerable pain before death's riptide. The ground rushes up to meet him, punching him in the face. He wakes with a start.

He is wet, his T–shirt sticking to his skin in damp patches. Turning his head gingerly on the pillow to check Lola is still sleeping, he climbs stealthily out of bed. Dawn has just broken and the first rays of sun are slanting through the gap in the curtains, creating a golden puddle on the floor.

In the bathroom, he peels off his damp clothes and

steps under the boiling water, aware of a tightness around his shoulders where they have caught the sun. He washes himself thoroughly, the soap and his hands taking the sweat of the night away. Making him clean . . . almost. Almost. And then he just stands there, forehead pressed against the tiled wall, letting the water beat down over the back of his head.

When he returns to the bedroom, Lola is still sleeping, face down, sprawled out diagonally now across the mattress. After drying himself and pulling on a pair of boxers, he rolls gently onto his back beside her, careful not to disturb her. Head propped up on his hand, he looks down at her sleeping form, her bare back exposed, the thin white sheet tangled between her legs. She is so painfully pretty with her translucent white skin, the delicate pattern of veins just visible beneath the skin of her neck. Her tousled hair catches the light slanting through the curtains, turning it golden brown, wisps hanging over her closed eyes. Lying there, she appears so young, so vulnerable. Asleep, she hardly seems to be breathing at all and it scares him. Awake, she has so much energy, is so full of life. Her speech is so animated, her gestures expansive, her laugh explosive. She is almost childlike in her zest for living. Running into rooms instead of walking, slamming doors instead of simply closing them, shrieking with mirth instead of merely chuckling. She is the girl who takes his breath away, who exploded into his life nearly two years ago like a small bright firecracker, fizzing with vitality, dynamism, spontaneity. Everything she does is filled with tangible exuberance – she only has to walk into a room for people to turn round, her presence like an aura of fire, igniting the air about her. She has a magnetic appeal for all those who come within her radar, her fervent lust for life contagious, her gregarious nature like a warm cloak of friendship, drawing everyone in. He has never met anyone like her before. Through her eyes, the world seems to come alive again. And he knows that with her by his side, he will get through this, and one day feel normal again.

His gaze travels the length of her jaw, down the curve of her neck, across the delicate line of her collar bone. The silver teardrop pendant nestles in the hollow beneath her neck, and he can barely resist leaning down and kissing that most delicate, vulnerable place. As his eyes travel up and down her sleeping form he thinks, *She is so lovely, she is so kind, she is so beautiful . . . What have I done? God, what have I done?*

After a lazy morning and a late lunch, they all finally descend onto the beach. By now the sun's rays have reached every corner of the sky, turning it a bright, startling blue. At the end of the garden, the grass gives way to stone and sand, and they scramble down the almost vertical path – steep, sandy steps cut into the rock. On one side, a high bank of tall grass stretches up into the sky; on the other, the ground falls away into the sea. Plateaus of rock jut out from the cliff like shelves, outcrops visible all the way down to the shimmer of blue water, so far below that it appears as still as glass, despite white froth forming around the rocks within its reach. The cool air has turned hot and dry, the sun pounding down relentlessly from a cloudless sky.

Mathéo turns and holds out his hand to help Lola down the last bit. As they emerge out onto the wide stretch of deserted beach, everyone stops for a moment. They are in the most beautiful place, golden sand stretching out to the foamy white line in the distance, almost blinded by the sun's dazzling rays, reflected up from the smooth expanse of cobalt-blue water. For the first time since school ended, Mathéo suddenly feels a sense of release in the air: he is free and light, cut loose from the relentless routine of training, school and homework for the first time in years, relieved of the pressure of getting good grades and winning competitions. It may only be temporary, but for now at least, he is his own person, finally able to put the hell of the past month behind him, forget about the nightmare of that one night, and extinguish the flashes of horror that have followed him around ever since. Although the black thoughts are still present, he is aware of no longer dwelling on them. Surrounded by blinding sea and bottomless sky, he is too overcome by the beauty of it all to continue to indulge such feelings further, and for the first time they find themselves relegated to the side-lines of his consciousness.

All together, they start to run, and moments later they find themselves standing at the water's edge, watching the wavelets inhale and exhale against the vast expanse of smooth, empty beach. Lola and Isabel squeal each time the water touches their feet, and even he and Hugo are hesitating to take the first plunge.

'Fuck, it's cold!' Hugo has waded in as far as his knees, and turns to the others with a grimace. 'Come on, Izzy, there's only one thing for it!' He exchanges glances with Isabel, and the two of them retreat several metres back from the water's edge before counting to three and racing into the water, yelling as they go. Hugo splashes in as Isabel follows at a slower pace, shrieking as the water reaches her thighs. Hanging back a little, Mathéo glances over at Lola, who has begun to inch her way forward, arms hugging her chest. She is wearing a yellow bikini and has the beginnings of a tan, her hair lit up by the sun. Mathéo bites his lip and follows tentatively, not so much because of the freezing water lapping at his calves but because he is still trying to drink all this in. As he follows Lola into the icy blue, he gazes at her back and thinks, *I love her. I love her so much.*

He catches up with her, smiling and wincing. 'Come on. We can do this!'

He holds out his hand. She takes it and yelps as he pulls her towards him, the icy water suddenly deepening, reaching their waists.

'Come on – quick and painful!' he says encouragingly; then, with a laugh, lets go of her hand, plunging forward. Engulfed by the glacial water, for a moment he fears his heart will stop in shock, but then finds himself staring up at the stream of bubbles rising towards the dazzling surface and, above that, the blurred contours of Lola's face as she stands looking down at him. It feels wonderful to be underwater again. The sea seems to be transforming him, turning him into the person he once was, giving him back what is rightfully his. He can sense it inside him; can almost feel the sordid memories begin to melt away. The world shrinks away above him. Liquid blue fills his vision, darkening and deepening down below. The new Mathéo is fresh and bright and clean like a child, a baby being reborn.

He pushes himself deeper, circles Lola's ankles with his fingers and, with one swift movement, pulls her feet out from under her, sending her plunging backwards with a muffled scream. He resurfaces, wipes his eyes with his hands, and for a moment cannot see her, the sun bouncing off the water, refracting shards of blinding gold into his eyes. Then, suddenly, she is by his side, heaving, grabbing his arm for support. 'You bastard!' she splutters.

'See?' he laughs. 'Quick and—' He is cut off mid-sentence as she throws her full weight against him, sending him back under, but he manages to grab hold of her as he goes, dragging her down with him. Then, before she can retaliate further, he sets off at a fast crawl, Lola shrieking and splashing in his wake.

When they finally stop and turn round, treading water, the beach is a long way behind them, Hugo and Isabel just bobbing heads in the distance, splashing each other and tossing something into the air.

He turns to Lola, breathing hard, hair plastered to his head, water streaming down his face. 'Keep on going?'

'Don't be crazy – we're already too far out!' she exclaims.

Mathéo takes a deep breath and slides down beneath her, swimming deeper and deeper into the darkness far below. Way up above, he can see Lola still treading water, waiting for him to re-emerge. He lets his breath out in steady increments, floating weightlessly, deep down near the sea bed. Above him, empty shards of golden light illuminate the surface. He feels calm, cocooned. As if he could stay here for ever.

He rockets out of the water with a splash, flooding Lola with spray.

'Oh my God, you're crazy!' she starts to shout as, coughing and gasping, he laughs at her horrified expression, tickled at having succeeded in scaring her. He follows her into shallower water where their feet meet firm sand. Pulls her into his arms, holding her tight, gasping against her ear, kissing the side of her head, her face. Lola turns towards him and his mouth meets hers – cold, salty lips, hands gripping his head, water from her hair dripping into his. Between hot, frantic kisses, Mathéo opens his eyes for a moment and finds the colour of the sea reflected in hers, droplets of water pearling across her cheekbones, down her forehead, hanging on her lashes, sparkling like tiny diamonds in the sun. The pale, freckled skin on her cheeks and nose is slightly burned; flashes of light refract from the water on her forehead. He feels her chest pressing against his, her leg against his thigh, their feet touching in the soft sand. And he thinks, *This is it.* He is back, alive, passionate, in love, and the nightmare that has haunted him over the last few weeks is gone for good.

He wants to capture this moment in time and hold on to it for ever, stay in it for ever, remain for ever right here, with Lola in his arms and the feel of her warm neck and dripping hair against his face. It's as if someone has found this day, created it just for him, like the most amazing present he could ever have wished for. He now knows that meeting Lola was always meant to be. He was always meant to fall in love with her and have his love returned. He feels light – so light, all dark thoughts erased, replaced instead by excitement and amazement and a happiness so pure it threatens to take his breath away. For the first time in ages there is not the slightest trace of pain in his body or his mind – no piercing shaft between his eyes, no throbbing ache in his head, no sick dizziness within his chest, no currents of electricity burning through his veins. The heavy fog that has been surrounding him has evaporated into the bright blue air – that static, stabbing, burning weight gone from his muscles, gone from his skin. His body has softened, as if something harsh and solid has been released from inside. And it's as if he has finally achieved what he has been longing for ever since that terrible morning: stepped out of his body and into one that is brand new; found a place where he can think and feel and live and breathe without hurting, without pain. He never knew not hurting could feel this good, this light, this gentle. He wants to hold onto Lola like this for ever. It's as if by merging his body with hers, she is dissipating everything dark and heavy and negative within him, allowing him, after weeks of unrest, to exist once more as a normal person . . .

After a game of Frisbee with the others in the sand, the sun seems to have lost some of its luminance, the air has turned slightly cooler, and the sea has retreated still further. Mathéo is reminded that time is moving on, that things keep changing. Casting patterned shadows on the sand, he returns with the others to grab towels, shove sandy feet into sun-baked sandals. He ignores the other two and keeps his eyes fixed on Lola, desperate for her to continue to provide him with the light and energy to keep the darkness at bay.

As they begin their ascent back to the house, leaving the beach and the dipping sun behind them, Mathéo keeps Lola's hand firmly clasped in his, the sand rough between their warm palms. When they finish climbing the steps and Hugo and Isabel drift quietly across the garden, discussing what to have for dinner, he holds her back for a moment and kisses her again, trying to stop her from drawing away.

Surfacing for breath, Lola smiles. 'Your cheeks have caught the sun,' she says, and then hesitates for a moment. 'Are you OK?'

He nods, feeling a genuine smile touch his lips for the first time in ages. 'Yes. Yes, I really am.'

That evening, everyone seems a little hyper, as if all that sun, sea and sand has stirred up a potion of exuberance inside them. After dinner, amidst guffaws of laughter, they play strip poker around the poolside table. As usual, Hugo and Isabel are losing on purpose: Hugo is already bare-chested, having chosen to divest himself of his T-shirt but keep his flip-flops. Isabel is down to her bikini. Lola has managed to find bits of jewellery to remove; Mathéo has lost his sandals.

Hugo laughs wickedly as Lola loses a round and removes her ankle bracelet. 'That's all the jewellery you've got. I'm gonna get you out of that T-shirt, Baumann!'

'Over my dead body!' she retorts.

Late that night, after emerging from his shower, Mathéo finds Lola already curled up in bed, light off, the room filled only with moonlight and the sound of the waves. Slipping carefully under the bedsheet as not to wake her, he stretches out on his front, the pillow cool against his sunburned cheek. After a moment, however, he feels her breath against his skin and is aware of her lips against his face – she is kissing him: tiny butterfly kisses, so light they barely seem to make contact. He waits, hoping for a change in their circular pattern, longing for them to come further down, to reach his lips, his mouth, his tongue. His lungs heave in a deep sigh and he opens his eyes a little, just enough to be engulfed by Lola's startling green gaze, tilting his chin upwards in the hope of catching a fluttering kiss on the mouth. They come closer, but not enough, and a small sound escapes him, a murmur of encouragement, until a kiss brushes the corner of his lips, setting them alight. He empties his lungs slowly and then fills them again, struggling to wait for her and not to respond. Craving a proper kiss, he finally has to raise his head off Lola's shoulder, and touch her jawline with a finger to guide her mouth towards his. But she turns to kiss his finger instead, and he follows the contour of her lips and feels the sharp, smooth enamel of her front teeth and then the soft, wet warmth of her tongue as she grazes his finger. Mathéo's sigh is deeper this time as his finger begins to tremble with a mixture of excitement and desire. And he realizes he wants to kiss her so much he is actually shaking with the urge, all the muscles in his body tensed in anticipation. He can hear the sound of his own breath now, shallow and rapid and increasingly frantic, his lips tingling. A small sound of frustration escapes him as he leans in towards Lola, only for her to turn away so that he barely manages to kiss the tiny downy hairs of her cheek instead.

He takes another steadying breath, but it seems to fill the room, and his voice, when it comes out, is tremulous and softly desperate.

'Lola, stop it, let me kiss you.' A breath. 'Lola, I really want to kiss you . . .'

'How badly?' she teases, a question they used to taunt each other with when they first started going out. And just like all those months ago, he feels himself tense so strongly that his stomach disappears into the hollow beneath his ribcage.

He gives a little laugh to let her know he remembers, but is so turned on he can feel himself shiver. 'So badly that – I'll bite you if you don't.' A tremor runs through him and he gives a brief, shy laugh. 'See?'

She kisses his neck and he tenses further. 'Lola, don't— Ah, shit, come on, please . . .'

She smiles, and her kisses follow a trail up his neck, over his chin, beneath his lower lip and . . . and then her mouth meets his: warm and tender, yet so fierce and passionate that it catches him off-guard.

With ragged breaths, he slides his fingers into her hair, each kiss deeper and stronger than the last. He wants her so much that his whole body thrums with desire and he holds her face between his hands, kissing her with a fervour bordering on desperation. Lola runs her hands slowly up and down his back, her fingers as light as petals, before circling round to his stomach and gradually reaching his nipples. Her touch sends small aftershocks rippling through his body, and just as he finds himself coiled as tight as a spring, her mouth meets his with such startling strength and passion that he gasps in shock, and he feels that electric bolt of excitement rush back through him for the first time in a long time. Such a long time . . .

Their clothes go flying. His T-shirt and boxers, her nightie, all tossed onto the floor. Kneeling naked on the bed, Lola is half laughing, half gasping. 'Whoa—'

Grasping her shoulders, he pulls her towards him, kissing her neck, her ear, her cheek, her mouth, his chin pressing into her face, his mouth hard and urgent against hers.

'Mattie—'

Hand holding the back of her head, he kisses her again, harder and harder still, then tries to coax her back against the pillows.

'Mattie, wait—'

He can't wait, not after all this time. Lola passes him a condom and he fumbles in his haste. She is back. He is back. They belong together and he is never letting her go.

'Mattie!' Hands on his chest, she pushes him away hard, alarm flashing in her eyes.

'What? No – you want me to stop?'

Keeping him at arm's length, she stares at him, hair wild and face exquisitely flushed; breathing hard. 'Look at me,' she says quietly.

He forces his eyes to meet hers. 'Lola, don't. I want—' He feels his windpipe constrict.

'Just go gently, my darling.'

'OK . . .' He takes a deep, shuddering breath, bites his lip, manages a reassuring smile. 'OK. Like this?' He strokes the side of her face, brushes his lips across her cheek, kisses her softly and feels her relax beneath his touch.

'Yeah. Like that,' she breathes.

She keeps her eyes open and stares up at him, warm, flushed and gently panting as he slides over her, enters her with an audible gasp. He forces himself to go as slow as he can, gazing back down at her, drinking her in as if for the first time. It's as if, since that terrible night, he has seen her only through a veil, but now that veil has been lifted, a thick fog has dissipated and he sees her afresh, anew. He notices all the tiny details that make her who she is, that make her unique. The gentle arch of her eyebrows, the soft curve of her cheek. Each individual eyelash, long and dark, framing irises of the deepest green. He sees her so clearly he can count the freckles that sprinkle her cheekbones. Holding himself over her, his arms vibrating slightly, he moves rhythmically against her, taking deep breaths in an effort to keep calm. He concentrates on the sweat glistening on her neck – her throat so white, so delicate, so soft against his mouth. The pearl-drop on her necklace catches the light of the moon, reflecting its rays into his eyes so that it seems to glow from the inside. Her hair is wild and tangled by his fingers, russet brown against the white pillow, small wisps curled into humid spirals framing her face. Her hands are pressed tight against his back, sliding up to stroke the nape of his neck, then moving over his head, into his damp hair, separating the strands between her fingers. He closes his eyes and inhales sharply as they make their way to his forehead, her nails skimming the contours of his face: his temples, his cheeks, slowly down the line of his jaw until they meet his mouth. They play against his lips; he opens his mouth to taste them, and they are cool and refreshing, like droplets of water. He fills his lungs again, opens his eyes, and she is smiling up at him – and he feels it in his heart. So much tenderness, so much understanding, so much love in that smile that it hurts him – but this is a good pain, one that makes him feel safe, and complete, and alive. She has woken him from his nightmare, brought him back to life, thawed the walls of a deeply frozen heart. He tries to say thank you, but the words won't come out, so he mouths them instead and her smile broadens, as if she understands, as if she knows everything and has forgiven him ... He closes his eyes as their mouths meet and he is forced to give way, pressing himself hard against her, shudders overtaking his body as he buries his face in her neck, softly gasping.

As they lie side by side against the pillows, their warm, naked bodies washed white by the moonlight, Lola turns her head so that their faces are only inches apart. He barely has the strength to speak – exhausted yet more alive than he can ever remember. She raises her hand and runs her fingers down the length of his arm. 'Sweetheart, you're trembling . . .'

He smiles at her concern, waits a moment to catch his breath. 'I'm OK.'

'Sure?'

He can't stop smiling. 'Yeah. More than OK. More than everything.'

14

'Breakfast?' Bare-chested, in his swim shorts, his hair still wet from the pool, Hugo turns from the cooker as Mathéo walks through the living room and into the kitchen. He is brandishing a sizzling frying pan and the air smells of bacon.

'Oh, cheers, but I think I'll pass.' Mathéo takes a seat at the breakfast bar, across from Isabel, who's wearing an orange sarong. She holds out the cereal box, but he shakes his head and takes an apple from the fruit bowl, forcing himself to bite into it. He wishes last night could have lasted for ever, just he and Lola together in their own private bubble, all other thoughts and memories banished to the outside world. But now it is morning, he has returned to the real world with a jolt, and the sun seems too garish today, its violent brightness cutting in through all the windows, illuminating the chrome kitchen, its light refracting from the silver cutlery. A warm cross-breeze, billowing gently through the open French doors of both the kitchen and the living room, carries with it the smell of sulphur and cut grass and roses. The wide window at the front of the living room reveals a sea as smooth as a sheet of glass, and gulls gliding in circles against a vast expanse of deep blue sky. There is a stillness in the air, a sense of time being suspended, of reality being put on hold. Even Hugo and Isabel, chatting and arguing and laughing at their joint culinary efforts, seem different here – too perfect, too contented to be convincingly real.

'Mattie!' Isabel's raised voice makes him start and he almost drops his apple.

'What?'

'You OK, mate?' Hugo asks, both he and Isabel regarding him with a faintly quizzical expression.

'Yeah, why?'

'Hugo was talking about going hiking,' Isabel explains. 'And you seemed to totally zone out.'

'Where?'

'Along the cliffs,' Hugo responds. 'Last time, Izzy and I found a brilliant picnic spot really high up the cliffs, overlooking the sea. And from there it's a fairly easy climb down to the water for a swim.'

'Cool,' Mathéo replies with a bright smile. 'Let's do it.'

Once Lola is up and finishes breakfast, Mathéo and

Hugo load the rucksacks in the kitchen. Mathéo glances out at Lola and Isabel standing at the edge of the garden, in deep discussion. Isabel has changed into a pair of cotton trousers and Lola is wearing denim shorts with a strappy white top, her feet weighted down by a pair of solid hiking boots and oversized socks that fall down round her ankles. Isabel has handed the binoculars to Lola now and is pointing out the picnic spot on the neighbouring cliff across the sea.

The four of them swing their rucksacks onto their shoulders and, with the girls following more tentatively, leave the garden and begin the hike along the wide chalk road flanking the coast. For the first half-hour or so the road is smooth and flat, snaking its way round rocks and inlets, keeping them aligned with the sea. It is still early – the forecast for today is clear skies and temperatures reaching forty. The plan is to reach the plateau by midday, then picnic in the shady enclave, thus avoiding the sun at its most powerful, then climb down for a swim. But right now, it is still cool and slightly damp, the air still. Alone on the wide swathe of road, beneath the morning sun, Mathéo feels as if they are the only ones on the planet – the empty road stretching out ahead: no houses, no people, no sound, except for the soft calls of fishing gulls and the distant wash of the sea below. It feels both eerie and strangely beautiful – the early morning light turquoise, making him feel like a stranger in this unusual hue. The bowl of sky above is a glaucous blue, splinters of white light emerging just above the horizon. They are in one of France's most beautiful regions, and it is so different to London or even Paris that Mathéo feels as if he might as well have stepped into a whole new world.

Now and again he feels himself shiver, as much from excitement as from the sea breeze now brushing his bare arms. Sleep has not entirely left him, its aura still surrounding his head, and his limbs feel stiff from yesterday's swimming. A tuft of hair refuses to lie flat at the back of his head and he feels light-headed and insubstantial in his blue T-shirt and faded shorts, as if only the weight of his hiking boots is keeping him attached to the ground.

For a while everyone is quiet, still fuzzy from sleep, as if afraid of breaking the fragile web of silence that surrounds them. Despite Hugo's warning about pacing themselves, Lola is striding ahead, her long legs moving soundlessly across the gritty road, her hair tossing about behind her. Holding hands and talking in hushed voices, Isabel and Hugo are not far behind. Mathéo wants to catch up with Lola and take her hand – aches for the feel of her skin against his – but is afraid of coming across as possessive since right now she appears to enjoy walking alone, face turned towards the gathering light in the distance. Watching her fills Mathéo with a strange kind of longing. For all her tall, slender frame, there is something robust about her. With long legs lithe and strong, she seems to move effortlessly despite the heavy rucksack, and he senses within her a healthy, durable energy, as if she could walk like that for ever.

By the time the sun's rays have reached every corner of the sky, turning it a bright, startling blue, they meet the coastal path. Here there is rough, uneven ground beneath their feet: dry, dusty soil that their thick soles send cascading away. The cool air has turned hot and dry, the sun pounding down relentlessly from a cloudless sky. Up on the cliff edge, there is no shade and they are at the mercy of its unforgiving rays. The pace has slowed substantially now, Mathéo and Lola hanging back from the other two as they begin to pick their way up through the forest. The first two or three hundred metres from the road are the hardest. The gaps between the trees are covered in rambling bushes, and the only way past them is to push through. As the ground begins to rise, the trees change into tall, ivy-choked columns, with massive gnarled roots that fan out across the earth. The air dips into shaded coolness, the vegetation thinning out from lack of sunlight. Occasionally the canopy of trees and bushes becomes too thick to pass through, forcing them to get down on their hands and knees and crawl along some animal track.

After nearly an hour of hiking, they find themselves at the bottom of a particularly steep slope. It is a tough climb, pulling themselves up by the thick fern stems to keep themselves from slipping back on the mud and dead leaves. Hugo is the first to reach the top, and almost immediately disappears over the ridge. As soon as Mathéo and the girls catch up with him, they stop with a collective gasp. The slope extends out onto a narrow shelf jutting out from the edge of the mountainside. Above them the cliff stretches up almost vertically into a canopy of trees.

The drop beneath them is enough to take Mathéo's breath away. So used to heights, yet he has never experienced anything as spectacular as this one: the drop to the deep blue sea below is the height of a tall building. At the foot of the cliff, the waves break into white froth against a cluster of rocks set back close to the shore. He can see why Hugo was so determined they hike to this spot: the view is spectacular. From here they can see right out across the bay, along the undulating coast and all the way to the nearest village, its houses nestling beside and above each other, stretching up the slope of the mountain. Matchbox cars crawl along the weaving coastal road, disappearing into the forest in the distance. Below them and to their left, Hugo's villa looks tiny yet deceptively close, surrounded by rows of cypress trees dwarfed by the dramatic landscape. Mathéo can just about make out the glint of turquoise of the swimming pool, the great lawn now just a tiny patch of green, and, below it, the narrow stretch of sand left behind by the high tide.

Moving towards the edge of the plateau, knee deep in bushy plants, Hugo gazes around with his hands on his hips, head cocked with a triumphant smile. 'Pretty awesome, hey?'

Isabel lets out a loud gasp and retreats back into the trees, Lola drops to her knees and shuffles forward to peek down, and even Hugo keeps well back from the edge.

'I'm starving,' Hugo declares. 'Shall we have lunch now and then climb down for a swim?'

'How do we get down?' Lola asks, sounding uncertain.

'Look, there are steps.' He points to the side of the plateau, where protruding rocks create the illusion of a giant staircase. 'The rocks go all the way down. I've tried it – it's easy enough. Like climbing down a ladder.'

Lola bites her lip and moves hastily back from the edge. 'It is an amazing spot! I'm going to take some photos!'

'It's scary,' Isabel counters. 'I think we should move further back inland. What if this rock crumbles or something?'

'It's perfectly safe!' Hugo mocks her gently, jumping up and down to prove his point. 'When the tide was higher, a bunch of daredevils from the next village used to drive over here on their motorbikes and dare each other to jump. Rumour has it that one of them hit a rock and died.'

'Cliff-diving, you mean?' Suddenly Hugo has Mathéo's attention.

'No, they weren't divers. Just nuts!'

'Have you ever tried jumping?' Mathéo asks him.

'Me?' Hugo snorts with laughter. 'Do you think I'm crazy? Hitting the water from this height – Jesus! And look how close the rocks are below!'

'Only at the foot of the cliff. You could clear them with a running dive.'

'Yeah, right.'

As Hugo and Isabel spread out the picnic blanket beneath the trees and Lola starts unpacking the sandwiches, Mathéo feels overcome by a rush of heat and nervous energy; a kind of invisible adrenalin that seems to fill the air around him. For the first time since he first set foot on the ten-metre platform all those years ago, he feels overcome by vertigo so strong it dizzies him: looking down makes him feel unsteady, light-headed, almost nauseous. Memories of his last dive come rushing back – the humid, chlorinated air, the echoing screams from the kiddie pool, Perez's booming voice. He remembers how scared he was, how disorientated, how rattled, and how convinced he was that he wouldn't succeed, filled with that deep pit of certainty that something was about to go seriously wrong. And suddenly, on the edge of this cliff, the feeling is back, even though there is no coach here, no impatient father, no panel of judges or even an audience of squealing teenage girls. There is no one here to judge him, to put pressure on him; nor is there a complex sequence of twists and somersaults he has to memorize visually and kinaesthetically. Up here he is free to just dive – it's so easy that it's almost laughable. A simple, pure dive from this height would be accompanied by the sensation of weightlessness, the feeling that you were flying . . . Back when he was seven and first took up diving, he used to feel like that too. That's why he wanted to join the club, start training every week. But now, ten years later, falling through the air at high speed has become a daily occurrence, more familiar even than brushing his teeth or packing his school bag. Gone is the adrenalin rush, the sense of flying, the feeling of being both everywhere and nowhere all at once.

As he kneels down on the dry earth to unlace his hiking boots and peel off his socks, he notices the others glancing over from their safe haven, well away from the plateau. Lola is saying something, holding out a sandwich wrapped in tin foil.

'What are you doing?' she asks him as he unbuckles his belt, slips off his jeans and pulls his T-shirt over his head.

'I'm gonna dive,' Mathéo informs them all quietly, turning to face the rising breeze, the bottoms of his swim shorts flapping around his knees.

Hugo stops mid-chew, one cheek bulging comically. 'What did you say?'

'With a running dive I'll clear the rocks.'

Hugo snorts and begins to laugh, but then breaks off when Mathéo fails to join in. 'You're joking.'

'No.'

Hugo hesitates, as if unsure whether to start laughing again. 'You mean you're going to kill yourself?'

Lola wipes her hands absent-mindedly on the side of her shorts. 'Mattie, that's not even funny.' She waves the sandwich at him. 'Do you want egg or ham?'

Suddenly he is fed up. Fed up with their disbelief, with their refusal to take his proposition seriously. They think he is being ridiculous, but what do any of them know about diving in the first place? What do they know of the risks he takes day after day, diving off a ten-metre board and plummeting towards the water at thirty-four miles an hour, twisting and turning and somersaulting through the air? What do they know of the pain of missing an entry by a tiny increment and landing on your shoulder or your chest, having the wind knocked out of you as if being slammed up against a wall? What do they know about having to climb out of the pool in front of thousands of spectators, trying to hide the fact that you are injured

so as not to give the other competitors a psycho-
logical advantage? Trying to hide how utterly gutted
you are that, after all those long hours at the pool, the
dive that you had perfected in training went wrong at
the exact moment it most mattered and the morning's
press will label you a 'choker'? What do they know
about the long hours before and after each competition at the Aqua Centre, trying out a new dive,
missing it, climbing out of the pool and going straight
back up to do it again, and again, and again – mistake
after mistake, the fear growing so vast you feel you
will never escape it? What do they know about a tiny
wobble on takeoff that fails to clear you of the board
by a few millimetres – nothing noticeable to the
naked eye, but enough to have your head clip the side
of the board on your somersault, and leave you gun-
shot and unconscious as you smack against the water's
unforgiving surface? What do they know of doing all
that, and then being led to a wood by one of the few
men you have ever trusted, slammed against a tree,
thrown onto the ground and assaulted in the most
heinous way imaginable . . .

Suddenly he is angry, furious even. What do any of
them know of nerves and pain and pure, undiluted
terror? He wants to show them – show them what it's
really like, how horrifying it really is; give them the
view from his perspective. He pushes his clothes to
one side, backs up against the rocky cliff wall so that

the plateau stretches out like a diving board, fixes his spot on the sun-bleached horizon and pushes his heel against the rock to propel himself forward. He is running in slow motion – five long strides, a shout from Hugo, and then he is propelling himself through the air, off the edge of the cliff and into the void.

Their screams follow him like an echo. The sun is blinding, both from the blue sky above and the blue sea below. He is not sure which way is up, but that doesn't matter: he is like an arrow, or a rocket, or a missile, plummeting downwards, headfirst, at over forty miles an hour. He can actually feel the wind resistance like a wall of air; the breeze pushing him towards the left, towards the rocks, the G-force so great that his face feels dug out of his skull and inhaling is impossible. The sound of rushing air obliterates even the roar of the waves; he can hear nothing but the shrieking wind, and the water is still nothing more than a sparkling patch of blue in the distance. He is at once moving at incredible speed and not moving at all – plummeting towards the earth and hanging in the sky. Maybe he will never land at all, or maybe he will die on impact. Unless he hits the water hands first and as taut as an arrow, landing on the sea's smooth surface will feel no different to landing on a concrete slab. And suddenly it's there, in front of him, beneath him. He squeezes his eyes tightly shut, every muscle in his body clenched and screaming, the wave of fear meeting him at last as he braces himself for the final smash.

The water wall is brutal. It knocks every remaining pocket of oxygen from his body and batters him as if in fury. But he was lucky: he achieved the perfect rip entry. Anything less and he would be in pieces. He shoots down beneath the surface, deeper and deeper, until gradually he feels his underwater descent begin to slow, becomes aware of the sunlight illuminating a patch on the surface a very long way up. He must kick if he is to surface without passing out, but his legs appear to have gone numb. It takes for ever to reach fresh air, and when he does, for a moment he cannot inhale, his lungs so emptied they seem to have collapsed. But then he is aware of a muffled retching, gasping sound, and feels his ribcage expand and contract like an old, creaky accordion, and finds himself floating, head tilted back, heaving in oxygen. His body has taken over and is doing all the work, his nerves and synapses shot to bits, and for a long time all he can do is float and gasp until he is aware of the rest of him. His arms are slowly coming back to life, aching from the impact, but his legs are dead weights, pulling him down. He manages a slow breaststroke towards the foot of the cliff, steering himself with his arms towards the rocks. There is a small patch of dry earth amongst the shrubs – if he could just pull himself up onto that and curl up and never move again . . .

A fold in time, and he is still floating, still trying to reach the shore, but now he is aware of shouting, and figures on the rocks scrambling down, their movements hurried and frantic. He finds himself drifting through thick weed: the edge of the forest is near, but still he fears he may never reach it. He hadn't thought about this part: swimming back to dry land, climbing out, surviving. By rights he should be dead.

'Grab my hand! Grab my hand!' Hugo is yelling.

It takes Mathéo a while to figure out exactly how to do that, to decide which arm still has enough strength to be raised, but as soon as he does, Hugo's hands clasp his wrist like a vice, pulling him through the weed and onto the sand, and then he feels smooth rock beneath him, and he is being dragged backwards towards the trees, the air here strangely cold, the sun obliterated by the thick canopy of foliage above.

'Fucking hell!' Hugo is flushed and sweaty and breathless, hair sticking to the sides of his crimson face. 'Jesus fucking Christ!'

Lola and Isabel run over to join him, equally flushed and sweaty, panting with shock and exertion, looking shaky and terrified.

'Is he OK?' he hears Isabel ask.

'I'm fine,' he replies, sagging back against the trunk of a cypress, still waiting for the nerves in his hands and legs to start responding. 'That was amazing. Just amazing!'

'You're a fucking idiot, you know that?' Hugo stumbles back between the roots, gripping a stitch in his side. 'You nearly killed yourself! We – we couldn't see you for ages! We were convinced you'd hit your head and drowned!'

'What?' He still feels comfortably numb, slightly dizzy and faintly euphoric at having landed such a faultless dive. At having survived! He isn't so pathetic after all! Their loud, panicked shock and bustle completely baffles him.

'You *knew* how dangerous that was!' Hugo is still shouting, his face a violent shade of crimson. 'It's not like you're some amateur. You knew! You knew there was every chance you'd fall on rocks, or the impact of the water would kill you, but you just went ahead and fucking did it anyway!'

'I just wanted to show you . . . I just wanted to show myself. I was just having some fun—'

'Fun?' Hugo retorts. '*Fun?* Lola tried to jump in after you. I only just managed to grab her in time. She was going to jump without the run-up and go tumbling down the side of the cliff!'

Lola . . . He turns his head to look for her, but she is standing some way off with her back to him, Isabel's arm wrapped tightly round her shoulders. She appears to be crying.

'Lola, don't be silly. I'm fine!' He lets out a nervous laugh and Hugo rounds on him again.

'You think it's funny? You actually think this is all just a fucking joke?'

Mathéo stares up at Hugo, and for a moment thinks Hugo is going to punch him – sees his right hand clench into a fist and begin to pull back, sees his eyes darken and narrow . . .

Then, suddenly, Isabel is there, grabbing Hugo's wrists, pushing him back. 'Babe, come on, leave it. There's no point having an argument. Let's just go home.'

Isabel turns to toss him his rucksack and boots, then follows the others without a word. Mathéo opens his bag and pulls his T-shirt back on over his soaked swim shorts, so waterlogged they feel heavy and cling to his thighs. It is only when he bends over to pull on his socks and boots that he notices. His leg, covered in bright red gashes from ankle to thigh. He remembers the skim of razors he felt just before reaching for the surface, and all at once it hits him. A rock. He dived in right beside a rock and grazed his leg along the side of it coming back up. A couple of millimetres further across and he would have landed on it, ending his life immediately.

As the water begins to dry on the exposed parts of his body, the salt coagulates in the cuts on his leg, making them sting. Hugo and Isabel have pushed on ahead – still in sight but only just, hands entwined and talking in earnest. As the shock of the dive begins to wear off and his brain starts to thaw, it dawns on him that Lola hasn't said a word to anyone since he got out of the water. Her shoulders are hunched beneath her rucksack, straggly hair falling into her face, head lowered, trudging solidly and rhythmically over the soft earth and twisted roots of the forest floor. She appears oblivious to him and everything else around her; lost, it would seem, in her own world.

Wincing, he increases his pace to catch up with her and reaches for her hand. 'Hey!'

At the touch of his fingers against hers, she reacts as if to an electric shock, pulling her arm back sharply, lengthening her stride in an attempt to increase the gap between them.

'Tired?' he asks her gently. 'Let me take your rucksack.' But as he starts to lift the strap from her shoulder, her arm knocks his away as if in self-defence, startling him so much that he almost loses his footing.

'Sweetheart, what's the matter?'

'Don't call me that.'

He jolts back, the words hitting him like a fist in the stomach. 'What d'you mean?'

Her hand shoots up to ward him off as he tries to touch her again. 'Just — just don't touch me, Mathéo. Just leave me alone, all right?'

He winces at her tone and shrinks back, stung. 'Lola, I'm sorry if I scared you.'

'Don't be,' she retorts. 'But when you next try to kill yourself, do it when I'm not around so I don't accidentally kill myself too, OK?'

He is aware of a hot, buzzing sound in his ears, the thrumming of blood in his cheeks. 'I – I wasn't trying to kill myself—' But suddenly he realizes this isn't quite true. Hadn't part of him wanted to die just then, just so he could wipe the slate, just so he wouldn't have to go on? Diving from that height between rocks was playing Russian roulette – he knew that, so why did he do it? Perhaps because it would be so much easier, so much cleaner than having to deal with the rest of his life.

'Whatever. If you want to go on pretending nothing ever happened, that everything's fine now; if you forbid me from ever mentioning the – the attack, then there's nothing I can do.' Lengthening her stride, Lola catches up with the others, and he has neither the strength nor the courage to try to catch up with her or speak to her again.

By the time the villa comes into view, everyone's pace has slowed almost to a crawl. Bruised from his dive, back aching and leg still bleeding, Mathéo feels light-headed from pain and exhaustion, ready to collapse on the side of the road. Lola has kept her distance the whole way home and is the first to reach the house – he can just about make out her silhouette striding across the lawn, Isabel breaking into a jog to

323

catch up with her as they go through the doors. Hugo stops at the edge of the garden, waiting for Mathéo, his face still hard with anger.

'I'm going for a swim,' Mathéo calls out to him, heading down towards the cliff steps. He really can't face an argument right now. Better let Lola cool off for a while.

He sees Hugo hesitate, then shrug and turn to go inside.

He walks to the far end of the beach, limping now, his feet blistered, face prickling with sunburn. Large boulders the size of huts cluster together at the foot of the cliff-face, creating a small area of shade out of view of the garden or road above. The tide is beginning to drift out, and he sinks down onto the damp but solid sand between the rocks; translucent wavelets lap over his boots and sting his scraped leg. He collapses on his side using his rucksack as a pillow, the wet sand slowly soaking into his clothes, cooling him down. Exhausted, he closes his eyes against the harsh light of the afternoon sun . . .

He is aware of a sharp, rapid, clicking noise deep inside him, resonating through his skull. At first he thinks he is being shaken, that something inside him must be loose and rattling; then he feels the ache in his jaw and is aware of his teeth chattering against the cold. It is dark – the sun has set and the moon has risen, illuminating the sea in the distance and turning the tide pools a glistening, eerie silver. He levers himself slowly to a sitting position, shivering hard, his muscles stiff and unyielding. There is a painful crick in his neck, a sore raised ridge on his cheek; his clothes are wet and he is freezing. For a while he just sits there, hugging his knees to his chest as the afternoon's painful memories slowly thaw in his brain. From his rocky enclave, he stares out at the smooth, wet sand, indefinable in colour but somehow shimmering all the same, and the edge of the sea, that foamy white line, so far out now as to be barely discernible. His watch reads quarter past ten, which means he must have been asleep out here for something like six hours. For a moment he is surprised the others did not come to wake him when it got dark – then he remembers their fury at his reckless behaviour, the kamikaze dive from that colossal height, missing the rocks below by mere millimetres. Hugo's accusation that he was trying to kill himself rings sharply in his head, and he wonders again – was he right? Was that actually what he was trying to do? Or was he just trying to prove to himself that he was still a world-class diver, as strong and determined as before the attack . . . ? He has no idea; is too cold and achy and shivery to think . . . He hadn't planned it, that much he does know. But he *had* wanted to take a chance; take a chance in the hope of maybe – maybe escaping something. Something he had done, but also something he still has to do, a confession he has yet to make, a secret he is waiting to unveil: one so terrible that it would change his whole world, destroy a family, rip loved ones apart, sever blood ties and wreck lives for ever.

After ascending the cliff steps and reaching the garden, he is met by the bright lights of the villa's living room and the fluorescent turquoise of the pool. Brushing the sand from his clothes and holding himself tight in an effort to stop shivering, he crosses the floodlit lawn and pushes open the heavy front door. The scene that greets him is not one he expected. Hugo is sitting on the sofa, his arm around Isabel. In the armchair opposite, Lola is curled up with a cushion hugged to her chest, eyes pink-rimmed and cheeks flushed. There is no chatter, no banter, no DVD and no booze. Not even a card game. All three are just sitting there as he shuffles in, staring at him, stock-still like waxwork figures.

'Hey,' he says hoarsely, still hugging himself against the cold that seems to have lodged itself permanently inside him. 'What – what's everyone been up to?'

'Where have you been?' Hugo asks, an unusual mixture of wariness and concern in his voice.

'Fell asleep on the beach.'

'We've been worried sick.' Isabel now. But she doesn't sound angry – a note of sadness in her tone.

'I'm sorry, I didn't mean to—' He looks over at Lola, but she immediately averts her gaze.

He can feel his heart. Can tell something is wrong. The earlier anger at his reckless behaviour has dissipated. Hugo and Isabel seem subdued as well as shocked, eyeing him with an air of what could almost pass as caution.

'Sit down,' Hugo says stiffly. 'I'll get you a drink. Coffee?'

'No, it's OK, I'm fine,' Mathéo says, moving slowly towards the stairs. 'I'll – I'll just go upstairs and have a shower before I cover the place in sand.'

'Wait. Sit down, we need to talk.' Hugo gets up, blocking his way. 'I think' – again, a glance at Isabel – 'maybe you should call your parents—'

'What are you on about?' His pulse is accelerating at an alarming speed. 'Has something happened to them?'

'No, they're fine.' Isabel takes over now. 'It's you, Mattie. We think you need help. We think you should tell your parents—'

'About what?' The words fire out, harsh and ragged.

'About what happened,' Isabel says. 'About—' He sees her swallow. 'About the rape.'

He can hear his breath shuddering in his throat and the ground begins to tilt, knocking him off balance, sending him stumbling back against the wall.

Hugo is staring at him in a faintly horrified way, while Isabel's expression holds a mixture of shock and pity. He looks over at Lola, still keeping her face hidden.

'You – you t-told them?'

A screaming stab of silence, and then she turns, cheeks damp with tears. 'I had to, Mattie! You nearly killed yourself this afternoon, and then you went missing for six whole hours! We searched everywhere and found your water bottle down on the beach. I thought you'd gone and drowned yourself or something!'

'But you *promised*!'

'They wouldn't believe me!' Her voice rises. 'Hugo and Izzy wouldn't help me search for you because they didn't think you were in any danger! I tried explaining how unhappy you were, but they didn't understand! You disappeared for half the day after throwing yourself off a cliff, Mattie! What did you expect me to think? What the hell did you expect me to do?'

He feels for the wall behind him to keep himself upright, his knees threatening to give way. 'Lola, you could have just . . . Oh, Lola, dammit—' His voice breaks. 'You promised. You *promised*!'

'Matt, listen, it's OK, we're not going to tell anyone.' Hugo moves towards him, hand held out in a gesture of solidarity. 'I'm just really sorry you had to go through that, mate. I – I can't imagine what it must have been like—'

'I don't need your fucking pity!'

'We're not pitying you, we're just concerned!' Isabel is approaching now. They seem to be closing in on him, trapping him, encroaching on his space, and he only just resists the urge to lash out. 'Something like that – sexual abuse – it's a huge trauma,' she continues. 'You have to let people help you. You have to tell your family, the people you love—'

'I told the only person I really love and she fucking betrayed me!' The pain stabs like knives – the pain of those words stabs him like a million knives, cutting him all over. Far, far worse than hitting the water after diving off the cliff. Far, far worse than cracking his head on the ten-metre platform. Worse, even, than that night. He had wanted to die then, but the thought of never seeing Lola again had kept him fighting. Slumped against the wall, he presses his hands hard over his cheeks, jamming his fingertips into the sockets over his eyelids. He wants nothing more than to get away from them all, but is suddenly disorientated – has no way of finding the stairs, no way of finding the front door.

Hugo puts his hand on his shoulder. 'Matt, I'm so sorry. I wish you'd told me. I can't think of anything worse. I'd have gone with you to the police. I'd have tracked him down, beaten the hell out of him—'

He shoves Hugo back with all his strength. 'Don't touch me, OK? Just don't fucking touch me!'

'We're just trying to help! We care about you, Matt!'

'I don't want your fucking help! You weren't supposed to know. Nobody was supposed to know!'

'It wasn't your fault, Matt—'

'You're damn right it wasn't!'

'Then why all the secrecy! You've got nothing to be ashamed of—'

'I fucking know that!' But Hugo has got it right. He does feel ashamed: ashamed and dirty and weak and pitiful. Damaged goods, raped, abused, messed up in the head. He knows now that nothing will be the same between them ever again; that Hugo, his oldest and closest friend, will always remember him as *my schoolfriend who was raped*. But worse, far worse, is the horrifying knowledge that the secret is out. If even Lola was unable to keep it to herself then he stands no chance with these two. Word will spread, gossip will run rife – his other friends will know, his diving buddies will know and, worst of all, his parents will know. And there will be questions. What he thought until now was a fairly watertight story about a stranger – perhaps a crazy fan – luring him into the woods will begin to fall apart under intense scrutiny. Even if he refuses to go to the police, people will ask questions, people will want answers, and people will start speculating . . . Others will have seen the guy. If they start asking questions at the Brighton Aquatic

Centre, putting together the pieces of the puzzle, joining the dots, then . . . they will find him. Him, the rapist. *And he cannot let that happen.*

'Matt – Jesus, you're hyperventilating! Calm down!' Hugo's hand is on his shoulder, but Mathéo grabs him by the collar and shoves him away with all his strength. As Hugo stumbles back, crashing into a lamp, Mathéo makes a dash for the stairs. Into the bedroom. Into the bathroom. Throwing off his wet, sandy clothes and turning the shower on full power. The freezing water scorches his sunburned skin, the bruises from the dive, the lacerations on his leg. The strength of the jet powers down over him like thousands of needles. But as the sand, salt and sweat are swept from his skin, disappearing down the plughole, he feels more exposed and dirty than ever, and, kneeling on the tiled floor, presses his face into his hands, choking on hot tears and icy water.

15

After dipping in and out of sleep all night, Mathéo finally gives up just before dawn and, extracting himself carefully from beside Lola's warm, sleeping body, dresses in the heavy silence of the room. He pulls a hoodie on over his T-shirt and jeans, slips his feet into his sandals and creeps down the marble staircase, letting himself quietly out of the still sleeping house.

The nightlights set in the ground surrounding the lawn are still on, but as he leaves the garden behind him, he sees that dawn is just close to breaking, the night sky turning purple, glorious in the first rays. A tiny sliver of sun has just begun to creep over the horizon, turning the sea violet, the first sparks of silver catching on water. The air is misty, cool and slightly damp. Zipping up his hoodie, he begins his descent, the beach path spinning out before him like a snake's tongue unfurling. At the bottom, the smooth sand that greets him, like the air around him, is tinged with blue, the tidal pools shimmering, stretching all the way to the wide, foaming line of the sea.

Mist veils the cluster of large rocks that sheltered him the day before; they stand as still as statues, their dents and edges catching the dawn sun. He reaches them and climbs atop the highest, settling himself into one of its smooth curves so that he can look right out across the sea, and with his eyes follow the coast-line into the misty distance. Behind him the house stands firm and solid, its whitewashed walls ghostly against the looming black silhouette of the mountain behind it. He takes in deep lungfuls of cold, salty air and watches the golden rays spread out across the water, the purple early-morning light pouring across the bay. Tilting his head back, he stares up as the wide swath of bottomless sky falters from purple, to Prussian blue, to violet – a pink smear cutting a path above the horizon like the mark on a child's finger painting. Haloes of light converge and cover the paling mist, turning it a sanctifying white as it falls like dust over the rocky headlands, the trees and bushes dark cut-outs against the rising sun. Below, the sea spreads out before him, whispering and wrinkled, sunlight dancing on the moving water. There is some-thing utterly heartbreaking about this violently beautiful, continuously changing scene. The sea rhythmically inhales and exhales in the distance, and as the chill blue mist wraps itself around him, Mathéo wishes he could just disappear into it, become part of this breathtaking view and cease to hurt, cease to feel, cease to be.

As gulls begin to circle the cliff-top, stirring the silence with their sharp, plaintive cries, Mathéo becomes aware of another sound – a scrabbling from below. He stiffens, expecting an animal of some kind, but hears panting, and then suddenly Lola's head and shoulders come into view as she pulls herself up using the tricky footholds.

He reaches out and helps her up. 'How did you know I was here?'

Standing there, her face flushed with exertion, she wipes her hands on the sides of her jeans and then turns to point back to the house in the distance. 'I saw you from the window.'

'Oh.'

She lowers herself down beside him, resting her arms on her drawn-up knees, her face turned towards the expanding sun. The smattering of freckles across her cheekbones has spread, the skin on her nose and forehead a sun-kissed pink. The dawn rays wash across her face, leaving the rest of her in shadow, and as the breeze picks up, she shivers, her golden brown unkempt hair streaming out behind her.

'Do you want my hoodie?'

'But then you'll be cold.'

'I'm fine,' he lies, pulling it off and wrapping it round her shoulders. 'Better?'

'Thanks.'

There is a silence as thick as the blue mist rolling off the surface of the sea. The gulls continue their crying overhead like a lament and, side by side, they sit together wordlessly for what seems like an eternity. Glancing across at her huddled figure, Mathéo aches to put an arm round her shoulders, move closer so they are pressed up together – but doesn't dare. The ache inside him is so great, it seems to fill the vast expanse of space around him, rising all the way up to the sky, stretching right out to the horizon.

'Did you come here to be alone?' Lola asks him quietly, her voice faint in the rising breeze.

'Yes . . . I mean, no.'

'I'll go.' She starts to get up. 'I just wanted to check you were all right.'

'Lola, don't.' He reaches out to stop her, his hand making contact with the warm skin of her arm, and as she sinks back down, forces himself to let go of her.

'Are you?' she asks, resting her chin on her arms, her gaze still turned away. 'All right, I mean?'

A pause. He doesn't know how to answer – determined to tell her the truth but, as usual, unable to find a way to do so. After a moment she looks at him, tilting her head to rest on her arms.

'No.' He gives her a small smile to make up for the

tremor in his voice, but she doesn't return it. He gleans a sadness from her expression, pain and concern in her gaze, her green eyes huge, flecked with gold. The gentle touch of her hand makes him start and he has no choice but to pull away, and quickly. He looks back out across the sea to escape the hurt in her face.

'Are you still angry I told them? Even after our talk last night?'

He takes a long breath, filling his lungs to capacity, and lets it out slowly in an attempt to keep his composure. He shakes his head.

'No?' Lola asks, her tone disbelieving.

'No.' The word is whispered, so he is not sure she has heard, but he keeps his eyes fixed on the horizon, on that curved gold line where the morning sun first reaches the sea. Something heavy and full begins to rise in his chest, and he inhales deeply again, trying to force it back, blinking rapidly.

'Why won't you let me hold your hand then?'

Because if you do, I'll fall apart.

He swallows hard, pressing his knuckles against the sharp edges of rock beneath him. 'It's just that – Lola, there's something I want you to remember—' He breaks off, taking another breath to steady his voice.

Despite being unable to look at her, he can feel her gaze focus sharply on his face. 'What?'

'It's really important for you to remember that whatever – whatever happens, I always loved you.' He turns to look at her now, 'I *always* loved you, Lola. More – more than I ever thought was possible to love anyone in this world.'

'Mattie . . .' She reaches out to touch him, and then, remembering, retracts her hand. 'I love you too, but why are you saying this now?'

'Because you've got to believe me.' He turns to face her, his breathing accelerating. 'It's just really important that you believe me, Lola, OK?'

'OK . . .' There is a wary note in her voice. 'But I still don't understand. What do you mean by you always *loved* me. Don't you love me any more?'

'I do. Of course I do.'

'Then why do I need to remember?' She gives him a tentative, hopeful smile but the wariness hasn't left her eyes. 'You'll always be here to remind me!'

He looks at her face, her beautiful, trusting face, and feels the blood thrum in his cheeks, pulsing painfully through his veins. He is unable to reply.

'Mattie . . .' A slight crease forms between her brows. 'What's going on? Are you – are you breaking up with me?'

'No! At least . . .' He inhales raggedly. 'I – I don't want to. I really don't!'

The tentative smile is gone from her face, her expression changing. Her voice fades to barely more than a whisper. 'Then why does it feel like you're saying goodbye?'

He turns his face back to the horizon, a sharp pain pressing against the back of his eyes. 'We can never be sure what might happen in the future.'

'But I thought we had it all planned. Drama college in London, and going back to work at that bookshop so I can travel to watch you compete.' He can feel her stare on his face, as if trying to read his thoughts, understand where all this is coming from.

'Things change,' he says doggedly. 'Things happen—'

He feels her tense. 'Mattie, what are you trying to tell me? What's going on?'

He shakes his head, looking away, biting down hard on the inside of his cheek. 'Nothing . . . It's just – it's just that, Lola . . . I have this feeling, I have this terrible feeling that—' He breaks off breathlessly.

'What?' she presses, her voice sharp with concern. 'This feeling that *what*?'

'That things are going to change between us.'

Silence. Deathly silence. Even the gulls seem to have gone quiet.

'Yesterday, that dive . . .' There is a shocked, brittle sound to her voice. 'You so nearly could have died . . . Mattie, look at me!'

He shakes his head, holding his breath, leaning away as she reaches up to try and touch his cheek.

'Mattie, you're scaring me. What's happening? Are you thinking of doing something? Are you thinking of hurting yourself?' The sharpness of her tone increases, rising in panic.

He empties his lungs in a rush, the air stuttering in his chest, tears cutting into the rims of his eyes. 'No . . . I don't know. I just can't live like this!'

Her fingers trace a path over the back of his hand. 'Do you want to talk about what happened?'

He shakes his head, pulling and working on the skin on the inside of his cheek. 'Lola, I love you so much.'

'I love you too—'

'But it won't be enough, it won't ever be enough! You have no idea what I've done to you, what I've done to *us*—' A muffled sob breaks through the last word, and he lowers his face into his hands, tears warming the tips of his fingers.

'Mattie—' She touches his arm and he pulls away violently, getting to his feet and climbing down off the boulder, skidding and grazing his hands and scraping the skin off the side of his arm in his haste. He starts to run, but the pain in his leg slows him and he strides out across the beach, following the cuts of white light on the pale sand towards the distant line of the sea.

Jumping up onto the small wooden jetty, heading resolutely towards the water, he soon becomes aware of the sound of gasping breath, the slap of sandals against the wooden slats behind him. 'Mattie, listen – you know I'll support you in whatever you decide to do. Do you want to go home? Do you want to speak to the police?'

'No!' Lengthening his stride, he turns just enough to see her following him, hair blowing across her face, cheeks flushed with exertion. 'You know what I want? To leave! To leave London for ever and never go back!'

Lola slows to a brisk walk as the gap between them closes. He can make out the rise and fall of her chest, the small puffs of exertion as she works to keep up. 'But why?'

Hugo's rowing boat is bobbing on the waves and rocking from side to side, in turn straining against the rope, then knocking up against the side of the jetty, the metal loop clattering against the slats.

'So that we can go away together. Just the two of us.' He is suddenly gripped by the idea. 'I know what! I'll take a year off from diving, you can defer your entrance to Central and we'll go backpacking round the world!'

Her face relaxes at the sight of his expression and she moves forward tentatively, holding out a hand. 'Come back here. What are you talking about – running off together?' She smiles at him as if convinced he is joking.

'I mean it. What's stopping us? Loads of people take gap years.' He backs away towards Hugo's boat.

'You're crazy, Mattie!' Lola laughs at him, her eyes sparkling in the dawn sun. 'But I tell you what – after the Olympics and when we've finished with university, we should totally do something like that!'

He can tell that she still thinks he is joking and a feeling of panic begins to rise in his throat. 'I'm serious, Lola. I don't want to wait four years. Let's do this now!'

'Fine!' she laughs. 'Where shall we go?'

'I'm not kidding.' He lowers his voice suddenly. 'I'm not kidding, Lola. I'm not going back. I can't.'

Placing one foot in the middle of the boat, Mathéo then gently transfers his weight and follows with the other. He is busy working at the knot as Lola approaches.

'Mattie, what are you doing?' But despite her words she looks excited, her cheeks pink from the wind, face and eyes alight. 'We can't just take Hugo's boat.'

'They won't be up for hours!'

'It's getting blowy!'

'It's not – it's beautiful out there at this time!'

After a moment's hesitation, she takes his out-stretched hand and gingerly climbs in, seating herself on the damp bench at the stern. Mathéo grins and tosses the heavy rope on the floor where it slides and coils of its own accord, like a snake. He places the oars in their rowlocks, sits down on the cross seat, braces his wet sandals against the footplate, and allows the oars to drop and catch the water. A few strong strokes later, and they are well clear of the jetty.

Moving swiftly away from the shore, the prow pointing out to sea, they head towards the glistening pink of the eastern sky. The choppy water makes for a bumpy ride: opposite him, Lola swings in reverse to him – up and down and side to side as if they were on a faulty seesaw. She grips the edge of the bench on either side of her to keep from sliding, but he can see the flush of adrenalin, the spark of excitement in her eyes as she gazes over his shoulder towards the rising sun.

'Wow, Mattie. The sky – the colours on the water – look, it's so beautiful!'

Grinning, he allows himself a quick glance behind before resuming the rowing – settling into a good, steady rhythm, careful to pace himself but also to keep the boat nice and central in the ragged semicircle of the rocky bay. Lola keeps pointing at the sunrise on the horizon, urging him to look, but he is content just rowing, putting as much distance between them and the shore as possible, watching the dawn light, soft and roseate, wash across Lola's sun-kissed face. She raises her arms as if to stretch, but tilts her head back, hair streaming across her face. 'I'm free!'

He laughs at her, into the rising wind. Yes, that is exactly it. They are free! Free of Hugo and Isabel back at the house, so serious and heavy with concern; free of all their ties back home in London – his father, Perez, his diving, his life . . .

Lola lowers her arms and grabs the sides of the boat as the prow smacks against a particularly big wave, jolting her off the bench for a moment, causing her to squeal in surprise.

Mathéo feels overcome by a sudden, unexpected rush of joy. It is the joy of freedom, of having a boat of your own. It is the joy of pulling on oars and feeling the boat surge forward with the rustle of tearing silk; it is the joy of the morning sun gently warming your back and making the sea surface flicker with a hundred different colours. Despite the choppy waves, this morning the sea seems bluer, more limpid and transparent, its surface striped with silver and gold. The sun-drenched coastline is remote, distant and beautiful. They are floating, just the two of them, floating in a void of space. A flock of gulls fly over, and one pauses to soar just above their heads – Lola stretches an arm up towards it and laughs.

'Will you row away with me?' he asks her.

Lola smiles. 'Like *The Owl and the Pussycat*? I wish' – she sighs contentedly – 'I really wish we could . . .'

'Then let's do it.'

'Now?'

'Yes!'

She laughs.

'I'm serious.'

She blinks at him. 'Mattie—'

'I can't go back, Lola.' Suddenly his heart is

thudding, his pulse thrumming in his ears. 'You have no idea what's waiting for me back home. I don't know what to do!'

'You could go to the police. But you don't *have* to do anything if you don't want to.'

'I do!' The words explode from his lungs. 'Dammit, Lola, you don't understand. I do. Otherwise someone else could get hurt!'

She stares at him, her body very still. 'Hurt . . . Like you were, you mean?'

'Yes.'

'Then we'll go home, sweetheart. You can give the police a statement, a physical description.' She leans to look over her shoulder, and when she turns back, some of the colour has drained from her face. 'Mattie, we're too far from shore. We need to turn back.'

'Not just a description. I'd have to turn him in.'

'Shit! Mattie, I'm serious. Turn the boat round.'

'Are you listening to me? *I'd have to turn him in!*'

Lola looks back at him and freezes, her knuckles white against the sides of the boat. 'Turn who in?'

'The guy – the guy who raped me.'

'You know the guy who raped you?'

The word bursts like a sob from somewhere deep inside his chest. 'Yes!'

The clash of two opposing waves sends a cap of white spray over the gunwale, jolting them out of their momentary stupor, drenching them both.

'Turn back! Turn back!' Lola shouts. Her hands are on his, struggling against the movement of the oars, fighting to turn the boat round. But maybe it would be better for them both just to keep on rowing . . . Her face is suddenly very close and he notices how large her gold-flecked irises are, how pronounced the freckles on her cheeks. It is as if he can suddenly see everything in much more detail, as if out here, in this wild freedom, a veil has been lifted, uncovering the tiniest details of life.

'Mattie!' Lola screams in terror.

Stunned back into reality, Mathéo feels his heart skip a beat as the boat lurches to one side and he almost loses an oar. He has managed to turn the boat round but the tide is tugging them out. He has been rowing enough times in his life to know that the swirls created by the oars should be fading behind the stern of the boat, but now they are barely moving. After several minutes of strenuous rowing on the spot, the swirls began to move to the front. The boat is being pulled backwards, out to sea.

'Fuck!' His arms feel like lead. He lifts the oars out of the water for a moment to try to catch his breath. 'I can't!'

Lola moves to swap places. 'I'll try, I'll take over!'

'No . . . You can't . . . The current's too strong. Just – just give me a sec—'

'Mattie, we need to keep rowing.' Her voice is

eerily calm, but when he looks up, he sees the panic in her eyes.

'Lola, it's OK, I can do this! I'm going to get us back to shore, I promise!'

Kneeling on the floor of the boat, she covers his hands with hers, helping him row against the current. Her jaw is clenched in effort, eyes narrowed in concentration, the colour returning to her face as they struggle together against the tugging tide.

'Fucking hell!'

'Just row, Mattie. Just row. Keep the rhythm steady. We're starting to move forward now – look!'

'I wasn't thinking – I'm losing my mind—'

'You're not. Your mind is fine. And you're strong, you can do it. We've just got to—' She is cut off as another wave breaks over the stern, soaking her to the bone and throwing her to the side. When she regains her balance he sees blood trickling down from her lip.

'Lola, get down on the floor and brace yourself against the bench! Get down, now!'

She does as he says, eyes wild with fright.

'It's going to be OK!' he shouts at her desperately.

'I believe you. Save your breath. Just keep rowing!' she yells back over the shrill whine of the wind.

The wave hits with so much force that it throws him off the bench and back against the bow, knocking the air from his lungs. For a moment it is simply impossible to inhale; then his rib meets something hard, the air forced back in by the shock of pain. The boat is rolling dangerously now; Lola is doing her best to lean towards the upturned side to try to weigh it down, but water begins to splash in as the waves repeatedly smack against the stern with terrifying force. Mathéo is hit by pain and adrenalin in dizzying waves. Down on the floor, Lola is managing to brace herself against the bench and the sides, shouting encouragement up at him, sea water streaming down her face.

Mathéo can feel his whole body shaking now – whether from terror or cold or exhaustion, he cannot tell. Every few strokes he compulsively turns to look over his shoulder at the shore, wasting precious time and energy, but it has to be getting closer – it *has* to! He can just about make out Lola's shouts of encouragement over the howl of the wind and the crash of the waves. 'Keep rowing, keep breathing – you can do this! Come on – you can do this, Mattie!'

But he is slowing down, he can tell. Can no longer feel his arms, his back, his legs – his muscles all turned to pulp. As the boat continues to pitch back and forth, waves sweep over the sides, more and more water accumulating at the bottom, weighing them down. Occasionally a large wave caps off, washes over them, drenching them and leaving them gasping. The spray coming up from the water hits his face like needles, making it near-impossible to see. He is so exhausted,

347

the boat is so water-logged and they are so wet, it's as if they have already drowned. He finds himself having to fight the impulse to grab Lola and swim with her to the shore – he knows too well that abandoning the boat would be the most dangerous thing of all, but right now it feels like the only option. The muscles in his arms and shoulders scream in agony and he bites down hard. *I won't let her drown, I won't let her drown*, he repeats to himself from between gritted teeth – but what starts off as an affirmation soon becomes a frantic, pleading prayer.

The boat falls off a wave and slaps down so hard, the top of the oar makes contact with his cheekbone. The crack sends him reeling. Waves whack at his kneecaps, and as spray rains down, he is reminded of a different kind of struggle, a different battle, a different kind of pain, and his mind screams against the repellent memories . . .

A fold in time. He is slumped forward against the side of the boat, the wooden edge cutting into his neck. The oars are inside the boat, wet and glistening, and the boat seems to be moving of its own accord, buffeted gently by the waves. The howl of the wind has died down, the sky has cleared and the sun is brighter. He squints against its light and sees that Lola is wading waist deep in water, pulling the boat along by its rope. In a daze, he watches her haul herself up onto the jetty, brushing wet hair back from her face, and secure the rope around its metal loop with a thick knot.

He wills himself to move, climbing out of the boat, following Lola down the wooden path, across the beach, up the cliff path, and back to the house. There are sounds from the pool, shrieks and laughter, but Lola keeps on upstairs and, dazed, he simply follows her. Showering and pulling on a T-shirt and boxers uses up the last of his energy, and he collapses onto the edge of the bed, head in his hands.

The edge of the mattress sinks slightly and he looks up to see Lola sitting on the bed beside him, cross-legged, with a towel and what appears to be a first-aid box.

'Christ, Lola, are you OK?' He levers himself up painfully and runs his eyes over her, folding his arms tightly around his waist to stop himself shivering. Apart from a small cut on her lip, she appears relatively unharmed.

'I'm fine, Mattie, but you . . .' She winces and draws in air between her clenched teeth. 'Hold still and let me have a look at those cuts.'

'I'll live.' But Lola ignores him, soaking a cotton swab in iodine and dabbing at his cheek.

His head jerks back in reflex.

'Ouch, sweetie, I'm sorry. But you've got a nasty gash on your cheek . . .'

He tries to hold still, letting his breath out in a rush. 'Fuck, I should never have . . . I'm sorry.'

But there is no anger in her face. As she leans in close to clean the cut below his eye, he feels her breath on his cheek, sees her eyes – wide, trusting, full of concern.

He turns away from her. 'It's OK now.'

The corners of her lips twitch into a small smile. 'Will you stop being a wuss and let me clean it?'

But it's not the physical pain he objects to. Having her so near, her hand against his face, the gentle pressure of her fingertips against his temples, the soft touch of the cotton wool against his cheek . . . He feels as if he might break.

Lola stops suddenly, drawing her hand back with a look of alarm.

'It's – it's just the iodine,' he tells her quickly. 'Makes my eyes sting.'

'But I'm using water—'

'Well—' His voice quavers. 'Well, that – that stings too!'

She lowers her hand from his face and gives him a long look as he clenches his jaw and blinks back tears. Pushing the first-aid box aside, she reaches out for him. 'Come here.'

'I'm fine.' He moves to get up from the bed, but Lola tugs him gently back down.

'No, I mean come here. Come right here.'

He sinks back down onto the bed and she pulls herself across his lap. 'You know what I was thinking when we were being pulled out by the current?'

'No.'

'That if I died – that if I had to die out there, drown at sea, at least it would be with you.'

Startled, he stares into her face, into her glistening eyes. 'Goddammit, Lola! I would have never let you drown!'

Her bottom lip quivers for a second. 'For a moment I thought that maybe – maybe you wanted to—'

'*Drown?*'

'You kept talking about leaving. Never going back. You were so determined to get away! I thought maybe the rape was making you wish you – you—'

'No!' He can feel his eyes filling, hot and heavy. 'No, Lola, I don't want to die any more. I want to live – but I want to spend the rest of my life with *you*!' The tears hang heavy on his lashes, threatening to fall.

'But that's all I want too!' Gently she slides her arms around his neck. 'Come back to me, Mattie. Come back and tell me what happened. Don't push me away any more. Tell me who hurt you. Tell me, Mattie. Please, darling, please . . .'

16

He must have fallen asleep, for when he wakes, Lola is gone and the room is filled with the thick, inky light of dusk. The balcony door is still open, the net curtains dancing in the breeze. The air has turned noticeably cooler, and outside the sky has begun to darken, the last rays of golden sunset falling in sparkled shards onto the glossy, deep blue of the sea. Mathéo can hear the distant buzz of voices rising from the floor below and wonders if the others have already had dinner. He thinks he can smell pizza or bolognese, and, still fuzzy with sleep, forces himself to sit up. He is famished after the day's exertions: if they've started dinner he doesn't want to miss it. Swinging his feet onto the floor, he rubs his eyes hard with the heels of his hands and then pads into the bathroom to use the loo and splash his face with cold water. Returning to the bedroom, he locates his clothes in the half-light and pulls them on, hovering by the mirror to run his hands through his unruly hair, rub the pillow crease from his cheek. Then he heads downstairs.

It isn't until he reaches the bottom of the spiral staircase and finds them sitting on the sofas round the coffee table, plates on laps, that he realizes they have been talking about him again. He is not aware of even having heard his name, yet recognizes the look on their faces – that incriminating look of having been caught in the act. The startled expressions, the voices muted mid-sentence, the sudden, heavy silence, the atmosphere thick with the presence of embarrassment and guilt.

'We didn't hear you come down.' Hugo is the first to break the wall of silence, his tone almost accusatory.

Mathéo pauses for breath, searching for a way to hold onto the feelings of relative peace and calm he woke up with only moments before.

'Sorry, didn't realize I was supposed to knock.' He manages to keep his tone light, his response jocular, eager to give them an easy way out. A quick change of subject is all that is needed. He won't probe – Lola will fill him in later: no doubt they were still digesting yesterday's news. But that's fine, that is the past; he has put it behind him finally, and now . . . He looks towards Lola and gives her a smile.

She doesn't return it. 'It's just that we were worried . . .'

'It's my fault,' Hugo says slowly, his tone strangely low and grave. 'I suggested it first.'

'Doesn't matter.' Mathéo shrugs quickly with a forgiving smile. 'As long as you've left me some of that lasagne—'

'So you agree with us?' Hugo looks surprised.

'About what?'

'About what we were just discussing,' Hugo replies. 'Going back to London tomorrow and telling the police.'

Mathéo freezes. The stupid smile seems stuck to his face. 'What?' He can hear his heart.

'Doesn't matter. We can talk about it in the morning,' Lola says quickly, glancing rapidly round at the others.

'But if we're flying back tomorrow, we'll need to book our plane tickets tonight,' Isabel protests.

Mathéo steps back unsteadily, meets a pillar, leans on it with some relief as his knees suddenly begin to feel weak. 'What do you mean? Why do we have to go home tomorrow?' Breath quickening, he searches for Lola's gaze but she refuses to meet his eyes, turning anxiously to look at Hugo for guidance instead.

Hugo stands up slowly. 'Matt, listen. Lola told us you know the person who – who assaulted you. This is really serious. If you won't tell us, then at least tell the police or your parents. Unless it was—' He breaks off for a moment, and Mathéo watches the horror

dawn on his friend's face. 'Unless it was your own –
oh, shit . . .'

'I don't – it wasn't—' Mathéo fills his lungs in an
attempt to steady his voice, but he is breathing too
fast, the air shuddering in his chest, making him
shake. 'It's gone, it's in the past, it's done with, Hugo.
I'm not talking to the police or anyone else!'

'But, Matt, for God's sake, man, you can't just let
this go! There's a fucking predator out there and you
know who he is!'

Lola jumps up, reaches towards Hugo. 'Please let's
not argue – we can talk about this rationally—'

'You don't think I know that!' Mathéo hears himself shout. 'You don't think that every waking second
I'm living in fear that this psycho, this – this predator
– might strike again?'

'Then for God's sake, do something about it!'

Lola is tugging at Hugo's arm. 'Come on, don't. We
agreed we'd all talk to him about this calmly.'

Mathéo feels the sweat break out across his back.
Suddenly, even the pillar supporting him doesn't feel
altogether solid. 'You – you . . .' He stares at Lola,
struggling to catch his breath. 'You agreed with him?
You planned to force me to go to the police too?'

Guilt washes across her face. 'Not *force*, Mattie.
But it's – it's – you said yourself it's what you had
to do!'

'I said I didn't know *what* to do! I thought you said

you'd support me whatever I chose. I thought you understood, I thought you were on my side!'

All three of them are standing together now, ganging up against him. Three against one. His Lola, his darling, amongst them.

She breaks away, moves towards him. 'Mattie, it's not like that! It's not about taking sides!'

Somehow, before she can reach him, he manages to move. Across the room and down the hallway and out of the front door. Through the garden, over the grass, right out to the cliff edge, and down the slippery, stumbling, uneven steps in the rock face – down, down, down towards the sea.

The tide is so far out it's barely visible. Miles of darkened sand seem to stretch ahead of him, striated with beams of orange and gold from the setting sun. At first he is running, but this morning's rowing has weakened him, and soon he is forced to slow to a stride, the muscles in his legs shaking with exhaustion.

'Mattie, where are you going? Mattie, wait for chrissakes!' He can hear the slap of Lola's sandals on the hard sand behind him, hear her panting breath, hear the panic in her voice. 'Mattie, wait for me, please. Just listen to me for a second!'

He feels her hand attempt to grasp his, but lengthens his stride. 'You were talking to them about it? You were agreeing with Hugo's shit?'

'Only because I'm worried about you!'

'Hugo doesn't know fuck about anything! He has no idea! No idea at all!'

'But he cares about you. And he's right, sweetheart! We *do* need to go home, we can't hide out here for ever! What happened to you was terrible – you need to tell your parents for a start. And Mattie, you said you know this guy so you've *got* to report him to the police.'

Lengthening his stride, he turns just enough to see her running, hair blowing across her face, cheeks flushed with exertion, eyes glistening with tears.

'Oh my God! You don't understand! Go to the police? It would be a disaster – a fucking disaster, Lola!'

'You wouldn't have to go through some dreadful court case. You are perfectly entitled to go to the police, say you don't want to prosecute, but just give them a name—'

'I'm not going to the police!'

'Then just put it in a letter. If he was waiting for you outside the Aquatic Centre there'll have been other people about – spectators and staff who can corroborate your story.'

'You're not listening to me! I'm never going to the police! I told you that right at the start – how can you turn against me now?'

Lola slows to a fast walk as the gap between them

closes. He can make out the determination in her face, the rise and fall of her chest, the small puffs of exertion as she works to keep up. 'You wouldn't even have to be directly involved! Write it anonymously and I'll hand it in for you! What the police do with him then is up to them, but at least you'll have done *something* to try to stop him from abusing someone again!'

'Why won't you listen to me? I don't *want* to do anything!'

'But sweetheart, don't you see? Hugo is right about one thing – this guy will attack again; maybe he already has! By doing nothing you are letting the sicko go free! You've been through hell already! How could you have that on your conscience?'

The line of the sea is gradually approaching, the shimmering white wavelets reaching out further with each exhalation, the water reflecting the light like glass, stunning in the evening sun. He will keep walking – keep walking until he reaches them, splash through the delicate veils of lace until they get deeper, covering his sandals, his ankles, soaking up the bottom of his jeans. He will keep wading until the weight of the water pulls him down, sucks him beneath the surface, wraps him up in the rising tide.

'On my conscience? On my conscience? Do you have even the faintest idea of what I have on my conscience?' He whips round to face her, walking backwards, sandals splashing in the shallows. 'I am dying here, Lola!' he hears himself yell. 'I'm dying inside. I wish I was dead!' He feels the punch of his fist against his own stomach. 'I wish he'd fucking killed me!'

'But – but why?'

'Because I can't tell. Not the police, not anyone! And by not telling, then yes, I'm fully aware I'll have to live with that on my conscience – the fact that he will most likely continue to – to abuse.' The wavelets wash against his feet, lapping against his sandals, working their way up the legs of his jeans. He turns round to see that Lola has stopped several metres back, still on dry sand, hugging herself against the wind.

'But Mattie, you're not making any sense! If you feel that way, why can't you just give a statement, or simply his name?'

'Because, Lola, that man – that man has a family! A family which will be ripped apart, destroyed, torn to shreds!'

They are both having to shout to be heard now, the wind out here so powerful it tugs at their hair, their clothes, almost threatens to knock them over. Behind him he is aware of the rising waves – the semblance of calm from a distance revealing itself as choppy sea and blustering air.

'Who the hell is it?' Lola shouts.

'I can't – I can't tell!'

'If he has a family, then all the more reason to tell! His kids could be in danger themselves!'

'That's why—' Gritting his teeth, he runs his hands frantically through his hair, ready to pull it out. 'That's why I don't know what the fuck to do!'

He chokes on a sob and stumbles backwards, the water was now almost reaching his knees. He thought it was going to be OK. She let him think he'd got away with it, buried it in the past. She allowed him to think he was safe – safe from ever having to tell, from ever having to live through it again. He puts his face in his hands. Between the cracks in his fingers he watches as, in the glory of the evening light, Lola approaches him tentatively, brow puckered with concern. 'Mattie, sweetheart, please don't cry. This pervert's family is the least of your concerns.'

Slowly, painfully, he lifts his face from his hands, cheeks wet with tears, shaking hard. 'Lola, oh God! It's the greatest concern – the greatest concern of all!'

'What?' She wades through the shallows to reach him, takes his hand softly in hers, pulls him gently back onto dry land. 'I don't understand, sweetheart. What on earth do you mean?'

Mathéo stares at her through the kaleidoscope of light refracting through the tears in his eyes and realizes that this is it. This is actually going to happen. There is no turning back, no running away; he has run out of options, of excuses, he has no choice now.

Perhaps he never did. Perhaps, after that horrendous night, every path available to him was always going to lead to this crucial, horrific point in time. One he wrestled and fought to escape without ever realizing that all along, it was totally out of his control. After that night there was never really any going back. The die was cast and, with the throw, this moment in time set by default on the trajectory of his new life. Unavoidable. Inescapable. Postponable for a time, but only until now. He bows his head and feels the acute pain of something breaking inside him – something permanent, something he knows will never, ever mend.

He lifts his head and looks into her eyes. Her gentle, loving, trusting eyes. Eyes that never once imagined him ripping her life apart, shattering her existence, hurting her beyond repair. He takes a breath and feels his world end. Feels *her* world end. Feels their love – their warm, passionate, all-consuming love – hover between them for one last moment, before being brutally snatched away. He stifles a sob of despair.

'*Because, Lola, his family is you.*'

17

She remains horrifyingly still for several seconds, her expression unchanged, as if frozen in time. Then slowly, very slowly, she starts to back away.

Mathéo stumbles towards her, his jeans weighed down with sea water, shivering hard.

'Dad? My – my dad? You're – you're saying *my dad* raped you?' Her face is so white, so bleached with shock, he fears she might faint.

He takes a tentative step closer. 'Lola, I swear, I will never tell anyone. But you were right, I had to tell you. You had to know, just in case he ever tried anything – did anything to you. I thought he must have to be gay, but now I just don't know, I don't understand—'

She lets out a small sound like a trapped animal and, wincing, takes another step back, beginning to heave, as if about to throw up. 'You're – you're claiming my dad's a – a rapist? A – a gay rapist?'

He stands there, witnessing her shock, feeling it permeate his own skin. 'Lola, I wish— Oh God, I'm so sorry!'

'You're sick!'

'Lola, listen—'

'How could you even think such a thing!' Clutching her stomach as if shot, she backs away still further, staring at him as if he were metamorphosing into some hideous kind of monster.

'No. Lola, listen to me. It's true. I would never lie about something like this. Lola, you *know* me!'

'Oh God, you've gone crazy! You're – you're traumatized, you're sick!'

He moves forward, reaching out for her, but she instantly shrinks back. 'Lola, I saw him, as clearly as I see you now. There was never any doubt. He didn't even try to hide his face—'

'No!' she screams suddenly, her voice louder than the gulls: a shrill, sharp shriek of despair. 'Stop it, stop it, shut up right now! You've gone crazy, Mattie! Whatever happened, it's fucked up your whole mind!'

'Lola, I'm not crazy. It happened. It was Jerry. You have to know because you can't go back home. I don't know if he was on drugs or ill or – or has some condition, or what. But I do know he's dangerous—'

'No! This isn't you, this can't be you talking! Take it back, Mattie. Tell me – oh please God, this can't be

363

happening. You can't have gone crazy. Please, Mattie
. . . please tell me you're just messing around!'

'Lola, I can't. Because I'm not. And you have to
know. You can't go back there, it's not safe!'

'Mattie . . .' She has begun to sob, bending forward
and hugging herself as if in agony. 'Why would you do
this? Why would you say something like this? Why,
Mattie? Why? Why?' She is screaming now, white-
faced and petrified, tears coursing down her cheeks.
'Do you hate me? Do you hate Dad? What the fuck
are you trying to do to us?'

'I hate your dad for what he did to me. But not *you*,
Lola. Never you! I love you – you know that!' He tries
to move towards her, arm outstretched, but she continues to back away, like a wild animal poised to flee.

'Then why are you doing this?' she screams.

'I had to tell you – you were going to go to the
police! They would interrogate me. Obviously I'd
have lied, but they're trained to see through bullshit
and my lies would immediately make them suspect I
was covering for someone I knew! They would
interrogate people close to me, including Jerry;
including Perez, who saw me go off with Jerry that
night. They would probably even find other witnesses
who saw Jerry in the area that evening . . . Don't you
understand, Lola? If I hadn't told you and you'd gone
to the police, your dad would have ended up in
prison!'

364

'But it's all a lie!'

'It's not a lie, Lola. I wish, I wish it was! You have no idea how much I wish—'

'Look at me, then!' she screams. 'Look me in the eyes and tell me my father raped you!'

He holds her gaze. 'Your father raped me, Lola—' His voice breaks as her expression distorts into one of disgust and she backs away from him still further. How did he ever think, for one insane moment, that he could tell Lola the truth and not lose her? Even if the near-impossible happened, if she confronted Jerry and he confessed, how could she ever forgive *him*, Mathéo, for destroying the most important relationship in her life? That one person who had cared for her since she was a baby, had been by her side all these years, had fed her, brought her up, looked out for her, become her confidant, her best friend?

'You know my dad would never hurt a fly!' Lola shouts. 'You know him! He loves you! He's always been nice to you! How *could* you!' She is crying so hard, she appears unable to draw breath; her lips are tinged violet. Tears course down her cheeks, dripping onto the jacket she hugs ever tighter round herself, as if it is a shield to protect her against his words. 'And what about me? I trusted you. I *loved* you!'

'Lola, I love you too!' he shouts, his voice splintering. 'That's the only reason I'm telling you! I've been agonizing over this ever since it happened, but you finally made me realize – I couldn't risk you getting hurt by my silence!'

'You didn't want me to get hurt?' she yells back, sobbing wildly into the rising wind. 'You've just destroyed everything between us, Mattie! You've just said the most hateful, disgusting, filthy thing anyone could possibly think of!'

'But it's true! Lola, you've got to believe me. You can't go back, you mustn't confront him – it could be dangerous!'

She stares at him, utterly aghast. 'Of course I'm not going to confront him! Did you think for one second I'd ever consider these vile accusations? That I'd believe you before my own father?'

Fear, like an electric bolt, streaks through his veins. 'Lola, no, you mustn't go back! I'll look after you, I'll protect you, I'll do anything to keep you safe, I *swear*!'

'D'you think I'm stupid? I never want to see you again, Mattie! I can never forgive you! Oh God, oh God—' She doubles forward suddenly, retching. When she straightens up, her face has taken on a ghostly, translucent look, as if she might suddenly disappear. 'I just don't understand . . .' she half whispers. 'Why would you do this? I trusted you. I trusted you more than anyone, Mattie!' Her slim frame racked with sobs so violent they threaten to break her, she presses a fist to her mouth, turns and begins to move away.

He immediately follows her, tries to reach out for her.

'*Don't touch me!*' She spins round and screams, a sharp cry of terror.

'Lola, please!' he shouts at her, tears choking him. 'Don't go! Don't leave me! I never meant – I'll take it back, I'll take it all back—'

'You can't!' she screams. 'Don't you see, Mathéo? Don't you realize what you've done? You've accused my dad of the most horrific crime imaginable! How can you ever take that back? How can you ever make up for that? And you believe it – look at you! You *still* believe it!'

'I believe in you, Lola! I believe in us! That's all I care about—'

'There *is* no us! There never was. Everything we had between us was a lie! You believed my dad was a rapist while – while making love to me? While pretending to love me?'

'I never pretended, Lola. I swear on my life! I loved you from the moment we first met!'

She takes a deep, shuddering breath, pausing for a moment in her retreat. 'How can that possibly be true?' she asks more quietly now, her voice shaking with barely suppressed fury and pain. 'If for some crazy reason you actually believe my dad raped you,

you wouldn't love me! How could anyone possibly love the daughter of a rapist – their rapist, their rapist's own flesh and blood?'

'Because you're not your father!'

'He's my family! He's my life! He created me, he brought me up, I share his genes – I'm a *part* of him!'

'That doesn't make you the same person!'

'I am his daughter! If you're deluded enough to believe he's a rapist, do you believe he's raped others?'

'Oh God, Lola. I don't know, but he could do it again! And I know you're his daughter and he loves you, but there's always the risk that he might do something – do something to you! Don't you see, I *had* to warn you!'

She appears to stop breathing for a moment, then heaves in a lungful of air and lets out a swift, sharp cry.

'Lola, I can help you through this. You've got to believe me. Whatever you father did, I love you just as much as before!'

'Love?' Lola screams. 'You call this love? It was all a lie – every second of it, every shared moment, every time I ever touched you. *I hate you, Mathéo!*'

'Lola, don't, please!' He heaves for breath, blinded by tears. 'You don't mean that.'

'I do! I swear on my life. I wish I'd never met you. I wish you were *dead*!' She sounds almost hysterical, as if being beaten, and continues stumbling back, further and further away from him, close to collapse.

'No!' he yells at her. 'You don't mean that. You don't mean that, Lola. You don't, you don't!'

'I do! I wish you'd killed yourself diving off that cliff. I wish you were dead, Mathéo Walsh! I wish you were dead, I wish you were dead!'

The pure, undiluted hatred in her voice hits him in the chest like a bullet. 'No!'

Lola stands still and presses her hands to her face. A long moment passes. Neither of them has the strength to speak. Then Lola lowers her hands and takes several long, steadying breaths. 'I'm going to pack and take the first flight home,' she says, her voice trembling with shock and exhaustion. 'I'll be quick, but don't come back to the house until I've gone.'

'No—'

'I mean it, Mathéo. If you follow me back to the house, I'll tell Hugo and call the police. I swear.'

He shakes his head. 'No,' he tries to say again, but this time no sound comes out. Tears spill down his cheeks. He feels as if he is choking. He feels as if he is drowning.

She takes another step back, seems to hesitate, then a brutal sob shakes her whole body. 'Goodbye, Mattie.'

He tries to follow her, but can't seem to move. She is gone, running across the beach, back towards the house, swallowed up by the gathering gloom.

The strength leaves his legs completely and he

drops to his knees on the wet sand, a puppet with its strings cut loose, useless, crumpled. 'Lola!' he hears himself yell. 'Lola!'

As she disappears over the cliff-top, he slowly falls forward and begins to cry – harsh, ugly sobs ripping through his body, making him retch and heave. *You should have killed me, Jerry. You should have killed me. I would rather have died . . .*

By the time he leaves the Brighton Aquatic Centre after the awards ceremony and all the press interviews, it is already dark. Perez and the rest of the team are heading for pizza up the road but, exhausted after the intensity of the competition, Mathéo declines their invitation, looking forward instead to getting back to the hotel and calling Lola to tell her the good news. As he waves goodbye to Perez and the others however, he is stopped in his tracks by the sight of a man pacing up and down, looking around anxiously.

'Jerry?' Mathéo feels his face break into a smile. 'Jerry! What are you doing here? I thought you couldn't come! Oh wow, this is such a great surprise! Where's Lola?'

But Jerry barely raises his head. 'Something's happened. I need your help.'

He sets off down the road so fast that Mathéo, shocked into action, has to break into a jog to keep up. 'What's happened?' he asks breathlessly, too stunned to think straight. 'Is Lola OK?'

'No. She slipped and fell.'

Fear courses through him as Jerry leads him down a side street, across a main road, then abruptly veers off between a gap in the trees and into the woods flanking the pavement. It is almost pitch black and they are both running now.

'Is it serious?' Mathéo gasps, momentarily imagining Lola unconscious, confused as to why Jerry would leave her side. 'Did you call an ambulance? Is it on its way?' But Jerry doesn't reply.

After a few minutes they reach a clearing of rough shrubbery and dry, uneven ground. Jerry stops and turns round, and by the light of the moon, Mathéo sees his expression change. He looks . . . He looks almost excited.

'Where's — where's Lola?' Mathéo asks, his voice suddenly unsteady. There is something strange about Jerry — he appears tense and on edge; his expression is not one that Mathéo recognizes. He isn't smiling, for a start; he appears to be grinding his teeth and his face glistens with sweat.

'Jerry, are you OK?' Mathéo takes a step towards him, and suddenly Jerry reaches out, resting his hand on Mathéo's shoulder, making him jump.

'Lola's in London, at the school ball. I told her I was working tonight so it could be just you and me for a change. Finally!' He is smiling. 'You dived really well today, Mattie. I'm so proud of you.'

Mathéo opens his mouth in reply but finds himself unable to utter a sound. Is Jerry drunk?

'Uh — thanks.' With an awkward smile, he begins to move away, searching for the lights of cars from the road in the distance. 'But if Lola's not here, then what are we doing in the woods?'

'I wanted to talk to you in private. Why the sudden rush?' Jerry takes a step closer — so close in fact that Mathéo can feel wet breath on his cheek, recognize the smell of stale sweat mixed with weed.

Jerry's hand leaves Mathéo's shoulder, sliding up his neck and cupping his cheek. 'I brought you here so we could be alone. So I could congratulate you.'

Startled, Mathéo takes a step back, knocking Jerry's hand away from his face. What the hell is the guy doing? Has Jerry gone mad?

'Hey now . . .' Jerry says softly, moving towards Mathéo and grabbing him by the wrist. 'I just want to give my favourite young man a hug for a job well done!'

Mathéo can hear the sound of his own breathing, shallow and unsteady, in the silence of the wood. His heart is knocking wildly against his ribcage like an animal trying to escape. 'Jerry, I think you may have had a bit too much to drink or − or smoke—' He lets out a startled gasp as Jerry pulls him into a fierce hug.

'Jerry!'

'What, I can't give my favourite guy a congratulatory hug?' Jerry asks, his arms wrapped tightly around Mathéo's torso. But as Mathéo gives him a quick pat on the back and tries to step back, Jerry's grip only tightens. 'Easy, Mattie. What's the rush? We've both been waiting for a moment to ourselves like this for so long.'

'I − I really don't know what you're talking about,' Mathéo gasps raggedly, trying to push Jerry away. 'Just − please let go of me. I think you're drunk—'

'Now come on, stop deluding yourself. I've spotted all your little signs,' Jerry continues in the same syrupy voice. 'Ever since we met you've been using my daughter as a reason to come round to see me, hang out with me, always staying as long as possible. Trying to spend as much time as you can on your own with me, having those private chats with me in the music shed . . .' He turns his head so

372

that his face is pressing against Mathéo's ear, into Mathéo's neck.

'Get the fuck off me!' What began as shock quickly changes to a burst of terrified adrenalin, and Mathéo tries to wrestle himself out of Jerry's vice-like embrace. 'You're — you're crazy! I come round to see Lola. I'm not — I've never been—'

'Hey, no need to be shy.' Jerry is beginning to pant now, struggling to keep hold of Mathéo. 'It's normal to want to experiment in your teens. And because I'm older, I can show you things, teach you—'

'Fucking pervert!' Mathéo shouts furiously. He tries to knee Jerry in the groin but catches the top of his leg instead, though hard enough to send him staggering back.

Then something snaps in Jerry's expression, and as Mathéo turns to run, he launches himself at him, grabbing Mathéo by the throat and slamming him back against the nearest tree with brutal force.

It takes Mathéo a moment to react. But when he does, all he can manage is to loosen Jerry's hand on his windpipe so that he can breathe.

'Oh, I see, you like it rough.' Jerry's face contorts into a strange smile. 'Playing hard to get turns you on, does it?'

'You're a fucking psycho!' Mathéo manages to gasp. Then, sucking in a lungful of air, he starts to yell.

Jerry smacks a hand down over Mathéo's mouth, and suddenly his smile is gone. 'Oh no you don't,' he begins, his voice shaking with suppressed anger. 'Lead me on for nearly two years and then just decide to change your mind? Make me out to be the bad guy?'

'I never—' Mathéo tries to reply from beneath Jerry's tobacco-stained fingers. 'I wasn't leading you—'

'Listen carefully,' Jerry says quietly, his face so close to Mathéo's that he can feel his damp breath on his cheek. 'I have a knife.' One hand still pressed against Mathéo's windpipe, he lowers the other from Mathéo's mouth, reaches into his jacket pocket and flicks open a switchblade. 'If you make any noise, or try to run or decide to play the innocent little victim, I will kill you, do you understand?'

Mathéo tries to respond, but Jerry's grip on his neck is too tight and he is running out of oxygen. Black spots dance before his eyes. He manages to nod.

'Good.' Jerry releases his grip slightly; brings the knife to the level of Mathéo's throat. 'Now get undressed.'

Gasping for air, Mathéo finds himself pinned between the knife and the tree. He tries to move sideways and feels the blade split the skin on his neck.

He freezes and finds himself babbling. 'Jerry, I'm sorry, it was my mistake. I never meant to— But look, we can work this out, I'll pay you as much as you want. I've got my credit card. You can have it. I'll give you my PIN. Or you can take me to a cash machine—'

'Shut up. You know I don't want your money. Get undressed or, I swear, I'll stab you right here, right now.'

'But – but why?' He feels sure this can't be happening. He is trapped in a nightmare. He just needs to wake up. 'Jerry, it's me, Matt. I'm your daughter's boyfriend. Why – why are you doing this?'

Grabbing the collar of his T-shirt, Jerry slashes at it with the knife. Mathéo hears himself shout, expecting to be stabbed. But there is no pain — just the cotton splitting apart and falling loosely to the ground around his ankles. Jerry still has his hand against his neck, pinning him to the tree. Now, the tip of the knife is pressed against his chest, right over his heart.

'You want to — to — to rape me?' Mathéo can hardly believe he is saying the words. Barely recognizes the sound of his own voice, so faltering and shaky.

'Take off your jeans.'

He finds himself beginning to beg. 'Jerry, listen to me — you know me. You don't want to do this. I never meant to — to lead you on. I — I really like you, but just not in this kind of way. Don't do this. Please. I'll do other stuff. I don't mind what. Just d-don't—'

The knife begins to cut his skin, and this time Jerry shouts. 'Shut up and get undressed! I won't tell you again!'

'No!' Mathéo suddenly finds himself yelling back. 'You're crazy! I'm not going to do this!' He hits Jerry's arm with all his might, and for a moment the blade is no longer pressed against him, and the struggle begins. Mathéo grabs hold of Jerry's arm and, with both hands, wrenches it backwards. The knife drops to the ground. But before he can reach it, Jerry kicks him in the stomach, and as Mathéo doubles over, knees him in the mouth. Mathéo falls back for a moment, but as Jerry lunges again, he manages to block the blow and deals Jerry one to the chest, another to his shoulder, another to his face. He feels his knuckles meet bone. There is a crack and a roar of pain, a splattering of blood from Jerry's nose, and suddenly he is stumbling back.

Mathéo starts to run. Makes it out of the clearing. Dodges trees, trips over the undergrowth. The road, the road . . . Is he even going the right way? Disorientated, he loses concentration for a moment and the toe of his shoe hits a small rock. He falls hard. Jerry is on top of him in a moment, grabbing him by the shoulders and bashing his head repeatedly on the ground. He's going to kill me, Mathéo thinks. He's going to kill me. I'm going to die, right here, out in the woods. And Lola will never know. She'll never know that her father is a – a . . . Darkness engulfs him.

He comes round to find himself lying on his front with his arms pinned behind his back. When he tries to move them, pain shoots down from his shoulders and he can feel the bones in his wrists grinding together, bound by something so tight, it is cutting into his flesh. Jerry rolls him onto his back and Mathéo kicks out at him, but he is too weak and barely grazes his thigh. Before he can try again, Jerry crouches down, the full weight of his body on his knee, pressed against Mathéo's chest, crushing it, so that Mathéo can barely inhale enough oxygen to keep from passing out again. As Jerry leans down and presses the knife against Mathéo's neck, he feels a warm trickle of blood.

'This is your last chance or I swear I'll kill you,' Jerry says, and it's at that point that Mathéo notices there is something wrong with Jerry's eyes. The pupils are dilated, huge, turning his irises black. Mathéo realizes he is high. On what, he has no idea, but he realizes that in this state, this man is capable of anything. Even murder. If he is to survive this ordeal, Mathéo realizes suddenly, if he is to stand any chance of surviving at all, he needs to comply and, in doing so, somehow remind the man that he is human, that he is just *a teen, a teen who will be too ashamed to tell, who doesn't need to be killed . . .*

Looking down, Mathéo can make out the red pressure stain on his chest, the way his ribs stick out as he sucks his stomach in, his skin pale and white in the light of the moon as he clenches every one of his muscles. Jerry slides his hand down Mathéo's stomach, beneath his jeans and the waistband of his boxers. Mathéo coughs to repress a scream and shuts his eyes tight as he feels Jerry's cold, rough hand close around his penis.

With one hand he is stroking him, squeezing him, massaging him, with the other he is fumbling with Mathéo's belt, the buttons on his jeans. After a few minutes he seems to get frustrated and stands up, yanking off Mathéo's shoes, then dragging down his trousers and ripping open his boxers. Mathéo keeps his eyes closed. What doesn't kill you makes you stronger, *he says to himself, and almost wants to laugh. Whoever invented that motto had clearly never been sexually assaulted. He fights to keep his mind elsewhere, occupied, as far away as he can from his body.* What doesn't kill you makes you stronger. *What song was that? Who was it by? He tries to remember the tune, the lyrics – he remembers playing it at full volume on his iPod after over-rotating his first dive. He has a whole playlist devoted to picking himself up in competition after a dropped dive. He needs it now. Surely he can remember . . .*

Jerry grabs him by the hair and shoulders, and rolls him over onto his front. Mathéo tries to concentrate on the sharp rocks and pebbles cutting into his shins, his hips, his ribs, as a crushing weight descends over him. Jerry is on top of him, his belt buckle cutting into the small of his back. He is still dressed but his trousers are undone — Mathéo can feel something hard and prickly pressing against his left buttock — warm and wet too. Jerry is gasping, rubbing himself against Mathéo's backside. Then, what begins as pressure turns rapidly into mind-numbing pain. Jerry is forcing his way inside him. Mathéo feels something tear and hears himself scream.

As Jerry continues to pump against him, Mathéo escapes into his mind. Waiting there he finds memories, snapshots of the people he cares about. Lola, Loïc, Mum, Dad, Hugo, Isabel. He remembers the first day of summer, the four of them chilling out in the park, Lola squealing as they swung her over the edge of the pond, threatening to let go. Threatening … OK, maybe that wasn't so nice. What else, what else? Playing cards in the grass, Lola's head on his lap. Yes, that's good. The freckles across her cheekbones brought out by the sun. Her green eyes squinting up at him against the light. She is saying something, but he can't hear her. Jerry's grunts fill the air. The pain is of a kind he has never experienced before — he's going to pass out, he's going to die. Concentrate harder, for God's sake! Lola, laughing. The sound of her laughter, the way her nose crinkles and her eyes shine. Why is she laughing? He must remember. It is imperative. Keep laughing, Lola, he tells her. Keep laughing and I'll remember.

And then, all of a sudden, it is over. The weight is lifted and Jerry is getting to his feet. He is zipping up his trousers and bending down to brush the dirt from his knees.

'You're not going to breathe a word of this to anyone, ever, are you, Mattie? Because you know you wanted it, you've been wanting it for ages.'

Mathéo tries to reply but can't get his voice to work.

'Answer me, dammit!'

'No — no of course not.' His voice is shaking, tearful. He sounds like a child.

'You'll never see Lola again if you do.'

'I — I know — I won't, I swear.'

'And you enjoyed it, right?'

'Yes — yes, I did.' Tears are rapidly filling his eyes.

'Tell anyone and I'll put you in a hole in the ground. And your kid brother? Pretty little boy, just like you . . .'

'Jerry, I'm n-never going to tell. I'd be t-too ashamed anyway. I'd never — please. I'll pretend it never happened. I swear, Jerry. I swear.'

Jerry wipes the sweat from his brow and starts to smile again. 'Then it'll be our little secret.'

'Yes — yes. Exactly.'

Jerry bends down to cut the rope binding Mathéo's wrists with his knife. Then, with his foot, he rolls him over.

He gives a short laugh, staring down at Mathéo's naked body. 'Come on, get dressed then, Mattie,' he says. 'Make damn sure you don't leave anything behind now!' He sounds almost cheerful.

'Yes. Yes, of course . . .'

And then Jerry is gone, striding off into the woods and vanishing into the darkness.

18

'But you must have had some sort of fight! What the hell did you say to her to make her take off like that?' Hugo is pacing between the seats of the near-empty airport lounge, mobile in hand. He has been trying to reach Lola ever since she left the villa by cab nearly five hours ago. Montpellier is only a small airport, and after quizzing several members of the check-in personnel, Hugo managed to find out that Lola had boarded the last flight of the day back to London. She must be almost home by now, leaving the three of them stuck here with their hastily packed bags, waiting for the next flight at dawn.

Mathéo isn't talking, and both Hugo and Isabel are getting increasingly frustrated. He wishes he could at least fob them off with the excuse of some argument gone wrong – but his brain cannot find the sentences, his mouth cannot form the words. It should have been easy enough to make up a reason, but since dragging himself back to the house he appears to be in some kind of trance: every movement has to be carefully orchestrated – his body no longer appears capable of moving of its own accord. Sitting at the very end of a row of metal chairs, his rucksack slumped between his feet, he stares out through the glass wall at the rain-soaked runway, glistening with artificial lights. A large plane taxis slowly into position, the roar of engines filling the air. He watches it set off and quickly gather speed, racing down the runway until it appears to be flying on the ground, then slowly lift off, its front wheels leaving the tarmac. And just like that it is in the air, rising and shrinking, an exotic silver bird, disappearing into the night. He can still hear its rumbling echoes, just as he can still hear Lola's anguished cry, and his mind – now almost running on empty – tries to catch up with her in thought. She must have reached home by now, must have called Jerry to come pick her up from Heathrow, and he will have asked, will have instantly sensed her distress, however much she tried to conceal it. She will have told him, blurted it out in her state of shock, hurt and anger, and so Jerry will know. He won't risk hanging around to see if Mathéo actually does go to the police or not – he will surely hastily pack some bags, lock up the house which they were only renting anyway, and drive off with Lola, perhaps under the pretext that he doesn't want Mathéo anywhere near her again. But he will run, of that Mathéo feels certain. And Lola will vanish with him.

His pulse accelerates at the thought, the unbearable thought of never seeing Lola again. It makes him dizzy: the bright lights of the airport lounge begin to bleed around the edges, spinning and blurring like a Ferris wheel. He can hear his breath, shallow and shaky, and so he closes his eyes, tries to calm his pounding heart.

'Jeez, what's wrong with you?' Hugo's voice is too loud, too raw, magnified by the almost empty lounge and his own confusion. 'Are you sick?'

Mathéo forces himself to open his eyes, look across at Hugo and Isabel, sprawled out in the seats opposite.

'No.' But his voice is just a whisper, unheard. He shakes his head instead.

'Well then, why won't you try calling her?' Hugo asks him, his tone accusatory. 'Not necessarily to apologize for whatever the hell happened, but just to make sure she's OK!'

Mathéo forces his eyes to meet his friend's. And shakes his head again.

'Oh, for fuck sake!' Hugo sighs loudly in exasperation. 'This is nuts. It was meant to be an awesome holiday! I'm gonna get some coffee.'

Out of the corner of his eye, Mathéo sees Hugo get

up and leave the seating area. Then, moments later, he is aware of Isabel coming over to sit beside him.

'Mattie?' She is looking down at his hands, twisting and pulling against each other in an attempt to disguise the shaking. He takes a deep breath and lets it out slowly, eyes fixed on the lounge's grey carpet.

'Listen. Two members of staff confirmed that she was on that last flight, so we can be sure she's back in London. You know how close she is to her dad, so I'm sure she'll have called him and he'll have taken her back home. They probably aren't answering the phone because they're having a long talk and don't want to be disturbed. I'm sure she just needs some time to cool off, and then you can go over and apologize or sort things out or whatever.' A pause, and he is aware of Isabel's hands covering his, attempting to hold them still. 'It's going to be fine, Mattie. Lola rarely loses her temper, but when she does, she gets over it really quickly, and you know she's very forgiving. I'm sure this will all blow over in a couple of days.'

The sudden, unexpected show of concern throws him. He swallows, unable to meet her gaze, clenching his hands together as hard as he can.

'Jesus, you're really shaking!' Isabel sounds genuinely concerned. 'I'm sure Lola's got home all right.'

'I – I know.' He pulls his hands out from beneath

hers and folds his arms across his chest, hugging himself tightly as the trembling spreads throughout his muscles and he finds himself barely perceptibly rocking back and forth. 'I'm just – I'm just a bit worried we won't get through this—' His voice cracks on the last word and he turns it into a cough, staring hard at the ground and trying not to blink. He sucks in his breath and holds it as his eyes begin to brim, and suddenly finds himself terrified he will burst into tears.

'That's ridiculous. It's just a road bump. I know you two will get over it,' Isabel says gently. 'You've been through this – this horrendous thing, and I know for a fact that Lola's worried sick about you. She keeps asking us what she should do to help you, and she's been borrowing my laptop every day since we arrived, looking up stuff about people who have – you know – gone through the same thing as you, to see how they got over it and how it affected them after. She's been looking into different types of counselling, she's anonymously joined this online support group and she's even ordered a bunch of books off Amazon! I saw it all in her browsing history, so don't tell her I said anything. But seriously, you're all she talks about at the moment, and she keeps saying she can't bear to see you hurting so bad. She thinks it was somehow her fault you felt you couldn't confide in her right away, and she told me herself she feels so, so guilty she wasn't with you that weekend—' Turning to gauge his reaction, she abruptly breaks off, her expression changing to one of alarm and palpable unease. 'Mattie!'

He wants to go and lock himself in a toilet cubicle but can't even seem to move. Instead, he finds himself hunched over, elbows on his knees, staring down at the floor and rubbing the side of his face in an attempt to shield his face from view.

'Damn, I don't have a tissue . . . Mattie – shit – I didn't mean to make it worse, I just wanted to make sure you knew how crazy in love with you she is, and how much she hates to see you suffering! Fuck, shall I go and get Hugo?'

He manages to shake his head and a small sound escapes him as the air bursts from his lungs and is sucked back in again. His face is burning but the tears are even hotter, scalding as they track silently down his cheeks before he has time to wipe each one away. The touch of Isabel's hand running up and down between his shoulder-blades makes him shrink back and forces words to the surface.

'No, don't – I'm – I'm all right, I'm just so tired!' He rubs the heels of his hands up and down his cheeks, his heart thudding with embarrassment, fighting to get a grip.

'I know,' Isabel says awkwardly. 'Rows are really draining, and you're worried about Lola so it's normal to be upset. But I know Lola: I know how much she loves you and how happy you make her and I don't think there is anything that could ever change that!'

He tries to cough to muffle a sob and lurches to his feet, pointing at the TOILETS sign at the far end of the lounge; Isabel calls out after him as he heads blindly towards it. But thankfully the men's is empty, and in front of the washbasins he catches sight of his flushed, tear-stained face and slams his fist against a metal tap, the cracking pain in his fingers strong enough to shock him into getting a grip. He spends the next few minutes splashing his face with cold water and concentrating on the pain in his hand until he is exhausted.

Returning to the seating area, he hovers by the window, keeping his distance. In the glass reflection he recognizes Hugo's blurred shape, returning with a tray of paper mugs. He sees Isabel get up to meet him, stop him a few metres away and lean in to talk to him in hushed tones, occasionally glancing over at Mathéo. And after a moment's hesitation the two of them retreat to the far row of seats, clearly keeping a respectful distance.

Mathéo concentrates on a plane coming in to land, pressing Isabel's revelations about Lola into the furthest recesses of his mind. It appears to hover for ever, motionless in the night sky, and for a fleeting moment it seems to Mathéo as if time itself is suspended. He feels on the brink of something huge, and realizes that his life and Lola's will never be the same again. He is no longer where he was; he is not yet where he will be; he is nowhere exactly. Simply adrift, a spinning atom in the ether, and although the thought horrifies him, he sees now, with utter clarity, that nothing more than chance has led him here. There is no meaning to be found in the random order of things; trying to predict the future is useless, a waste of energy. Hit with the revelation that he may never recover from the consequences of what has happened, he is increasingly aware of spinning out of control, descending into an abyss of his own making. It is the first time he has felt truly acquainted with madness, and as he wanders the dark caves of his mind, he realizes with a start that this madness, this insanity, is more than capable of carving its own reality.

By the time they board the plane at dawn, Mathéo has devised a way to keep himself in check, to keep himself moving. He fixes his gaze on a single point – the boarding gate, the seat in front, the rain-speckled window – and freezes out everything else around him. He feels drugged – when Hugo asks him a question, he is unable to even turn his head. But under his breath, he repeats to himself: *I'm not going mad, I'm all right. I'm going to get through this, I'm all right. I'm on the plane home to find Lola, we'll be all right. This is really happening, but it's going to be all right. I love you, Lola. I love you so much. If I keep saying it, you'll have to feel it. I know you can feel it. I love you, Lola. I love you. I love you . . .*

In the taxi speeding down the M4 back into central London, he realizes that some of the horror has drained from his veins. It is a bright, fresh morning, they are back on familiar ground, and he reminds himself of what Lola said to him, screamed at him, just hours ago on the beach. That *of course* she wouldn't confront her father. That *of course* she would never believe Mathéo's heinous accusations. And he realizes suddenly that this is good, that this will keep her safe: safe from being whisked away by a panicked Jerry, safe from disappearing out of his life for ever. And Jerry would never harm his own daughter – of that he is certain, *has* to be certain. Mathéo will plead amnesia, insanity, post-traumatic stress, anything – *anything* in order to be able to retrieve the accusations. And, with time, Lola will forgive him. She will, she must, because without her there is no life, there is no future.

For a moment he allows himself to imagine that Jerry never abused him at all. That it was someone who just happened to look like him. All those sleepless nights when he wished, prayed it could have been someone else – anyone but his girlfriend's father. What if it had just been a stranger? There is no definitive reality, he reminds himself, only the individual's perception of it. And if in his mind, in his memory, he replaces Jerry with someone else, then everything can go back to the way it was before. Everything *has* to go back to the way it was before. Perhaps, if he believes it enough . . . He wasn't himself when he made those accusations, hadn't been himself for ages. Lola knew that. So she will forgive him. She will give him another chance. Because she knows him, she understands him, she loves him in a way that no one else has ever loved him before, or possibly ever could again. His whole life is wrapped up in that one loving, kind, funny, bright spark of a girl, and he cannot, *will* not let her go.

The taxi has pulled up to the kerb. They have arrived outside Lola's house. It looks bright and unfamiliar in the morning sun, and Mathéo hears Hugo breathe a sigh of relief.

'Well, looks like she's back all right,' he says, pointing towards the front window at Lola's bright red backpack tossed onto the couch inside. 'Do you want us to come with you?'

'No. No.' Relief coursing through his veins, Mathéo stumbles out of the cab, his knees weak, the weight of his rucksack nearly knocking him over. 'Look, Hugo, I'm sorry about the holiday. I really am.'

Hugo sighs. 'Yeah, well, I'm just sorry about what happened to you, mate. But coming back and telling

389

the police is the right thing to do. Good luck with Lola, OK? Give me a call when things have calmed down.'

The taxi pulls away, disappearing down the road, and for a moment Mathéo just stands there, absorbing the quietness of the street, the faint chirping of birds, the smell of the oak tree, its branches laden with lush, thick green leaves. The normality of it all. Everything so tranquil, so still. He feels his heart slow to its usual rhythm, his breathing soft and steady again. Even if Lola was thinking of mentioning the argument to her father, she won't have had time. Jerry is on a shoot: the van with all his equipment is gone from the driveway. Rocky is barking at him from behind the garden fence, just like always. They wouldn't have run away and left him, nor would they have left the kitchen window open . . . Thank God. Oh, thank God.

He knows he should be thinking through exactly what he is going to say, how he is going to explain his earlier madness and retrieve his crazy accusations, but right now he just wants to see her, reassure her that he has come to his senses. Let her know that it was nothing more than a blip in his crazy mind but that he is OK now, and in no way suspects Jerry. Never will again. The person in the woods has morphed into a stranger – someone he has never met before. Pushing open the garden gate and striding down the side path, he calls out to Rocky, then presses his finger to the bell.

Rocky is whining for attention now. Mathéo reaches over the garden fence to ruffle his coat. There is no reply at the door, no movement from inside – but that is to be expected. Lola is undoubtedly still furious and upset. He calls to her through the kitchen window.

'Lola, it's me. I'm so sorry. It was all a mistake. I was having nightmares, my mind was playing tricks on me. Open the door and I'll explain everything!'

Still nothing, so he climbs into the garden to retrieve the spare key from beneath the rosemary bush and lets himself in.

'It's just me!' he calls up the stairs. 'I'm only asking you to give me five minutes. Just hear me out, Lola, OK? I wasn't well, I went a bit crazy out there. Maybe it was post-traumatic stress or something, but I promise you I'm fine now.'

Rocky follows him into the cool of the hallway. Mathéo drops his rucksack to the floor and calls out again. 'Lola, I know you're in your room. Just hear me out. I know you're really mad, and you've every right to be, but I was delusional, I lost my mind for a moment. But I realize that now, and I just want to tell you how terribly sorry I am for all the crazy stuff I said.'

His voice echoes in the penumbra of the small

house, and after waiting a few more seconds, he takes the stairs. Her bedroom door is closed. He knocks, calls out again. Turns the handle, expecting to find it locked, but to his surprise it swings open. The clothes she was wearing yesterday lie discarded on the bed, her Birkenstocks creating a sandy patch on the floor.

He turns from the empty room in surprise. 'Lola?'

Across the landing, the bathroom door is tightly shut. He recognizes the sound of water in the pipes overhead and knocks. 'Lola?'

Still no reply. He listens for the sound of the shower but cannot hear it. Suddenly his heartbeat is picking up again. 'Lola, just let me know if you're in there and I'll wait! There's no hurry . . .'

Nothing. He turns the handle. Locked. 'Lola, come on . . .'

Why isn't she replying, if only to tell him to go away?

He raises his hand to knock again, and feels something give beneath his feet. The carpet. A spreading stain, moving out towards him. Water. Water trickling out from beneath the door.

He doesn't give himself time to think. He moves back as far as he can go, takes a running jump and throws the full weight of his body against the bathroom door. The small bolt inside loosens from the wall but refuses to come off entirely. He kicks the door repeatedly with all the strength he can muster.

Slams himself against it again and again. A splintering noise, and the door finally crashes open, its bolt hanging loose by a single screw. Mathéo trips over the threshold and goes skidding across the wet floor, smack into the basin, the enamel edge hitting him in the ribs. It's just a trickle but the bath tap is still running, the tub overflowing, and in it . . . in it . . .

'Lola!'

Submerged beneath the water, her hair spread around her head like a dark halo, she appears to be floating, her body white, wide green eyes staring straight up at him. For a second nothing happens – she doesn't blink, sit up, or react at all. He waits a moment, waits for the splash as she emerges, waits for her laughter at giving him a fright. But there is no flicker of movement from her. A roar of horror fills the room, so deafening, so animalistic that it appears to come from some other being. He plunges his arms into the cold water, grabs her by the top of her arms and drags her out of the bath. She is unusually heavy, slippery, limp. Her head lolls back, and then she falls on top of him as he slips backwards on the wet floor. For a moment he thinks she is giving him a hug, her dripping hair covering his face – yet she is like a rag doll, her body weighed down as if filled with water. Kicking the towel rack out of the way, Mathéo shoves her down against the tiles, bumping her head against the floor as it falls back, her face white, still, lifeless.

Gasping for air between repeated bellows for help, Mathéo kneels over her and begins compressions on her chest. Water begins to bubble from between her lips. Yes! He can pump it out of her. He can drain her lungs. She can't have inhaled that much. He pumps and pumps and pumps – listens for a heart-beat, feels for a pulse. Nothing. He does it again. Her face is translucent, her lips a deep purple, the area around them tinged with blue. He tries to give her mouth to mouth, but no oxygen will go in, water merely trickles from the corners of her lips. He turns her onto her front, thumping her back to empty her lungs, but only a little comes out. He turns her back again, tries to pump harder, afraid now that he is breaking her ribs. But this doesn't matter. He just needs to get her heart going, he just needs to get her breathing again. He has been taught how to resuscitate as part of his training, has been resuscitated himself with no ill effects. Any minute now and she'll begin to cough – that's how it happens, that's how he's seen it happen, that's how it's meant to happen – but why isn't it happening yet? He pumps and pumps her chest again, but a thin line of water just continues to trickle down her cheek and there is no heartbeat, no cough-ing, no breathing. Nothing. Nothing. Nothing.

It's been ages now – he knows because his arms are so weak he can barely apply any pressure, and her body is limp and blue and cold – so cold. She must have gone into shock; she needs professional help.

When the paramedics come – he doesn't remember calling them – they have to forcibly drag him away. Their radios fizz and crackle and they are rushed and noisy, crowding into the small bathroom all together, all at once. They have equipment: machines, pumps, defibrillators – thank God! They will get her heart started again, drain the water from her lungs, give her some oxygen. But gradually the buzz and commotion begins to dial down: he can see one paramedic just standing there, unmoving. From somewhere the words *sleeping pills* and *drowned* and *dead for hours* swirl around him, and he starts to protest, starts to shout: why have they stopped? Why isn't she coughing? Why is it all taking so long? What the hell is happening?

They carry her out on a stretcher – good, she is stable enough to be taken to hospital, she must be breathing unaided now. He tries to follow them so he can hold her hand in the ambulance, stroke her hair, reassure her that she's going to be all right. But they have covered her in a white plastic sheet – not just over her body but over her face as well. Her face, Lola's face, Lola's beautiful face, he can't see her any more! Why are they doing this? She won't be able to breathe, she won't be able to see, she will be terrified! He needs to get to her, he struggles to get to her, but he is being restrained by someone so strong he can barely move.

'She's gone, buddy. We did everything we could but her heart had stopped a long time ago. There was nothing anyone could have done to help her.' One of the paramedics is standing in front of him, his face looming large as the sun. 'Are you family? Is there someone we can call?'

'She's not dead.' His voice sounds harsh, loud and hurts his head. 'You're wrong. She's not dead.'

'She is dead, son. I'm so sorry. She's been dead for some hours.'

Shrouded in white plastic, strapped down against the stretcher, Lola is beginning to disappear down the staircase as the other two paramedics manoeuvre her round the tight bend at the bottom.

He tries to get to his feet, tries to run after her, but is still being held back against the wall and so starts to scream. 'She's not dead! She's not dead! Look at her, for fuck sake – she's not dead!' But they ignore him, and the stretcher carrying Lola, his Lola, so witty and fun, so loving and full of life, disappears from sight.

'Lola, don't do this!' he screams. 'I'm sorry, I'm so sorry, I didn't mean it. I love you! Come back, Lola, come back! I'm so sorry! Come back!'

Come back, come back, come back . . . He has been saying those words for what seems like an eternity, like some kind of mantra, even though he has almost completely lost his voice by now. Someone gave him a shot in the arm, and as a result he can barely move, sitting on the landing propped up against Lola's bedroom door. One of the paramedics squats down in front of him and asks him questions – his name, age, next of kin, a parent or guardian they can call. Another emerges from the bathroom wearing white rubber gloves, says something about a bird and holds out a folded piece of paper to his colleague. A pale blue origami crane. For a moment he cannot move, then Mathéo throws himself forward, managing to snatch it from the paramedic's clasp. With clumsy hands, he unfolds its wings. At first his eyes won't focus, but then slowly Lola's neat, slanted handwriting swims into view.

Mattie, I'm so sorry. You were right. He broke down and told me. I don't understand, I don't know what I feel or who I am any more. But I do know that I'm so sorry, sweetheart. I'm so sorry for what he did to you. I'm so sorry for not believing you, for saying all those hateful things, which even at the time weren't true. I'm so sorry about everything – me, coming into your life and almost destroying it. If we had never met, this would never have happened to you, but as selfish as that may be, I still can't bring myself to wish for that. I never stopped loving you, Mattie. I never will. You are the best thing that ever happened to me. You are the kindest, sweetest, funniest person I've ever known. You made me happier than I ever deserved to be. Even with everything that happened, I'm still glad I was born and had this life because it meant meeting you, loving you and being loved by you. And being loved by you was the best feeling in the world and one I can't imagine living without. Even though it's over now, you made it all worthwhile, you brought me the greatest joy a person can experience. I just hope that before this happened, I made you happy too. All I want now is for you to get better, my darling. All I want is for you to forget him, and to do that you need to forget me too. Once I've gone you will be free to move on with your life. Free to love again, but this time without getting so brutally hurt. Oh, I so wish I could wash away what happened along with myself, but at least without me you will one day find a way of putting all this behind you. This is the best way I can think of, this is the only way. I can't continue to live with his blood inside me, I can't continue to live with the knowledge of the suffering my love for you ultimately caused, and I can't continue to live knowing I can never see you again. So this is the best way. One day, I hope you'll understand. I'm not afraid, Mattie, honestly. I don't care about myself any more, I don't even know myself. I only care about you. I just want you to live a long and happy life, and without me, you will. Please find happiness, my darling. Please find love again. Find the life you deserve. Live it to the full, for what we dreamed of, for what could have been. Live it for us. Live it for me.

I love you.

Lola xxx

Epilogue

It would appear that summer has arrived again. Another summer, another end to an academic year. He is sitting in the long grass at the edge of the university campus, down by the water, down by the river. Between lectures most of the students hang out on the lawns behind him, in pairs or in groups: guys with their arms slung proprietarily around their girlfriends' shoulders; amoeba-like clusters picnicking from pizza boxes and beer cans, celebrating the end of exams. It's a particularly warm day in June, and today feels like the first proper day of summer – the kind of weather where you can kick off your shoes and enjoy the feel of the soft, cool ground beneath your soles. The sun is a pure, transparent gold, stroking the campus with light and filling it with delirium. His friends are in the distance, beneath the shade of an oak tree – they know not to disturb him when he comes to sit here.

Next year will be his last one as a student. He will miss university life. St Andrews, up here in northern Scotland, has been good to him. Overall, he has enjoyed studying English Literature – has made good friends, ones that he will probably stay in touch with, even when this chapter in his life comes to a close. He sees little of the ones back home in London: Hugo went to college in Boston on a sports scholarship; they drifted apart over time and rarely speak now. He lost touch with Isabel too – the last he heard she was doing voluntary work in Africa. She used to send him emails and an occasional postcard, but they petered out when he failed to reply. Jerry's parole date must be coming up – he turned himself in when news reached him about Lola, but Mathéo rarely thinks about him now. There was a trial: Mathéo signed Jerry's statement but refused to give evidence, refused to attend.

His parents found out about the rape when the paramedics called them, that terrible morning, when he was still slumped against the wall of the Baumanns' landing, clutching Lola's paper crane. They both took the news hard, but in very different ways. His father initially reacted with fury, demanding to see Jerry, threatening to kill him. But when he found there was nothing he could do, he retreated, burying himself back into his work, as if trying to forget it had ever happened. His mother explained that he blamed himself – for having pushed Mathéo into diving, for not having been able to protect him. But when his mother took a year off work to look after him during his illness, Mathéo became acquainted with her gentler side. Although he doesn't often go back to London, Mum and Loïc fly out regularly to visit, and Mathéo enjoys their company, enjoys showing them around. Loïc likes it here, says he wants to come and study architecture, and he probably will.

Mathéo likes this part of the river, likes watching the swans glide by with their long, slim necks, their heads held high. Lola's paper cranes come to life . . . He likes to sit in exactly this spot, close enough to see the sequined light dancing off the water, listen to the gentle trickle of the moving current. But no closer. It reminds him of too many things . . . He was once a competitive diver, tipped for Olympic gold. Not many of his friends here know about that part of his life, although some claim to have heard of his name. But although he still gets team updates from Perez, he hasn't been back in the water since that summer, three years ago. Three years . . . Time has passed so quickly, yet in some ways has not passed at all. He took a gap year, but not to compete in the Olympics – he didn't even watch his old teammates on TV. For a while he was quite unwell – maybe eight or nine months. Glandular fever, some doctors claimed, others said it was chronic fatigue syndrome. Of course, no one wanted to accept the truth: that he was bed-bound out of choice. That he chose not to eat rather than was unable to. That for many months he refused to leave the house, rather than being too weak to do so. He lost so much weight that he had to spend nearly two months in a specialist hospital. His parents paid for him to be treated by top psychiatrists, psychologists and therapists, all specializing in abuse. But no one ever suggested bereavement counselling. Perhaps because he refused to talk about her – still does. Some things are too painful to put into words, too personal to hope that anyone could possibly understand. Lola now exists only in his memory and he will do everything to protect that memory, will share her with no one. Many times he thought seriously of ending things, but Lola's note held him back. It still does.

They say he is better now. He gets good grades, pursues other sports, has become a keen wildlife photographer. His doctor is even talking about tapering off the anti-depressants and sleeping pills. He doesn't think about dying so much these days. But 'better'? It is a strange word. He isn't even sure what it means any more. How do you get better after losing someone like Lola? He has learned to function again, yes. Has learned to have fun again, at times. Has learned to mix with others, to make new friends. And he has a new chapter in his life waiting for him, plans for what to do after university – a time he is beginning to look forward to. People talk about moving on after losing someone, and that is what he has done – is doing. But nothing takes the pain away. You learn to live with it, that's all. You find new ways of getting through the day, new people to talk to, new friends to trust. But the pain is always there. Not a day passes when he doesn't long to see her smile, feel the touch of her hand, hold her in his arms, even if it is just for a moment. Not a day passes when he doesn't think of her and ache for her all over again. The hurt will never go away – he understands that now, and he wouldn't have it any different. Lola will always be his greatest love, and not a second will pass when he doesn't long to be with her again, wish beyond everything that she were by his side. He only has to close his eyes to see her, watch her smile, hear her laugh, feel and remember how much she loved him. And he realizes how lucky he was to have known her, to have had any time with her at all. He doesn't always cry, but sometimes, like today, he does a little.

And then he hears voices calling his name: George and Kirsty, suggesting a game of Frisbee. And so he takes a deep breath, wipes his eyes, raises an arm to signal he is coming and jogs back away from the river to join his friends.

Acknowledgements

Writing this novel was no easy task and would never have been accomplished without the help and encouragement of some very special people. I would like to thank my extremely patient and talented editor, Ruth Knowles, for her expertise and belief in my writing. Annie Eaton pushed for the book's creation and always trusted I would get there, even when I doubted it myself. I am profoundly grateful to them and the whole team at Random House for their hard work and boundless faith in mine.

Via a competition, three young adults ended up contributing to the creation of the book's cover. Brigid Gorry-Hines came up with brilliant design; Bartosz Madej took the evocative photograph; Wojciech Kisek brought Mathéo to life. I cannot thank them enough for their talent and creativity.

The support of those closest to me has been invaluable. My sisters, Thalia Suzuma and Tansy Roekaerts, offered me encouragement and feedback. My brother, Tadashi Suzuma, shared travel anecdotes which often found their way into the story. My little brother, Shin Suzuma (aka Tiggy), inspired me with his breath-taking concerts on his path to becoming a concert pianist and even provided a live soundtrack to write to. I couldn't be more proud of him. I am also extremely grateful to my godson, George Manchester, who has always been like a son to me. He is the light of my life and keeps me going through even the darkest times.

Finally, none of my books would have existed without the help of the two most supportive people in my life. Akiko Hart is more than my best friend; she is also my soul mate, my advisor, my confidante and, undoubtedly, the person who knows and understands me better than anyone. Not only has she been there for me during my hours of need, but she supports me and encourages me throughout each of my books. She is the one person I can always turn to when I am stuck, she supports me through the disappointments and is as thrilled by my successes as if they were her own . . . The other rock in my life is my mother, Elizabeth Suzuma, who painstakingly proofs every word, often staying up through the night to do so. I am so grateful to her, even though I'm not always very good at showing it. She is, without doubt, the unsung hero behind every one of my books.

Hurt is **Tabitha Suzuma**'s sixth novel for young adults. Her debut novel, *A Note of Madness*, was shortlisted for the Branford Boase Award, and since then her novels have won and been shortlisted for many other awards, including the Young Minds Book Award, the Carnegie Medal and the Waterstone's Book Prize. *Forbidden*, Tabitha's controversial 2010 novel, won the Premio Speciale Cariparma for European Literature.

Tabitha has always loved writing and would regularly get into trouble at the French Lycée for writing stories instead of listening in class. She used to work as a primary school teacher and now divides her time between writing and tutoring.

You can visit Tabitha at:
www.tabithasuzuma.com
@TabithaSuzuma
facebook.com/tabitha.suzuma